Black Dawn

by

Morgan L. Brautigan

Copyright 2012 by Morgan L. Brautigan
Cover art and design by Tony Branch
Second edition 2013

ISBN – 978-0615599342 (Maranth Press)
ISBN – 0615599346

This book is dedicated to
my father, Bertis E. Long
Who has been my inspiration not only
in my love of books
but in how I live my life.

I love you, Dad.

Morgan L Brautigan

Acknowledgements

As with every project, this book was hardly the work of only one person. I would like to thank the following:

To Julia and Chris who were the first to express belief that it could be done.

To Kathy and Randy who gave me the computer and the motivation to do it.

To the clerk at the copy store who read the first page when she printed it out and liked it.

To Lois Bujold for introducing me to the wonderful world of military science fiction.

To Neil Norman and his CD "Greatest Science Fiction Hits IV" for his music to write space battles to.

To my girls, Missy, Angie, Jenny, Ariel and Corrie who were the first and best BlackFleet fans.

To my best friend in the entire universe, Tony, who gave me encouragement, belief, battle strategy suggestions, and the most wonderful artwork I could have imagined.

And to my Lord for allowing me to use my love of writing in such a fun way.

Thanks all

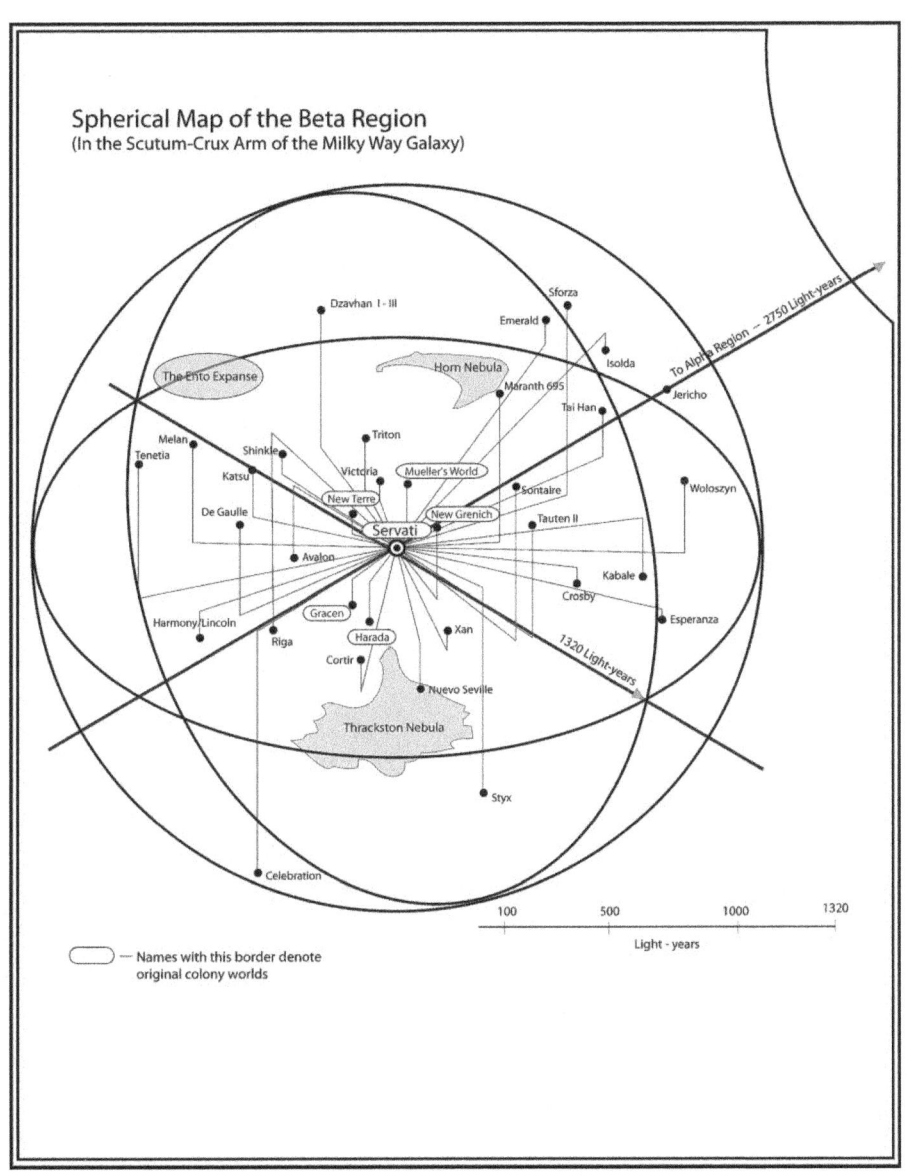

Spherical Map of the Beta Region
(In the Scutum-Crux Arm of the Milky Way Galaxy)

⬭ — Names with this border denote
original colony worlds

Morgan L Brautigan

Chapter One

The air was thick with battle. The sights, the sounds, the smells, filled one's senses with death. The flash of a plasma beam, voices shouting in desperation, the stench of burnt metal, burnt material, burnt meat.

Smoke hung over everything like fog obscuring the view of the asteroid terrain. Here and there one could make out a body--a mound of charcoal that used to be a friend. And in the midst of it all, fifty horrified civilians, totally bewildered at this disaster that should have been their rescue.

If only Aubry had come a little sooner, they could've gotten everyone out. If only Aubry hadn't come at all, then he would still be alive...

"Hey you! Yeah, you, the Rigan."

The voice jerked Coy back to the here and now. Back to this dismal space station commonly referred to as the "End of the Universe".

C-space travel had been established, making regular journeys outside the solar system, if not instantaneous, at least practical. When man at last began reaching out into space away from the arms of Mother Earth, their homes were developed on planets within 2000 light years of Sol. This first generation of colonies was referred to, rather unimaginatively, as the Alpha Region. Technology marched on and when people again needed elbow room they were able to travel even farther out. The Beta Region contained 34 formal colony worlds spreading out around the planet Servati, which sat at the center of the officially mapped 1,320 light-year sphere. It also contained the typical amount of asteroid mines, space stations, and orbital stations offering jobs, get-aways and "exotic" ports of call. Or less exotic ports...such as this one.

When Alluria Station had been built, the asteroid belt it accompanied had been thought to be a wealth of treasures. It had turned out to be a wealth of disappointment. But the station struggled on, servicing mostly wanderers and drifters. All around the room, people hunched over empty bottles, empty glasses or simply empty tables. Most sat alone. This was the kind of place you came to drown your sorrows, forget lost loves or hide from just about anybody. But yourself.

Even the station itself seemed depressed. The gray walls had not seen a cleaning or paint job in a long time. Half of the vending machines, which lined the walls offering anything a credit token could buy, were out of order. The ones with life still in them blinked dully from under a layer of dust and grime. Which meant the air handlers and filters were probably in the same state of disrepair.

Coy looked over at the gaming tables in dim acknowledgment of the hail. Coy Lamont knew no one on this scrap pile, was not wearing Rigan clothing and had not spoken for anyone to hear an accent. Indistinct race, indistinct age, chin length hair hanging limply around Coy's face, except for one detail, someone would be hard pressed to guess where in the large nexus of inhabited worlds it had come from.

"It." That was the detail. The one thing that transmitted Coy's place of origin was its gender. Or genders. Riga Colony was where hermaphrodites were created. Along with any other variation on humanity that someone was willing to pay for. *Most* Rigan labs *usually* worked within the laws concerning what one could and couldn't --or shouldn't --do to a human body. But anyone with enough money could find a lab willing to do just about anything.

And of course there was always the rare case when a customer cancelled an order and some poor prototype was left to fend for themselves. As Coy had done until eventually making a life for itself as a mercenary.

Former mercenary. The thoughts rolled full circle, coming back to the reason Coy was sitting there alone drinking away the last of its credit. It sighed and considered the card players.

"We could use another hand," a large, gaudily dressed man smiled.

Seeing the empty bottle on the table, they probably assumed they had an easy mark. No point in telling them alcohol had no effect, thanks to the lab back "home". It thought a second more, then got up and came over. "What are we playing?"

The rules were explained, the cards dealt and the game began.

Several hands later, the circle of contenders was thinning as the crowd of onlookers grew. All around the room people had dragged themselves up out of their drinks and wandered over to watch. It was an unusual event for anyone at Alluria Station to have enough money to make a game worth caring about. These people obviously had plenty. What they were doing in such a place no one dared ask.

At last it was down to three players: the large, loud man who had made the invitation, a small reserved man wearing an expensive silk business suit, and Coy itself. The pile of winnings had shifted between them rather regularly. At the moment Coy was in possession of quite a bit more money than it'd had in its entire life. But it was not over yet.

The stakes were raised again. And again. In addition to the currency, credit chits, jewelry, chronos, and a tiny ornate stunner had crossed the table.

All eyes were now on the quiet little man. He looked at his cards and at the bare table before him. Finally, he reached into a pocket and pulled out a document disk. He laid it carefully on the pile.

"What's this?" bellowed the other.

"Land. A rather expensive piece of land on Servati."

The big man picked up the disk and fingered it while he thought. He glanced at his own hand. "All right." He added his own disk to the other. "My ship," he announced.

The crowd gasped. The man beamed. Coy laid its cards face down and cleared its throat. The best hand of its life and no way to stay in the game.

"You're out?" the man bellowed again.

"I have nothing to match those bets."

The man grinned hungrily. "Sure you do, Rigan. Your kind always has marketable - talents."

Coy stared at him, realizing finally just what type of person it was playing with. It had seen the type before, most often as customers of the "specialty" labs on Riga. He appeared to have the wealth to custom order just about anything he wanted.

"I'm good," Coy drawled, "but not worth a ship."

The crowd chuckled, but the big man only grinned more.

Coy looked at the cards again. It's life for a card game? This was insane. It was suicide…or worse. Coy wouldn't do it. It couldn't. It…looked at the other player for confirmation.

The Servati shrugged. "I'm a businessman. What I don't want for myself I can always sell." He nodded in agreement.

Coy nodded as well and the bet was made.

The little man spread his cards for all to see. A great hand. He smiled confidently.

Until the big man put down his. A terrific hand. The other wilted, conceding his defeat.

Everyone looked to Coy, who was sitting with its head down, clutching its cards. It looked up at the ship owner. *'He'll kill me where I sit,'* it thought. *'All the crap I've been through and this is how I die.'*

Very slowly and carefully it spread the cards out. The best hand possible.

The crowd was absolutely silent. No one so much as breathed as they stepped carefully back away from the game.

The owner of the bar, backed by a large bouncer, came over and tossed a transaction scanner on the table, breaking the tense silence. "I don't want no trouble," he growled at all three of them.

The big man looked at the scanner sitting on top of the pot and then at Coy in apparent disbelief. He stared for several moments, rubbing his lip, contemplating the person before him. "Would you have honored your bet?"

Coy nodded sickly. "Probably."

He blinked in surprise, then frowned, perhaps not having a lot of experience with honesty. "Why?"

Coy tried to think of an easy answer. There wasn't one. How to explain the whole nightmare of betrayal, loss and self- hatred? It said simply, "I've had a bad week."

"Hmph," the man grunted. "Looks like it's improving. At my expense." He picked up the disk and scanner and began signing over the title. "What's your name?"

"Cap.. Coy Lamont."

He glanced up at it a moment, seemingly amused. "Cap..? As in Captain? A herm captain? Now, who would…Oh, well, it takes all kinds I guess. A mercenary, no doubt." Coy managed a small nod. The transaction complete, he handed over the updated disk. "Congratulations, you're an Owner. A very nice ship, I might add. The crew, I keep. They are all, well, specially trained for my service. But you can have the pilot."

Coy was very surprised but very glad at this bit of information. Jump pilots were a very expensive commodity. It was *technically* possible to fly a ship without one, at least between transition points. Coy itself had the training. But some people were just born to be pilots. They had some sort of special gift, an ability to merge themselves with their ships which was absolutely essential when holding a transit point open long enough to get a ship through. Not to mention safely navigating through C-space to the next point. In the past large companies had been known to pour a lot of money into searching out and sponsoring the training of someone with especially promising pilot skills. More and more often however pilots were being created. Genetically skewed before birth. Again, paid for by organizations which would in turn benefit from their unique skills. All of which made it unusual for someone to give one away. Unless he wasn't any good, burnt out, or unbalanced.

"So, now you can go be a commodore or whatever it is that mercenary ship owners call themselves." He paused, all amusement gone. "And if you'll take some friendly advice, I recommend you take your ship and leave Alluria as soon as humanly possible."

Well, that explained the generosity with the pilot. Coy looked him over, beginning to think of reasons someone might want to be rid of 'a very nice ship'. "With no crew? Take it where?"

The man nodded at the other transaction now taking place across the table. "Servati, I would imagine."

Long after it was over, Coy sat studying the specs on its new possessions. It decided - belatedly - to find out whether either had mortgages, liens or if they were even legally owned to begin with. Somewhat to its surprise, everything seemed to check out.

The property on Servati turned out not to be merely a piece of land, but what was essentially a villa. What it was supposed to do with such an acquisition, it had no idea. It turned to the more familiar territory of the ship.

A very nice ship indeed! The description of the huge ship was almost as overwhelming to absorb as the villa.

While it was skimming through the mass of information, three men approached the table. Coy recognized them from the mob of spectators from the game. It glanced up, then returned its gaze to the scanner readout feigning disinterest at their curiosity.

"May I help you?" it looked up and asked after a moment.

From the nods and nudges from the other two, one man seemed to be their spokesman. He cleared his throat and straightened his stance. "We were watching. Thought you could use some engineers."

The man appeared to be pushing forty, slim and weathered. As if he was more used to hostile environments than spaceships. The two men with him were darker but looked weathered in a similar manner.

Coy put down the scanner and motioned for the one to sit. It leaned back and crossed its arms. "I haven't even decided what to do with it yet. So I can hardly offer you a steady job. Which means beyond the game winnings, I have no guarantee of pay."

"That's okay." He paused at Coy's raised eyebrows. "This ship has bunks and meals?"

Coy indicated the scanner. "Apparently."

"Then we'll sign on."

Coy considered his accent. And all the issues that came with it. "You're Haradan. You understand my gender?"

The man paused again. "Aware, yes. Understand, not really. But if you're asking will we still work for you, the answer's yes."

"No better offers, huh?" Coy noted the discomfort this truth caused. But the man seemed sincere, and Coy appreciated that. "Well, I can use the help. Any mercenary experience?"

"No."

"Military of any type?"

A stricken expression appeared on the man's face, then quickly disappeared. Like the twinge of an old wound. "Y-yes."

"I see."

It was a well-known fact that Haradans were fanatical about the military being the beginning and end of all honor. Leaving the military life obviously had caused this man pain. It struck a chord in Coy. Another lost soul in search of a new beginning.

How many others like them were there out in the universe? People who had to start over because of some decision-good or bad-that ended up costing them everything. Decisions like Coy's. When it had chosen to do what it felt was right and necessary, knowing it was not technically correct. Coy wished this man no heartache, yet it was somehow comforting to know there were others.

Coy thought a moment, trying to size them up. They could indeed be engineers as they claimed, but would ground pounders be of any use on a spaceship? It focused on the one seated. The others seemed to defer decision making to him automatically. "An officer?"

He nodded briefly. "Lieutenant. But that was… awhile ago."

One of the others spoke up. "And you're really a mercenary?" He glanced dubiously at his companions. Now that was more the Haradan attitude Coy was familiar with.

"Yes , as a matter of fact," it told him. "Although I'm presently, ah, on my own."

"Not anymore, Commodore," the Lieutenant grinned.

Coy frowned, but put out a hand. "Captain. Captain Coy Lamont. Lieutenant...?"

The other took it. "Raeph Bon. This is Luka and Palo."

Coy stood to shake their hands. Luka took the outstretched hand with a smile and only the slightest of hesitations. Palo, however,

444444444444444444

seemed as skeptical of herms as he did of mercs. After a moment, and a look from Bon, he allowed Coy to shake his hand. Coy pretended not to notice. "A crew of five. Well, it's a beginning." It gathered its documents. "Let's go see this ship of ours, shall we?"

Even though Coy had read through the schematics, the ship was a surprise to it as well as the engineers. It was like nothing in any of their varied military experiences. It was a luxury liner such as they had never seen. Sleek and black. The fins on either side of the ship, used to transmit the beam that opened the portals to jump through space, swept up like elegant wings. Yet for all that, it was heavily armed and armored.

Lamont stood looking out of the station viewport at the ship in amazement. "Nevermore," it breathed to itself.

"Commodore?" Bon asked.

"It's Captain," it corrected, again, "and it's just a line from an old pre-jump Earth poem about a black bird." *And a grief stricken man searching for answers.*

"Well it is that, sir. Very black."

Unfortunately, parts of the interior were much as Coy *had* imagined from its assessment of the card player's character. This was no cruise line. The passengers on this ship had apparently cared only for gambling and entertainment - in all their most twisted and exotic forms.

The main rooms and corridors were pleasantly and artistically decorated with real wood trim, dramatic lighting and expensive looking artwork. The "guest" rooms however were a different story. Palo and Luka examined the furniture and equipment with fascination. Artwork depicting perversions of every kind lined the walls. Coy merely stood, pale and serious, struck with the knowledge of what losing that card game would've meant.

"Orders, Commodore?" Bon seemed to think the title was a nickname rather than a rank.

Coy was too distracted and vaguely nauseated to correct him this time. "Rip it all out. Melt it down and shove it out the airlock."

The engineer nodded understanding. "Aye aye, sir". Then, "Kinda good you had the hand you did, eh?" he added quietly, and walked away to begin carrying out his first orders.

Between the pilot, Hoffman's knowledge of the ship, Coy's schematics and Bon's "know-how", it didn't take as long as they had feared to learn the systems of the ship (which Coy had christened the *Raven*). By skipping such mundane interruptions as eating and sleeping, they were able to check out most of the essentials before preparing to leave the station.

Although, in truth, Eric Hoffman spent most of his time on the bridge, sitting in his pilot's chair, barricading himself from Lamont and Bon with a wall of resentment. He answered direct questions and little else. He had probably worked very hard for what he considered a prestigious position. He would not get the perks or tips with a mercenary group that he would've in his former employers crowd, and he was angry and bitter at the loss. Coy could sympathize with life's plans getting blown to pieces and left him to himself as much as possible.

About the middle of the second day, Lamont was wandering through an amazing length of corridor, peering into cabins that were nothing less than luxury suites. According to the floor plans the computer had willingly presented to them, the Raven was equipped with everything from tactical room to ballrooms. Thoughts of using the latter filled Lamont with amusement. Thoughts of using the former filled it with terror.

Among the more surprising items was when it went into one of rooms across from the officer's gym and discovered the swimming pool! A large sphere, the bottom half of which was set into the deck, contained real honest to goodness H2O. The spherical shape led one to imagine being in a scientific experimental container or perhaps an aquatic animal kept as a pet. But the shape had little or nothing to do with aesthetics and everything to do with containing all of that liquid in the event of the artificial gravity being disrupted.

Small amounts escaping, say one's teacup, during moments like that was amusing at best, messy at worst. Especially if you missed some of the floating brown blobs with the hand vacuum and ran into them. Aubry hadn't seen the humor. Coy smiled in memory of his impeccable uniform covered in...abruptly Coy remembered the last time it had seen Aubry himself and the smile evaporated. It turned and left the gym and continued its investigation.

It stopped in front of the captain/owner's quarters. It hadn't felt like picking quarters yet. What sleep it had gotten was a couple of hours on a cot in Sick Bay. But it couldn't do that forever. It opened the door and went in. Dim lights came on automatically.

Coy froze in surprise. This was not a cabin. This was an apartment. It was, in fact, larger than some planet side homes it had seen.

To its left was a generously- sized food prep area, with two doors leading off. One door led to a sleeping room with a bed the size of most ship's quarters! The other led to an adjoining office. Straight ahead from the main entrance was a huge ornate desk with a view port at its back. To the right and down one step was living space. Three couches and a couple of chairs in a semi circle around a cocktail table, lots of shelves filled at the moment with more perverse artwork, and a long dining/conference table.

Coy thought of its cabin on its last command. A tiny rectangle barely large enough for bunk, desk and wardrobe. It gave a loud sigh. It did not deserve this. It wasn't right. People like Aubry deserved to live like this. Heroic people. But Aubry would never see anything he deserved.

Coy suddenly felt overwhelmed. The depression it had been fighting for so long seemed to be winning the battle. It closed its eyes and tried to take a calming breath. It came out ragged. It tried to think of something, to focus on something, but every thought that came led to some mistake it had made. Something it had done wrong.

Going against the Admiral's orders had been stupid. Not telling Aubry had been stupid. Letting him stand there had been stupid. Betting itself in a card game had been stupid. One card different and its life would have been forfeit. The *if-only's* and *what-if's* became consuming. It looked around the room again and couldn't care about owning the most magnificent ship in known space. It couldn't care about anything. All Coy knew was that it was tired. And it hurt. And it was tired of hurting.

Just then Bon interrupted with excited summons to the shuttle bay. Coy straightened up with an effort, put on a commanding officer face and went to join him. The lights lowered once more as the door shut behind it.

Coy stood in the cavernous bay and looked over the three ships parked there, but didn't see Bon. Shuttles, they were designated in the files, although one was sleek and very large, even by combat drop shuttle standards. The hatch on the large one opened and Bon appeared. A very enthusiastic Bon appeared.

"You *have* to see this," he grinned. Inside he showed Lamont eight cabins, a Sick Bay cubicle, and what appeared to be a passenger lounge.

"A yacht," Coy guessed.

"Quite a yacht," Bon was still grinning. "This thing apparently has jump capabilities. Plus the shielding and weapons would match military specs on half a dozen worlds. I don't even want to try to estimate the cost."

"I doubt if money was an issue," Coy said. "They undoubtedly ferried high paying … customers… in this."

Bon nodded at the walls, indicating the shielding. "High paying and paranoid."

"Perhaps with reason."

Bon's enthusiasm subsided a little. "You know, no one out there is gonna know there are new people in here. Suppose we bump into some of those reasons?"

They looked at each other, possibilities blooming in their minds, but said nothing more on the subject. Silently they investigated the other two ships. Except for extra shielding, they appeared to be more typical passenger shuttles. One of the few typical anything on board. Bon's mood bubbled up again every time they found more "goodies". Coy remained

subdued, however, as they finished up their tour. Bon noticed and wondered about his new commander's dark moods, but drew the line at asking any personal questions…yet.

Ship's stores was the final eye opening experience. Enough standard, processed food for a thousand guests (the hydroponics bay they had found did not look like it had ever been used), manufacturing computers designed to create fashions to suit any taste, quite an interesting array of personal weapons and armor and the most elaborate set of wrist coms any of them had ever seen. Those, they put to use right away. Once someone located an operating manual.

Coy took a little time out to fiddle with the clothing computer to come up with a proper ship's uniform. Something serious and practical, yet fitting in with the elegant lines of the ship. It modeled its efforts for Bon at the first opportunity.

Bon tried not to stare outright at his commanding officer. Coy had taken the time to tie its hair back in a small tight tail at the nape of its neck which enhanced its appearance as much as replacing the baggy cast offs it had worn had. But surely it was the uniform that he found so appealing. After all he had been raised in a military society. It was perfectly logical that he would like someone in uniform. That is, a uniform on someone.

"Black," was his only external comment.

"Seems fitting," Coy told him, unaware of the engineer's discomfort. "Black ship, black uniforms...."

"Black moods," Bon braved, but Coy didn't comment. "You're right. It fits." He took the pants and jacket Lamont offered him. "So we have uniforms. And a whole shuttle bay full of ships down there. And what are you going to do with this little black fleet of yours?"

Lamont shook its head. For one to plan for the future, one had to *care* about the future. And the moments it cared were few and far between. "I don't even know yet."

"We've got a lot of potential here, Skipper."

Coy gave a skeptical 'humph'. "To do what?"

Bon gazed around the room they were in. "Suppose this has a point to it. A reason it all came together."

Coy stared at him for a moment. "You really believe that?"

Haradans were not known for any belief in events supernatural. But after a moment, Bon gave a sigh. "It would be kind of comforting to think I'm alive for some reason. After we got cashiered out...." he shook his head. "I don't know, Commodore. I really don't."

Coy looked thoughtful. "Maybe you can stick around and help me figure it out."

"Well, like you said, I've had no better offers."

Before Coy could respond to that, they were interrupted by its wrist com. "Luka to Lamont."

"Lamont. Go ahead."

"Captain, there are some people here at the docking tube that want to see you," he reported.

Coy frowned at the device. "Some people?" Great. Right when they were finally ready to pull out. They shouldn't have delayed. They should have learned the ship after they were space borne. But that hadn't seemed safe either. Too late now anyway.

"They want jobs." Luka added.

Bon's brows rose in hope. "Terrific!"

Coy, as usual, did not look nearly as excited. "All right, have..." it paused and thought. "Have Hoffman escort them to the briefing room."

"Oh. Ah, okay."

"Is there a problem?" Coy asked at his hesitant tone.

"Well, could *you* tell Hoffman, sir?"

Coy gave a hint of a sigh. "Yes, I'll tell him. But I suggest you at least attempt to work together."

"Yes, sir. Thank you , sir. Luka out." The com cut off.

Bon shrugged. "Sorry, sir. But you can hardly blame him. Hoffman hates us all. I find it a bit unnerving to know our lives are in his hands once we're in space."

"He's a pilot. He won't harm his ship just to get to us," Coy assured him. "But off the record, I sympathize with his attitude. He's understandably upset this is suddenly a mercenary ship. It's hardly what he signed on for."

"Considering his former boss, it's got to be a giant step *up*, mercenary or not," Bon persisted.

Coy waved him off and called up to the bridge.

"Hoffman. Go ahead," came a sullen voice.

"There are some new recruits at the docking bay. Escort them to the starboard briefing room."

"To the what?"

"The starboard lounge on deck B is now a briefing room. I explained that this morning."

"Yes, *Captain*."

Lamont and Bon looked at each other again.

"I think I'll cross my fingers every time we make a jump," Bon mumbled.

Coy let it go and went to meet the recruits. Happy or not about being an escort, Hoffman delivered five people to the correct location and after a stern look from his new employer even waited in the corridor. Coy let them stand alone in the huge room for a moment before going in. It
would have preferred to have a guard at its back when entering, for protocol as well as safety sake, but everyone was busy except Hoffman. And it didn't think having to battle for the man's co-operation would present the image it wanted.

Even alone, Coy had their attention. It returned their skeptical gazes and looked them over judiciously, eyeing the empty holster on one--an older man, dark, wiry and intelligent looking.

He caught the look and explained, "Your man did a fairly competent weapons search."

Coy raised a brow at the man's tone. Critiquing, rather than complaining.

"I understand you want a job," it spoke to them all. "Why?"

A laugh came from one. "Why do people usually want a job? To work maybe? To eat?" He eyed Coy disgustedly. "Look, be a good herm and go get the captain."

Coy was momentarily caught off guard at its sudden annoyance, bordering on anger, at the man's words. It had heard worse insults its whole life, both to its face and behind its back. What made this time different? "Actually, I am the Captain. Are there any other opinions?"

Another was impatient. "So what's the drill? I've worked for a dozen merc outfits. They've always been happy enough to have a warm body in the suit."

Lamont ignored that one completely and spoke directly to the man with the empty holster. "And you?"

He came to a casual attention. "I'm a soldier."

One thing Coy Lamont had been made to do was make quick evaluations of people and circumstances. There was something about this man that felt right. But Coy found it hard to trust its own judgment after....

"So why aren't you a soldier at home?" it stalled.

"They don't have soldiers at home."

"Oh, what do they have?"

His body tensed and his eyes hardened. "Mines. Lots of filthy mines."

Something clicked. That connection Coy couldn't even have named. But it knew.

"What is your name?

"Schiff. Walter Schiff."

"Mr. Schiff, welcome to the *Raven*." Coy turned to the remaining two. One of which was a timid appearing young woman. "Why do you want to be part of my crew?" it asked her

She looked around slightly panic stricken, as if caught in a pop quiz. Finally she sighed and admitted, "To be honest, I need off this station. I need to be, I don't know. Doing something. And I'm medically.
trained. I could help your Med Tech..." She started to wring her hands, stopped herself, took a breath and looked Lamont in the eye. "I would do my best."

"Your name?"

"Ah..." she paused, beginning to panic again.

"What you wish to be called will do fine."

"Oh. Okay." Relieved, she thought only a moment. "Ceal Byars."

"And..?" Coy asked the last candidate, but the man appeared only marginally sober and simply shrugged. "Very well. Mr. Schiff, Miss Byars, please stay. The rest of you--thank you for your time."

After closing their gaping mouths, the three muttered some expletives and shuffled out to be escorted off board. By their attitude, they could have caused some damage on the way out, except that Hoffman was armed and they were not.

After they were gone, Coy spoke to Schiff. "You are a soldier. Combat experience?" A nod in answer. "Good. You're our only one so far. I guess that makes you in charge" It looked him up and down again, studying his body language. Authoritative, but... "Is Sergeant all right for now?"

Schiff blinked. "Ah, yes, sir."

"And Byars, about helping the Med Tech...as of now, you <u>are</u> our Med Tech. Congratulations." It nodded understanding and a little sympathy at their expressions. "My name is Captain Coy Lamont. This is my ship. I've owned it about two days. Counting you two, we now have seven people to run it. Still interested?"

The two prospective mercenaries stared. Schiff composed himself quickly. "What's first, Captain?"

Coy relaxed, knowing it had been right about these people. "First? You can pick your quarters. There's plenty to choose from. I can show you the gym and the armory. Byars, I'll show you to Sick Bay. Everything here is pretty much top of the line so I don't expect anyone to be an expert yet. Poke around. Learn the ship. I'll get uniforms and contracts issued as soon as possible. Any questions?"

Byars was looking at the floor. Schiff was still more or less at attention.

"Then follow me for the quick tour. We'll stop off at Ships Stores and get you a wrist com and measured for uniforms."

As they walked, Byars gathered her nerve. "Captain, who exactly do we work for? I mean do we have a name or anything?"

Coy thought of Bon's comments earlier. "The BlackFleet."

"Fleet." Schiff repeated dryly. "Seven people. Interesting size for a fleet."

"Well," Coy said just as dryly, "I might hire a few more. If I find the right people."

They both accepted the implied compliment and followed their captain through the empty corridors.

Among the several others who showed up before they broke dock, Coy found three more that "fit". A navigator and two more troopers. Parker, a woman nearing Schiff's age, seemed to have no trouble working up on the bridge with Hoffman. Coy suspected that she could either get along with, or overpower anyone she cared to. Buried carefully beneath her gruffness, Coy had caught a glimpse of her pain. After a life of military service, sacrificing everything, including her family, she was retired. Which led to boredom. Which led to wandering. Which led to Coy.

The troopers, Rebel and Pedula were put to work relieving the overworked Palo and Luka. After Pedula made a quick visit to Sick Bay, that is. There Byars broke in her new Med Tech status by administering her first hangover antidote. Not the most glamorous beginning of a career, but she felt glad to be contributing to the cause. Whatever it was.

After leaving Alluria, the crew of ten worked themselves almost to the dropping point running the massive ship. When the troopers weren't working out in the gym, they relieved someone on the bridge. The engineers took their turns helping with everything from Sick Bay to communications.

However, now that there was a Med Tech on board, no one was allowed to go days without sleep or skip very many meals. Ceal surprised herself as much as everyone else with how seriously she took her job. She wore her new uniform with obvious pride, and even clipped her strawberry blond hair into a short no-nonsense style. And the times she wasn't running a scanner over someone, or clucking over eating habits, she doubled as the supply officer, relaying needs to the, now, Commander Bon.

Bon himself had also drawn double duty being Chief Engineer and First Officer. Coy was all over the ship, helping with minor repairs here and there, taking a turn as pilot or com officer or composing fleet manuals…and the promised contracts… until its eyes blurred. On top of which it managed to take time everyday to connect with a member or two of the crew. Discuss a favorite piece of music, listen to a description of back home… some small indication that they were a person that someone cared about.

Everyone was exhausted. They had no idea where the ship was headed, or why. The only thing they did know, was that for some reason, Captain Lamont had chosen them over other, often seemingly more qualified, applicants. For most, if not all, it was the first time in a long time anyone had believed in them.

And they were determined to live up to that belief.

However, no one protested when Coy decided to dock at the next Transit Portal station and take a breather. While some went off ship to relax, Med Tech Byars took the opportunity and headed straight to the captain's cabin.

"Enter," Coy responded to the door buzzer.

She found her CO sitting on one of the small couches occupying the living area of the quarters. Scanner, disks, printouts, half of a sandwich and an empty mug were strewn all over the couch as well.

At one time in human history, almost all communication technology was so small that it was virtually impossible to hold. Eventually it became necessary to download everything into a port people had implanted, typically, but not always, at the base of their skull.

Then people started being affected. After a couple of generations of paranoia, disorders, and insanity, growing by leaps and bounds through the population, progress had to take a giant step backwards. Mankind stopped hardwiring their brains, the tools grew back to a size comfortable enough to hold, and the health professionals all breathed a collective sigh of relief.

Ceal, however, frowned at the mess. "What happened to time off?"

Coy shrugged instead of answering. "What can I do for you, Ceal?"

"I hope that was supper and not lunch," she nodded at the partial sandwich.

Coy looked at it and then at its chrono. "The first half was lunch. I'm not ready for supper yet."

Ceal rolled her eyes. "I should've believed him."

"Whom should you have believed?"

"Bon. He said you never eat enough."

"I eat."

"You intend to live on half of a sandwich a day?"

Coy sighed. "I eat what I need to. I'm...a genetic. They fiddled with my metabolism. I really don't get hungry very often."

"Hmmm. Anything else I ought to know? As your medical officer?" She sat down in a nearby chair. Startled out of what she was going to say next by the comfort of the furniture, she unconsciously sighed
and stroked the arm. When she glanced up and saw Coy watching her, she put her hands in her lap and forced her thoughts back to her reason for coming. "I've been running scans on the others to get at least some sort of baseline information to start their file until I can do real physicals."

Coy nodded approval. "Good idea."

"But I must admit, ah..."she faltered, trying very hard not to look at Coy's body.

"You've never dealt with hermaphrodites before," Coy finished for her.

"I've studied everything … I've just never had practical experience."

"Well," Coy put down what it had been reading and paused. "Like I said, I've been fiddled with a little, but my basics are straight-forward enough. Herms don't have unusual organs, just, ah, more of them."

"Your physical - arrangement- doesn't *bother* me ."

Coy's expression went blank. "Then, what's the problem?"

"I didn't say there was a problem. I just..." she reddened ... "Alright, so I'm plain old fashioned curious."

"You want to know whether I like males or females best? Or if I'm sex obsessed? Or whether someone who can't make up their mind what they are can be trusted to make decisions in a crisis?" Coy's words came out cold and filled with anger.

Ceal stared in disbelief at the sudden hostility. "Captain?" she asked carefully. "Are you okay? What kind of trigger did I hit, any-way?"

Coy blinked and shook its head as if to clear it, then looked blankly at her for a second.

"Captain?" she asked again.

"I don't..." Coy stammered, then cleared its throat. "I'm sor-ry. That was inappropriate." There was a moment of awkward silence. Then, "You were asking about my biology?"

Perhaps it was right and a more concrete medical approach was safer. "You said you had been 'fiddled' with. By Riga, I assume?"

Coy obviously hesitated before answering. Ceal took a chance and forged ahead anyway. "Your personal issues are not my business, I admit, but that sounded physical, and that is in my job description, I do believe. Besides, Captain, I'm your Med Tech. Nothing goes any further".

Lamont let its gaze relax just a little. "I was a military experi-ment. A lot of chemicals have little or no effect on me. For interroga-tions, I assume. I was supposed to be able...." It paused again. "I've got a file that explains some of it. I can give it to you."

"I would appreciate it." Ceal said simply. She actually would appreciate its life story. *A military experiment?* She admittedly had very
little experience in the greater universe but that sort of thing would be illegal on most of the worlds she had had contact with.

Coy was watching her again. "You're very good at this you know. Being a medical officer. I was fortunate that you came along."

"So am I." She smiled sincerely. "Even if I'm still not dead sure why we're all here. What is it we're all working so hard to do?"

Coy paused again, then finally sighed and said, "I've been thinking a lot about that lately. With this ship I have an opportunity. Have you ever been in a position when there was no good answer? There was something you *had* to do? People that needed help. And there was no 'right' way to help them? I've decided I want a unit to be able to do what needs done without the chains of command or red tape. Without having to get permission or....To be able to go where we're needed and do what we have to do."

Ceal was quiet for a moment. "Yeah. I know exactly what you mean..... Who were they?"

"They?"

"The people who needed your help and you couldn't because of red tape."

Ceal couldn't even begin to guess the myriad of emotions that were passing behind Coy's eyes. She mentally kicked herself. So much for any bedside manner. She kept opening tender wounds. "When do you suppose things will slow down enough for me to do proper physicals on everyone?" she changed subjects again.

Lamont gave one of its short, tired sighs. "I couldn't tell you, Ceal. Hopefully soon. I would like to run this outfit as properly as possible no matter what its size." It forced itself to sit up straighter. "Look, I'll set a precedent. Schedule a time for mine and I'll bring my file."

She returned the smile. "Thank you, Captain. I appreciate..." she paused. "Well, I appreciate it all. Your trust and support. I don't know what I would've done. I couldn't stay there any longer."

"Should I be aware of who's after you? For the Fleet's sake?" At her shocked look, it added. "I'm your Captain, Med Tech. It would go no further."

"I guess I owe you that, don't I?" She took a breath. "It's my uncle. He took over when my father and the others were... killed."

"Took over what?"

"The government. The planet. He's my guardian until I'm 25. I couldn't stand being there under his control so I ran. His agents catch up with me every once in a while. They found me on Servati in Med school. That's why I'm a Med Tech and not a physician. I left before I graduated. I was afraid if I stayed on Alluria any longer they'd find me again."

"What would happen if they did?"

"I, I don't really know. Best case, they would take me back. Worst...I'd rather not find out." She looked Coy in the eye. "Does this change anything?"

It shook its head. "No, you definitely belong here. And as your commander, I'll do my best to protect you from your enemies."

Ceal stared, eyes filling with tears. "I have a feeling you mean that."

"Would I lie to the person in charge of all the hyposprays?"

She smiled again at the hint of levity. "Thank you, Captain," she said sincerely. "I guess I'll go schedule that physical." They both got up and Coy walked her to the door. She paused halfway through and turned back. "And , Captain?"

"Yes?"

"Eat your sandwich."

Ken Butler sat in the bar staring blearily at the drink before him. He hadn't even had a sip and the world was already out of focus. It had been out of focus for days now. He squinted as he tried to remember how many days it had been. Since he hadn't slept in between any of them it was hard to calculate.

Hadn't slept, hadn't changed clothes, hadn't eaten much, come to think of it. He ought to check and see if he had enough currency left to get some food, but the effort of getting it out and counting seemed overwhelming.

The thought shook him into pseudo-alertness. Had he really sunk so low so quickly? Obviously so, he told himself. He shook his head but it wouldn't clear. This was crazy. He had to pull himself together.

He pushed the drink aside and stood, a little shakily. Perhaps he could trade it in on a sandwich or something. There, a plan. A goal. Life was looking up. He staggered over to the bar, glass in hand.

The bartender was talking to some people in black uniforms.

"That's some ship," he was saying. "There's rumors all over the station what it is."

"Just a ship," one of the men answered. "A big empty ship."

"Yeah? What's it supposed to be full of?"

"Mercenaries," a second man spoke up. "We're just a little understaffed at the moment."

His companions snorted at that.

"I know a hundred mercs who could sign on in a second. Just let me spread the word…"

"No," the first man cut him off with a shake of his head. "The Skipper is a little more particular than that when it comes to hiring."

Ken couldn't resist. "Particular about what?"

All four turned to stare at him. At his red eyes, his hollow cheeks and wrinkled clothes.

"About what kind of people it hires," a woman in the trio told him.

"It?" Ken asked.

"Herm," she explained.

"Really? A real one?" He wondered if he sounded as inane to them as he did to himself. Evidently he did. They shrugged him off as a nosey drunk and turned back to their own conversation. But unwilling to be dismissed so easily, he put a hand on the arm of the older man in the group. "What kind of people does it want?"

"Why?"

Why. Good question. Why was he bothering these mercenaries? Was he really desperate enough to seek employment with pirates? Soldiers of fortune? But these people hardly looked like pirates, trim and neat in their black uniforms. Weapons gleaming, boots polished. They wore no markings or insignia of any kind, though.

"I..." he began, then followed the man's gaze down to the hand on his arm. He removed it and tried again. "I need..."

"We don't take applications," the man said. "You want a job, you go see the captain."

Ken blinked. "Yeah, okay. Where is he? I mean it?"

"The *Raven*. Docking Bay 106."

"106. Thanks." Butler left the drink on the bar, forgot about the sandwich completely and headed off in search of Docking Bay 106, not entirely sure why.

When he found it he understood the barkeeper's comments. It didn't look like any mercenary ship. Not that he was up on that sort of thing. But this didn't even look military. It looked...elegant. Smooth and black. Like the uniforms. Must be a theme here.

Uniforms. He looked down at his own clothes in shame. He tried to smooth them and his hair with his hands. Nothing he could do about his eyes.

The guard posted at the tube connecting the big ship to the station, was watching all of this. Probably in amusement. Gathering what shreds of dignity he could, Butler walked over to him and looked him in the eye. To his surprise, there was no amusement.

"I'd like to see Captain..." he faltered, realizing he hadn't even asked the name.

"Lamont," the guard supplied. He raised his wrist to his face and spoke into an expensive com. "Luka to Hoffman. Gentleman to see the captain," he announced.

"On my way," a voice answered, blandly.

The guard nodded at Ken and lowered his arm again to stand at parade rest. It was only a minute or two before another merc appeared through the end of the tube to escort him.

The man had the tattoos of a Jump Pilot. Millions of dollars of specialized training and the JP was doing grunt work? A little under-staffed indeed.

"This way," he said without ceremony. He turned back and led Ken through the massive ship to a door. They had not passed another person on the way. The pilot pressed a buzzer.

"Enter," came the command through the com speaker.

The door opened. Butler looked to his guide for moral support, but the man was already walking away. Okay. Great. Taking a breath he walked in.

Whatever he had expected – this wasn't it.

This was obviously personal quarters he had been led to. Large and, yes he had to say it again, elegant, quarters. The person before him was dressed in the same black uniform as the ones in the bar. Still no markings. It looked female to him at first glance. It was sitting on a couch in front of a low table.

"Come in, Mr. Butler. Do you drink tea?" It indicated the table which was set with china cups and teapot.

"Ah..." Ken's mind whirled. It knew his name? Tea? Did he drink tea? "Sort of , I guess."

Lamont gestured at a seat. "Sit down. When did you eat last?"

"What?" Awkwardly, he sat.

It frowned. "When did you eat last," it repeated, slightly emphasizing each word.

"I, ah, don't remember. Exactly."

Coy nodded and handed him a cup. "This, first then. To take the edge off."

"Oh, right. Thanks." He stared at the tea for a moment, then took an experimental sip. It was warm and sweet. Before he realized it , he'd drained the cup. He looked at the captain and shrugged.

With a small smile, Lamont gave him a refill. "Now, then, I understand you're interested in a job with us."

"How...?" he pursed his lips. "It sort of depends on who 'us' is."

Another nod. "We are a new, and I mean brand new, outfit. This is your proverbial ground floor opportunity. We call ourselves the BlackFleet. Who we are, what we do is still pretty much on the drawing board. I think I know what I want to do, but..." It took a drink.

"Which is?"

Lamont put down its cup and leaned back against the couch with a tired smile. "I want to be a hero."

"To who?"

"Anyone out there who needs it. Planetary systems can take care of their own area, but what about in between systems? 'Open water', so to speak. Who is there for them?"

Butler cocked his head. "And you really think there's a market for that sort of thing?"

The smile faded. The tired remained. "Yes, there is."

"Any money in it?"

"I don't know."

"I see." He looked at his cup again and swirled the last little bit of tea around in it. "Then you do it just because."

"Basically, yes."

"You plan on eating? Paying for all this?" Butler waved his hand vaguely around.

"We'll eat. This ship is paid for and fully stocked..."

"With everything but a crew from what I heard. You could have a lot of people if you wanted..." he paused. "Of course that would be more to feed..."

Lamont gave a sigh. "I don't want *people*. I want the *right* people. People who care." It got up suddenly and paced to a view port. It looked out for a moment before adding quietly, "People who have been there."

Butler didn't ask where 'there' was. It probably wasn't a place. Maybe a situation. Maybe a time when they could've used a hero. A time like...

"I think I'm in the wrong place," Butler mumbled. Self-consciously he set the cup back on its tray. He looked up to find Lamont peering at him curiously. "I'm no hero," he explained.

"Are you sure?"

"The whole reason I'm on this stinking station is because I couldn't..." he swallowed. He looked at Lamont looking at him, trying to decide what he saw in the other's eyes. Curiosity. Encouragement. And something else. Something he hadn't seen in quite a while. Acceptance.

"I'm ...was... a commander. Third officer on the flagship," he began haltingly. "My brother got our father's titles, I got a military career. It's kind of how things are done..." he straightened defensively. "Not that I didn't work for my commission. I did.

"Anyway, here we are out on maneuvers and the skipper slips a gear. Making stupid commands and forgetting the name of the queen. But it's not that bad. And he's still the captain, right? Right? Still the man I swore loyalty to." Butler's voice rose with his agitation. "The rest of the crew didn't see it that way. They thought the exec should take over. I guess they were right about assuming command in a crisis or something, but he deserved some dignity. They even..." another swallow. "I couldn't be a part of it. He wasn't that loony." He paused again.

"Go on."

Butler shrugged. "One day I had enough. I punched the exec. Mutiny, they said. I ask you, how is mutiny against a mutiny wrong? Two wrongs and all that I guess....I was thrown in the brig...These people were in the Queen's Service for heaven's sake! They acted no better than common..." he stopped himself just short of 'mercenaries'. He glanced quickly at Lamont, but either it didn't catch what he'd been about to say or politely pretended not to. "They didn't even wait to go home for a trial. They stripped me of my rank in front of the crew. And when we passed by here, they dumped me. So here I am. The hotshot protégé of the fleet."

"What about your family?" Lamont asked gently.

"I'm sure they told my brother I deserted."

"You could contest that."

"My word against an entire crew? I might as well save time and behead myself."

"If you allowed pentha..."

He shook his head. "Truth drugs aren't allowed on Mueller's World. Sacrilegious or something. No, face it, Captain, I'm a bad bet." He stood. "Thanks for the tea."

"You're welcome, Commander. Would you like dinner before or after you select quarters?"

Butler stared.

"I told you, I wanted people who had been there. People who had the integrity and guts to make tough choices." It smiled. "People who need a bed and a meal badly enough not to quibble over a paycheck."

Butler stared a moment longer before he let a return smile grow across his own face. Lamont came over and put out its hand.

"Welcome aboard, Commander."

"Thank you, Captain." They shook hands. "Captain Lamont, isn't it?"

"Yes. Coy Lamont."

"Ken Butler."

"I know."

"You know a lot."

"My officers called to say you were on your way. The bartender knew your name."

"Oh. Right." So simple. "So who actually owns this outfit?"

"I do."

"You and what Bank?"

"Just me. It's a long story. But it is mine. And it needs an exec."

Ken grinned. "Ironic, somehow. Now, I have to take it . As long as you don't have any young upstarts that go around punching officers. Besides, you mentioned something about dinner?"

Coy added his name to the roster. Eleven people. Could anyone save the universe with eleven people? *Don't be silly, an inner voice mocked. You'd need at least twenty to save the **whole** universe.*

A large ship docked at the station drew the attention of a number of people seeking employment. However, the next few who turned up on the doorstep Coy sent packing quickly. They left saying very uncomplimentary things about Rigans in general, hermaphrodites in particular, and Captain Lamont specifically.

Commander Butler did them an undeserved favor by keeping Schiff and Rebel from taking them apart and spacing the pieces. Coy quietly watched in approval as Butler held his ground and earned a grudging respect from the two troopers.

An hour before leaving dock, an earnest young man came begging an interview for himself and a friend. Coy met them in the smaller of the two lounges turned briefing rooms.

Upon entering the room, they both came to attention and saluted- one a beat behind the other. Coy returned them , blandly.

"At ease. What can I do for you gentlemen?"

"We've come to apply for positions aboard your vessel. Sir, ah, sir."

" 'Sir' is fine," Coy assured them. "What exactly do you offer that the people I've turned down didn't?"

They exchanged a bewildered look. "Turned down?" the second said. "We heard you had lots of openings."

"I do. But they are very specific openings." Curious, Lamont cocked its head. "What have you heard?"

"Not much," the first answered. "We hit the station less than an hour ago. To be honest, we're here because we ran out of money to go any further. Someone at the port said this ship was hiring on mercenaries before she left, so we gave it a shot. I didn't realize you needed specialists."

"I see." Coy sat down. They stayed at attention. "Where have you served before this?"

"Me? On merchant ships, sir."

"Oh? They salute a lot on merchant ships?"

"Well, *actually*," the young man drawled the word out, "they were my second choice. I started out in military school."

"You've had academy training?"

"Technically, yes. But not command. Computers. A little communications work. That sort of thing."

Coy blinked in disbelief at this gift landing in its lap. Aloud it said, "From military to merchant to mercenary. Do you have difficulty deciding what to do with yourself?"

He shuffled his feet a little. "A merchant ship was the quickest way off planet at the time."

Coy tried to look stern and encouraging at the same time. How did Commodore Aubry always do it? "Away from what?"

"I, ah, needed to put some distance between myself and my father's people."

"Your father's "people" ?"

"He's a, ah, businessman. Mostly. Sort of."

Coy made a few mental assumptions and cleared the young man. It focused on the other. "Are you tech as well?"

"No, s-sir. I've never worked for anyone with a real army. Just security work. You, know, warehouses, rent-a-cop and so on."

Lamont frowned a little. "What makes you think you can be a soldier?"

The two looked at each other. The former security guard swallowed, and with an effort, turned back to Lamont. "If I have to explain that in words, I guess I won't make it. When Dev suggested we give it a try, it seemed like a good idea. It seemed..." Coy watched hopefully while he struggled for words and nerve. Finally, he found both. "You're not pirates, are you?"

Coy blinked in surprise. "If I were, would I tell you?"

He shrugged.

"No. We are *not* pirates."

Something in Coy's tone made him smile. "I didn't think so. I would hate to think I'd left everything just to end up on the other side after all."

"The other side of what?'

Another swallow. "My folks were killed by pirates. Everybody back home thinks I'm just out for revenge...but it's not just that. There's more people than me that needs..." He gave a small frustrated sigh. "It's...like I said. I don't know how to explain it."

"What is your name?"

"Randy Sweggert, sir."

"And..?" to the other.

"Devyu Aziza."

"Very well. My name is Capt. Coy Lamont. I own and command this ship. Welcome to the BlackFleet. Mr. Sweggert, I will introduce you to Sgt. Schiff. He will get you situated. Mr. Aziza, there is a communications console up on the bridge waiting for you."

Both of their faces lit like candles.

"We're in?!" Aziza exclaimed. "I mean, yes, sir. Thank you , sir"

Coy smiled at their enthusiasm, called Schiff and added their names.

Numbers fourteen to twenty-two came quickly at their next few stops: Andrea Pierce, a stunning blond with a wicked kick and deadly aim. Anton Vennefron, quick minded but pessimistic. Barry Donalds, cool and confident. Cori Swift, a bubbly red-head and Helen McKnight, her tall dark counterpart. Tony Knepp, one of the few with actual military training and talented as either trooper or tech. Orson Terrell, who signed on as a tech, but after listing first aid as a talent was snapped up by Byars for a corpsman. Sammy Nathon, a born tinkerer.   And lastly Sren Erhardt, a lonely young clone who needed a chance to live his own life.

Each with their own version of the Story. Each with something they desperately needed; each with something they desperately needed to give.

The day the last one signed on, Coy sat staring at the roster. People under its command. Did it really want this again? Now that it had them, what should it do with them? '*What are you going to do with this fleet of yours?*' It hadn't lied to Butler. It knew what it wanted. But it went against all of its training and its....Coy paced and thought and calculated all through the sleep cycle. It was afraid to think it might actually be caring about something. And the fear was as unaccustomed as the caring.

In the "morning" it took a deep breath and called a meeting with Bon and Butler.

"We're ready," it told them as they sat around the table in the port briefing room.

"Ready?" Bon asked. "Ready for what, Commodore?"

"To get down to business. The BlackFleet is on line."

Butler blinked. "You're kidding, right? We have , what, nineteen people now? Not counting the three of us. What are we going to do with twenty-two people?"

"Numbers are not the issue. It depends more on motivation. Training."

"Motivation, I'll take your word for, but half these people are *not* trained," Butler insisted.

"So train them, Exec. I want you to sit down with Schiff and work it out so everyone is trained. I have their assignments here," it gave the data to him. "Raeph, you have 6 people under you counting Pedula, although I want him as shuttle pilot. If you need anyone else in a pinch request Knepp. Or Aziza if he's not on the bridge."

"Okay. I won't even mention that I could use a staff of twenty all by myself."

"Thank you for not mentioning it."

"Then I will," Butler said. "Why ? I mean, this isn't permanent. Is it?"

Coy paused. "I don't know. Possibly. I want a small team. This ship , even at its size does not need a lot of maintenance. Yes, we all will be pulling long shifts. But what I want to do can best be done with a small, tightly knit unit. When you have intimate knowledge of your team mates abilities and reaction times your efficiency is phenomenal."

Butler tried again. "You really think we can go out there," he waved his arm in a large circle, "and be vigilantes or something? Playing hero ? That's *really* what this is all about? Then give me an army to do it with!"

Coy crossed its arms but said nothing.

Ken opened his mouth to protest further, but Bon gave him a nudge and a shake of the head. "This is the people it wants, this is the people we have, this is the people we'll work with."

Butler contained himself with an effort. "Bootlicker," he mumbled.

Lamont nodded. "Now that it's settled, talk to Schiff. We break orbit in four hours. I'm calling an all crew meeting in one. I want the schedules then." It stood and they followed suit. "Right now, I have an appointment with our Med Tech."

Twenty-one people occupied the large lounge-turned-conference room. Which left a lot of empty seating space. The few who had been aboard since Alluria spoke to each other in quiet, familiar tones. Others looked about the room warily, or at their hands nervously. The newest recruits just sat, wondering. In an outfit this new, four or five days gave a person a lot of seniority.

The doors swished open and the captain entered. Lamont strode to the front of the room and looked over the group. Its first crew since... They all looked back with various degrees of puzzlement and curiosity. It was very glad none of them had seen it pacing the corridor outside this room , doing battle with its warring desires.

There was no need for gavel banging or throat clearing. Everyone's attention was locked to the person before them.

"I believe", Coy opened, " in doing what is right. And I believe in doing what is correct. And I have found they are not always the same." There was a murmur of agreement around the room.

"Perhaps you have wondered what kept you on board when so many others have been sent away. It is my understanding from talking to each of you, that you, each in your own circumstances, have had to choose between right and correct. Between honor and duty. It is not an easy decision. Many of us have paid dearly for our choices. We have lost family, homes, careers and friends. But those choices led you here, to this moment. To the BlackFleet."

Some of the puzzlement melted away. A myriad of expressions took its place. Old pain, damaged pride, skeptical hope.

"Many have asked what you were hired for. What the Black-Fleet is going to be. Well, ladies and gentlemen, we are going to be heroes. For anyone who needs us. Profit is not going to be our first priority. If it is yours, let me know now, while the other side of the airlock is attached to the station." Coy paused. Did they understand what it was asking of them? Had it read them right during those, often hasty, interviews? It went on. "Another belief of mine is that everyone deserves the right to prove - and improve - themselves. Many of you have military experience, which has been considered, but it is not the only grounds for an assignment.

"As of yet we have no rank insignia. We will, however, be professional. I expect you to follow proper form and courtesy whether someone is wearing a pin or not. As you know, I am owner and captain of this ship. You will address me as such. Commander Butler..." a nod and he rose from his seat... "is second in command and Executive Officer. He's the one you tell your problems to." Coy gave him a small nod. He returned a grimace. "Commander Bon..." Butler sat and Bon rose. ... " is our Chief Engineer and third in command. Which makes him responsible for anything that doesn't work." Bon saluted and sat. "Jump Pilot Hoffman," he remained seated, "that's rather self explanatory. And you don't bother him with *anything*." A small spattering of chuckles acknowledged the value of the JP. "Med Tech Byars is in charge of bumps, bruises and migraines. Lieutenant Parker is Navigation and Weapons. Lieutenant Aziza is Communications. Those, for now, are the officers.

"Sgt. Schiff is our hand to hand expert and is in charge of ground troop training and crew fitness. We will all get to know him very well over the next few weeks. His second is Cpl. Rebel. Troopers are, Pierce, Vennefron, Sweggert, Knepp, Donald and Erhardt. Bon's second in Engineering is Cpl. Luka. Techs are, Palo, Nathon, Swift and McKnight. Pedula will be our shuttle pilot. Terrell is Corpsman. "

Myke Pedula gave a small sigh at the announcement. Having noticed his discomfort during the last jump, Coy discovered upon further conversation that he was, more than likely, a natural born pilot. Assigning him to the shuttle was the first step toward ultimately getting the training that would allow him to reach his potential. Assuming he could overcome his ingrained opinion that his abilities made him abnormal.

"Those are primary assignments. You will each have secondary and tertiary training. In an emergency everyone is a tech, everyone is a trooper and everyone better know first aid and stasis prep. Anyone who, for personal reasons does not wish to be frozen and revived can put that in their file and it will be honored." Coy stopped and looked them over again. "Any questions?"

A hand raised and Coy nodded at it.

"Do you prefer 'sir' or 'ma'am' ?"

"I have no preference." That should answer their unspoken question as well. "I tend to go by 'sir' because it is more universally accepted by military. Next?"

Pierce stood up. "Do we *always* wear black? It's not my color."

Coy watched her toss her long blond locks over her shoulder and recalled her interview. Strikingly beautiful, Andrea Pierce had been pre-judged and underestimated her entire life. Having finally had her fill, she had decided the only thing to do was to turn the flaw into a feature. Taking part in her world's civil war, she had been able to get into places no other underground agent could. The last thing many an enemy saw was a blinding smile and that toss of curls.

"Our uniforms are black," Coy told her. "What you wear , or don't wear , off duty is your business."

She grinned, saluted and sat down.

Another hand. "Why does Commander Bon call you Commodore?"

Coy scowled at the chief engineer. "An old joke. Irrelevant as well."

"What about relationships among crew?"

Coy pursed its lips for a second. Didn't anyone have any *military* questions? It reminded itself of the varied backgrounds represented here. Some, like the Haradans, did not have mixed crews in their military.

"Relationships are an expected part of life. However, I will not tolerate any past time that interferes with the performance of duty. If it is easier to fight alongside of people with whom you are not emotionally entangled, you had best take that into consideration." It went very serious as it added. "Any *relationship* that exploits another crew member for rank or privilege will not be tolerated. The offender will be dropped off at the first oxygen bearing location – no matter where that is."

"How will we be paid?" someone finally asked a practical question.

"Each of you now has an account. As income comes in, it will be divided according to rank and performance. All food, uniforms, and equipment will be supplied by the Fleet."

"Does the Fleet have more than one ship?"

Coy worked hard not to glance at Butler. "As of now, it is one ship. As of now, you are the crew. That is all I know...Anything else?" There were a few more queries pertaining mostly to duties, ship functions and equipment. When there appeared to be no more immediate questions, Coy nodded to Butler and stepped aside.

Commander Butler stood and faced the others. "Today you will be given regulations manuals, ship schematics and Fleet procedures. Read them. Study them. Sleep with them. There *will* be a test....And only I know when.

"This is a large ship and a small crew. We have the luxury of being comfortable and the burden of maintaining it. Pulling your own weight is your basic job description.

"There are two gyms, officer's and crew. Don't mix them up. Officers also have the option of dining in their quarters. All crew will take their meals in the Crew Mess. All officers are housed on Deck D, everyone else on Deck E. Decks A, C and F will not be used for now. Life support will not be on in those places. If you go exploring, don't expect a rescue squad to bail you out.

"You have six hours before we leave dock in which to learn your way around. Duties will commence as soon as we break orbit. Sgt. Schiff has the schedules for training, Byars has one for physicals. No exceptions for either. Your daily duty roster will be continuously updated. Check your console last thing at night and first thing in the morning."

He stepped back. On cue, Schiff stood stiffly. "Attention!"

They all stood. Most stood correctly. One or two were still a little bewildered. Coy came forward and inspected them.

"Nevermore ," it said, "will we be alone. Nevermore will we be outcasts. Nevermore will we be searching for a place to belong. Starting today, we are The BlackFleet!" Chins came up. Spines straightened. Coy blinked at the effect its words had. "Dismissed." Everyone filed out, those who did not have military background imitating the stride of those who did.

The senior officers remained at Coy's side, watching them.

"Well," Bon grinned, "Here we go."

Butler gave a dramatic sigh. "I don't know about a couple of these guys, Skipper. You really think they can make it?"

" I do."

"And what if you're wrong? What if they get blown away trying to play hero?"

"We're not playing, Commander," it told him gravely, and walked

Chapter Two

In the months that followed the BlackFleet crew was put through a grueling training process. Physical endurance was pushed to the limit and a little beyond. Even Coy was surprised at Schiff's skills in martial arts and weaponry. And he was insistent that everyone else master them as well. On top of that, they had safety drills, battle armor drills, medical emergency drills, technical repair drills, shuttle drills, rescue scenarios and battle simulations.

More than one trainee was seen dragging themselves to their quarters for a few precious hours of rest, mumbling about mutiny and murder. In the end, twenty stuck it out.

Donald came to Lamont and Butler one morning. Without a word he dropped his wrist com on the floor at their feet. He then secluded himself in his quarters until their next stop. Sweggert, Knepp and Rebel tried to talk to him over the door com, but he answered no one.

Nathon came to the hatch when Donald left and also turned in his com. He looked Lamont in the eye with great difficulty. "Make no mistake, Skipper. I know what I'm losing out on. But I just can't cut it. I'm sorry I let you down."

Coy watched them leave silently, trying to decide if it were disappointed that they were giving up, or relieved that they were going to stay alive.

Lamont watched the events in engineering from the communications station up on the bridge. Bon had been particularly merciless in the last training exercise and now six hands were flying over their engineering consoles in an attempt to keep the *Raven's* fusion reactors from 'blowing up'.

The engineers had caught the problem and corrected it in minutes. But these were troopers sweating over the switches. And considering that fact, Coy was pleased that they had even noticed the booby trap -- let alone had a clue as to how to fix it. Sgt. Schiff must have truly put the fear of something into them when it came to studying specs.

There was a throat clearing over by the door and Bon wandered over to join Schiff and Butler who were watching as well. He moved quietly so as not to disturb the "techs".

"So," Butler opened in a low voice, "are we dead yet?"

"Not yet. They're getting it."

"In time to stay alive?"

Schiff frowned at his skepticism, but said nothing.

"Give them a chance, Ken. If Lamont hadn't thought..."

An alarm interrupted, filling the room with its raucous death warning. The trainees frantically hit switches, and routed information on the panel, in an attempt to activate the emergency fail safes in the brief interval of time now left to them by the exercise. Two minutes later, a buzzer sounded that time was up. The panel in front of them simply read "boom". A chorus of groans went up from the troopers. Sweggert flopped back in his station chair in disgust. Pierce and Vennefron froze for a second, then turned to Bon in defeat. After a moment, Randy Sweggert reached over and silenced the panel.

Bon gave a small sigh. "It's always darkest...."

"....just before it goes completely black," Butler finished. He shook his head and walked out of engineering.

"Why don't I just hit self-destruct at the beginning and save us all a lot of trouble," Randy sneered.

Schiff strode over to him and jerked him out of the chair . "Get back to the gym and run laps until I say to stop," he hissed, then turned to the others. "Your comrade has just died in a hostile takeover. It's up to you two to save the rest of us." He gave them a cold glare. "I, for one, expect to live this time." Turning to go, he gave a nod to Bon.

The engineer stifled a smile and proceeded to set up another exercise.

Lamont turned off the vid and waited, knowing what was coming.

Butler reached the command deck just as Devyu Aziza, hair still damp from the gym, relieved Lamont at communications.

"Sweggert just blew the ship to pieces again," the commander announced. "We're all floating debris."

"I saw. What's Bon's opinion?"

"Skipper, the man was *smiling*. Like they were doing good!"

Lamont shrugged. "Perhaps they are. It's his domain. He knows what he's seeing." Coy made a quick tour of the stations, manned and unmanned, then motioned for Ken to follow out into the corridor. "Schiff said Rebel and Knepp were both shaping up great. Potential officers there."

"Officers over who?"

"Whom."

Ken scowled. "Whatever. The issue is manpower. Not grammar."

Lamont paused and looked at him a moment at that. "Would you like a cup of tea, Commander? It's great for stress."

"We'd better start serving it by the gallon, then," Butler growled, gave a half-hearted salute and turned back towards the bridge.

"There's an old Earth saying," Coy said to his back. "It's always darkest...."

The hatch shut behind him.

".....right before the dawn," Coy finished thoughtfully to itself.

A shrill scream jerked Lamont awake. It lurched to a sitting position and looked wildly around the dark room. But the only sound breaking the silence was Coy's own adrenaline fed heartbeat.

Coy raised its wrist and spoke into the com link that was always strapped there. "Lamont to Bridge."

"Bridge. Go ahead, Captain."

The voice sounded calm. The only emotion was perhaps surprise at the middle of the "night" call. In a second, Coy realized where the scream had come from and felt like a fool.

The person on the other end was still waiting. But then, there was no way for the bridge crew to know if this was an actual emergency, a drill, an inspection ... or a bad dream.

"Status report," Coy said in its best inspection voice.

"All quiet , sir. No reports since shift change. No incoming communications. Cpl. Rebel is on Watch."

"Very good. Carry on. Lamont out."

As the adrenaline rush passed and Coy's heart rate slowed to normal, it tried to blot out the memory of the scream. Of the whole nightmare. The same one that had been plaguing its sleep more and more often these past few weeks.

Now that the initial flurry of activity surrounding owning a ship and planning her future was settling into routine, the possibility of actually leading a raid was becoming a reality.

Coy lay back against the pillows, tired, but unwilling to let sleep, hence dreams, take it back to the scene of its greatest failure.

After a few minutes, it got up to make a gallon of tea.

Lamont fell heavily into the chair at the galley table the next day and looked at the food sitting there on the tray. Nothing appeared terribly appetizing, but it had been quite awhile since meals had been anything but

nutri-bars, coffee and of course the occasional cup of tea. A real dinner was probably in order.

Besides, Ceal Byars would be checking around to see if her commander was eating right.

"Is this a private party, or can anyone join?"

Lamont looked up to see Ken and Ceal hovering, trays in hand. Coy waved a hand at the empty seats around the table, inviting them to sit.

Ceal eyed Coy's plate approvingly. "I'm glad to see that."

Without replying, Coy took a bite and forced it down.

Ignoring their interplay, Butler gazed around the large mess hall, peopled at present with only a handful of BlackFleet crew. He opened his mouth, but Coy cut across whatever remarks he was about to make.

"I know we're down to 20 people and I don't feel like any *'why don't we increase the size of the fleet'* arguments today."

"You're making assumptions," Butler put on a frown. "How do you know that's what I was going to say?"

Lamont cocked its head in unspoken question.

"Well, okay, so it was. But still...."

"Case closed."

Butler made some frustrated sounds. He took a breath and let it out slowly. "Make me understand."

Coy collected its thoughts for a time. "I...I don't know that I can lead more than what we have." It pushed the tray away, leaned on the table and sighed. When it spoke again, Coy's voice was low. "I don't know that I can lead anyone."

Ceal and Ken looked at each other in amazement. This was not the ongoing feud Butler had expected. This was deep and real. And a little scary.

"You can't lead us?" Ken choked out. "Then what in blazes are we doing here?"

Coy's head came up and its eyes met Butlers. "To heal....we have to help others heal."

"I thought it was to be heroes."

Inwardly, Coy chastised itself for bringing it up. But not answering was not going to help. The damage was done. Another saying came to mind about closing the barn doors too late. Whatever a barn was.

"And what," Ken asked carefully, "did you mean about not being able? I've seen you training these guys. I've seen them grow. Just what is it you don't think you can do?"

Coy shook its head. "I don't know. Maybe it will be okay. Just...just always have contingencies. I'm not above doing really stupid things."

Butler cleared his throat. "This is all very comforting, Captain. Would you please tell me what the hell you're talking about?"

Lamont glanced around the room. "Not here." It stood and walked out of the galley. Two crew members just entering snapped to attention and saluted. Lamont absently returned the gesture and continued on. With a shrug and an 'after you', Butler and Byars followed.

Coy led them to its cabin. In the corridor, waiting for them was Bon, having been summoned by Lamont enroute. Without comment, Coy opened the door and went in.

Bon frowned at the other two. "What's up?"

Butler gave an elaborate shrug. "I'm hoping to find out myself."

Once in the cabin, they followed Coy over to the couch area. Coy itself stood, back to them , gazing at the wall. After a minute, it turned and nodded at Bon, who, along with the others, had settled back against the cushions. "We were discussing my ability to lead this unit...." it began.

"*We* were doing nothing of the kind," Butler objected. "*You* were discussing...."

"All right, *I* was," Coy admitted. "I realized that although I required everyone to tell me their story, I've never told anyone mine."

"And you think somehow this story will disqualify you?" Ken said, a bit impatiently. "Whatever happened to the creed of the Fleet? Second chances, and all that?"

"Ken, shut up for a minute," Ceal told him.

He shut his mouth, crossed his arms, and looked at Coy expectantly.

Lamont took a breath and began. "I was a captain in *Corbet's Commandos* . A pretty typical bunch of mercs. I was glad to be a soldier. I was literally made to… ," it paused and glanced at Ceal before continuing , "…even though the jobs we took were pretty safe, boring little jobs. Then we stopped on.....we stopped at an asteroid mine to resupply. Some of the miners came to the Admiral in secret and begged we help them get out. Their lives were no better than slavery. Horrible conditions." It shook its head in memory. "But the Admiral said no. We, Commodore Aubry and I , tried to talk him into it, but he wouldn't budge. He never liked getting his hands dirty....Anyway, they came back to us later, right before we left the asteroid. They were so desperate....I smuggled them onboard my ship and dropped them off at the next transit portal station we came to." Coy paused again.

"I assume there's more to it," Ken said, in what was for him, a patient tone.

Coy looked at the stars. "There were a lot more than the ones I got off. So I went back....and this time I got caught. We were pinned down by the mine security. I don't know what all they did there, but they had some pretty tough weapons for security guards. I thought it was all over. The miners panicked. Some of them tried to go back. The guards mowed them down. Just then Commodore Aubry shows up to save our tails. He was standing next to me laughing, saying , ' I knew you were going to do something like this someday, Kid' when he got hit by a plasma beam. One second he's my only friend in the universe. The next he's a pile of ashes."

Ken and Ceal remained attentive. Bon was looking at his hands.

"By the time we got out of there and met up with the rest of the fleet, I would've agreed to anything."

"What did you agree to?" Ceal asked cautiously.

"The Admiral asked for my resignation. He could've hanged me for mutiny." Coy sat down at last. "There have been times I wished he had."

No one spoke for several minutes. Bon got up and went to the large port behind Coy's desk and looked out at space.

"So," Coy broke the silence, "you see I'm not the hero I've insisted everyone be. I directly disobeyed my CO. My crime was real."

"Did you get the miners out?" Bon asked.

"Most of them. Not all."

He turned around. "You're right. Your admiral could've executed you. But he didn't. Maybe you're not as guilty as you think."

Coy looked frustrated at their inability to understand. "I got my only friend killed, because he followed me out there. I thought I wanted command...I do want command ...but I can't..." It sighed. "How can I ask you to trust me?"

"But you did ask." Butler interjected, "And we agreed. And here we are. And my opinion hasn't changed. You lost your command because you did what you thought was right. Right, even when not correct. Isn't that the way it goes?"

Coy didn't comment.

Ken looked to the other two. "Am I wrong here? Am I missing something?"

"Not as far as I'm concerned," Ceal said. "Captain, you once told me that as my commanding officer you would defend me against my enemies if they ever caught up to me." Coy nodded. "I don't think you comprehend what that means to me. I've never had someone on my side like that before. I know a lot of the guys around here feel the same. Technically, I'm still a minor back home. It was against the law for me to even leave without permission. Does that mean I shouldn't...."

Coy stood up. "You don't..."it began angrily.

"Don't what?" Bon interrupted. "Hate you? No, we don't. You're on your own there."

Coy looked taken aback. "You think this is self pity?" it demanded.

"To tell you the truth, I don't know what it is." Bon rubbed the back of his head as he thought back. "I was tossed out of the service for not following orders. Minor detail the orders were cruel and inhuman. It's still mutiny. I could've been killed. But instead the charges were swept under the rug and I was let go. Dishonor is a hard thing to deal with on Harada . Or anywhere." He looked back at Coy. "It's been years for me. I've had time." He raised one brow. "That's why you made that bet wasn't it? Some sort of self-punishment?"

"What bet?" Ken asked.

Bon remained looking at Coy. After several moments, it gave in and turned back to Ceal and Ken

"I used myself for collateral in a high stakes card game. That's how I won the *Raven*."

"You won the *Raven* in a..." Ken began, then realized what Coy had said. "Wait. Bet *yourself*?!" he sputtered in disbelief. "To be...I mean, to..."

"We've all lost part of our selves. But we've gained this chance," Ceal said quietly. "This was meant to be."

Butler looked at her, and then at Bon. "You mean like 'It's always darkest right before....'"

He was interrupted by Coy's wrist com. "Aziza to Lamont!"

"Lamont, go ahead."

"Skipper, we've intercepted a transmission. It's the Tenetian consul on Melan. They say they have ten dignitaries held hostage on the new Melan orbital Station. They assume terrorists. It was a record-ed message, but the old guy sounds desperate. The message was tightbeamed - probably to a Tenetian vessel - but there's nothing as close as we are."

Coy thought for only a second. "Send back: 'Message re-ceived. Help enroute.' On the same frequency."

"Aye, aye."

"Lamont out." It turned to Butler. "Do we know anything about Melan station?"

"I think so." Butler went over to Coy's vidcom and brought up all the stations they had been collecting information about. "Some basics. Building design. Some sketchy info about the governments. Tenetia is a monarchy, I know that."

Coy nodded. "Gather as much as you can. Full crew meeting in the Starboard room."

Butler was speaking into his own com even as he hurried from the room. "Butler to All Ship. All crew to the Starboard briefing room. All crew, starboard room. Vennefron, report to I &S ..."

Byars hurried out after him, on her way to prep her Sick Bay for whatever was necessary. Bon hung back a moment. "It would seem the time for discussion is past."

Coy gave a short nod, but said nothing.

"Want a pep talk?"

"Such as?"

"Such as all the things you already know. How you've made sure these guys were trained right. How you're the best ship captain I've seen, whether you see it or not. How everyone here is here be-cause it is their desire to be here, doing this, with you."

Coy looked him in the eye for a long moment. "Butler's right," it told him finally.

"About what?"

"You are a bootlicker."

Bon grinned, saluted and they both dashed out.

There was no relaxed conversation at this meeting. For all they knew, this was one of Schiff's endless drills. But you couldn't tell by their faces. Drill or not, they were primed and ready. Coy felt a wave of… was that pride?

"We have our first job," Lamont announced. "There are ten people being held on a space station we assume by professional terror-ists. Our job is to get them off safely." Butler and Vennefron entered from Intelligence and Security, a small room dedicated solely to the gathering of information. Lamont had recently discovered Venn's talent for sifting large amounts of data for relevant information and had assigned him to help Butler whenever necessary. Butler nodded at Lamont to indicate the information was ready and sat down. Coy returned a nod of thanks and continued speaking as it pulled it up onto the vidcom. "How many of you are aware of the Trojan Horse scenario?" Every hand went up. They had better. It was standard BlackFleet drill. They had been over it dozens of times in theory and practice. "We are going to offer them something they can't refuse to open their gates for."

Rebel spoke up. "If a message was sent, won't they assume someone's coming?"

"Yes. And we'll allow them to keep track of us. The *Raven* will continue on its present course, at moderate speed, alternating shield frequencies. Hopefully, at least one of those frequencies will be read by them so they will believe they are tracking us. It will be manned by Bon's staff and the bridge team. Everyone else will be on the *Blackbird*. It may look like a yacht, but it has full jump capabilities. We will leave the *Raven* and jump beyond Melan, then head back to it at full speed. If they are keeping
their eyes on Bon, hopefully they won't expect so blatant a trick. We'll simply knock on their door and offer our gift."

"Which is...?" Bon asked for everyone.

When Coy told them, smiles of appreciation rippled across the room.

"Melan Station! Come in please!" the desperate voice called over and over.

"What the ...." the terrorist manning the com network punched on an audio only channel. "This station is not in operation. Move along or be used for target practice."

His comrades chuckled at that, but the pilot of the small ship didn't give up. "Look, this stuff is gonna blow anyway if I don't get help. This is not worth my cut, I mean commission." He paused, perhaps reading a gauge. "Come on, man! It's getting hotter!"

"What is?" the terrorist couldn't resist asking, despite orders.

"This stuff. The Duromite. It's more unstable than they said. It's not worth any fortune to me if I'm dead or maimed."

"Duromite," one of the other terrorists breathed. "A fortune is right. Get the commander up here."

The com man spoke to the pilot again. "Hold your current position. We'll see what we can do."

"I can't...." he began, then swallowed. "All right," he said shakily and cut off communications.

Within moments the senior officer had joined them. "What do you think you're doing? You're not up here to play traffic control."

"Sir, this guy has a load of Duromite."

The commander whistled. "That stuff's not due to be out of the labs for months."

"He's a smuggler. Gave himself away. He's scared to death it's unstable and he's going to die before he can collect."

"Hmm," the commander rubbed his chin. "Where did he come from?"

"Can't tell. But his engines are over heating according to the sensor trace. He's been running flat out."

"And what about our BlackFleet friends?"

"Still coming," another man answered. "Two hours at present speed and course. They're being real cautious."

"Two hours. Okay. Get me the smuggler on vid." A holo image came up of a young man, sweat trickling over his pilot tattoo. " I understand you want our help?"

The pilot nodded. "I'll never make it to my buyer. This stuff's worth a lot. If you've got a lab there to contain it....Look, I'll sell it to you. Cheap. Just let me dock."

The commander smiled and cut the audio. "Do we have anything to contain it here in case he's peeing his pants with reason?" he asked his people.

"Yes, sir. These folks built a pretty decent lab."

He flipped the audio back on. "Very well, we'll give you one percent of what your buyer was."

"One percent!" the pilot yelped, then glanced at his gauges. "Okay, okay. Where do I dock?"

"My officers will direct you." He cut the link and turned to those officers. "Shoot him as soon as he hands over the stuff. It could be worth more than our guests."

"Yes, sir."

The ship came to dock, the flex tube attached and the hatches opened. The terrorists watched from the vantage points, waiting for their opportunity. At last someone stuck his head out of the hatch. It was the pilot from the transmissions.

"You guys want this stuff? Help me!" he called then ran back in.

The officer in charge nodded to one of the snipers. Weapon still at ready, he approached the hatch. Without pausing he went in. The weapon discharged and then a voice came over the helmet com.

"Got him!" And then, "You should see all the stuff he has in here! Crates and crates!

Grinning, the officer and his snipers slung their disrupters across their shoulders and headed for the hatch as well......

Moving quietly down the corridor, the only sound Coy could hear was its own combat armor ventilation unit. Even the footsteps of the rest of the team were muffled by the soft soles of their boots. In the event the terrorists decided to turn off the artificial gravity, those soles would stick to almost any surface for a few precious seconds. Theoretically time enough for a trained soldier to orient themselves. Trained soldier. Theoretically. Of course if they chose to blow a hole in the side of the station and let space itself deal with the BlackFleet, what boots they were wearing wouldn't matter at all.

That had been the choice. Battle armor or space armor. Coy had made the guess that the lives of the hostages were important enough that blowing that hole would not be their first reaction.

Choices. Guesses. All these lives depending on Coy making the right ones. And what if....No. This was not the time to indulge in more self pity. Gritting its teeth and firmly ignoring the voices from the past, it moved on.

"Skipper," came Vennefron's voice from the present. "They know something's up. Their coms just went silent."

"Understood." Alright, so having Venn stay with Pedula on the *Blackbird* and monitor the internal communication lines had been a good choice. "Randy, how close..?"

Sweggert stared at his hand scanner. "We're right above them."

"Team one, cut through right here. Team two, we go down a deck and go in the front door. Team three should be nearly to the command center."

The only acknowledgment of the orders was the silent movement of team members as they got into their positions. Ken Butler was in charge of the actual rescue through the ceiling. Coy led the frontal attack, but was connected to all three teams via its command helmet.

Lamont's team came to the tubes. Stepping in they let the flow take them gently downward. At the next level they swung out of the portal and landed on the deck. Even with their silent boots, it made a thud when three bodies wearing armor, hit the floor.

They heard a voice from around the corner, "What the..."

Pierce and Sweggert immediately took up positions on either side of the "T" in the corridor. Before long, one of the terrorists came cautiously around the bend.

"Hey big fella," Pierce crooned in a sultry tone.

He turned in her direction. "Huh..?" and received an expert kick to the groin.

Randy got him point blank with a stunner. As the man crumpled to the floor, he held up the weapon and showed it to Pierce. "As I recall the plan...."

Pierce shrugged. "Sorry."

"Yeah, right."

"Move," Coy growled at them both.

Another voice floated down the corridor to them. "Nes! What the hell you doin' down there?"

Coy froze. The readout on the inside of its command helmet faceplate showed a steady countdown until Butler would need the diversion. The seconds ticked by as Coy and its team waited. 3..2..1.. "GO!"

Lamont, Sweggert and Pierce blasted around the corner, weapons firing. One door guard fell, dead before he hit the floor. Another crouched and returned fire, but without armor he didn't last long.

Sweggert straightened from his firing stance and stepped up next to Coy. "Some fun now, eh Skip....."

The shot hit him square in the chest. He flew backwards and slammed into the wall behind them. *One minute he was my only friend....* Furious, Coy raised its weapon and shot blindly in the direction of the attack.

Through its rage, it heard Butler's account of rescue in progress. "We've cut through... Watch it! Don't let it fall in... Drop down. I'll cover you...We're in, Skip...Damn! They've cut the air! Terrell, get those masks...Have we got enough?....."

Another voice was heard, muffled since it was coming over the channel from outside Ken's helmet, "Please, my aide...No, no, he was alive just a moment..."

" It's okay. We'll take care of him..." There were sounds of voices, some moaning, "Captain, we've got them," Butler spoke to Coy. "One for stasis, one float pallet, everyone else is walking. We're on our way back to the ship."

"Understood." Coy spoke through gritted teeth, firing all the while. That left only Schiff and Knepp's mission up in the control center of the educational station. It concentrated on the information coming on the other channel. A short bit of static which it took as someone hotwiring the access panel. A surprised yelp and then a lot of stunner fire. Schiff's team couldn't afford to use hot weapons in the control room and risk damaging essential equipment. Their only objective was to secure the commander and command station to keep anyone from firing on them as they left.

Its thoughts were interrupted by a steady stream of swearing in Randy Sweggert's voice. Coy stopped firing and looked over at him. It closed its eyes briefly in relief. "Welcome back, Mr. Sweggert. Can you travel?"

"Yeah. Just knocked the breath..." More swearing as he tried to straighten up.

"Damn fine armor, Captain," Pierce checked the readings on Randy's medical telemetry. "Just gave him something to complain about."

"We're clear!" Schiff reported in.

"Alright!" Coy broadcasted to them all. "Everybody out!"

The three teams each made their way back to where the *Blackbird* was docked, encountering some half-hearted opposition now and again. Upon the loss of their commander and further orders, the terrorists seemed to care little about anything but personal survival.

By the time Coy reached the bay, Butler already had the released hostages on board. Lamont stood at the end of the tube and hurried its troops through. Upon a last hasty look around, Lamont spotted a lone terrorist standing in the shadows. They stood, weapons raised, staring at each other for a long moment.

"Who are you?" the man asked, desperately. "This was supposed to be so easy... No one around..."

Now that the adrenaline was wearing off, Coy suddenly felt weary. "I'm Captain Coy Lamont. Commander of the BlackFleet," it answered literally. While they continued staring at their mutually deadly weapons, Coy quietly pulled out a small ornate stunner with its other hand and fired. Once on board, it called to Pedula up in the little ship's command center. "All in. Go."

"Aye, aye, Skipper. We're gone."

Lamont stood in the small medical chamber of the *Blackbird* next to the anxious Tenetian ruler. They both watched Byars and Terrell work on the former hostages. Most sat in a daze, slowly awakening to the fact that they were indeed safe.

At last Ceal joined them. "The stasis prep was textbook . The other patient is stable and able to be transferred safely to a medical facility."

King Frederic took her hands gratefully. "Thank you, Doctor."

She smiled a little nervously. "I'm a med tech, sir. And you're welcome." She pulled her hand free carefully and returned to the refuge of her duties.

"Thank you, too, Captain," he said turning to Lamont. "I cannot possibly thank you enough. Whatever price my government agreed to pay, they got their money's worth."

"Actually, Sire, we never made an agreement with your government. We thought our element of surprise would be compromised had we taken the time for negotiations."

"Is that so," the man said in amazement. "Then you did all of this as a personal favor?"

Certainty clicked into Coy's brain. Sometimes, the universe worked, it mused inwardly. "Yes, Sire," it said without missing a beat. "And that's all I ask in return."

"A favor? What is it you want? My word, you'll have it."

Coy smiled. "That's good to know."

"And what is this favor you need?"

"Oh, not now. Sometime. Someday, I'll need something."

"And I'll owe it to you?"

In answer, Coy looked around the room at the safe and recovering people. The monarch followed the mercenary's gaze.

"Yes, you're right." He motioned to one of his aides, who promptly came to them. "Witness this." He pulled a round disk on a clasp from his cloak and handed it to Coy. "The commander of the BlackFleet Mercenaries, bearing this brooch is entitled to whatever favor they ask of the Royal House of Tenetia." He looked Coy in the eye. "Will that do?'

Lamont gave a small bow. "Thank you, Sire. I shall leave you now to rest. We'll let you know when we are in range of your vessel." Another small bow and Lamont left the chamber.

Sometime later, the *Blackbird* mated in space with the incoming Tenetian ship. Coy went on board and oversaw the hostages being settled into yet another medical department. Everywhere it turned people were thanking it for averting the war that surely would have been the outcome had things continued. Coy was persuaded to accept a modest monetary compensation (over and above the Favor), and was headed back to the *Blackbird* for rendezvous with the *Raven*.

The combat squad sat silently in the passenger area watching their hands and feet and waiting for a word from Lamont. The captain itself sat across from Butler, staring ahead, but seeing who knew what.

Eventually, it blinked, noticed it was looking at Butler and nodded. Remembering the payment, it also pointed to a minicomp clamped near Butler's seat. He handed it over wordlessly. Coy stuck the token in, read the amount and raised one eyebrow. After pulling up some other notes and files, it switched off the scanner and returned it.

Coy leaned back in its seat and closed its eyes. "I have never," it began quietly, "seen a mission go so well. I was very proud to be a member of the BlackFleet."

There was no cheering. Only a lot of held breaths being released.

As usual, Pierce was the first to speak up. "Shouldn't we celebrate or something? All those party rooms on the *Raven* should be for something."

Lamont opened one eye and peered at her. "I want people to stay functional."

"Oh," she frowned, thinking seriously, "I suppose we could manage that."

Coy closed the eye. "All right. Go for it."

"Yes!" she clenched her fist in victory. "Thanks, Mom. Or Dad. Or Whatever."

Coy resisted the temptation to glare at her. It was probably what she wanted, anyway.

When at last they reached the *Raven,* Bon and the others did greet them with a cheer as the first trooper stepped through the hatch onto the
mother ship. Bon personally clapped Butler on the back and shook his hand.

"Well, done, Commander!"

Last of all, Captain Lamont emerged from the *Blackbird,* cool and silent. Bon started over to repeat his congratulations, but at Lamont's expression he wisely tampered down his enthusiasm.

"You've trained a good team, Skipper," he said, sincerely.

Coy nodded. "I understand there's to be a victory celebration. It may commence as soon as helmet recorders are collected and troopers are debriefed." Coy turned to Butler. "I'll be in my quarters," it said quietly and strode off.

Butler caught up with Lamont before it reached the cabin door. Coy glanced in his direction but continued palming open the door lock. "I don't need any hand holding, Commander."

"I heartily disagree, Captain," he returned cheerfully. "As your next in command, your emotional health is extremely important to me."

Without a word, Coy entered the cabin and brought the lights up only about halfway. But it did not stop Butler from following. Ken went to a chair by the desk and made himself comfortable.

Coy paced for only a moment , then sank down on the seat behind the desk. It sat, looking at its hands, which trembled very slightly. "That was .....so hard," Coy's voice was almost a whisper. "I kept waiting for the automatics to kick in, but they never did. I had to think about each step. Doing it all on sheer will power. I could've gotten us all killed."

"But you didn't. Autopilot or manual, you got the job done. I think that's what counts."

Coy shook its head. "Not to me. I have to *know*. I used to know...I," it stopped and gave a long sigh. "...am so tired."

After a long silence, Butler took the hint and stood. "Remember something, Captain. There's a whole ship of people here that believe in you. Run on that for awhile if you have to." Lamont didn't answer. Butler remained were he stood, waiting for some sign that Lamont would be all right. He had to admit, his CO's continued depression concerned him.

"You haven't asked what we got paid," Coy said, suddenly.

"You said you'd take care of us. Besides, most of us needed a meal and bed badly enough not to quibble about a paycheck." He stopped and grinned. "But as long as you brought it up..."

Coy looked him in the eye. "Nothing."

The grin froze. " Pardon?"

"I didn't charge them anything."

Ken opened his mouth, but nothing came out. On the second try he managed, "Oh."

"That meal and bed still enough for you?"

The commander cocked his head. "Am I going to be graded on my answer?"

Coy went to the vidcom and punched up Fleet finances. "They did volunteer a token payment, which covered expenses. Which means we basically break even."

Butler came and read over Coy's shoulder. "I'm going to make the assumption you know what you're doing."

Coy pulled out the gold disc and handed it to him. "That's our real payment."

He turned it over and over, hoping it was more valuable than it looked. "What is it?"

"A favor. We may redeem *that*," Coy pointed to the coin, "for one Royal favor. Any time. Any size favor."

Butler looked thoughtful. "Guaranteed?"

"Guaranteed."

"*Any* favor?"

"Anything we want. Back up, a ship, weapons, supplies, an alibi, a place to hide, any one of a multitude of things that cash couldn't easily buy."

The grin spread back onto Butler's face, growing wider as he absorbed the possibilities. "Is this going to be procedure from now on?"

"It just might. I think I like it."

"When are you going to tell the crew?"

"I should as soon as possible. I hope they understand. Anything extra that we get will be divided between everyone as I said. Twenty people are a lot easier to fund than your normal fleet of thousands. Besides, if we're ever desperate, I have some property on Servati that I could liquidate."

"Property, huh? I'm not even going to ask where you got it." He handed the disk back. "Let them party tonight and tell them at the morning briefing. Which reminds me, I'd better debrief them so they can get to the party." He paused. "Are you coming?"

Coy managed to find something fascinating in the computer files. "I may. Don't hold your breath. And..." it added as Ken was leaving. "Make sure senior staff stays functional."

He saluted, still grinning and exited.

Coy turned off the computer, locked the door and stared out into the blackness of space.

The *Raven* streaked along in space, lurching at another direct hit on the shields. They returned fire, but their pursuers' shielding was as good as their own.

Captain Lamont braced itself against the changes in gravity and remained peering intently at the tactical display, trusting the pilot and weapons officer to keep them alive long enough to use the brilliant plan it was still trying to come up with. There was a flicker in the small representation of the large enemy vessel behind them.

"What was that? Bon, what happened to them?" Coy called to the chief engineer.

Bon studied his own monitors. "They have a fluctuating shield."

"Parker!"

"On it," the weapons officer called as her fingers sped over her targeting console. And a few moments later, "Shield is down, Captain."

"Keep up the firepower."

"She's turning," Aziza announced, "protecting that side."

"Good. They'll be out of pursuit position temporarily. Let's see what we can do with that. How close is that transit portal?"

"Ten minutes," Hoffman answered through gritted teeth at the abuse "he" was taking. No one but pilots themselves understood the complicated relationship they had with their ships. The headset physically connected their brain to the navigation system, allowing them to weave the ship through Transit. The ship was, from the pilot's perspective, an extension of themselves.

Coy knew and understood Hoffman's feelings, but now was not the time for sympathy. "Make it five". Lamont thought ahead to what was on other end of their trip. "It's time to call in a marker."

By the time the pursuing craft had followed them, the *Raven* was nowhere to be found.

This was a system with two major Transit portals relatively close to each other. The two inhabited planets they served had been at each other's throats in an intra-system war only a short time ago. But rumor had it that a third party had helped them begin to settle their differences peacefully.

While calculating where their quarry could have gone, the commander of the pursuers contacted the system's portal station.

"Why should your chase concern us?" the officer responded. "This Portal is not under any blockades or restrictions. We do not harass passersby."

"These are not passersby. They're mercenaries. Thieves. We are only attempting to stop them and retrieve that which is ours."

"I'm sorry we cannot help you. Your vengeance means nothing to us. We have our own concerns. Good day."

The commander growled as the image from the transmission faded to nothing. He looked again at the computer displaying the area and his choices. "Can't you pick up any traces?" he snapped at his sensor officer.

"Yes, sir. In fact, lots of them." the man reported nervously.

"What do you mean?"

"According to all this, I'd guess at least five ships have moved through this area within the last hour. Either these folks are doing a great commercial business or..."

"Reinforcements. Damn."

"Orders?" the pilot asked.

His commander glared at him. "Do you want to take on fresh warships with an exhausted crew and buckling shields?" He punched the nearest control board in frustration. "Take us back. And pray we survive the debriefing."

Later, the five decoy ships came back through the Portals and returned to their home station. As they came into dock, the *Raven* gracefully left it, and with heartfelt thanks set their course away from the system.

Coy stood up from its station chair and stretched. "Good work everyone. Commander, let's deliver this package as promised. I'll be in my quarters. You have the conn."

"Aye, aye Skipper, I have the conn," Butler replied, slipping into the chair Lamont had just vacated.

The *Raven* waited in orbit as Captain Lamont, Commander Bon and Sgt. Schiff escorted their cargo down to its anxious owners. The officers exited the shuttle and were met by company officials, led by the Chairman of the Board himself.

Everyone watched as Bon and his engineers delivered four float pallets of crates. They conferred briefly in low tones about temperature, stability and other factors that no one outside the techs would've understood had they been able to hear.

The CEO grabbed Lamont's hand and pumped it excitedly. The BlackFleet troopers acting as guards snapped into defense positions at the sudden movement but relaxed at a gesture from Lamont.

"Captain, I can't possibly thank you enough. We have security, but nothing equipped to handle pirates such as those."

"That's our job, Mr. Chairman. To help out where we're needed."

"Now, about your compensation. My assistant tells me you do not intend to turn in a bill for your services."

"That is correct."

The man shook his head. "I can't imagine your motives. But I can't afford the reputation of not paying my debts. What kind of arrangement can we make?"

Coy smiled. "All I ask of you is your word of a return favor should I ever need it."

"A favor? What kind of favor could I do for the commander of a mercenary warship?"

"Off the top of my head I could think of a number of ways the owner and operator of such a large shipping business could come in very handy."

The other pondered this for a moment. "I somehow get the feeling it would be cheaper to simply pay cash now. What would happen if I decided not to redeem my word when you ask for it?"

Coy's smile became just a little cooler. "A man that couldn't afford the reputation of not paying debts wouldn't even need to ask such a thing. And very surely wouldn't break his word. To the commander of a mercenary warship."

He gave a humorless laugh. "I see your point. You have my word."

Coy gave a small bow. "Thank you." Lamont collected the others with a look and went back into the shuttle. The guards followed behind the officers and engineers and they lifted off.

In the shuttle, Bon watched Coy for a moment, as it sat gazing out at the stars. "You're accomplishing what you set out to do, you know."

It looked over at the sudden statement. "What do you mean?"

"Think back a couple of months. The beginning days of the BlackFleet. I would walk down those amazing corridors and you know what I would see? A couple of drunks, a recluse or two, some refugees, and at least three potential suicides."

"And what do you see now?"

Bon's spine straightened automatically. "Heroes."

Chapter Three

Captain Lamont walked into the briefing room, wearing a serious expression. Butler, Bon, and Schiff seated around the conference table, watched anxiously. Lamont carefully loaded the contents from the data disk it had brought into the room's vidcom. Information came up on holo-screens all around the table. All the BlackFleet personnel present read through it quickly.

"This," Lamont spoke evenly, "is the proposed job. The Regent has verified that four very important political figures are being held behind their enemy lines. Our mission is to get them out."

" 'Behind enemy lines' sounds just a little vague, Skipper," Butler commented. He pointed to his screen. "I don't see an address here...."

"Venn should have the location pinpointed by the time we arrive."

"We use the shuttle?" Schiff guessed.

Coy shook its head. "Both of our shuttles do have enough extra shielding to drop at the speeds we will need, but I want the *Blackbird* on site for close air support faster than a shuttle could lift."

Butler looked up at that. He locked eyes with Lamont, but said nothing.

"Manned by whom?" Schiff asked it for him.

"Pedula, Vennefron and Luka."

"Just three...!" Butler spat out before he could stop himself.

Lamont stared at him with no expression. "Yes, Commander?"

Ken looked as if he were having an internal debate, but finally shook his head.

Coy went back to its notes. " All right, here is the plan...."

They went over logistics, attack plans, and time frames, as the *Raven* sped through space.

Hours later, the planet loomed below them. Coy had never been to this system before and it was struck by the beauty of the world. Even as contingency scenarios played through its mind, it marveled at the swirling pale blue clouds surrounding the aqua colored ball. Every planet was an artistic masterpiece in its own right. Coy would never tire of seeing new ones. It gave an internal sigh and focused its thoughts on the reality that could be awaiting them beneath those clouds.

The *Raven* went into a high orbit, the *Blackbird* dropped like a rock through the atmosphere to their planned landing site. Although the '*Bird* normally had artificial gravity as did the larger ships, the power from the A.G. units had been diverted to shielding in order to protect them from the friction with the atmosphere due to the speed of their descent. As a consequence, everyone would have been smears of goo on the ceiling had it not been for the seat straps and padding.

Lamont stared as straight ahead as possible, feeling the adrenaline rush building. This was the closest the BlackFleet had come to a true commando drop raid. Eight people. Hardly a commando squad. But they knew their stuff, and that's what counted in the thick of it...Wasn't it? Quality over quantity. The BlackFleet creed.

With a heart-stopping *thud*, the yacht landed, ending the wild, ear-popping ride as suddenly as it had begun. Coy had often marveled at, and was grateful for, the technology the ship's original owner had installed into his vessels. Very few ships could match their versatility. But now was not the time for pondering ship design anymore than it was for second guessing its choices.

With well practiced precision everyone unclipped straps and hurried into formation. Coy spared a look to the pilot.

"I'll be ready if you need me, Skipper," Myke said confidently.

Coy nodded once at him and then at Schiff. Now.

The troopers poured out of the side hatch, weapons ready. On Schiffs cue, they started moving across the field where they had landed , taking advantage of whatever natural shielding they could.

The target was a small compound just ahead. Even as they maneuvered closer, soldiers came out to meet and greet them with weapons.

BlackFleet hit the ground and returned fire.

"Pedula! Cover us!" Lamont shouted into its headset above the din.

The *Blackbird* took off instantly and swooped down, flying barely above their heads, firing ahead of the squad. The enemy fell back hastily. The BlackFleet advanced, following Pedula's scorched trail. As he reached the buildings, he veered off, and went back to his holding position.

The troopers battled for the last few feet on their own. Once at the compound, two person teams searched each building. At the third one, Schiff's voice came over the com.

"Got 'em Skipper. There's six, not four."

Randy Sweggert, Coy's partner gave a grin. " Does that mean we get a bon...."

His words were cut off as the enemy, evidently not believing the hostages worth the fight, blew the building.

"Sergeant!", Lamont shouted and began heading through the rubble even as the dust and pebbles rained down on them.

"We're...." his voice choked back, "It's Pierce! She's...."

Coy checked through its headset channels as it ran. Yes, Schiff's was intact. Pierce's was still transmitting, but just barely. Medical. Medical. Telemetry came up. With bad news.

"*Blackbird*, keep everyone busy. We're on our way!"

By the time Coy and Sweggert reached the site, Knepp and Rebel had arrived as well. Coy took in the scene. More people were on the ground than on foot. One was in black armor.

Knepp, doubling as corpsman for this trip pulled the collapsible stretcher from his pack and stretched it out next to the unconscious Andrea Pierce.

"How many hostages do we have?" Coy barked.

"Five," came Rebel's reply. "Maybe six, if we try a portable stasis."

"Bring them all. Our ride is ready."

Knepp hooked an emergency backpack onto Pierce's battle armor. The medical program came back on line and instantly released a combination of chemicals into her system. She was placed carefully on the stretcher, one hostage was put on another, and they all headed back the way they had come.

By the time they got back to the field, the yacht was ready to lift. Vennefron and Luka took up positions on either side of the open hatch, and shot cover fire over their heads.

Almost there. Coy looked up at the beckoning hatchway just in time to see a grenade land on the ramp. Swinging his plasma rifle like a golf club, Vennefron attempted to knock it away...

It stood in the door of sickbay and surveyed the scene. Nearly every bed, and two stasis chambers so far, were occupied.

"Captain?" came a thin voice.

Coy had to force itself to turn and look at the speaker. Pierce. Beautiful Andrea Pierce, now a burnt and bloody imitation of the strong blond soldier Coy knew. It came close to the bed.

"We got 'em out didn't we?" she whispered.

Coy swallowed before answering. "The mission was success-ful. Everyone performed magnificently. As brave as anyone I've ever seen."

She smiled a little through her drug haze, and closed her eyes. When she didn't open them again, Coy anxiously checked her readouts, but her heart and breathing plugged on.

A hand touched Coy's arm. Ceal led it away from Pierce's bed. "I have a battle victim I need your help with, " she said.

"Anything," Coy replied quickly, looking at the various pa-tients. They all appeared to be resting. Corpsman Terrell walked among them with a scanner, checking vitals.

Ceal shook her head. "This patient isn't in bed--but should be. Surface injuries were minor, but they seem to have affected a lot of old scars. And being in here, punishing itself is *not* going to help any of those wounds heal."

"I see." Without another word, it walked over to the stasis unit, and looked down into Vennefron's still features. "I'm not a mar-tyr, Ceal. I just...."

"You're our commander, Coy, not our parent. And we need a commander with its head on straight. Now more than ever." She paused at the expression on Coy's face. If only she had an anesthetic for that pain. "Please get some rest, if not sleep, and check in with me later." She started to say something more, but Coy shook it's head.

"I'm okay," it lied. "I'll----be in my quarters. If anyone joins Venn, let me know."

"Of course I will." She had to say something more. It was in her job description to heal people. "You do realize that with a different commander they might have all joined Venn."

Coy looked at her, but said nothing. Another glance at the wounded and it left.

Butler was out in the corridor, waiting.

"Now how did I know where you'd be..." he began.

"I've had my quota of patronizing," Coy cut him off quietly. "Did you need something?"

Butler held a hand reader. "Status update."

Coy took it, read silently, and handed it back. "Keep me post-ed. Anything else?"

"Nothing *new*," he said gravely.

Coy's eyes narrowed at his tone. "If we increased the size of the fleet, things like this wouldn't have to happen," it recited a new version of the old argument.

"The phrase 'adequate backup' does spring to mind," he admitted. This wasn't the time to come down on Lamont, but he was unable to keep it to himself any longer. "A handful more troopers, and..."

"And Vennefron wouldn't be frozen meat. And Pierce would still be in one piece, and Erhardt would have two working arms. I know what happened. I can't forget it. The rest of my *life*, I won't forget it. But it doesn't help anyone now."

"But it might next time. We could avoid a next time, Captain."

"We have Friedhoff and Doutaz now. That will help until the others are back on their feet...."

"You're not listening," Ken said angrily, realizing that a conversation like this back home would've gotten him shot, easily. "Two people, one of them a tech, does not improve our survival odds. We need *ships* full of soldiers. We need a fleet."

Coy took a breath and sought for the right words. "I don't want a fleet as you mean. I want a covert team. I want *this* team and this ship."

"*This* team just got blown to hell. If we'd had more perimeter men in place..."

Fury welled up inside Coy suddenly. "Don't--tell--me--how--to--command," it bit out.

"Well somebody should," Butler growled back. "When I signed on, I was not aware that this was going to stay a closed society. I *thought* the idea was to be the vigilantes of the universe--not some personal therapy of yours that *we're* paying for!"

Coy's eyes narrowed. It was nearly a minute before it spoke. "Are you through, Commander?"

The coolness in Lamont's tone cut through Butler's hot anger. He opened his mouth to answer, but instead, took a calming breath. He had just maneuvered himself into a nasty corner, and he knew it. Lamont probably wouldn't shoot him outright, but his career was forfeit he was sure. "I guess I probably am," he admitted.

Lamont ignored the concession in his voice. "I'm sure you have duties," it said coldly, and brushed past him.

For a moment, Ken merely stood still. What had he just done? Besides stand in an open corridor and blast his commander, that is. Was mutiny in his blood or what? When he finally focused and looked around, he found Bon gazing at him. Had the engineer been there the whole time? He hadn't even noticed.

"Feel better?" Bon asked sarcastically.

Ken drew himself up defensively. "It needed said."

Bon glanced at the lift tube into which Lamont had disappeared. "Where I come from, we don't tell commanding officers how to do their job."

"It might not be correct, but what if it's the right thing to do?"

Bon looked back. They stood, eyes locked for several seconds. "I believe we both have duties," Bon said, finally.

Ken nodded and they separated, each to his own tasks.

It took the *Raven* a week to reach Servati in order to check Vennefron into a hospital for re-animation.

The doctor there echoed Ceal Byars' prognosis of a good recovery. He was very happily impressed with the stasis-prep, and babbled on about the problems that a bad prep always caused.

Lamont waved the physician quiet. "Take the best possible care of him. Cost is not an issue."

At that, the talking stopped and treatment began.

Coy and Ceal wandered out of the hospital and stood looking at the city skyline. Servati was literally the center of the entire Beta Region. The core of the sphere. And the oldest of the colonized worlds. The technology base was therefore older, more entrenched. And more diversified. Other planets may have advanced in certain fields, but on Servati you could find just about anything you wanted. Tourists came from all over the region to see the original landing spots of the Alpha Region Immigrants and to sample the varied entertainments offered.

"Now what?" Ceal asked, as they looked out over the blend of two centuries of architecture. Evidently a little of every style had been tried. Stone spires competed for attention with round silver domes. Ground cars drove along under a moving ceiling of hovercraft. Servati's capitol city was nothing if not eclectic. "A little R&R would do you good."

They began walking vaguely back in the direction of the local transit system.

"I do have some property here that I've never seen. I suppose I should look in on it at some point."

"Sounds like a good idea. You and Ken could check it out."

Coy stopped walking and turned to stare at her. "Ken?"

"You two need to talk."

"We talk."

"No. You give orders, and he says 'Yes sir.' He's just biding his time waiting to be dumped somewhere - again."

Coy looked truly surprised. "Dump him? Why?"

"For telling you off."

Lamont began walking again. "I see."

"I don't."

"He won't be 'dumped' because his point was not wrong."

"Then why the cold treatment?"

"His method was."

They boarded the public tram and headed for the shuttle port. Being a cosmopolitan planet, their uniforms received only minor curious stares, but they had a car to themselves none the less.

"Shouldn't you tell him this? You can't let him keep wondering forever."

"I'll take it under advisement." The subject seemed to be closed and the two continued the trip without further comment.

Ceal sat watching Coy's face. There was a tension that she hadn't seen since the first days of the BlackFleet. A grief, if that's what it was, that she had hoped it had dealt with at last. It seemed she was wrong. But
could she, and should she, say something? Her status as medical officer gave her an inside line that others, even command staff didn't have, and Lamont had opened up to her on more than one occasion. She did not want to abuse that and lose it. But when would it be any more private than it was right now? "So, what else is up?"

Coy attempted to keep up the stoic expression for a little longer. As it lost the attempt it turned to face out of the port. "People died."

"Yes."

It turned back to look at her. "One of *my* people."

She tried to keep her voice as professional as possible. "He should recover. The stasis prep…"

"I could've lost." Its voice was anguished.

"Yes," she agreed again. "That is always a possibility."

"Not for me."

"Why not?"

Coy looked at her as if perplexed. "I need to win," it said as if that explained something.

"Everyone wants to win…"

"I don't *want* to. It's my …my job to succeed."

Now she was the one who was perplexed. "According to who?"

Coy paused, unable to answer.

She tried again. "Coy, what's really going on? In your head? Right now?"

Coy took a steadying breath. "I want…I want to command…but it's not…"it seemed to have to work hard to get the words out. "Riga. They didn't make me to…I get angry, and sad and , and things I don't even understand. I'm not supposed to." It gave a sigh. "Everything is changing."

Ceal frowned, trying to sort out the speech. "You're not supposed to feel things?"

Coy gave a small nod. "Emotions get in the way."

"Of winning?" she guessed. "Of succeeding?"

"Exactly."

Ceal thought back to other conversations she and Lamont had had about its past. "Riga purposely suppressed your emotions? But human beings need emotions. Pride and loyalty can help you succeed…"

"I'm not a…"

"Don't tell me you're not human." She cut it off. "Conceived or constructed, you're still a person. I'm a med tech remember? I have your scans and files if you want proof. Besides. You obtained the *Raven*. You started the Fleet. You give us our missions. Not Riga. You don't belong to them anymore."

From the way it stared at her, she knew she had gone a step too far. It retrieved its stoic face from before and crossed its arms, building an instant wall. "You're right. We should be able to recover all of our personnel." It glanced out of the port as the tram car slowed to a stop and said nothing more.

It's wrist com bleeped just as Coy stepped onto the shuttle for the trip to the *Raven ,* breaking the silence.

"Lamont. Go ahead."

"Skipper, we have a message for you from New Terre. Coded and personal," Aziza informed Coy.

"New Terre? They want us to do another job for them?" Rescuing some of their ambassadors had been one of the Black Fleet's earliest missions.

"No clues."

"All right, I'm on my way up. Shunt it to my quarters."

"Aye, aye, sir."

After viewing the recorded message, Lamont had Butler see it as well.

"That's all?" Ken exclaimed. " 'Dear Captain Lamont, come to tea.' "

Coy gave a short nod. "Whatever it's about, he didn't want to say on record."

"And he thinks you're going to waltz right over, with no back-up?"

"He did mention that I should come alone. As I recall, a lot of people in his government did not like the idea of a mercenary ship on their doorstep."

"They didn't mind us dropping their people safely on that doorstep."

"True enough." Coy leaned back in its desk chair. "I haven't decided whether to take the small shuttle or commercial transport. Either way, by the time I get back, Vennefron should be up and around. This would also be an opportune time to put in some of the modifications Raeph has been itching to do. I might even call in a big favor and see if this "quad" cannon that BetaTech was bragging about is all they say it is. I've got the capital for the parts. Our shipping company favor should be able to get everything here in time. You can rotate shore leave for the crew as well."

"You're not serious."

"Shore leave would be good for everyone."

"Very funny. You can't go alone."

"The invitation clearly stated only myself."

"What if it's a trap?"

"Then you would inherit command. And given the Black-Fleet's job description I would expect a timely rescue."

Butler's jaw dropped. "Skipper..."

Lamont got up to pace. As usual it ended up staring out of the large portal. "You were out of line the other day, Ken. This is my fleet. I own it. I command it. I make the rules. You signed on, agreeing to obey those commands and rules."

Butler could think of no response other than, "Yes sir."

"However, you forced me to see some things. My own contradictions. I want command. I've worked and dreamed and sweated for it as much as any officer in space. I don't understand what keeps me from..." It stopped, shook its head as if to clear it, then straightened, and said to the stars, "Either we're vigilantes, or we're not. But..." It turned and looked directly at Butler. "...if you ever have a problem with my command decisions, you will follow proper protocol. Is that understood?"

For a moment Ken was speechless. Instead of being jobless once again as he deserved, his position was being confirmed. He replied with an amazed, "Yes, sir."

Coy gave him a nod to indicate the subject was closed. "However, I still don't want a huge business with tons of people tripping over themselves. I *want* small teams."

"Teams." Butler managed. "As in plural."

Coy managed not to sigh. "It is probably more… realistic. But I will not compromise the BlackFleet standards. Anyone hired has to match the precedent we've set."

"Yes, sir." Butler heroically tried to keep the victory he was feeling out of his voice.

"So we'll need an updated plan of operation. What would we need to do the job right , keeping in mind..."

"That you don't want tons of people tripping over each other," Ken finished.

Lamont looked at him with an expression Butler could not read. After a moment's pause, it said, "While I'm gone, I want you and Schiff to sit down and work on the plan."

"Gone? You're not seriously going alone."

"Tony Knepp is probably the best all around trooper we have. He will accompany me. But that's all."

"But..."

"Don't push your luck, Ken. I don't concede too many things in one day."

Just the hint of a grin and, "Yes, sir."

Coy walked along beside the President as he spoke of his gratitude to the BlackFleet for having saved his advisors and their families. Coy smiled and nodded acknowledgment, wondering all the while where this was leading. The rescue, however dramatic, was old news. Why had Coy been summoned here, now?   Not even the Fleet, just Coy.

It had taken flat out pulling rank to even be here. Bon had been just as unhappy as Butler about trusting Coy's intuition. It had to admit, it probably would not have let either one of them go, had the situation been reversed. But it wasn't. Coy and Knepp had traveled on a commercial passenger liner, since so far Hoffman was the only JP and Coy would not leave the *Raven* flightless.

While its host talked and Coy pondered, the corridor they were following led them to one of the main docking bays of this space station orbiting above their world. They paused before the tube. The President placed his hand almost affectionately on the sealed hatch.

"This is one reason I've asked you here, Captain. I would like your professional opinion on something."

A nod, and a bodyguard/trooper unlocked the seals and cycled the airlock.

"Come with me."

Coy obediently followed, glancing uncertainly at the two guards bringing up the rear, immediately behind Tony, wondering if it were as stupid as Butler had thought.

At the other end of the tube, they entered the ship. The President rather pointedly stepped aside, and waved an arm to indicate the entire vessel.

"An honest opinion, Captain."

Coy spent most of the afternoon poking around, peering into empty cabins, checking engineering schematics, running through non-secured computer files. Which, to Coy's surprise, meant all the computer files. There was only one name on the manifest. Guillermo, the jump pilot.

At the end of the lengthy inspection, which had included a quick lunch in the main mess for the entire entourage, Coy began trolling for answers.

"A very nice ship, Mr. President. Actually much nicer than I would have expected from your situation as I recall it."

"Better than this planet is capable of producing? You're absolutely right. We could no more afford these kinds of ships than we could an army of our own." He nodded at Coy's mercenary uniform, recalling their former relationship. "This vessel was commissioned off world to be my presidential ship. Unfortunately, by the time it was ready..."

The President broke off and gave a small nod to the guards, who promptly exited. Knepp took up station just outside the door, leaving them sitting alone in a small conference room.

"Captain, there have been several changes in our government since we spoke last. Number one, I lost the election."

Coy had no appropriate comment on that, so kept quiet.

"I'm not surprised, however disappointed I may be. The point is, I have no faith whatsoever in my successor honoring our debt to you."

Coy paused for only a moment. Here it was, their first taste of the central flaw with the whole Favor system. "I see. Kind of you to let me know."

The president either read Coy's expression or expected its assumption. "I have no intention of defaulting on what I owe," he said defensively. "My problem is time. Or lack of it. Mere days in fact. This is my solution."

Coy cocked its head. "Sir?"

He waved around, dramatically. "This ship. I hope your evaluation was honest. I know you were supposed to choose your favor, but as I said, I'm out of time. You can use her, sell her for cash, or trade her for a favor you do need."

Another ship. The BlackFleet had just doubled in size.

"Ah, sir, this is a generous gesture..." Coy began.

"It's not a gesture. It's a fact." He reached into a pocket and pulled out a data disk. "It's in your name. At least the name Coy Lamont. You may transfer it however you wish." Coy hesitated at taking the disk. "I'm sorry Captain, I am profoundly sorry, but I must wash my hands of any political connection to you as soon as possible. This is the best I could do."

Coy took the disk and shook the offered hand firmly.

"I am glad our association has been mutually beneficial. Your world has lost an honorable leader."

The soon-to-be-former President studied Coy's face, searching for sarcasm, or hollow politics. He found neither. He nodded his head in acknowledgment. "Your pilot should be boarding even as we speak. I realize the three of you hardly make a crew, but I do urge your hasty departure. This is only mine to give for a short time longer." He stood.

Coy stood as well, wondering if every time it got a new ship it would have to run like hell with it. "I understand. I wish you well."

"Same to you, Captain. And to your crew." With no further comment, the President gathered his bodyguards from the main hall and departed.

They were gone only moments when the door chime sounded. "Enter," Lamont called.

The door slid open to reveal a young man with the coveted tattoo of a jump pilot. Knepp followed him in, eyebrows drawn down in confusion. "Captain Lamont?" the young man asked.

A nod. "Pilot Guillermo?"

"Yes, s--ah---sir?" He frowned. And reddened.

Coy considered what it knew of New Terre's culture. Doubtless they had even less engineering for genetics than they did for spacecraft. " I'm a hermaphrodite. 'Sir' is fine."

The pilot blinked in embarrassment but nodded.

"I'm going to run some checks. Go ahead and get clearance and plot a course for the Transit point. But don't move this ship a centimeter until I give the word."

"Aye, sir." He started to leave, then paused. "I'm a mercenary now, aren't I, sir?"

"Yes Guillermo, you are. Not a personal aspiration, I take it?"

He shrugged. "Never thought about it." He grinned suddenly. "Would sure shake 'em up back home."

"You enjoy shaking them up back home?"

A dark cloud passed over his face briefly. "I became a pilot," he stated. As if that explained everything.

"I see." Without the use of genetic engineering, Guillermo must be a natural born pilot. Coy knew some worlds saw people such as that as almost mystical. No doubt his family had hoped that he would use his "gifts" for something less commercial than flying a spaceship around.

"I doubt it."

Coy raised a brow. "You might be surprised, Guillermo. And yes, we mercenaries tend to make a living out of shaking people up."

The grin returned to the pilot's face. "It's Gil."

"Pardon?"

"Everyone calls me Gil."

"All right, Pilot Gil, how about that clearance?"

"Yes, Sir!" He gave a somewhat amateurish salute and trotted off to the bridge.

Tony watched him go, then turned back to Lamont. "Sir?"

Coy sighed. "It seems, like it or not, the BlackFleet has acquired a new member." It waved around the room to indicate the ship.

Knepp's eyes went wide. "This ship? They just gave us a ship?" Then he paused. "Who's gonna fly it back to the Fleet?"

For one of the first time in its life, Coy gave a very genuine smile.

Ken Butler forced his eyes open and raised his wrist com, softly chiming for attention, up to his mouth.

"Butler. Go ahead," he intoned sleepily.

Friedhoff's voice came back. "Sorry to disturb you, sir, but we have an incoming message."

"From who?" In the back of Ken's mind he thought about Coy Lamont correcting the "who" to "whom."

"It's the Skipper."

Ken was now awake. "Pipe it down, Karl."

"Aye, sir."

In a moment, Coy's image appeared on Butler's vidcom, wearing a very guarded expression even for Lamont.

"Hello, Captain Butler. An interesting thing happened to me on my little visit. I have acquired another ship. I'm calling her the *Nighthawk*."

Coy's face disappeared and was replaced by the visual representation of the ship. Not a sleek and elegant cruise liner like the *Raven*, but an actual military vessel; technically a light cruiser. Coy's face returned.

Butler was staring openmouthed. " A ship. A whole new ship. Just like that?"

"The President signed it over to me to pay off his debt. I'm still trying to decide what to do with it. I assume you have that plan ready?"

"Yes, as a matter of fact, we do. Another ship! This is great!"

Coy raised a hand to fend off Butler's enthusiasm. "I'm sending along the schematics for you and Bon to go over. We'll talk more when I get there. Right now the crew consists of myself, Knepp and the pilot, so we're a little busy." It paused as if to say more, but evidently changed its mind. "Lamont out."

Ken stared at the dark screen where the holo-image had been. Of all the things Lamont had said, one replayed in his mind. 'Hello, *Captain* Butler.' A mistake? Not likely. A few moments earlier, he had been a Commander.

But two ships meant two captains. As the more inexperienced of the two, he would probably get the *Nighthawk*, and leave the *Raven* as the flagship of the two-vessel fleet. Anticipation of these events, even though they were unconfirmed, welled up inside him, and he waited anxiously for Lamont's arrival.

When the *Nighthawk* at last flew into visual range, everyone watching from the viewport gave a murmur of approval. Well, almost everyone. Bon gave a small moan.

Butler turned to him, reluctantly tearing his eyes away from his--the--ship.

"What's your problem, Raeph?"

"Oh, I was just remembering the first week on *this* ship. No crew, four or five people doing the work of thirty. I don't suppose the Skipper has sent along on updated crew list or anything?"

"No. As far as I know, it's still Lamont, Knepp and the JP," Ken admitted.

"Not even an engineer? Not *one* engineer?" Bon groaned. "Terrific."

Schiff listened to all of this, disapproval on his face. "The Skipper knows what it's doing," he said firmly.

"I'm not criticizing Capt. Lamont," the engineer told him. "I am merely remembering the good ol' days."

Despite his complaints, Bon was up front, wearing a grin of excitement when Lamont's shuttle docked.

It stepped out of the hatch and into the *Raven's* bay. The senior officers snapped to attention and saluted. Most of the rest of the crew were on duty, and unable to immediately satisfy their curiosity.

Coy returned the salutes and nodded at Butler , Bon and Schiff. "I know you want to go look at our new toys, gentlemen. And then we need to talk."

"Alright," Lamont opened as the four of them settled into the port briefing room. "How can we use our new acquisition?"

"These schems are really accurate?" Bon asked.

"They seem to be. The president was pretty particular about his design as I understand it."

"Well, it will fit in very nicely with some of the concepts that Schiff and I have come up with," Butler opened some files of his own to let Coy read the notes they had made in its absence.

Lamont read in silence for a while, a frown growing as it read. "Six ships?"

"I figure that would give us an acceptable spread in a space battle."

The frown deepened. "And why are we involved in a space battle?"

"This is why," Schiff sent a report to his commander's vid. It contained a list compiled by Aziza in Vennefron's absence of distress signals they had heard or heard about. "These are from all over this part of the region. Somebody is attacking everything out there."

"What do you mean 'everything'?" Coy asked, its frown mutated from annoyance to puzzlement.

Ken counted off on his fingers. "Cargo ships, merchant ships, private ships, passenger ships, you name it."

Coy re-read the information. "The same   people attacking?"

"No," Schiff shook his head. "Different ships, different attack styles, different places."

"It's an epidemic," Ken said. "Pirates and mercs all over the region have caught it."

"And you think six ships is the antidote the galaxy needs?" Coy asked him.

"It stands a better chance than one ship and 20 people," Ken answered, and at Coy's look added, "and I mean that in the most humble, respectful way."

Bon cleared his throat at that. "Anyway, back to the _Nighthawk_. It's a good start."

"I don't want six ships. What can we do with the two we have?"

Butler sighed. "I sort of figured that was going to be your response. But we actually have three, counting the _Blackbird_."

Lamont thought about that for a moment. "You want to cut it loose from the _Raven_?"

Bon leaned forward eagerly, "It's got the shielding and weapons. And you know how versatile it is. Recon, troop carrier. A little more remodeling and it could be anything you wanted."

"And by the time Raeph's remodeling was done, Pedula could be done with his training to pilot it," Butler added.

"So that means we need to find two more ship commanders," Lamont said.

"Ah, two?" Ken asked puzzled.

"One for the _Nighthawk_ and one for the _Blackbird_," Coy stated, and watched Ken's face work to stay neutral.

"I see."

"Assuming I give you the _Raven_."

Bon didn't bother to muffle his laugh at Ken's shocked expression.

"You _what?_"

"Command, not ownership," Coy explained.

"I know, but..."

"If we're going to have three ships, I'll need to command the fleet, not a single ship."

Ken blinked. "But the _Raven_ is your pride and joy!"

"Yes, it is," Coy agreed. "I'm making the rash assumption that I'm placing it in competent hands."

"And whose competent hands are you placing the _Blackbird_ and _Nighthawk_ in?" Schiff asked.

Lamont raised its eyebrows at him in inquiry. "I thought you might have a suggestion for the *Blackbird*, at least."

"Rebel," he said without hesitation. "He should've been an officer all along."

"I was thinking the same thing about you."

Schiff shook his head. "I'm happy where I am."

Coy raised an eyebrow. "Funny, that's what I thought, too. But if this keeps growing we may all find ourselves in new places." It looked back at its notes. "We concentrate first on the *Blackbird* upgrades. Manning the *Nighthawk* will wait until after that."

"Then we can keep her?" Butler asked, sounding more like a little boy who had brought home a puppy than a ship commander.

Lamont tried not to smile at the image as it nodded to Butler. "Yes, Captain, we will keep it. Now let's get Rebel in here and give him the news about his promotion. You're still Fleet Exec, as well as flag Captain, so on top of your regular duties, his training will be up to you. "

Butler rose and snapped off a salute. "I live to serve, Commodore Lamont."

Coy rolled its eyes. "Speaking of epidemics, you've caught it from Raeph."

Bon grinned, "Yes, but now you can't complain anymore. If you're commanding three ships, it's proper. Besides if you bump Ken up, you move ahead of him."

"Consider it one of those new places you were just talking about," Ken added.

Lamont did consider it. Its gut reaction was to protest. Which made less and less sense, the more it thought about it. Finally it sighed as if surrendering. "Well, at least it keeps me on top of him."

Lamont, Butler and Rebel sat at a small cafe down on a transit station sipping too-strong coffee, and comparing notes on staff and crew. Pierce and Erhardt were back on limited duty, and Vennefron was completing his post-trauma counseling and would rejoin the fleet in a couple of weeks. And so far for the *Nighthawk*, they had signed on an Engineer and three techs, a Navigator, a Communications officer, and a headstrong but apparently capable young Corporal to run the troops. The troops that he was intended to run as of now consisted of four people. And they still needed to fill such minor slots as Medical officer, and Ship's Captain.

"If you want my opinion", Butler leaned as far back in his seat as he could go without toppling, "you're being too picky. You took awful chances with the *Raven's* crew because you swore you saw potential, or raw talent, or however you put it. They proved you right. In fact, they
turned out *so* good, I think you're spoiled. But you're not necessarily going to find people that good to start with again."

"Spoiled *and* picky, eh?" Coy raised an eyebrow.

Butler grinned. "Sir."

Rebel looked back and forth between them. Being so recently promoted to commander of the *Blackbird*, he was not quite used to the open banter that went on among the senior officers.

Lamont noticed his not-quite-bewildered expression, and gave him a small nod of encouragement. "What do you think, Adrian? Am I being too cautious in my hiring?"

"On or off the record?" Rebel wanted it perfectly clear that he was not going to pay a price for his honesty.

Coy glanced at Butler and then back. "I asked the question. I'll take an honest answer."

"Well, I don't know exactly who it was that you took the chance on before--if it was me, I'm sincerely grateful, but I'm not really inclined to trust in people's potential when we're talking about life and death situations. I'd much rather see some proof of qualifications. So if it were me..." he glanced at Butler, "I'd probably err on the side of caution."

"So where do we find these qualified people?" Butler countered. "Not on this station. And if we move on to look elsewhere, we do so with a half-staffed battleship. Where's the safety in that? No, I say trainees are better than no crew."

Coy Lamont nodded at him. "I'm rather glad you feel that way, because if it comes to that, you may be commanding her, and her trainees, after all."

Butler opened his mouth, but evidently thought better of his retort, and closed it. Rebel smiled, knowing that the Commodore was the only one in the fleet who could out-maneuver Captain Butler. He turned to brave a comment of that nature, but Lamont was suddenly staring across the promenade. Butler noticed too, and they both looked at the two women who had captured Coy's attention.

It seemed obvious that the women had been waiting to be noticed. One of them, a woman with a coffee-and-cream complexion and long dark hair, looked straight at Coy, as if asking for an invitation. Coy stayed glued to its seat, but gave a tiny careful nod.

She and her companion, a strong-looking woman of very dark complexion and short military hairstyle, came to their table. The first one smiled tentatively, and put out a hand.

"Captain Lamont?" She seemed to notice it's uniform for the first time, and the smile turned down a little. Coy did not correct the rank. It did not budge an inch. And for a second, it didn't even appear to acknowledge the hand. It took her hand and shook it hesitantly.

"Doctor Durand," it said rather gravely.

The doctor looked relieved. "I didn't suppose you'd forget us but...and it's Rose, by the way."

Coy nodded and released the hand.

She turned to her companion. "Mara, this is Captain Coy Lamont. This is Captain Mara Hendricks."

Hendricks put out her hand as well. "It's a privilege, Captain Lamont. Rose has told me how you saved her and the other miners."

Coy's face froze in a polite smile, and it had to consciously let go of her hand to keep from squeezing it in the wave of tension that swept through along with the unwanted memories. The conversation seemed to freeze along with Coy's smile.

Butler was one who believed ice was for breaking. "Captain of what, may I ask?"

Hendricks and Rose glanced at each other a little sadly. "That should be former Captain, I'm afraid, ... ah?"

"Ken Butler," he supplied, leaving off his rank intentionally, Coy was sure. He probably thought there was a surplus of Captains in the conversation.

She eyed his uniform for clues, but found none on the insignia-less black fatigues.

"I *was* in command of a ship in our Reserve forces. But when the new regime took office recently, the defense budget was slashed. And since I had, ah, annoyed a few people who were suddenly in high places..."

"When the chopping block came around, your neck was too near the front of the line," Butler finished for her.

She nodded and turned back to Coy.

"When Rose told me who you were, I thought that perhaps you could help us get passage away from here."

"To where?"

"Anywhere closer to Servati."

"I see." Coy thought for a moment. "Dr. Durand is going back where I dropped her the first time, I assume. And your interest?"

Hendricks shrugged. "It's a good hub. A lot of employment possibilities."

"Such as passenger or cruise lines?"

Coy watched her attempt to swallow her pride and say yes, but she couldn't quite manage it. Coy relaxed for the first time and motioned for them to sit.

"I'm afraid that Dr. Durand is slightly out of date with her information about me. When we met I was in a completely different situation. I don't give free rides anymore."

The two women looked at each other.

"And what do you do now?" the former captain asked.

"It's Commodore Lamont now and I have a fleet of my own to run."

"Your own mercenaries?"

"The BlackFleet."

Hendricks was silent for a moment. "The BlackFleet." She was clearly impressed. "You know, I met a guy not too long ago who was trying everything to find you. Had his own ship and everything. Wanted to sign on or something like that. Said no merc in the region could get a job but you guys. You have quite a reputation."

Coy's eyes widened a little in surprise. "Do we? And what is that?"

"You guys are supposed to be the heroes of the universe or something. Saving everyone and never asking to be paid. Actually," she said with a knowing smile, "I never believed that part."

Durand frowned curiously. "What are you doing on a place like this?"

"I was wondering the same thing about you."

She sighed. "Mara's government-the former government-had wanted to import off-world medicine. I volunteered to be part of the team. After all that time in virtual slavery it seemed my big chance at independence."

"Let me guess," Butler said, "More budget chopping."

She nodded, then looked again at Coy.

"And you're here because…?"

"We have a new ship…."

Mara sat bolt upright in her chair. "You're hiring crew?"

"We hire a very specific number of people for very specific jobs." It let those words hang for a moment. If Hendricks did indeed know anything about the BlackFleet, she would know they did not advertise. It looked at her barely contained enthusiasm. "Would you be willing to lose your rank and begin as a trainee?"

She paused only a second. "If there are suitable advancement possibilities."

Both of Lamont's brows rose at her bravado. Butler laughed outright. "All placement and promotions are made due to abilities demonstrated to senior officers," it recited, "Ultimately to me, of course. Advancement is always possible for those with talent and drive."

Rebel finally joined the conversation at that.

"Lieutenant Rebel, Ma'am. Trust me, it happens."

"The Lieutenant commands one of our ships. As of very recently, as a matter of fact," Coy explained.

"Well, lower rank beats no rank at all, which is what I have if I stay here," Hendricks agreed.

Coy put out its hand again. "Then welcome aboard, Trainee Hendricks."

She happily shook all three officers' hands.

Rose cleared her throat. "I'd be no good as a mercenary soldier. Can I still get a ride?"

"That depends on how badly you wish to get back---and how soon," Lamont said.

"Why is that, Ca--Commodore?"

"Because ships need medical staff." Coy cocked its head."It would be a rather big chance at independence."

"You want to *hire* me?" she stammered.

"It is a battleship, not a hospital or a passenger ship. I won't belittle the danger. But I need staff, you need a ride, and I've seen you at work. I know your qualifications." Coy cast a sideways glance at Rebel, at that.

"What if it didn't work out?"

Butler started to make impatient sounds, but Coy frowned him down, knowing very well where her hesitation came from.

"You would not be bound by an unbreakable contract. We work on word of honor. Anyone who is a member of the BlackFleet is so because they have a desire to do something with their life. Something they were not allowed to do elsewhere. To make a difference."

Resolution settled on her features. "Count me in, Commodore Lamont."

They all stood to escort their new crewmembers to the *Nighthawk*. Coy fell in beside Butler. "Spoiled and picky," it murmured.

Butler rolled his eyes and shrugged surrender.

As Exec, Butler gave the two women the official tour of not only the *Nighthawk*, but the *Blackbird*, and *Raven*, as well.

"I'm confused by one thing," Hendricks admitted as they shuttled from the '*Bird* back to the *Raven*.

"What's that?"

She frowned. "I'd heard so much about the BlackFleet... stories here and there about people being rescued, and worlds saved...." She trailed off, trying to put her thoughts into words.

"Yes?" Butler prompted.

She waved her arm at the empty seats. "Where is everyone?"

Ken had learned he could argue till he was blue with Lamont about crew numbers – in private. But he would never appear to disagree with it in public again. So he grinned and nodded at her question. "You two will make thirty-two. And that's it so far. The *Raven* and *Blackbird* put together have a crew of twenty."

Hendricks stared. "Then all those stories..."

"Are absolutely true. The Commodore is very particular about who it hires." Ken smiled to himself at the memory of Schiff giving him the same lecture. "Quality, not quantity. If you don't pass, you're not in."

"Pass what?" Rose asked.

"The Commodore's standards. And don't ask what they are. Only Coy Lamont knows."

"When do we know if we've passed?" Hendricks asked.

Ken raised an eyebrow. "You already have, or the Skipper would've left you at that table on the station."

"I don't understand. All I said was that I screwed up and got myself axed."

The brow came down. "Is that what happened? You performed your duties incorrectly and left the authorities no alternative?"

"The 'duties' they asked me to perform were incorrect, and I told them so. That was my mistake."

"You regret telling them so?"

"Y--no. Not really. They were wrong. But what difference does it make? Slovenly duty or insubordination? I still got axed."

Ken's smile returned. "It makes all the difference, Trainee Hendricks. All the difference in the universe."

A few hours later, Butler stood before Lamont's quarters, pushing the door chime.

"Enter," came the reply that opened the hatch.

Ken stepped into the room and found Coy working at its large desk. Behind it, out the viewport, Petrov Station floated silently.

The *Raven* was detached from the Station, as was the *Blackbird,* but remained in holding orbit until the *'Hawk* was ready to cut loose. Even Bon could find very little to modify on the new ship, but it stayed docked until the new crew was settled.

"Yes?" Coy looked up from the files it was reading.

Ken handed over the tiny data disk he was holding. "As you said, Durand knows more about medicine than anyone I've met. In fact she's already asking about remodeling the Sick Bay to make it possible to add a re-animation section for stasis patients."

Lamont looked shocked. "Is that possible?"

"I asked Ceal. She said that, between the technologies on the two ships, it's theoretically possible. But you'd have to have someone experienced to do it."

Coy leaned back in its chair. "The mining station had a working stasis section. I don't know Rose's personal expertise, though. But we ought to look into it. Our own re-animation unit..."

"Would you like me to call her up and let her explain...?"

"No," Lamont said, a little too quickly. The sight of Durand down on the station had brought up far too many memories. The thought of bumping into her everyday was almost more than it could handle. Perhaps it had been a bad idea to hire her.

Butler waited politely for Lamont to finish, but it seemed to have no explanation. A few moments later, Coy focused again on current issues.

"And Hendricks?"

Ken pursed his lips. "She's good. She passed the simulator with a near perfect score. But there's something.... she'd make a wonderful First Officer."

"For whom? You? Should I resume command of the *Raven* and send you over to the *'Hawk*?"

Ken gave a hint of a sigh. "To be honest, that's not my first choice, anymore. But it's your decision Skipper."

Coy nodded, acknowledging all the meanings of the statement. "She's been burnt by the authority she trusted. We've all been there. I think we've run into her before she's been able to deal with that completely."

It was Butler's turn to nod. He well remembered his state of mind when he had met the BlackFleet. And Coy's own pain. And everyone else's. Yes, they'd all been there.

"I don't mean to judge her harshly. But I'll stick with my recommendation against handing her the reins too soon."

Unexpectedly, Lamont smiled. "When's the last time I told you I appreciate you?"

Ken blinked, then returned a grimace. "You want me to send my things over to the *Nighthawk*?"

"No, I want you to send *my* things over. We'll see how she does with her C.O. breathing down her neck. Besides, I need to keep a closer eye on our new Bridge team. I almost wish I'd held out for a different communications officer."

"Carson got you worried? Besides being spoiled, she knows her stuff."

"Spoiled. She's used to Admiral Daddy bailing her out when things got uncomfortable. No matter how much she detested him doing it, she's still used to it."

A bit of a wicked gleam came into Ken's eye. "A little academy hazing would sort that out."

Coy shook its head. "No need. If I take the *'Hawk* out on a few maneuvers with a crew of eight, she'll get all the hazing she can handle. Or have you forgotten the good ol' days?"

"According to Bon, I missed the *really* good times."

"Well, unfortunately, you may get to see them. If I go ahead and launch the *Blackbird* to fly independently, that leaves the *Raven* with a crew of thirteen. Twelve if I'm on the *'Hawk*."

"Yes, I'd---ah, thought of that. So we need to be looking for more people besides the *Nighthawk* crew."

"When have you known me to *look* for crew, Ken? We fly with what we have in four days. If they don't come in that time, they will at the next stop. Either way, they'll come to us."

It seemed a ludicrous way to run a military organization. Except that Ken Butler knew that it was true. He'd seen it. He'd been there. And there was no one he trusted more than the officer on the other side of the desk. He stood and snapped a salute, without a hint of skepticism or sarcasm. "Yes, sir. I'll arrange for your belongings to be sent over."

Lamont returned the salute. "Thank you, Captain." For everything.

Two days later, Coy had settled into the Captain's quarters on the *Nighthawk*, and proceeded to run the small crew ragged.

Everyone pulled at least double shifts learning their primary and secondary positions, as well as filling in wherever else they were needed.

Lamont passed an exhausted, smudged Drea Carson in the corridor between second and third shift. Second was supposed to be her sleep period, but she was trudging from the direction of Engineering.

She almost passed before she remembered to salute. Coy returned it without expression.

Before she moved on through, she said, "Commodore?"

Coy stopped and turned to face her, an expression of polite inquiry on its face. "Yes, Trainee Carson?"

She opened her mouth, but then shut it, shook her head, and moved on. Lamont continued in the other direction. Just before she rounded a bend in the corridor, however, she turned and blurted out, "How long is
this going to go on, sir?"

"Is what going to go on, Trainee?"

She waved helplessly at the walls and the ship around her. "This! Working us to death."

Lamont frowned. "You look alive to me."

Drea sighed. "Yes, sir."

"Was there anything else?"

Another sigh. "No, sir."

"Good. Carry on, Trainee."

Mara Hendricks stood before the Captain's quarters, nervous, but determined. She tugged on her new, black uniform jacket, straightening out some non-existent wrinkles.

Finally, she took a breath, and pushed the buzzer to announce her arrival.

"Enter," came the Commodore's voice over the com speaker. At that word, the door opened and she stepped into the room.

"Trainee Hendricks reporting as ordered, sir." She came to attention before the desk Lamont sat at and saluted.

Lamont returned the salute. "At ease, Trainee. This isn't a review."

She relaxed her stance, and clasped her hands behind her.

Lamont nodded at the other person in the room. "Sergeant Schiff and I are plotting some emergency drills for the crew. I would like your input on how well you think they'll do."

"The Troopers or the Techs?"

Coy shrugged. "Either. Both."

Hendricks thought only a moment. "The best trooper under duress that we've got is McKinney. Reinhart and Cook are good fighters individually, but they don't have the necessary teamwork."

"Hmmm. And Meiser?"

Hendricks smiled. "You want me to out predict a fortune-teller? Okay, my best guess is that she will do as she's told, and little more. Personally, I think she lacks the---initiative--to be a mercenary."

Lamont raised an eyebrow at Schiff. The sergeant nodded his head in reply to some unspoken message. So far the assessment had lined up exactly with the sergeant's. Lamont turned back to Mara.

"What about the Techs?"

"They're good. I'd trust Phil Torren with my life. He's quiet, but he has those engineers hopping. Biggs may complain a lot, but he knows these type engines in and out. Savalo is one of those *born* techs. Edwards may be learning the ropes, but he's coming along. He was a good bet."

Lamont looked at her thoughtfully for a moment. "You seem to have everyone analyzed." Mara gave a careful shrug.

"I like to know the people I work with."

"Very good. Bridge officers."

"Nathan sucks up a little too much for my taste, but he's a good navigator, as far as I can see. Carson's...." she grimaced.

Coy gave a small frown. "I was under the impression that she was coming along."

"She is. She knows how to run the com equipment. She would just rather be running people."

Schiff barked a laugh.

Coy frowned him quiet. "She needs this chance as much as anyone else here."

"Yes, sir." Hendricks remained standing at parade rest.

"Anyway," Coy continued, "you seem to have a handle on the crew. I want you up there on deck, keeping an eye on things during the drills."

"Yes, sir!" she repeated, only with much more enthusiasm.

Coy kept her a bay a few moments more. "It's not going to be much of a surprise to anyone if I hand command over to you, is it, Trainee Hendricks?"

Mara hardly batted an eye. "*If*?"

"Yes, Trainee, there are other contingencies," it said lightly. "The next few drills are going to be essential to my final evaluation."

Hendricks pulled her stance a little tighter, and added more respect to her tone. "Yes, sir."

Coy eyed her. "Very good. Dismissed."

She saluted again, and practically marched out.

"Spunky thing," Schiff grinned. "What exactly are you waiting for?"

Coy thought over its motives. "Respect."

"You just got that."

"I noticed."

"Anything else?"

Lamont gave a very small sigh. "Nothing substantial. She just doesn't----transmit----what you or Butler did when we met."

Schiff blinked. "What in the hell did I 'transmit'?"

Coy recalled the conversation as if it had been moments instead of months before.

"A loathing of your former situation. Intense pride and professionalism, associated with being a soldier. An intent to be something more than the people back home thought you could."

The sergeant's jaw dropped. "I said all that?"

"No, but that's what I heard. Was I close?"

"Dead center."

"Good. I heard the same type message from Bon, and Ken Butler. I don't hear it from Mara as plainly."

"What do you hear?"

"That we're a stepping stone. A path chosen out of desperation, to get another command."

Schiff frowned. "That's rather harsh."

"I know. I'm hoping the drills will change either her message, or my interpretation."

"And if it doesn't?"

"Butler gets the job, and she's his Exec until *something* changes."

Unexpectedly, Schiff nodded agreement. "Don't ever give in, Skipper. Don't ever forget that all this is yours."

Coy stared at him and this seemingly irrelevant comment. But Schiff said nothing more on the subject. After an awkward moment, they turned back to designing some 'interesting' drills for the *Nighthawk* crew.

Coy was watching the *Nighthawk's* troopers working out with Schiff when it got a call from the *Raven* that Vennefron's shuttle had arrived.

"On my way," it spoke into its wristcom even as it turned to head down to the shuttle bay and get a ride over to the flagship.

Once onboard, it hurried into Sick Bay to find Ceal waiting at the door. "I'm glad you're here," she said.

"What's up?" Coy asked, worried that something had gone wrong with the re-animation process.

"I just think he needs to talk to you," she said. And with no further explanation, led Coy in. Vennefron was seated on an exam bed looking grim.

"Anton!" Coy greeted him. "Welcome back!"

Vennefron looked up with his typical bleak expression. No, this was even more bleak than the pessimistic young man had usually looked. "Hello, sir."

Coy frowned briefly at Ceal. "Is everything okay?"

"Physically, he's more fit than when he first came to us," she reported.

Coy looked back at Venn. It had known one other fellow crew member who had been reanimated. That man had never been the same. Eventually, he had left the fleet and disappeared. It was just too hard for some people to come to grips with the experience.

It walked over and looked Venn in the eye. "It must be strange to come back."

Vennefron looked a little relieved that someone understood. "Yes, sir. They gave us tons of therapy at the hospital. Told us all about the physical changes as they happened. Helped us get back in shape. They just never really seemed to prepare us for going back and facing people who knew we'd been..." he swallowed, "...knew I'd been dead."

Coy nodded, even though it really didn't understand. "It may seem different to you for awhile. But if you want to know how we feel... You make the BlackFleet complete again. We weren't whole without everyone."

Venn gave a small, not quite heartfelt smile. "Thank you, sir."

"And when I think you're ready, I'll have a nice medal to give you."

"A medal for being stupid enough to hit a live grenade?"

"Or for saving the life of your CO, all of our rescuees and your teammates."

His expression lightened a little. "Just returning the favor, Commodore," he said sincerely. "If you hadn't signed me on..." he shook his head instead of finishing. "In fact, this makes two times you've given me my life back. Seems I still owe you one."

Coy shook its head, but had no idea how to express how it felt. In the end, it merely gave Venn a little clap on the shoulder, reiterated its welcome, and fled back to the *Nighthawk*.

It was a week later, Vennefron had settled back into his duties and the 'hazing' period had slowed a little when the 'screamer' on Lamont's wrist com went off smack in the middle of its sleep shift, jerking it awake with an adrenaline rush. Coy hit the button on the unit as it lunged from the bed, killing the alarm.

"Lamont to bridge." Slipping into black pants and boots, it was again grateful for the voice activated coms that allowed a person use of both hands during emergencies.

"Bridge," Schiff's voice came back. "We've got a live one. We've picked up a mayday close by. Appears to be a yacht being chased by pirates."

By this time, Coy was pulling its jacket on and heading out the door and up to the command center. "Best time?"

"This thing's less than an hour away."

Lamont swore. "Pirates this close to a system?"

"Brave or stupid," Schiff commented; his tone indicating which it was that he thought.

Coy entered the lift tube at the same time as Hendricks. She raised an inquiring brow. Coy nodded at her. "This is real."

Hendricks said nothing. Her mouth set determinedly, she swung out of the tube right behind her Commodore.

Phil Torren reported in via com from his post in engineering, Durand did the same from Sick Bay. Nathan sat at Navigation, but Schiff himself still manned the com board.

"Where...." Hendricks began just as Drea Carson dashed into the room and to her station. Her uniform would never pass inspection and her normally flowing dark curls had been hastily pulled into an untidy ponytail.

"Your quarters are closer than mine, Trainee," Hendricks stated simply.

"I know Ma'am but...."after a look at Hendricks' and Lamont's faces, she wisely halted her self defense and with a red faced "Yes, ma'am", turned to her station.

Schiff gave her the seat and quietly brought her up to date.

"Com, I want a link to all ship commanders," Lamont said crisply.

"Y--aye, sir, " her hands flew over the board. "Link established."

Once all three ships had co-ordinates, they set off in the direction of the conflict. As Schiff had stated, it took less than an hour.

But it was not a yacht. It was a passenger liner. Dead in space and surrounded by small ships. Nathan gave a low whistle as he counted. "Twenty-six fighters. Looks like a feeding frenzy."

Coy Lamont, hailing from a world with virtually no wildlife, had never heard the reference before, but gathered the meaning easily enough.

"Com, broadcast to them."

"Aye, sir." She was much more together now, and had even straightened the ponytail a little, during the flight.

"This is Commodore Coy Lamont commanding the BlackFleet Mercenaries. Move away from the liner. You have two minutes to comply."

A few seconds later, a holo-image formed above their console.

"Who the hell do you think you are, and what the hell do you think you're doing?" the image of a grimy, aging man bellowed.

"I told you who I was," Coy stated calmly. "And I'm breaking this up. You have a minute 30."

The man laughed. "On whose authority?"

"My own. A minute fifteen."

"'Till what?"

"Until we open fire."

The man's eyes went cold and hard. "Wrong answer."

The image disappeared. At the same moment, the small ships began to move.

"Shields on full power!" Lamont shouted out and heard acknowledgment from all three bridges. It looked at Hendricks. "You have command here. I'll be in Tac."

"Aye, sir. I have command."

Before Coy could turn to leave, the first volley hit their shields. The deck shook under their feet.

"Pack quite a punch for such little guys," Butler's voice came over the command link.

"They'll go for the *Blackbird*," Lamont told them. It went down the corridor at a jog, and swung into the Tac room. The scale holo-model of local space in the center of the room lit up upon Coy's entry, displaying everyone's position. Sure enough, a swarm was heading for the '*Bird*.

"We're ready," Rebel announced.

"Offense or defense?" Butler asked.

"We'll draw them away," Coy ordered. "You use the *Raven's* shields to help cover the gap in the liner. I'm showing them bleeding a lot of air."

The Tac comp also showed a circle of ships around the *'Hawk*, powering up their weapons. They fired simultaneously. The *Nighthawk* shook once more as its shields were battered.

"No permanent damage," engineering reported immediately. "Back ups on standby."

"Weapons?" Lamont barked.

"Full power," Nathan assured it.

Coy gave a grim smile. "Fire at will."

Nathan blew a path straight through the swarm. Over on the *Raven*, Kensie Parker did the same, even as the flagship sidled up to the bleeding liner, enveloping her with the *Raven's* shields.

Lamont focused its attentions on the *Blackbird*. "Get them off Rebel's tail," it ordered the *Nighthawk's* gunner. "This is not the time to test the limits of her defenses."

"Aye, sir." Nathan mumbled distractedly as he lined up his shots.

The pirates' speed and numbers against the BlackFleet's size and power was making for an interesting battle. The swarm's tactics seemed to be to send in wave after wave of fighters close to the surface of an opposing ship, using high relative speed and pinpoint targeting in an effort to overload the bigger ship's shields. They were staying too close to the hulls of the *Blackbird* itself to target the small ships safely. Nathan, too, had to wait and time his shots for when a ship swung out away from their prey.

Down in the Tac room Lamont studied the scene in frustration. "Hendricks, move the *Nighthawk* as close to the *Raven* as possible without touching shields. Rebel, make a pass between us."

"You gotta be kid...!" came Myke Pedula's voice over the com line.

"What was that, *Blackbird*?" Coy asked.

"We said, 'aye sir'," Rebel answered as the ships began to move together.

The maneuver quite effectively scraped the fighters off of pursuing the *Blackbird*, and out into space. It also served to temporarily disrupt the small ships' carefully coordinated attack, so neither the *Nighthawk's* nor the *Raven's* gunners wasted any time locking on to the suddenly exposed and confused fighters. When a good third of the pirates' fighters had been destroyed or disabled, they at last began to withdraw.

The grimy man with the cold eyes came on the viewer one last time.

"Commodore Coy Lamont of the BlackFleet Mercenaries, you've made an enemy today."

The image stared at Coy for a moment as if memorizing its face.

"Does my enemy come with a name?" Coy asked.

A frightening smile tugged at the man's face before he disappeared without answering. The swarm took off at top speed, leaving their damaged comrades to limp along on their own.

"So much for honor among thieves," Butler's voice commented.

Lamont ignored him. *"Blackbird, damages?"*

"We're a little crispy in places," Rebel replied. "Life support is on line. Engines are operational. Shields are on emergency power only. I'm not sure what magic tricks Luka conjured up to make them hold on as long as they did."

"No injuries?"

"No. But we need more full time bridge personnel, that's for sure."

"Noted. Dock in the *Raven* as soon as Butler gives the okay." Lamont checked in with everyone, then made arrangements to meet with the captain of the liner aboard the *Raven*.

Before leaving the *'Hawk*, however, it made a quick visit to its cabin and then back to the bridge. Everyone was still there. Coy walked straight to the Navigator/Weapons station.

"Trainee Nathan!"

The surprised young man leapt to his feet.

"Sir!"

Coy put out its hand. "Well done-----Lieutenant."

Somewhat in a daze, Ezra Nathan returned the handshake and felt a small piece of metal pressed into his palm. He looked down at the rectangle pin bearing the thin stripe of a Lieutenant.

Coy then turned to the engineer, and repeated the gesture. "Excellent job, Commander Torren."

The almost-albino flushed with pleasure.

And next to him, as dark as Torren was pale...

"Congratulations, Captain Hendricks."

Mara took her pin with more grin than grace. "Yes, sir. Thank you, sir."

Drea Carson sat with her back to all this, dutifully managing her console.

"Trainee Carson."

Drea turned, stood, and faced Lamont, head held high and proud. Coy took in the personal shame behind the proud eyes. "Do you want this?"

She knew what it meant, and it wasn't just a piece of metal for her collar it was talking about. This job, this opportunity. This responsibility. "Yes, sir. I do."

"Then carry on, Ensign."

Ensign, not Lieutenant. That carried a lot of meanings in itself. Yes, she could be a Bridge officer, but she had a lot of learning to do. Still, Carson stared almost in disbelief at the insignia it held out realizing it was probably the only thing in her whole life she had earned on her own.

"Sir, I..."

Coy gave her a firm nod, and for the first time in as long as she could remember, Carson felt as though someone believed in her. Everything about the whole horrible morning was momentarily forgotten---except for that nod. And the small pin in her hand.

Lamont spoke to them all. "According to BlackFleet tradition," which it had just made up on the spot, " you may wear your rank insignia for one duty day---then it will go on your dress uniform permanently."

Captain Hendricks snapped to attention and saluted. Her crew followed suit. Lamont returned them, collected Schiff and headed toward the shuttle bay.

The Fleet stood watch over the crippled passenger liner while it made emergency repairs to its hull and whatever vital systems had been damaged. The *Blackbird*, likewise sat nestled in the *Raven's* bay, having her wounds tended.

Which gave everyone plenty of time to analyze the experience.

"You know what we need, don't you?" asked Ken Butler at the command staff meeting. "We need some of those little guys of our own."

Lamont merely stared at him without saying a word.

"Ah, Skipper," Rebel interrupted the silence. "I'd have to agree. If there's going to be any more incidents like this one, that is."

"Which we don't know," Bon said.

"If we met them once, we could meet them again." Hendricks remembered quite well the pirate's parting remarks.

"Fighters," Lamont said without inflection. "Which means pilots, and support crew, not to mention somewhere to dock and launch them."

"I didn't say it would be quick and easy," Butler defended, "I said it was necessary. Sir."

Coy blew out a long breath. It looked over at Schiff, whom it always invited to sit in despite his lack of command rank. "Any comments?"

The sergeant thought a moment. "I've always been a ground trooper. Space battles are not my area of expertise, you might say. But whether you're on the ground or not, you need the right tools to win."

Lamont paused in thought a few moments more. "Well, unless by some miracle the owner of this cruise line has a load of fighter ships they want to give us in return for our good deeds, I think this subject will have to be tabled for a while." It looked at Butler, but the captain made no more comments. "Our immediate Fleet needs are personnel and to build up our information network."

"For more jobs?" Rebel asked.

Coy nodded. "That plus tracking down who these guys were and where they disappeared to."

"You want to go looking for them?" Hendricks asked. "I mean, you *want* to meet up with them again?"

"I want to find out who was behind them. Who our "enemy" is. This," it jabbed a finger angrily at the table for emphasis, "is exactly the type of thing we exist to put a stop to. People who think they can fly around attacking civilian targets and not pay for it." Coy looked around the table at their faces and saw its own determination mirrored in them. It took a calming breath. "To begin with, I sent Lieutenant Aziza over to the liner to help them with any computer damage. While there, he just happened to collect quite a few names of contacts at the various stations on the line's route. Not only company personnel, but also several others who could possibly have information on activity in this area. He's sitting down with Vennefron right now working on the list." Its eyes narrowed. "No matter what it takes," a look at Butler, " no matter what tools we need to have, the BlackFleet is going to stop this.

Chapter Four

Coy sat in its cabin, slouched on the couch, staring at nothing. A mug of tea sat on the table, untouched, slowly cooling off. Coy heard a small clink of china and focused on the here and now. The cup was now steaming . It thought back. It had all started with its com link chiming its familiar call.

"Butler to Lamont."

"Lamont. Go ahead."

"Skipper, we have another one of the passengers here to see you."

It had had about a thousand things going through its mind at the time and really hadn't wanted to talk to anyone. But several of the people they had saved from the pirates had not only been extremely grateful, but extremely wealthy as well, and had guaranteed not a few Favors over and above the one from the cruise line itself. Well, except for the liner's piano player who had offered his services should the BlackFleet ever happen to need a lounge singer. But perhaps this was another of the ones who had means. It could well be worth the time.

"Have them escorted to my quarters."

"Aye, sir."

The man who arrived at Coy's door turned out to be one Rogelio Asch, a passenger from the economy section who had barely paid his fare. He was trembling with nerves but determined to pay off his debt.

"How?" Coy asked bluntly.

"I can work it off."

"This is a battle ship. What do you propose I have you do?"

Asch looked at his hands. "Whatever you want me to do, I'll do. I owe you my life. I can never repay that enough."

Coy relaxed back in its chair. "My crew is handpicked. They are the finest soldiers - the finest people. What exactly is your training?"

Asch looked crushed. "I-I'm no soldier," he admitted painfully, "I'm nothing."

Coy had responded to his obvious grief. "Everybody is something. What have you done in your life?"

"Before I lost everything, I owned a restaurant." Bitterness tinged his voice.

Coy sat up straighter. "You ran a restaurant?"

"Yes."

"Ordered supplies? Food? Equipment?"

"Of course."

Coy blinked. "Why is that nothing?"

Slowly, Asch went on to explain his family history. How his military and politically important parents had scoffed at his desire to go into the restaurant business.

"What about a career as a ship's steward? Or Acquisitions?" Coy asked.

He shook his head. "It would've been a compromise simply to please them. And that's no way to live."

"I see," Coy said thoughtfully. "So you would be opposed to a job with us doing just that?"

"Doing what?"

Coy smiled. "We could very well use someone with knowledge in acquisitions, accounting, that sort of thing. If you're interested."

"You don't have someone doing that sort of thing?"

"I have myself. And frankly, I have enough other ways to use my time."

Asch paused. "Commodore, I passed up all the benefits and education my parents offered because I was arrogant enough to think I was right. Are you sure you want to hire someone like me?"

In answer, Coy put out its hand. And Asch took it.

So now the Fleet had an acquisitions officer who decided, in his "off" hours to double as Lamont's personal steward. Coy objected at first, not having any experience with a servant of any kind. But Asch seemed to have an almost telepathic ability to know what his commander needed and when. No more cold tea. With a faint disapproving frown, the cup would disappear and a fresh hot one would take its place.

And Asch was just as efficient with Fleet business .Even though the job had been growing as steadily as the fleet itself had. They were now at three ships and forty people.

Butler still wanted more, of course. And who knew what could fall into their lap next week? Coy Lamont sure didn't. It got up from the couch and began pacing. Fall into their laps. That was the problem. The whole reason it was in such a mood tonight. The way the *Raven* had fallen into Coy's lap was an ongoing mystery. It had been rather easily pushed to the background in the manic first days of the BlackFleet. But now that many of the routine jobs had been delegated to others, Coy had more time to ponder such mysteries.

The huge black craft was any shipmaster's dream. Precision built, as elegant in design as it was deadly in battle. Who in their right mind would wager such a possession in a card game? *Someone who wanted to get rid of it quickly and cleanly.*

Possible scenarios played through its mind again as it paced. Number 1- the man had not been in his right mind. Possible, but not probable. Number 2 - The man had owed someone a lot of back payments. More probable, but somehow it didn't ring true with Coy's assessment of his character. Number 3 - It was hot and whoever the rightful owners were got too close. Unfortunately for Coy and the BlackFleet that one seemed the most possible and probable. Now why someone would steal something that large and easily identifiable was still another question. Could it have been cover? A smoke screen to hide an even more valuable theft? Something more valuable than the amount that a ship like that would've cost to build. And, as Bon had pointed out early on, someone out there didn't know the *Raven* had changed hands.

The mystery branched out in several directions from there. Who they were, what they were doing to find their possession, what they would do when they did find out...The only thing that wasn't a mystery was how the BlackFleet would respond. It was their ship now. And woe to the force that tried to take it from them.

Coy smiled a very unhumorous smile at that thought. They would make more enemies that day.

'*Commodore Coy Lamont of the BlackFleet, you've made an enemy today.*'

The quote echoed in its mind. The parting remarks of the pirate leader. No, it corrected its own thought. Not the leader. The battle leader perhaps, but hardly the person pulling the strings. Little ships like the ones they had used needed a lot of backup. A mother ship and technical crew. Someone bigger was out there somewhere, and they were mad at Coy.

Terrific. The *Raven*'s original owners mad at it, pirates mad at it -- maybe it should start a collection. See just how many people in the universe it could piss off at one time. It sighed. It would be a whole lot simpler if all of these potential enemies were one person. It's a lot easier to aim at one target..... Coy sank slowly down into a nearby chair as it thought about that one.

What if someone were pulling the strings for all the raids that had been ever increasing. Sure, with industry in the area growing so quickly everyone was prepared for some increase in incidents, but no one had been prepared for what was happening now. Coy spent the rest of the evening and most of the night (much to Asch's disapproval) pacing and pondering and pouring over records of every incident reported so far.

The next "day" Coy called a meeting of all senior staff as it had been in the habit of doing. After routine ship reports, however, Lamont put forth its fledging theory of one source behind the raids.

"The only common denominator so far is timing." Coy pulled up the data it had been working with the night before on all their vidcoms. "You can see a normal spattering of raids and trouble for most of the time Beta Region has been populated. Then suddenly the amount spikes up in the last year. It does not follow the growth curve of trade as I would have thought. It's almost as if they were all influenced by the same catalyst. The question is who would benefit," it finished up.

Butler stared. "You're serious. You think some person, somewhere is strong enough to orchestrate all the pirates and thugs in this whole part of space?"

"They wouldn't have to 'orchestrate' them," Schiff told him. "Just hire each group to do a job."

"Not even that," Rebel added. "Assuming the objective is not the loot itself, but some outcome brought about by the activity. If no one was counting on splitting the spoils they wouldn't have to hire anyone. Just make sure they had names, flight plans, cargo manifests. Enough to encourage the strike without being directly involved."

Coy nodded along with Rebel's reasoning. The two of them often thought alike it realized. Not like it and Ken Butler who seemed to always be butting heads. No, that was unfair. Ken's job as Lamont's exec was to play Devil's Advocate and point out all of the flaws before they became plans. And that was exactly what he was doing right now. With enthusiasm.

"You're all paranoid," the captain was saying. "We can't run our daily business looking over our shoulder for the Boogeyman all the time."

Bon cleared his throat. "Excuse me. Pretend for a moment that I'm just a poor uninformed techie and explain to me what our 'daily business' is."

Everyone paused a minute. They looked around at each other like students caught without the answer.

Coy nodded at Bon. Good idea. Time to refocus.

"Well, we're..." Rebel drawled and with a hand gesture passed it off to the next person.

"Heroes," Schiff said firmly. "We help who needs our help."

"Right now everybody in the galaxy seems to need help," Hendricks commented.

"And the best way to do that is to stop the harassment. Hence..." Coy began.

"We have to find who's harassing them," Butler said and gave a melodramatic sigh. "So now this is Operation Boogeyman."

Lamont became more serious. "This is not an imaginary monster in your closet, Ken. There is a real something out there causing all of this."

Butler was serious as well. "Skipper, going after one pirate at a time is one thing. But you're talking about something big. Really big. Really bigger than us. We don't have the manpower or hardware to fight a real war."

"We won't be fighting the war for awhile. We'll be investigating. Every rescue we make holds a clue."

"What about local skirmishes? Civil Wars?" Rebel asked. "The jobs that don't have anything to do with pirates."

Lamont shook its head. "Don't make the assumption it's not related. If it upsets things in the area it could be part of the picture. I believe you said it right. The..." it looked at Butler " 'Boogeyman' could be mainly interested in an outcome that all this upheaval is only contributing to.

"But as much as I hate to admit it, Captain Butler is right." Coy ignored the feigned look of shock Ken wore. "Eventually we are going to need more guns. If we get any leads through our network of a good deal, I'll look into it. Also I need to delegate some of the hiring. Captain Bon and Major Schiff will both be authorized to interview recruits."

Both men stared openmouthed as Coy handed them each a pin. As usual, Schiff was the first to recover.

He looked straight into his commodore's eyes. "You're sure."

"Yes."

Bon couldn't decide which was the bigger surprise, the promotion or the policy change. "Commodore," he began, then merely smiled.

Lamont gave him a nod in return. It stood, indicating dismissal and returned their salutes.

Schiff paused as everyone filed out. "Gym?"

"I'll be there." Coy frowned at his empty collar. "Are you forgetting procedure?"

Without expression, Schiff clipped it on, saluted again and left. Lamont smiled, knowing the new major had hoped to avoid the scores of congratulations he would now receive. Oh, well, one of the hazards of being a hero.

Thump! Talk about hazards. Coy tumbled over its head and landed flat on the mat, a victim of Schiff's perfectly timed tai-otoshi throw. The last several minutes had been an exercise in striking and blocking, with little ground gained. The strain was beginning to tell on even these two frequent sparring partners.

"Who was that for?" it managed to pant.

"Pierce." As Coy had predicted, Schiff objected to all the congratulations he had been receiving since the promotion. "She practically kissed me."

Lamont got to its feet, although it still couldn't quite straighten up all the way. " Oh, right, there's a horrible fate."

Schiff frowned. "She's under my command," he said as he feinted in and out of Coy's reach, searching for an opening.

"She's under mine, too."

"Commodore..." Schiff's frown changed from subtle teasing to inquiry.

Coy waved it off. "No, I haven't. But, come on, Walter, I'm half male, and she's gorgeous. Don't tell me you've never thought..." before it knew what had happened, Coy was again down, gasping for air.

"Keep your mind on business," Schiff advised.

From the floor, Lamont raised a brow at his obvious double meaning. "You don't think I do?"

Schiff paused then shrugged. "It's not my concern."

"You don't bring up things that aren't your concern. It's one of the reasons I talk to you, Walter. I always get a honest answer."

"And what is it you need an honest answer to?"

"Do you think Fleet regulations are too strict?"

"Why? You want to ask Pierce out?"

"Or Bon." At Schiff's surprised look, it grinned. "You forget. I have options." The Major was in the midst of launching a flurry of strikes, but slowed abruptly as much in shock at the grin as the subject matter. To cover his surprise, he said " I thought we came here to work out, not...."

Breath or no breath, Coy was not going to pass this one up. After only a moment's struggle Schiff went down with a very satisfying thud. When oxygen was flowing correctly again, Coy made it as far as hands and knees. "How about a nice game of chess next time?"

"Sissy game," Schiff commented, still lying on the floor.

"Maybe, but you're not *sore* the next day." Lamont got the rest of the way up and came to stand over the trooper. It offered a hand up which Schiff ignored for a moment. "Come on, let me gloat over my one good throw of the day."

With a shake of his head, he let himself be hauled to his feet. "You're out of shape, Kid," he told his commander.

Coy had the sick feeling what was coming, but had no time to throw up its guard...

It massaged its shoulder absently as it sat at a table in the crew's mess with Ceal Byars. She noted the gesture, professionally.

"Been playing with Walter again?"

Coy merely grimaced.

She took a bite of sandwich and chewed thoughtfully. "He came to see me. He was concerned about you."

Coy frowned. "He thinks I'm that out of shape?"

She shook her head. "No, he said...he said you were grinning and joking."

Coy paused mid drink, tea mug almost to its lips. Then it continued the drink and set the mug down carefully. "I see."

"Well, I don't. You said..."

"Perhaps I said too much."

"Coy , everybody needs to unload sometimes."

"Unloading will not change anything."

"How do you..."

"We are here to have lunch," it told her firmly. "Not therapy."

Ceal knew enough to drop the subject for now. She swallowed her frustration and washed it down with coffee. "So where's yours?"

"My what?"

She nodded at the mug sitting by itself in front of Coy. "Your lunch."

"I had breakfast."

"So?"

Coy sighed. "All right, fine. I'll get..."

A sandwich landed on the table next to the mug. Lamont looked up to see a grinning Ken Butler.

"If you two ever decide to conspire in a mutiny, I'm in trouble."

"Ha," the captain winked at Ceal and took a seat with them. "It's on to us."

"Guilty of conspiracy to do lunch," Byars admitted.

Lamont obediently took a bite.

Before it could even swallow, its wrist com let out a long shrill tone. It wasn't hard to figure why the distress call indicator was called a "screamer". Coy stood up.

"Ahem!" Ceal nodded at the sandwich.

Coy picked it up, wrapped a napkin around it, and headed out and down the corridor to the Int/Sec office. It knew that in all three ships, every member of the BlackFleet was hurrying to their primary duty stations at the same time. "Lamont," it said into its wrist com. "What's up?"

"Aziza, here, sir. We've got a general distress. Small and close."

"How small?"

"At a guess, I'd say a pod. Maybe a shuttle."

A guess? Lieutenant Aziza had spent countless hours listening to every known signal ships could make. Devyu took his description of communication officer very seriously.

Lamont reached I/S barely in front of Schiff. Vennefron was there already, taking the data that was coming down from Aziza's scanners and making a detailed comparison of the facts they had so far - known trade routes, types of ships in the area etc.

"Whatever it is," he said over his shoulder, "it's close."

Coy read over the data. "Anything due to be out here about now?"

Venn shook his head. "Nothing that we know of."

"Aziza said it could be a pod. That would mean a larger ship should be within our scanning range."

"Unless they dropped it and jumped," Schiff speculated.

Coy straightened up and looked at him. "You don't suppose it could be bait?"

" No message or identification," Venn added.

Schiff frowned at that. "That doesn't sound promising."

Coy read over Venn's information once more. "No need to take chances. We go in with shields on max."

A few hours later, the BlackFleet made visual contact and found it to be a shuttle, not an escape pod. The *Raven* hailed them repeatedly with no response. Coy, connected to all the ship commanders via the com system, stood in the Tac Room studying the holovid display.

"It is small," Butler's voice said. "We could haul it into the bay and then open it up."

"I don't care to be on the other side of a Trojan Horse," Coy told him, "and have the *Raven* blown apart from the inside."

"Well, it was only a suggestion..." Butler trailed off.

Somewhere in the back of Coy's mind it wondered if it should worry whether Ken was serious at times like that. But, for now on with the problem at hand. "Anyone see anything we're missing?"

"It seems like someone is trying to compensate for their drift now and then," Bon answered, "Otherwise I'd think it was a derelict with an automated beacon."

"Could they be scared the wrong people picked up their call?" Rebel asked.

"Why wouldn't they have responded to our hails?" Hendricks wondered.

"They still wouldn't know for sure who we were." Lamont thought for only a second more. "Hendricks, take the *Nighthawk* to their starboard side. Rebel, take port. Butler, take us around to face them point blank. Keep shields up, people, looks can be deceiving." A chorus of 'aye, aye' and the ships maneuvered into their places. "All right, open a vid channel."

"You're on," Aziza said.

"Shuttle, I am Commodore Lamont commanding the Black-Fleet Mercenaries. We picked up your distress signal. Do you still require assistance?"

A few moments later the *Raven's* holovid showed a young uniformed man, much the worse for wear.

"Commodore, thank you for coming to our aide, ah, ma'am" he said hesitantly.

Coy acknowledged the gratitude despite the lack of trust in his voice. "Our pleasure. And it's not ma'am. At least not entirely."

Relief spread over the man's features as Coy's meaning registered. "I'm really glad to hear that, Commodore."

"Indeed?" Coy was not used to the revelation of its gender being met with such enthusiasm.

"There are none where I come from. I'm willing to bet you are who you say you are."

"And who do you say you are?"

He straightened automatically. "Lieutenant Edwin Drake, of the, well, of nothing I guess...." His proud statement trailed off in confusion.

"How can we help you, Lieutenant?"

"I have 12 men here, five wounded, all exhausted and hungry. We've been drifting for a couple of days. We only got the beacon working this morning."

"I understand. We will send a shuttle to mate with yours."

Drake nodded.

Lamont cut the transmission and called to Schiff. The major had his troops suited and ready. Orders were given and the rescue launched.

The bedraggled soldiers were hustled to Sick Bay as soon as they set foot on the *Raven*. The last to leave the shuttle was the lieutenant himself. Lamont met him at the hatch.

"Lieutenant Drake, welcome aboard."

The young officer gave a grateful sigh and put out his hand. "Thank you, commodore." He paused, "Is it sir or ma'am?"

"Sir is fine," it said wondering how many hundred times that it had said that. "Sick Bay is this way." In the corridor they met up with Ken. "This is Captain Butler, my Exec and commander of the *Raven*."

"Sir," Drake, fighting the impulse to salute despite the foreign uniform, again offered his hand.

"So, what happened, Lieutenant?" Butler asked.

"I was second Lieutenant on an Imperial Navy vessel out of New Grenich. We were returning to our ship after a routine drill when it was attacked."

Coy and Ken couldn't help looking briefly at each other at that. A clue already? "By whom?" Coy asked. They were nearly to Sick Bay, now and Drake had not so much as glanced at the elegant interior around him. Most people on their first tour through the huge ship couldn't help ogling at every turn. But he was much too miserable to notice his surroundings.

The lieutenant went pale. "Our own people. Evidently another coup back home and nobody bothered to tell us. The captain and most of the senior officers were already dead. Some of the crew openly joined the rebels. The others were either convinced or spaced. I," he started to choke, blinked and continued, "I couldn't. Even if some of their political points make sense, the manner of ... Anyway, at the hatch we broke free and some of us made it back to the shuttle. Only it wasn't set up for long flights. No food, not enough med packs or air. I was beginning to think the airlock would've been better. At least quicker. Then you came." He stopped and looked at Lamont. "We owe you our lives."

Coy smiled. "We like to give a hand when we can."

"But mercenaries aren't like national service, right? You work for money. We can't repay you. We don't have any..." he froze as if something had just occurred to him. "We have nowhere to go."

"You've been through a lot, Lieutenant. Yet, you took care of your men. You are a good officer. If the right side comes out on top, I'm sure they'll need people like you."

"And if the wrong side does?"

"Let's get you all clean and fed and we'll discuss a few options."

Behind Drake's back, Butler rolled his eyes. "Thirteen in one pop? Don't ever complain to me about numbers again."

Lamont merely raised an amused eyebrow at his 'insubordination' and followed Drake into Sick Bay.

Later Coy sat down with everyone who had come with Drake and discussed the possibility of joining the BlackFleet. Most had good motives for wanting to remain with the mercenaries instead of being sucked into the ongoing fighting back home. One such person was a teenage boy who was apparently in some sort of officer's training position. It turns out that their society had the habit of leapfrogging young aristocratic men and women into positions of authority by sending them out with the military and assuming they would learn what they needed to know before they were killed in battle.

Coy had heard of such practices back on ancient Earth sailing vessels, but had no idea that anyone in modern space still did such a thing. Especially since Jimmy Dobbs, the young man in question, did not seem to have any aptitude and had spent several miserable months in the service.

Then, helping out in Sick Bay at their arrival changed everything. He not only had aptitude for medical duties but a lot of enthusiasm as well. Coy thought Ceal would be thrilled when it took Jimmy in to talk to her.

She was not.

Jimmy, standing next to Asch, watched the officers intently as they debated his future. Unconsciously biting his lip, his eyes darted back and forth between Commodore Lamont and Med Tech Byars.

"He was on a warship before he came to us," the commodore was saying. "If he wishes to serve on a better one, I would commend him – not stop him."

"He's a child," Byars ground out through clenched teeth.

Coy raised a brow. "By what planet's standards? Yours maybe, but not his."

Ceal opened her mouth to protest more, paused, then said quietly, "This is different."

Coy didn't even answer. It continued to look at her steadily until she slumped in defeat and turned away.

Coy turned then to Jimmy. "Asch here will get you situated with your uniform and cabin assignment."

Jimmy's eyes opened wide. "I can stay? Yesss!!!" He stopped just short of leaping into the air. Taking in Coy's sudden frown, he took a breath and calmed down. "I mean, yes, sir, that is, aye, sir. Thank you, sir."

Coy watched them leave the room before turning back to Ceal. She was still facing away, doing something, or pretending to do something, with her files.

"You want to tell me what this is really all about?" Coy asked gently.

"Children shouldn't be soldiers," she answered too steadily to be natural.

"He asked to work here with you, not out on the field with Schiff," Coy reminded her.

"People can get..." she began, but stopped. "It doesn't matter. You've decided."

"Yes, my decision is made. But it matters that you are this upset."

No answer.

"I could make it an order."

Ceal turned around at that, but still didn't speak.

Coy tried again for a voluntary response.

"I've never been at odds with you, Ceal. If this was Butler I was talking to, I'd be relieved that everything was normal. But not with you. What is wrong with Jimmy serving with the Fleet?"

Ceal sighed sadly. "He's 17."

"Yes. And...?"

"My...my kid brother is, was 17 when the fighting broke out in the capital. My father thought he was old enough to help defend our...our home or honor or something. They let him go out with the palace guard. He acted like a kid playing soldier. Like it was a game.....Right up until he was hit."

Coy stood quietly, picturing the scene. Knowing all too well the pain of watching someone dear to you cut down before your eyes.

"Thank you," it told her sincerely. "If Jimmy chooses to serve the Beta Region by helping in your Sick Bay, he may. But he will have the same training every BlackFleet member has had. I can't promise you he will never be hurt. Any more than I can promise that you or Sweggert or Vennefron will not. But I can promise you he will never think it is a game."

And it left Sick Bay.

A few days later, the BlackFleet shuttle docked at the New Grenich Transit portal station. Drake stood at the hatch in his new black uniform as the three who had chosen to return home prepared to exit.

"Take care," he told them.

They stood uncomfortably for a moment.

"Come on, Lieutenant Come home. This is wrong. You're deserting," one of his men pleaded.

Drake stood his ground. "My own countrymen tried to push me out into space. These people saved my life. I'm here until that debt is paid."

"You don't owe these mercenaries anything. You owe the Service."

"I'm sorry, Albert, I know you don't understand. Or agree. But this is what I have to do. Maybe my destiny is different than yours."

"If you don't come back now, you can't come back at all."

Drake nodded. "There is that chance. I'm willing to take it."

"You're wrong. And you're taking nine guys down with you."

"If the BlackFleet didn't exist you and I wouldn't be alive to be here having this disagreement. I believe this is worth doing. I love my home world, my people. That hasn't changed. But I don't believe in the Service like I used to. They didn't warn us. They didn't help us. I'm sure they had orders and reasons, but that's exactly why this Fleet is here. To
cut through all that and help people anyway. You're a good soldier, Albert. You'll be a good officer. I hope they pin a medal on you when you get home."

Albert looked at him a moment longer. Finally, he saluted gravely despite the different colors they were wearing. "Good bye, sir."

Drake returned the salute and watched them disembark. He turned to find Butler behind him. "The commodore mentioned that your situation was similar to mine. Did you have to say good-bye to your men like this?"

"Nope," Butler forced his voice to his usual flippant tone. "They kinda said good-bye to me." He cocked his head a little. "Regrets?"

"I regret what I know they're walking into."

"Well, if the Skipper has its way, we'll be saving the whole galaxy eventually. Maybe they'll be okay   until we get back around to them."

Drake had to smile despite his worries. With one last look at the hatchway, he mentally shook off his old life and prepared himself for his new one. Although the real break had been earlier in his cabin when he took off his battered tan uniform. He had stood looking at the black suit for a long time before carefully putting it on and eying the stranger in the mirror. Albert was right about one thing. There was no going back now. His choice was made. "I hear my training begins today."

"Why do you think I'm here, Trainee Drake? Commodore Lamont, for some reason, thinks you have officer potential. Let's find out, shall we?"

Barely a day later Drake was broken in when the next mayday was received. Aziza did his best to clean it up before sending it down to Lamont.

"....under atta...engines....please.....ambassa....Tau....." It faded to static, then to nothing.

"Sorry, Skipper," Aziza's voice followed the transmission.

"It's enough. Keep monitoring."

When they came upon the battle, Butler swore. A stately, if elderly, vessel was being attacked by another swarm of fighters. "Tell me those aren't who I think they are."

"Nope," Bon told him, checking the scanner readouts closely. "Different design altogether. Much older. In fact, I didn't know anyone still used these things. And the big ship, what shields she has left she's rotating to... ouch, a hit, mid port."

"Let's break it up and send them to their corners until we sort it out," Coy ordered.

Parker's first volley exploded exactly in the center of the battle, but hit no one. One could almost sense the puzzlement of the combatants. '*Where did that come from?*' But it was only a pause.

The swarm continued.

She lined her next shot across the bow of what appeared to be the leader of the fighters. That caused more than a surprised pause.

A very angry man appeared on the *Raven's* vid. "Who the hell are you?"

"Commodore Lamont commanding the BlackFleet," Coy gave its customary answer to the customary opening question.

"This is none of your business, mercenary."

Coy gave him an icy look. "The galaxy is my business."

"Oh, shit, you're those blasted vigilantes," He muttered. "Look, you have no idea what's going on here."

"Enlighten me." Blasted vigilantes? It didn't realize quite how far their fame had spread.

"I don't have time..."

"Enlighten me or we can blow you apart. We are answering a distress call. Which makes your, ah opponent our clients. Which makes *you*," Coy's look changed to a glare, "the enemy."

The image disappeared abruptly, but the fighting ceased as well.

"What the...?" Butler frowned. "Who are these guys?"

"I think you got his attention, Skipper," Rebel added.

"Devyu, get our 'clients' on the line," Lamont ordered.

"Aye, aye sir."

The next person to appear was a desperate looking woman, graying hair escaping from barrettes.

"Captain," Coy opened with a nod, and repeated its introduction. "How may we assist you?"

In obvious relief, the captain pushed a strand of hair back into place. "Commodore, if you are responsible for breaking off the attack, you have already assisted us." She took a deep breath. "I am Captain Romex. We are transporting our ambassador home on a gravely important mission. If you could keep those fighters at bay until we can get reinforcements we would be deeply in your debt."

"How deeply?" Butler murmured.

"We would be quite willing to help," Coy told her, glad she couldn't hear Butler. "May I ask what nature of mission we would be assisting?"

"I guess that's the least we can do." Captain Romex agreed. Another breath. "The planet Sontaire has become an unbearable thorn in our side. The ambassador is going home to recommend war."

Drake, as part of training, was manning a com station in the Tac Room with Lamont. He sat up at the mention of war. "What is there, an epidemic?"

Coy was staring at the holovid image. "I see. Please remain where you are while we investigate."

"Investigate? What do..."

"I suggest you use this cease fire for emergency repairs. Lamont out." Coy spoke to the bridge. "Get me that other captain. Now."

It took several repeated hails before the man appeared.

"Yes, Commodore? Is it time to blow me apart?"

"It's time for you to enlighten me."

"Why do you care?"

"If you don't want to talk I can always go ahead and escort them safely home."

He paled. "Oh, don't do that."

"Again. Why?"

"If they reach home, they declare war."

"Now, why would they do that?"

"Because our idiot ambassador insulted their idiot ambassador and now a million people will pay for it. The only thing we knew to do was stop him from reporting."

"Won't they just transmit the information?'

The fighter captain shook his head. "Wouldn't do any good. It's in the code. They need a physical document delivered by a sworn appointee... What does it matter?'

Coy thought for a moment. "Captain, would you be willing to come on board my ship for a meeting?"

"My turn. Why?"

"To try and stop a war."

He heaved a desperate sigh. "What do I have to lose? When and where?"

The same agreement was made with Romex and her ambassador. Escorts brought them separately to the briefing room. The ambassador stopped in his tracks at the sight of the fighter.

"What is the meaning of this?"

Coy indicated the chairs around the table. "We are having a peace conference."

"This is preposterous! By whose authority...?"

"My own. And since it's my ship, my guards and my weapons that are superior here, I get to make the rules. Now sit."

Reluctantly, everyone sat, one eye on the guards at the door, the other on Ceal Byars, also seated at the table.

Coy leaned forward, and clasped its hands on the table. "And now for my ground rules. First of all everything in this room is being recorded. Secondly only the truth will be spoken."

Romex snorted. "How do you intend to enforce that?"

"That brings me to number three, pentha."

"What?" the fighter asked.

"Pentha. You will all be questioned under a truth drug."

Protests exploded all around.

"You can't do that!"

"What right...?"

"How dare you..."

Coy waved a finger at them. "My ship, my rules, remember?" It nodded to Ceal. "My medical officer will now test each of you to make sure you will not have an allergic reaction." Byars did a skin test on all of the intended, ah, volunteers. When all the tests turned out negative, Coy chose the fighter captain to be first.

A few moments after Ceal administered the hypo spray of pentha, he relaxed in his seat with a totally blank expression, all resistance washed away.

"What is your name?" Coy asked him.

"Aldolf Sondrie the 4th."

"What planet do you come from?"

"Sontaire."

"What is your position?"

"Captain of the Blue Wing Strike Force."

"Why were you attacking the large ship?"

"To stop them."

"To stop them from doing what?"

" Reporting home."

"Why don't you want them to report home?"

"They'll start a war."

"Why would they start a war?"

"Tamaz was insulted by Fodor. Fodor said his face looked like a ..."

"Stop. Who is Fodor?"

"Our ambassador."

"And where is he now?"

"In the Capital prison."

"Why?"

"He's under arrest."

"On what charge?"

"Treason."

"Hmmm. Thank you, Captain."

Ceal administered the antidote and a dose of something to help the typical post-pentha hangover. Then she stepped to Tamaz.

"I refuse to sit here and be..." he tried to stand. Ceal pressed the spray against his neck and he melted back down.

Lamont repeated the interrogation. "What is your name?"

"Tobias Tamaz Santiago."

"What planet do you come from?"

"Tauten Three."

"What is your position?"

"Ambassador to Sontaire."

"Where were you going before your ship was attacked?"

"Home"

"Why?"

"To give the king the declaration of war."

"Why?"

"Because he wanted me to." Pentha subjects always answered as literally as they could.

"Your king wanted you to declare war?"

"Yes."

"On what grounds?"

"On whatever grounds I could find."

No one breathed. The room seemed to drop several degrees. "You were under orders from your king to create a war with Sontaire however you could?"

"Yes."

"Why?"

Santiago paused and fought for control for a moment before giving in to the drug again. "To disrupt trade."

"Why would your government want to disrupt trade?"

"I don't know. It has to do with a deal he has."

Coy's heart stopped. "With whom does he have a deal?" it asked very carefully.

"I don't know."

"How would this deal benefit your king?"

"I don't know."

Coy tried a few more questions, but the man didn't seem to have any more helpful information. Ceal gave the antidote and medicine. The sick look in his eyes, however, had little to do with nausea.

He glared at Sondrei. "We don't imprison traitors. I will be killed."

"Like the civilians, the parents and children who would've died in your war?" Coy ground out.

Everyone got very quiet at the tension that filled the room.

Captain Romex cleared her throat quietly. "May I have a dose of that please? I want it on record that I had nothing to do with any of this."

Coy nodded agreement. She was drugged. And cleared.

Once again, no one spoke for a few minutes. Finally Tamaz mustered a shred of haughty dignity. "None of this is your affair, anyway, mercenary."

With an effort, Lamont refrained from shouting at the man. "Anytime helpless people are on the verge of being slaughtered, it better be someone's affair." It paused to contain its sudden , and unexpected , anger. "I am going to send a copy of this meeting to both heads of state. And may I remind everyone involved that according to all evidence, this ship alone has more firepower than either of you have. And I have more ships."

"Meaning?" Romex asked.

"Meaning that if I hear about a war, I will be back. And I will stop it. Is that understood?"

No one said anything. There was no need.

After the declaration was disposed of, they were escorted back to their vessels. Bon and Butler came into the briefing room as Lamont watched the ships disappear off the monitors.

"Commodore, do you know what you did?" Bon asked.

"Besides dramatically overstepping my authority?"

Bon grinned. "Besides that, yes. You saved a hell of a lot of people."

"Couldn't help it," Coy shrugged. "It's in my job description."

"I don't suppose we can count on any favors coming from this little experience," Butler said.

Lamont sighed in frustration. "We almost had something better. We came this close," it measured with its thumb and forefinger, " to finding our Boogeyman."

"You think the deal his king had was with the same guy that's ripping off cargo ships?" Bon asked.

"Yes I do. Disrupting trade seems right up the same line as the rest of the trouble going on."

Butler put on his best belligerent look. "Skipper, do you have any clue at all how you intend to find this guy?"

"As I said, every job is a clue. A piece to the puzzle. I just have to figure where this one fits."

"We could always kidnap the king and give *him* a dose of pentha," Bon half joked.

Lamont looked thoughtful. "If I thought it would help, I would be tempted. But anyone this intent on winning would not leave that obvious a trail."

Butler put a hand on Coy's arm and raised his eyebrows in disbelief. "You wouldn't really, would you? I mean, a *king?*"

Commodore Lamont looked at him steadily. "Remember, Captain, I'm intent on winning as well."

Sometime later, on the other side of the region, Lamont solemnly handed over the data file to the Prime Minister. As it did, it mused once again at the amount of trouble that had been caused by such a small item.

It had seemed a rather straight forward assignment at first. The tiny world had needed information about their enemies' movements and installations, but lacked the long range ships to gather it.

The "enemy", however, had turned out to be their own colony gone renegade. Very quickly the BlackFleet had found itself in the middle of a civil war.

"How do we play hero when we can't tell the good guys from the bad guys?" Ken Butler asked.

"I guess this time we can't," Coy had reluctantly admitted. "But we can finish the job for the people we gave our word to."

But then the rebel colonists had spotted them and attacked. And Coy had to hang in space and let them take pot shots at its beloved *Raven.* Nothing beyond the paint job and a few articles that fell from shelves was damaged, but every hit had seemed a personal blow. Yet if they had returned even minimal fire, their superior technology could've wiped out the planets forces.

Tempting after a while, but not what they were there for. A negotiated truce was the best-case scenario. And for that, their employers needed more information. So they had taken the abuse, along with the data, and returned.

The Prime Minister looked frighteningly like he was going to weep as he clutched the disk. "This is the beginning step toward peace," he told Lamont. "I understand our agreement was for an exchange of favors, but we must do something to express our gratitude now."

Commodore Lamont smiled at the familiar plea. "It's the way we prefer to do business, sir."

Captain Butler, standing at Coy's elbow, leaned forward to whisper, "Ask if he wants to pay for a new paint job before Bon..."

Lamont frowned him back in place.

"Something wrong, Commodore?" the PM asked.

"No, sir. Internal Fleet business.... And I repeat, the guarantee of that favor is truly all I ask."

The man looked at the disk thoughtfully for a long moment. "If this says what we believe it will...." He looked back at Coy. "Would you consider doing one more thing in our behalf?"

For another favor to call in someday, Lamont would indeed. "What do you have in mind?"

"I need to go over this with my ministers. Can you remain in orbit until I have an answer for you? If we discover we don't need your services, I will give you that guarantee and you can be on your way."

Lamont glanced at Butler, and at Asch, who as always stood close by. They both nodded in agreement.

"Very well, sir, we will remain in orbit until I hear from you."

The PM smiled and took Lamont's hand. "Thank you, Commodore. I will contact you as soon as possible."

It was the next 'day' ship time, when the call came.

"Commodore," said the holo-image on Lamont's console, "we have come to a decision. According to the data you brought to us, the rebels are as lacking in technology as we thought. Which would've made it very easy to stop their annoying attacks on you. I personally thank you for sparing their lives. Bloodshed is what we are attempting to avoid."

Coy acknowledged his thanks with a short nod.

"I spent all evening meeting with the ambassador from the colony. Since I had the proof of their troops and resources, there was no reason for bluffing.

"The agreement we came to is the reason I needed to talk to you. As a preliminary step of good faith, we have decided to reduce our own arsenal to even up the sides."

Lamont's brows rose. "Disarming yourself? Are you sure you can trust their word that far?"

"The deaths must stop. One way or another. As you are aware, these are our brothers we are fighting. Unfortunately, due to past experiences, it is *they* who have every reason not to trust *our* word." The Prime Minister's image shook his head sorrowfully. Then he straightened his shoulders. "This is where I need your help."

"What do you want us to do?" Coy asked seriously.

Coy took the proposal to the Senior Staff.

"As part of the negotiations, each side in the war has agreed to reduce their arsenal," Lamont began. "How all of that is going to be disposed of, I don't know. But we have been asked, in order to help out in the cause of peace, to take part of that arsenal off their hands. A favor which cancels itself out, I believe."

Faces lit up all around the table. With a smile, Lamont switched on their vids. And watched those same faces freeze.

Butler pointed to the decrepit looking freighter. "What is this, a joke?"

"This," Lamont answered him. "was on the top of their adversary's list of things to dispose of."

"The phrase, 'so what' springs to mind," Butler persisted.

"I don't get it either," Hendricks said. "Why would they need to get rid of a merchant ship?"

Instead of answering, Coy looked directly at Bon. "I think I'll call it the *Rook*."

The engineer looked puzzled. He glanced at the ship, back at Lamont, then more closely at the ship. Then he began to grin. "Are there any schematics to go with this charming little picture?"

Coy obliged.

Bon hadn't studied them very long before his grin turned into open-mouthed amazement. "Do they know what they are giving away?" he asked, incredulous.

"Yes, actually, they do."

"Is it just me," Butler interrupted "or does anyone else want to know what in the hell is going on?"

"A rook," Coy explained, " as well as being a relative of the raven, is another word for a bluff. The potential firepower of that little ship is roughly the equivalent of the *Nighthawk*. An armed merchant vessel. Its engines are not comparable in power to a warship, unfortunately. However the bright side of that is that when she flies into someone's territory the power signature, along with her appearance, writes her off as no threat."

Rebel immediately picked up on the possibilities. "You could get in pretty close to someone before bringing those weapons on line. What about shielding?"

"Merely standard issue." Bon answered, "Which more than likely accounts for the beat up exterior. With those engine designs, it can't be as old as it looks."

"I don't understand," Hendricks frowned. "Why are they giving up all those guns if they could win their war with it?"

"Because they don't want to take the time to win it," Schiff guessed. "They want to stop it."

"That's right. Even though it has great potential for us as an espionage tool, for them it's just seen as a weapon of death and destruction." Coy agreed. "In all honesty, I did make sure they understood what they were giving up. The Prime Minister merely said he was glad we found it useful and to please take it out of their space."

Butler rose his hand. "One word. Crew."

"If Bon can upgrade the shields to my satisfaction - which will entail calling in a marker - I intend to shift the B*lackbird* crew, with a few additions, to the *Rook*."

Coy couldn't tell from Rebel's expression how he took this news. On one hand, Rebel seemed the most excited about the new ship's possibilities. On the other, the *Blackbird* was an elegant little ship, and Rebel's first command. Would he see this as moving up, sideways or... Coy appreciated the steady gaze the young commander was returning. "My plans are to make your crew a very elite corps within the BlackFleet. The cream of the crop, I heard it put once. It will be an achievement to be chosen for the *Rook*. She could get in the tightest situations. The nastiest scenarios. You will have to have the people to handle it."

Rebel tried to look cool and collected. "I already do."

Schiff murmured agreement, while Butler and Hendricks shifted in their seats in vague competitive spirit.

"Everyone made the first cut simply by being BlackFleet," Coy reminded them all and let their ruffled feathers smooth for a moment. "For now, let's turn our attention and efforts to bringing it up to BlackFleet standards." There were a couple of cleared throats and humorless snorts. "Besides, maybe it doesn't look as bad on the inside."

Lamont was quite right about that. It was worse.

The *Blackbird* crew picked their way through the rubble that littered the main corridor. At each crossway they peered down in all directions only to see more trash and garbage.

"When was it exactly that this tub was used last," Sweggert asked. "And what exactly was it used *for?*" He stopped and shook his head. "No, forget I asked that. I don't think I want to know."

Pedula agreed. "I don't want to either. I just hope we have another favor from these guys. And let's hope the Skipper makes it a good one."

"That's enough," Rebel snapped.

Randy decided to risk the insubordination. "C'mon, Commander. We're standing in the proverbial pile of ....."

Rebel merely pursed his lips and pushed ahead of the group without letting him finish, stomping up to the bridge where Lamont and Bon were conferencing.

His crew watched his retreating back in silence. Then almost as one they turned to Tony Knepp.

The new Sgt. held up his hands to ward off questions even before they were asked. "Our current task is to get rid of it, not comment on it." He thought for a moment. "I suppose the easiest way to do that is to haul it all down to the docking bay, close the doors and blast it all to ashes. I'll have to talk to Captain Bon first about that. And we'll need more pallets. For now, split up into teams and start hauling it down."

They all saluted and left without any more grumbling -- at least until they were out of Knepp's earshot. Tony called Asch to ask for more pallets and went up to join the senior officers. He found the three of them staring rather tensely at each other. Lamont's arms were crossed and it was frowning. Rebel was frowning back. Bon looked like he'd rather be anywhere else.

Knepp cleared his throat. "I've got the crew started on cleaning."

Rebel nodded.

"And I was wondering if I could ask Captain Bon a couple of things."

Bon didn't even bother hiding his relief as he made his escape. After they had left, the discussion resumed.

"And what if the shields can't be improved enough?"

"Then we sell it. It still has to be cleaned either way."

"And if we sell it, I go back to the *Blackbird*."

"Yes."

"And Drake...?"

"And Drake waits a little longer for a command of his own. I'm not making either of you promises. I'm making plans. And plans can change." Lamont paused. "I was shipmaster for several years, Adrian. I do understand. This is not a glamorous ship. It is a tremendously useful ship. If that's not good enough I'm sorry." Coy's expression grew stern. "But you are not a child and these are not toys. If you insist on glamour, you can always rejoin the *Raven's* crew. And Drake, or someone else will get this shot."

Rebel's hands were clenched at his sides. He took a calming breath and looked around the bridge before speaking. He had just opened his mouth to request more help for the cleanup, when a puzzling fact belatedly dawned on him.

"Something wrong?" Coy asked, seeing his frown deepen.

"You said this was a functional warship."

"Yes."

"It has no weapons station."

"It doesn't?" Coy put on a frown of its own.

Rebel started to say something more, but after a look at Lamont's not-quite-believable expression, decided to double check it himself. He took a slow tour around the asymmetrical bridge. The station chairs were set here and there with no apparent care for design.

The captain's chair sat in the middle of the room facing the entrance. The engineer's place was at the "back" of the long narrow room. The JP was off to the side in his own little niche. The other stations, Nav, Com and a freight monitoring system were clustered up at the "front". But

no switches, buttons or anything else that reminded Rebel of any weapons system he had ever seen.

"I don't see any," he said, trying hard to keep the annoyance out of his tone.

"Good," Lamont surprised him by saying. "Hopefully any freight inspector won't either."

"Freight inspector?"

"Our *Rook* is very good at hiding its true nature." Coy walked over to the monitoring display and started to push something, then stopped and waved Rebel over. "I think you should do this, Captain."

Rebel stepped closer. "Do what, sir?"

"Push these in quick succession," Coy indicated certain buttons.

Adrian did as he was told. And watched in amazement as the entire work station flipped and slid until some more recognizable elements were in its place. Cannons, lasers, missiles... He tried hard to think of something to express his rapidly changing opinion of the ship, but all he came out with was, "So...what else can it do?"

Coy actually smiled a little as it pushed yet another secret switch. Rebel's mouth hung open as he looked at the Tac Room hidden behind a blank wall. It was small of course. More like the *Nighthawk's* than the huge master control room on the *Raven*.

"Is there anything she can't do?" Rebel said in awe.

"Yes," Lamont told him. "It can't look elegant."

Rebel looked up from the systems board he was inspecting and straight into Coy's eyes. "Understood. And, I'm sorry, sir."

Coy nodded. "I'm glad you can see the worth..."

"No, sir. I mean, yes, I regret acting childish and stupid about this ship. But mostly sir, I'm sorry I ever doubted you. I should've known you would always give us the best." He straightened and saluted. "The *Rook* and I will do you proud, sir."

Coy looked at him thoughtfully. "Do yourself proud, Adrian. That's the least and the most I will ever ask of you."

The Captain's quarters that Coy and Rebel located were virtually indistinguishable from the rest of those on the abused ship. All living spaces were exactly the same. A fact, which seemed to annoy Coy far more that it did Rebel himself. But Lamont had ordered part of a bulkhead removed in the midst of all the other work, thereby creating captains quarters and attached office. Rebel did appreciate the effort but nothing was going to top the surprises up on the bridge.

All other BlackFleet duties came to a temporary halt. All personnel took their turn working to make the *Rook* habitable. And slowly, the ship began to take shape.

Further remodeling was undertaken as well, when Coy discovered the ship had no gym or weapons range. Bon held his tongue and rolled up his sleeves, hoping devoutly that his CO wouldn't suddenly desire a swimming pool.

At their next layover opportunity, Bon and Schiff both performed their new duties and presented the BlackFleet with more capable hands. The former *Blackbird* technical crew, plus some additions, moved over to the *Rook*. Drake began his training to command the *Blackbird*.

The fleet was growing almost daily. And so were Coy Lamont's self doubts. This was ridiculous, it told itself, it was a soldier and an officer. Commanding 60 people was still not like running most single ships. It had to buckle down and get over the dread it felt every time it looked at the crew list.

So it stopped looking. Coy turned over even more of the administrative jobs to Asch and buried itself in whatever other duties it could find.

At the next senior staff meeting Coy sat and watched from its chair, absently tapping its fingers on the armrests, as the rest of the command staff entered the room and found their places. Due to the white color-coded rank pins, these weekly meetings had come to be dubbed the "White Meeting." As they settled into seats, the vidcom units embedded in the conference table came on. One by one their expectant expressions turned to curious frowns at the lack of information. They were used to the screen containing agenda, notes, reports and the usual Fleet business.

"Ah," Butler began, "either mine's busted or we don't have anything to talk about today."

A few smiled at his typical humor. Others were more concerned about what the absence meant. No news could always be worse than bad news.

Coy quieted its fingers and leaned forward. "There is no information there yet because you all are going to help me put it there." It got up and began to walk around the long, beautiful table and the people seated at it. Chairs and heads turned to follow its progress. "We have two mysteries, at least two main mysteries that we need to solve.

"What or who is the force behind all the violence going on in the shipping routes. Unfortunately, we don't seem to have any new data on our Boogeyman. Which leaves Mystery number 2 - Where did the *Raven* come from and why do we have it?"

That one caught most by surprise.

"Excuse me," Drake said, "Are you saying that you don't know where you got this ship?"

"What I know is that I won it in a card game." There was a muffled laugh or two until it dawned on everyone that Lamont was serious. "A card game that looks more and more like it was rigged the more I think back on it. The man I was playing against went to a lot of trouble to get me into the game, keep me in the game and, I believe, let me win. At the time I was like most of you when you came to the BlackFleet; life shot to hell, nowhere to go and not a soul in the universe who cared whether I was breathing air or vacuum. I didn't spend very much time investigating the facts. It seemed so astonishing to be suddenly in possession of something I could use to rebuild my life. I took the ownership documents and information at face value."

"They looked good to me," Bon put in. "Besides if we hadn't believed everything was on the up and up, we never would've started all of this."

Coy appreciated the engineer's use of "we", as if he could take some of the responsibility for the Fleet onto his own shoulders. It was true that if it hadn't been for Bon's timely support the BlackFleet would never have gotten off the ground. Coy would be forever grate-ful for that support and eventually, dare it admit it, friendship.

"True. But while it may have been to our benefit to ignore re-ality at the time, it isn't any more." Lamont continued around and back to its own seat and screen. What it put into its console would come up on everyone's. "Let's look at the question of why anyone would get rid of this ship."

"They were scared," Hendricks said immediately.

Coy made a note. "Of what?"

"What was this person like? The one in the card game," Rebel asked.

"Overweight, over dressed, talked loudly and demeaningly to everyone around him. Seemed used to getting his own way. Unfortu-nately that's all I know except the name on the transfer documents, which is probably false."

"That doesn't sound like a captain. Was he the owner?" Butler asked.

"So he said."

"But why would he give away his own possession? It makes more sense for someone like that to give away someone else's stuff," Rebel commented.

Coy looked thoughtful. "Not owner or captain? But scared."

"Wait a minute," Ceal Byars put in, "maybe this is a stupid question, but wouldn't Hoffman know all of this?"

Lamont sighed. "That would've made life a whole lot simpler, yes. However, it seems he had been hired only days before I took over. He barely knew the guy, but was paid well enough that he didn't care to ask questions. Even he didn't know if this Mr. Hessemen was the owner or merely a representative of the owner. He did seem to command the ship at least for those couple of days. Although even Hoffman was not impressed with his command style."

"That's right," Bon said. "I think the only positive comment he made in those first days was at least Lamont didn't act like it was right out of a bad adventure vid."

"What happened to the old pilot?" Drake asked. "Could you track him down through the Guild?"

"Hoffman got the impression he was dead."

Everyone paused in thought at that.

"Okay," Butler said, " You think maybe someone killed the pilot and this Hessemen ditched the ship to cover his disappearance because he was scared he would be next?"

Rebel whistled. "What in the universe could he and the pilot know?"

"The real owner?" Drake guessed.

So far everyone's reasoning was following Coy's own private surmising. "I had Vennefron put the word out in our network to see just where the *Raven* had been the past year."

"And...?" Butler turned to the Intelligence officer.

"No where," Venn answered. "No one anywhere had ever seen it before we started using it."

"That's crazy," Hendricks said, "Somebody would have had to notice a ship like this. It's not exactly a common design. Where would it have been hiding?"

"Good question," Coy said. "Where could you hide a ship like this?"

"You would have to stay out of systems," Bon put in. "Use shuttles to haul passengers back and forth."

"The *BlackBird*," Drake and Rebel said almost together.

"But still someone, somewhere would have seen it," Butler frowned. "Refueling stations, maintenance bays, someone."

Vennefron shook his head. "That's where I checked first. Of course, there's a lot of turnover in places like that. Temporary workers, industrial accidents, all sorts of reasons. But there aren't any records of a ship like the *Raven* docking for fuel or repairs. The only docking record I found was for Alluria Station and that's where the Skipper met up with her."

"Industrial accidents?" Hendricks raised her brows. "How many 'industrial accidents'?"

Venn frowned at his information. "I don't have a number. Why?"

"It just seems an easy way to keep people from reporting that they saw something."

Coy hadn't thought about that. "Is there any way to find out if there were periods of a large turnover? If it silenced a whole bay of workers every time it docked..."

"We could trace its path by the disappearances," Vennefron finished and made himself a note. "I'll see what I can do."

"If that's true it means we could *hypothetically* have a dead pilot, a scared captain *and* missing refueling techs?" Hendricks continued. "Commodore, I don't think we want to know who this owner was."

"No, but he probably wants to know who we are," Coy reasoned, " Which is the reason for all of this. He probably would like his nice ship back and I would like to be prepared for when he gets here. *We* aren't hiding from anyone, after all. He could show up anytime."

"So why hasn't he?" Drake asked. "Is he too busy killing someone else?"

"Nasty thought," Rebel mumbled.

Bon had been quietly scanning through some of his own records and notes. Suddenly he looked up. "C-space!"

Butler stared at him. "Good answer, Raeph," he said sarcastically. "What was the question?"

"That's where you could hide a ship this size and pretty much guarantee no one ever seeing you." He pointed to his own screen. "A while back, Masters was doing some routine study of the systems and he keeps trying to tell me that we had too much shielding. He said it was using way too much power to run and that the only reason anyone would need that much radiation shielding is if they lived in compressed space for years at a time." He looked a little sheepish. "I hardly listened at the time. You know Bruce. He always has to know more than anyone else about everything. I thought he was just trying to impress me again. Sorry."

Coy shook its head at the apology. "We have the clue now, and now is when we can use it."

"Terrific. So unless Vennefron's disappearing dock workers leave a trail, we can't track the *Raven's* movements. What about the *Blackbird's?*" Drake asked.

"We're trying," Vennefron said. "But it's a much more ordinary design. A yacht picking up a handful of passengers is not that unusual. There are hundreds of dockings. *Thousands*. And if they used phony names and designation codes, I don't know any way to track it."

"What about shield frequency?" Bon asked. "If the '*Bird* was in C-space almost as much as the *Raven* the shielding would have to be similar."

"Do docking stations check your shielding?" Byars asked, surprised.

"It's in the numbers," Schiff spoke for the first time. "It would be picked up by a routine identification scan, but no one would think to look at it unless they had reason to."

"Alright, what do we have so far," Lamont looked over the notes it had been making. "The *Raven* was owned by someone who lived in C-space and possibly killed people as important and expensive as Jump Pilots in order to remain anonymous. What kind of clientele would use a cruise ship run like that?"

"People who wanted to remain just as anonymous."

"Criminals?"

"At the very least people with a lot to hide from the folks at home."

"A flying Bad Boys Club?"

" A whole ship full of people like that? Just think of the nasty things they could come up with."

"They could plan major trouble."

"Or a lot of little ones," Coy said quietly.

The room became silent.

"The Boogeyman," Butler said without a single trace of his usual flippancy.

"And what do we do with this information?" Ceal asked. "How does it help us?"

"At the least, we might be looking to solve one problem instead of two," Lamont told her. It gave a small sigh. "I know that doesn't get us any further in finding him. But we're still gathering clues. I have a feeling we'll know more soon."

"One way or another," Hendricks added ominously.

"Anyone have any other brainstorms?" Lamont asked and looked around the table at each officer.

"Can we go back to the card game?" Rebel asked. "It seems if anyone wanted to hide from someone so bad that he would give up something like the *Raven,* why would he sit down at a card game in a room full of people?"

"Very good question," Coy nodded approval. "So whom was I playing against?"

They all pondered that for a second.

"Someone from a bad adventure vid." Schiff said.

"An actor?" Butler sounded unconvinced. "This is getting a little complicated."

"The whole thing is complicated," Byars sighed. "Give me a nice simple wound to put back together. I'm no good at being a detective."

"Think of it as an epidemic," Bon told her. "All we're trying to do is trace it back to the beginning."

"So maybe that's where we should go. Back to the beginning," Coy said.

"I hate to ask," Ken began, "but do you mean literally or figuratively?"

"I mean, as soon as the *Rook* is up to par we head to Alluria."

"On a trail a year old. Looking for a man you don't even know the real name of." Butler looked at Coy . "That seems a little crazy. Even for us."

"Pick your insanity," Coy answered the look. "Doing this again and again," it indicated their notes, "or going on a wild goose hunt?"

Butler looked at it quizzically for a moment. "Just tell me one thing," he said seriously. "Where do you come up with these sayings?"

Long after the meeting was over, Lamont sat in the conference room staring at the comscreen. "Who are you?" it whispered to the notes displayed there. "Where are you? And..." it sighed wearily, "why me?"

Coy walked into the bar on Alluria Station with a mixture of emotions and thoughts. It looked around at the dirty walls, dusty vending machines and sparsely occupied tables. Nothing had changed. Coy glanced over at the man behind the bar. No, not even the bartender.

That was a bit of a surprise. Coy would have thought that in a place like this the spot would have a high turnover of drifter employees.

"So this is where it all began," Butler murmured at Coy's side. "Reeking of potential, isn't it?"

"Potential is often hidden under a layer or two of dirt and disappointments," Coy murmured back, thinking of a certain rumpled young man who had turned up on its doorstep a year ago.

Ken obviously made the connection as well and grinned a little sheepishly.

On Coy's other side, Raeph Bon was also peering around the room. "I really never thought we'd be back here. Seems a lifetime ago, doesn't it, Skipper?"

"That indeed was another life," Coy had to agree.

The bartender was eyeing the group of uniforms standing in the doorway with a frown. "Something I can do for you?" he asked gruffly.

The three officers began moving toward the bar. The troopers that had come with them remained standing "casually" by the entrance.

Coy propped one foot on the low railing that went around the bar and leaned on the top. "Good day," it said with a smile. "My name is Coy Lamont. Exactly one year ago I sat at that," Coy pointed, "table and won a card game. And I was wondering if you had any information on the gentleman I was playing against."

The bartender looked at the table it had pointed to and then back at Coy. He had an unusual expression on his face. "Now how would I know who played a card game here a year ago?"

"Large, expensively dressed man who went by the name of Hessemen," Coy continued as if the man were co operating.

The barman hesitated just the tiniest bit. "So does he owe you money or what? You said you won. What do you need him for?"

Coy raised its eyebrows at the hesitation. "Yes I did win. In fact with my winnings I was able to start my own fleet. Maybe I just want to thank him."

"Your own..." the man stared at their uniforms for a moment, searching for a name or insignia. The lack of one told him everything he wanted to know. "The BlackFleet. You started the BlackFleet with..." He grinned absurdly. "Now that's irony for you."

Ken and Bon looked at each other. "Something you want to let us in on?" Ken asked him.

The bartender shook his head, still smiling. "Can't. It's amusing, but not worth my life." He looked Coy over carefully again. "You're a herm." He grinned more. "A herm at the helm of the fleet that's got everybody jumpin' at their shadows. Better and better."

Coy straightened up and blinked. "You seem to have a lot of information about the very people we want to find. How about you and I and a shot of ..."

"Pentha?" he finished for Coy and shook his head. "You wish. But only if you want me dead and useless."

"You're not rippingly useful as you are," Ken growled.

The bartender and the three officers stood looking at each other in assorted states of amusement and frustration for a few moments.

"Look," Coy finally said in a level tone, "People are getting hurt. Lots of people. Really hurt. And you are standing here with information that could help. Who and what do you work for that keeps you from answering?"

The man began wiping a cloth back and forth over the clean bar as if in thought. He glanced back at the table Coy had indicated.

"Hessemen, you say? Never heard him use that one before. He comes here whenever he needs to fence something quick. Always looks different. Always sounds different. Always a different name. But it's him."

"How do you know it's the same man?" Bon asked.

Another grin. "I know."

"Does he know you know?" Coy asked.

"We never discuss it. Makes it easier on everybody."

"How often does he come here?" Ken asked in a less than patient voice. Coy looked at him sideways. It didn't think pushing this guy was going to help in the least.

"Never know. Once or twice a year. Once or twice a month. Never know." He pulled some glasses out from under the bar. "Can I get you something while we're chattin'? I usually listen. All this talkin' has got my mouth dry." He pulled out a bottle and set it by the glasses. "Our house specialty you might say."

"N…" Coy started to refuse, despite Ken's sudden enthusiastic expression, when it noticed the label on the bottle. It was the same as what was stocked on the *Raven* when Coy had taken it over. Was the man trying to pass some kind of clue? Or was Coy ready to clutch at straws? Surely he wouldn't try anything as trite and obvious as drugging them – especially with the two guards at the door. The man locked eyes with Coy over the bottle, but gave no other hint of information. It nodded at the glasses. "Alright." Coy picked up the half full glass and swirled it around but didn't drink. "How different does, whatever his name is, look each time?"

"Oh real different. Sometimes heavy like you saw. Sometimes skinny as a rail. He never looks too healthy that way, come to think on it."

"And you have no way of knowing when he might show up?"

He shook his head. "He don't exactly book reservations."

A few more questions got them a few more non answers. Eventually they took what information they had along with the bottle of liquor and left.

Once back on the *Raven,* Coy held a handpicked White meeting in its quarters. Asch happily served coffee and tea to the department heads seated around the long table as Coy and the others passed on what they had learned.

"So how long has this guy been tending this bar in the middle of nowhere?" Venn asked. "Years?"

"Some of his comments would seem to indicate that," Coy agreed.

"Years of just being friendly and listening to people. So if this Hessemen, or the Boogeyman or anyone else showed up and asked about us he'll be just as friendly," Schiff said with a frown.

"Probably," Coy agreed again.

"So how are we going to track this guy? This Hessemen?" Bon wondered. "If he really looks that different every single time someone sees him."

Ceal was looking thoughtful. Coy watched her think for a while before interrupting.

"You have an idea?"

She looked just slightly embarrassed at contributing to the conversation. She rarely if ever had any input for their typically technical discussions. "I was just thinking that if he really looked that different each time – I mean drastically different body weight- he is probably paying for body sculpting at a clinic somewhere."

"Wouldn't he use various places?" Ken asked.

She shook her head. "Not if he does it that often. Unless someone really knew him, and he trusted them, his health just wouldn't hold up for long. Even a few treatments like that can be hard on anyone's system. I would bet he has someone on retainer."

"But we still can't trace him without some kind of ID, can we?" Bon asked.

"DNA" she said simply. "No matter what name or description was on file, the DNA would have to be real."

Ken held up two fingers. "One, we don't have his DNA, and two, how would we know what clinics to search?"

Venn spoke up. "The list of clinics in the entire Region may be huge, but it is finite. If we knew what we were looking for, we would find it." He nodded confidently at Coy.

"Okay, so we still have number one," Ken persisted.

Coy looked at Ceal seriously. "What would we have to have to know his DNA? He used to live on this ship, you know. In these quarters, I would assume."

She looked around uneasily as if the idea made her uncomfortable. She noticed with a smile she wasn't alone. "Anything. Hair, skin follicles, body fluids…"

Coy suddenly had a very distracted look on its face as it replayed the card game in its memory. It rubbed its lip as it thought. "How about perspiration?"

She nodded, but frowned at the question.

"Even year old, dried perspiration?"

She thought a moment. "I could try…"

Bon frowned quizzically. "Skipper, what are you thinking?"

"I'm thinking, he wiped his upper lip, then picked up the data disk with the *Raven's* registration information, and handed it to me. It's been touched very little since that time." It looked at Ceal to see if she still thought it would work.

"I'm willing to give it the old BlackFleet try," she grinned.

Coy smiled back at her. "You know, if this works, it could well be the biggest break we've had to date."

Ceal looked at all the expectant faces around the table and swallowed.

"But no pressure," Bon assured her.

Chapter Five

The three ships flew between the stars in a graceful "V" formation, the *Raven* in front, *Nighthawk* at her port flank, *Rook* to her starboard. No one could guess from their quiet and peaceful exteriors how much activity was going on inside. Even with the Fleet members more than tripling in numbers, it still meant only skeleton crews. There was activity around the clock navigating and maintaining the massive ships, not to mention the troopers working out, officers scanning information, and new crewmembers being put through their intense training.

Coy walked through the *Raven*, thinking it should be pleased with the level of business going on all around. It should be calming to have everything in place, everyone doing what they were supposed to be doing. But something just didn't … feel… right. It hesitated at the choice of wording. It never liked basing anything on "feelings".

The corridor lighting began its scheduled evening change as Coy continued. One of the many things the designers of the *Raven* had taken into account was mankind's planet based biology. So many things, from bio rhythms to emotions were known to be effected by something as simple as the amount of light in a person's daily life.

Running along the base of the wall at floor level were dim lights that were only on at "night", along with pinpricks of light on the ceiling that could be programmed to represent the stars as seen from a thousand different worlds. At the top of the walls, pinkish to orange lights simulated dusk and dawn, while the bright overhead lighting was on during the bulk of the "day". All ships had some sort of day shift/ night shift variations in lights, but few as subtle and sophisticated as the *Raven's*.

Right now the overhead units were dimming and the orange "dusk" coming on. Butler had commented often how the system was great for internal clocks, but it still made him want to look around for the sunset. Coy on the other hand, had spent virtually its whole life in either secluded laboratories or space ships. Yet, in some way it could not explain, the day and night cycles usually gave it a sense of balance. Maybe it should take the time to see some of these sunsets, it mused. Maybe it would help the decidedly un-balanced way it had been feeling lately.

There was that word again. Feelings. It decided to track down Bon. Talking to him often helped sort things out. A quick check with Int/Sec informed Coy that he was in his quarters.

Coy stopped in front of the engineer's door and pushed the com button to announce its presence.

"Come," came Bon's voice to unlock the door.

As Coy came into the room, it automatically looked around to locate the owner of the voice. It found him studying his computer intently.

"Sorry, am I interrupting?" Coy apologized.

"That's okay," Bon mumbled distractedly in reply.

Coy smiled, amused by Raeph's absorption. "Studying some technical?"

Bon finally looked up. "No, something…metaphysical." He cocked his head as if questioning his own choice of words.

Coy paused in the process of sitting down, surprised by the answer. "Excuse me?"

Bon paused as well, trying to come up with a way to explain himself. "Don't you ever feel that there's More than us out here?"

"More what?"

"Purpose. Reason. A reason."

Coy thought back to another conversation they had once had. "You mean like, there was a reason we all came together just at the time this ship fell into my lap?"

Bon remembered the occasion as well and smiled in appreciation. "That and more. A reason for everything. A reason for life itself."

Coy was quiet at that for a while. "You're not talking metaphysics. You're talking religious."

Bon thought for a moment. "Yeah. Maybe so."

"Which one?"

"Which religion? Well, that's the question. I'm not so sure there is more than one. Every person, every people, every culture that has asked this question has come up with an answer."

"Yes, different ones."

"Different slants, yes. I'm looking at all of those slants that I can to find the common thread, the baseline truth."

"And what will that prove?"

"I believe when I find the common truth it will be the Truth."

"What if there is no 'the Truth'?"

"That's what I mean to find out."

Another pause.

"I've heard of people," Coy said carefully, "who were religious. Some destroyed everyone around them who didn't have their slant on things in order to prove themselves 'right'…"

"Not the most effective way to make converts, I wouldn't think," Bon interjected.

"…and others who stopped fighting at all and disappeared from society." It looked expectantly at Bon.

"And you wonder which one I am?"

"Let's just say I don't wish to be blindsided by either."

He scratched his head. "Both seem a little extreme to me. I've found reality to usually be somewhere in the middle." He looked at Coy seriously. "You have my word I would never let you or the Fleet down."

Coy nodded in response to the promise, but made no other comment.

"So what did you want to see me about?"

"Nothing. Nothing specific. Just visiting."

"Oh. Okay," Bon returned to his computer.

Having been sidetracked from what it had wanted to talk about anyway, Coy stood to leave. "I didn't think Haradans believed in this sort of thing anyway."

"I didn't think herms were usually fleet commanders." Bon smiled at the surprised look on Coy's face. "I guess we both like to shake up the statistics a little."

"Hmmm," was Coy's only response to that. The comment had been to make a point, it was sure, but it struck a very deep nerve. Feeling even less settled than when it had gone in, Coy left Bon's quarters.

In the corridor, it practically ran into Ken Butler. Butler took one look at Coy's face and shook his head in sympathy. "Let me guess, you've just had the 'Meaning of Life' speech."

Coy felt compelled to defend Bon. "He has a right to believe in…something."

Ken threw up his hands. "Far be it from me to stop him from wasting his free time." He grinned and gave a sketchy salute. "I however am going to turn in like the rest of my shift is doing. Good night, Commodore."

"Goodnight." Coy watched him continue on down the corridor and turn into his own quarters.

Command staff, like everyone else, was grateful for the times they had to themselves to relax a few minutes in some personal choice of activity before collapsing into their bunks. And everyone dreaded the times when the screamer went off during those precious sleep periods.

Like this time.

As usual, Commodore Lamont headed immediately to the Intelligence/Security office located adjacent to the Tactical Room. There it found Vennefron already communicating with Aziza on the bridge, the two of them organizing the incoming information into a report for their commander.

The situation appeared to be a lone ship in distress sending out an automated message. The order was given to move the Fleet to the coordinates. They could only hope that the situation would remain stable until they got there.

By the time they were within visual range Lamont was in the Tac Room and linked to the bridge of each ship through its command channel. The holovid in the center of the round room showed a miniature version of local space. The distress call came from the small ship in the center of the representation. The *Raven*, *Nighthawk* and *Rook* slowly moved in from the side.

Captain Bon sat at his station monitoring the status of the Fleet. Lieutenant Drake also was present, watching the three stations that were direct links to the bridges of the BlackFleet ships. Two more stations were dark. One was the link to the *Blackbird*, which at the moment was docked inside the *Raven*. The sixth station was not as yet designated for any task.

"All right," Coy spoke to the three commanders, "Take your places everyone. Aziza, get me someone to talk to."

The ships slipped into position as the *Raven*'s com officer made repeated attempts to hail the vessel.

"It looks like a derelict," Butler's voice said.

"The shields are down," Bon offered. "I see minimal energy output of any kind."

"Are we too late?" Rebel asked.

"They don't look that beat up," Hendricks commented. "What could have shut them down?"

"We'll soon find out," Lamont said decisively. "Schiff, take your party over and search for survivors."

"Aye, sir. We're ready to roll," the major answered from the docking bay.

Coy couldn't help but smile a little at his choice of phrase. One didn't "roll" in a shuttle, one flew. But Schiff had spent most of his years as a ground pounder and the dirt-side phrases were still part of his vocabulary.

The commodore regretted not being part of the boarding party. Watching others go into unknown situations was the hardest part of command. Not that sending someone into a dead ship was the worst it had had to do in its career. "Keep me posted, Major," Coy told him unnecessarily.

"Aye, sir."

Now there was nothing to do but wait until Schiff contacted them with an update on the situation.

The shuttle slid from her berth inside the *Raven*, and edged closer to the darkened hulk of the derelict ship. Nothing moved. There was no hint of life from either visual or electronic scanning.

Burney brought the shuttle alongside, making a long slow pass over its exterior. He adjusted their ship's course, bringing it to what appeared to be the main exterior docking hatch. The shuttle mated hatches, and pressure was equalized. Schiff lined up his group in standard cover formation, and gave them his standard "speech".

"Heads down, eyes peeled and cover your partner's backside."

They opened the hatch. Dim lighting met them as they edged into the mysterious ship's passageways. All was quiet and still.

"We're in," Schiff reported. "There's no one in visual. We're moving out into the ship."

"Understood." Lamont shifted position and crossed its arms as it waited for the next message.

"Commodore," Hendricks' voice sounded urgent. "We're picking up some kind of energy signature in the area."

"Pin it down. Butler, are we getting anything like that?"

"No." He sounded puzzled. "That's funny. Our long range..."

"Damn!"

Coy whirled around in surprise at Bon's exclamation.

"Our shields are down!" the engineer reported, shock in his voice.

"Theirs just came up," Drake pointed to a station screen, indicating the "derelict".

"We've got company!" Kensie Parker announced, but Coy had already seen them in the Tac holovid.

A large ship and a mass of small fighters poured out from behind a dead moon.

"Can we get our shields up?" Coy tried to keep from shouting.

"Nothing is responding. No shields. No weapons control. No maneuvering control. It's like all the programming has been wiped, or overridden or something."

"Keep trying. Find out what it is."

"How can they do this?" someone asked.

Coy had a sickening feeling it knew who and how someone would know the *Raven*'s systems, but it didn't have time to fully articulate any of that at the moment. "Check the com channels for hidden carrier wav-"

"Incoming!" Butler's voice sounded throughout the ship.

Safely in the center of the *Raven*, no one in the Tac Room felt more than a slight rocking motion. But in order for them to even feel that meant they had taken a hard hit.

"Status!" Butler barked.

Drake switched to the *Raven*'s station. As he, Bon and Butler handled the flagship's immediate problems, Lamont concentrated on the Fleet's. It desperately wished that *all* the station chairs were filled right about now.

"Portside damage to Deck H, weapons section. Four crewmembers injured..."

Lamont listened to the report of damage to the flagship with growing alarm. The images of the *Nighthawk* and the *Rook* were still outlined in blue, which meant they still had shielding. The large ship held off, but thirty-three fighter craft swept at high speed toward the trio of BlackFleet ships. The fighters came in close, using hit-and-run tactics, firing heavily upon each pass. They moved so quickly that targeting was difficult.

"Hendricks, Rebel; report your situation." Lamont ordered.

"Shields are holding. Weapons at full," came Hendricks' reply from the *Nighthawk*.

"We're not toasted yet, able to maneuver," from the *Rook*.

"We have no shields. Rebel, can you target and deflect any of the hits we're taking?"

"On it."

Rebel brought the *Rook* alongside the *Raven*, taking up a defensive position. The *'Hawk* continued evasive maneuvering.

"Bring us in...," Hendricks spat out coordinates. "I want a full spread of all weapons at a range of 4,000 kilometers as we pass."

The *Nighthawk* shot toward the large vessel in an attack run, all forward guns blazing. The big ship sent massive amounts of particle beam energy at them as they came on. Hendricks gripped her chair tightly as they came through the hail of fire. Forward shields held, but barely. Nathan gave the enemy ship all he had with the port guns as they passed. The big ship held steady, *its* shields apparently easily able to absorb the punishment. It continued firing at the *'Hawk* the entire time that they were in range, but itself remained in a stationary position. Instead, it turned its attention once more to the *Rook* and the *Raven*.

The *Nighthawk* sped away, circling around for another pass. Not alone, however. The smaller warship continued to be harried by a number of the attack fighters, which flew after it, darting in and out of weapons range, and slowly wearing down its shields, too.

On the Tac display, some of the small red dots representing the fighters now began skimming along the *Raven*.

"Drake, we changed the frequency of the *Blackbird*'s systems during some remodeling. They shouldn't be able to mess with it. Take the *'Bird* out and see if you can knock some of those fighters off."

"Aye, sir." He dove out the door at a dead run. A klaxon sounded through the *Raven* calling the *Blackbird*'s crew to their stations.

"Byars to Lamont."

"Lamont. Go."

"The *Blackbird* is down by two people. I've got some engineers here in sickbay."

Coy swore to itself. "Butler, do we have a crew count? Can the *Blackbird* launch?"

There was a moment's wait on the other end while Ken scrambled to reorganize personnel then, "Got it covered. The *Bird* can fly."

"We've got another problem," Bon said. "The bay doors won't open to launch it."

In any battle situation, commanders had to deal with problems on every side. It was a normal part of the job. And with Coy's inherent talents it was usually the one part of the job it handled the best. Now, ironically, and frighteningly, it was the one thing it couldn't seem to do. It had to make a conscious decision not to be overwhelmed. "Do whatever it takes," it said. "Get them opened."

"Bon to Hanger Bay. Bypass the electronics. Open the doors manually."

"Aye, sir. We're trying."

"Are we getting any sort of detailed reading on that big ship from scanners?" Coy asked.

"Negative. It's similar to a Haradan *Vega* class heavy cruiser; slightly larger than the *Raven*; but it's an unknown configuration. We're getting no specifics on its shield capabilities, number or type of weaponry, or engine capacity. Same for the fighters. Unknown design, no definite readings other than location and speed."

"Carrier wave activity detected, Skipper," Aziza suddenly announced. "That's how they did it, alright. A hidden sub channel on the com frequency we used in trying to hail the derelict."

"Can you lock out the signal?"

"Negative, sir. They're no longer sending it. Once in, the wave seems to have had a coded subroutine which has affected the shields, weapons, and engine systems like a virus. It's a temporary thing at best. I can isolate it, and purge it from the systems, but it's going to take some time."

"Let's not waste the time talking to me about it. Get someone on it. And not you, you're going to be fully occupied with keeping me in touch with what's going on out there. Raeph, who could handle that?"

"Mark Penway has expertise..."

"Get him up here," Coy snapped, nerves beginning to show despite its resolution.

Bon stabbed the com button on his console.

" Penway to the bridge, on the double!" he said.

"He's gone to a lot of trouble to set us up," Coy mumbled to no one in particular.

Bon glanced up at its tone. "You think you know who?"

"Don't you?"

Another tremor shook the *Raven*.

The small attack craft were nimbly sliding between the *Rook* and the *Raven*, using the flagship as a shield against being fired upon.

"Rebel, can you maneuver closer to us, protect at least one side of the ship?"

"I can bring us a little closer, but if you're not perfectly still, it'll be risky."

"We're not going anywhere. Do it."

Coy looked at the vid from the hangar bay, noting which door was being worked on.

"Rebel, maneuver close to the starboard side. The *Blackbird* should be launching out the port."

"Aye, sir. Starboard side ."

"We badly need another weapons platform out there," Coy surveyed the scene around the *Raven*. " How are we coming in the shuttle bay?"

"They report nearly ready," Bon replied. "Crew entering now. Still working on the doors, but almost there."

Coy began getting the vid feed from Drake. He saw everyone hurriedly strapping in and going into emergency startup procedures. After only a few minutes, the crew signaled ready.

Bon paused, listening, and then reported, "Doors are down. The *Bird*'s away. And Penway's on the bridge."

"Good," Coy replied. Then it turned to another vidcom display. "Schiff! "

"Schiff. Go ahead."

"What's your status?"

"We've got a situation. We're cut off from the shuttle. Armed troopers. They have our codes. Our armor is on manual override."

"Don't go to the shuttle. There's a war outside."

"Understood. We'll hold our own. Schiff out."

Out in the shuttle, Burney listened to the trooper's communication. They were cut off from him? Should he wait on the chance they would make it eventually after all? How could he best help his…His thoughts were interrupted when a fighter shot past him at high speed. It didn't seem
to take notice of the small vessel sitting like an open target attached to the not-so-derelict-after-all. But before he could breathe a sigh of relief, another fighter came by and paused only long enough to line up a shot.

Burney was knocked completely out of his seat by the direct hit on his engines.

"Shit!!" Snapping his helmet closed, he dove headfirst out the shuttle hatch into the ship, just as the shuttle exploded behind him.

Coy saw the blast in the monitor and looked at Drake for the explanation.

"The shuttle," Drake reported. He scanned the rest of the information. "Looks like Burney is on board the ship. Medical shows…heartbeat up a bit, but okay."

Bon and Lamont caught each other's eyes for a moment. "It's him. Your Boogeyman," Bon stated.

Coy gave a small nod. "I can only assume your tinkering has kept them from being able to access everything. They could've bled our air a long time ago and avoided all of this."

"Three cheers for remodeling," Butler's voice came over the com, where he'd been eavesdropping.

Lamont grimaced in unspoken agreement and looked again at the vid.

The *Nighthawk* maintained its defensive maneuvers, soaring in and out of the battle zone surrounding the *Raven*. It continued to be harassed by fifteen of the attack fighters. This time, when it came into range, the big cruiser unleashed a terrible volley of fire upon it, battering its shields in a few swift strokes.

"Shields down to 37 percent on the port/bow quarter," Hendricks reported. "We've taken out a number of the fighters, and are continuing to attack, but we need some help here. We're not going to be able to maintain for long."

"Rebel," Coy spoke over the com, "Can you get a shot at the big cruiser from here?"

"We can try."

The *Raven* rocked again.

"This is not good," Bon peered at his information. "Those damn fighters."

The *Nighthawk* circled around the big ship, attempting to get into the blind area behind its engines. But the enemy ship spun about wildly in its fixed position, denying the shot. Meanwhile, it continued to hammer at the *'Hawk* and the *Rook* as well.

The *Rook* fired repeatedly at the enemy vessel. It was also attempting to deflect some of the shots taken by the passing fighters. However, by maintaining position in protecting the *Raven*, it was taking a real beating itself.

"Great," Rebel said, holding onto his chair for support as his ship rocked. " And I didn't think that it was possible for this ship to look any worse."

The *Blackbird* now sped through the battle outside the *Raven*. It added its firepower to that of the *Rook's* broadside guns in targeting a fighter. The small craft was instantly vaporized. Pedula swung the armed yacht around the *Raven's* bow, chasing another one. Yacht and fighter craft traded shots. After several more moments of the pursuit, all of the *Blackbird's* combined weapons fired, then again, hitting their target. The fighter's shields flared and overloaded. The *Blackbird's* next shot shattered the enemy craft into fragments.

Other fighters noticed the new entry into the fight for the first time. Now seeing the *Blackbird* as a threat, they began to fix on it. Drake hung on, as three fighters rocked their ship with repeated hits. The *'Bird* continued firing at them, even as it dove back toward the *Raven*, giving chase to still another small group of the fighter craft which were heading toward the flagship. The enemy craft returned to skimming close along the black ship's outer surface, firing continuously at the hull.

Lamont swore again. "They're staying under the *Rook's* guns. Drake, lead some away from us. Rebel, Hendricks, try to clean some of these things off of each other."

There was a very slight pause. "Aye, sir. Nathan says he only hopes Bard is as good a shot as he is."

The *Blackbird* looped away from the flagship, firing all the while at two of the fighters, and drawing three more away in the process. Again, the enemy fighters targeted the small ship.

At the same time, the *Nighthawk*, with a cloud of fighters still surrounding it, sailed toward the area where the *Rook* and *Raven* hung in space. It flashed directly past the *Rook*, where, for just a moment, both ships had a few of the fighters in a crossfire. Three more of them were destroyed. However, the large enemy ship began to hit the *'Hawk*, as it came once more into range.

Lamont watched their light cruiser's evasive maneuvering with growing concern. The dotted blue outline around the *Nighthawk* showed a dangerously low level of shield power to both its starboard and port aft quarters. Suddenly there was an emergency from another front in the battle.

"Man down." Schiff's voice sounded from over on the "derelict".

Coy centered attention on the vid access from the troopers. "Burney?"

"No," the major told it. " He met up with us a minute ago. It's Knepp." Walter leaned over to check Knepp's readouts. With their armor on manual, he couldn't access it from his command helmet. "Tony?"

Knepp looked up at him. "I'm fine. Leave me."

Schiff instantly understood and muttered, "G'luck Kid." Then, shaking his head at the 'loss', he turned to the rest of his team. "Move! They'll pay for this!"

Even though they moved quickly, they were outnumbered. Schiff realized they were being herded, but at the moment couldn't do a bloody thing about it. They retreated down a long corridor, hoping to regroup at the far end. Opening a large door, they fled through it. Suddenly, the door slammed shut behind them and the corridor was plunged into darkness. The vid feed from them was cut.

Coy clenched its jaw, shaking with the effort of fending off its emotions until a more appropriate time. It stared at the Tac vid, trying to take in information from all of the ships. The access from the *Raven* caught its attention.

"Is the bay door closed yet?"

"They seem to be having trouble..."

Before it could wonder why that would be taking so long, its thoughts were immediately interrupted.

"We're being hailed," Aziza announced.

"Alright," Lamont straightened and looked directly into the vid.

A strange man was on the other end; not anyone that Coy had ever seen before. Just how many people were in the Boogeyman's employ, anyway?

"Well, well, the infamous Commodore Lamont at last," he said. "You seem to be having more trouble saving yourself than you do others."

"It's far from over," Lamont said coolly.

"Oh, really? We have your boarding party. Some of them are still alive, too. It would be a shame to lose the rest." He shook his head in mock regret at the waste. " Now, let's talk, shall we?"

They were interrupted by a panicked voice from the hanger bay. "They're coming in! They're com..."

The man on the other ship smiled. "You were saying, Commodore?"

Bon scanned the internal monitors. A heavily armed boarding party of several dozen invaders wearing space armor had come in through the hangar bay doors before they had been fully closed. The vid showed them rushing toward the lifts.

"They're in alright," he said. "And on the way up."

The smiling face on the vid disappeared as Lamont cut off the outside communication and channeled its next remarks to wrist coms only. "Lamont to Bridge. Fall back to Emergency Bridge. Evacuate Sick bay. Now!" With a swipe it turned off the Tac vid and said gravely to Bon, "Let's go."

Sealing the doors behind, and sprinting down the corridor to the aft lift, the Bridge and Tac room crews crowded in, and the lift took them swiftly to Deck D. A similar sprint down that corridor followed. Then, up a flight of stairs to the engineering area on C Deck. They manually sealed the stairwell behind them. The access panel outside the Emergency bridge scanned Coy's retina pattern and fingerprints, then the security door slid open. As with their drills, three minutes and twenty seconds later, everyone was assembled there.

"Status report," Coy ordered.

"Hangar bay under control of hostiles," Butler said. "They have now arrived on G deck, making for the bridge. We still have no weapons, shielding, or maneuvering. We appear to be locked out of all other systems except the new communications systems, and the internal vid systems; we have nominal environmental and power systems control."

Lamont reestablished communication with the rest of the Fleet, hoping their guests would not hear them on this frequency. Or if they did, would not make sense of the messages.

"Attention : code V."

"*Shadow Two*, check," came the reply from the *Nighthawk*. Hendricks had received the coded message on the emergency frequency, understood, and would respond only in code for the duration of the emergency. The other ships also replied in short order.

"Message coming in from the derelict," Aziza said. "Voice-only frequency. It's Tony Knepp."

"Situation red," Knepp's voice came over the console. "Condition Lambda. Please enable."

"Damn," Butler muttered. He knew as well as Coy the meaning of that code. Tony was the only member of the boarding party free.

"Is Lambda Option seven-oh-seven available?" Coy asked in response.

"Yes."

Coy thought for several moments, weighing the possibilities. Then it reached a decision.

"Execute seven-oh seven; variation *cobra*, repeat *cobra*."

Someone on the bridge gasped.

"T. M. twenty-three," Lamont continued. "Pinewood retrieval. Copy?"

"Copy." Knepp replied and immediately cut the communication.

Butler leaned close to Lamont. "Tell me you're not doing what it sounds like you're doing."

"I'm doing whatever it takes," it said in a level voice.

The boarding party had sped effortlessly through the *Raven*, meeting token resistance and beating it back easily. They arrived at G deck, and made their way to the bridge. The leader held a remote transponder, and as he held it up, keyed in a sequence. Security doors parted and the group rushed in, guns at the ready. That sequence was repeated at the bridge hatch, and it too, opened easily to the invaders. To their amazement, the bridge was completely deserted. The group's leader set his men immediately to work. Then he threw back his head and laughed.

"Sir," Penway said. "I had the 'virus' isolated before we had to evacuate to the emergency bridge. I started a program to purge it from the systems. But now, something they're doing on the main bridge is keeping that program from running. I can't seem to get at it from here."

"Understood," Lamont said. "Keep trying. Aziza, give me the *Blackbird* on coded channel."

"Coming right up, sir."

Coy checked its chrono. Once the connection was made, it simply said, "*Shadow Four*; Pinewood retrieval. Coordinates; Beta One. T. M. twenty-one. Copy?"

"Copy," came the reply, and the connection was cut.

"I hope they remember their training," Butler sighed.

"So do...," Coy began and then turned to look at Ken. "Training," it repeated slowly, then spun around to Bon. "Training exercises. Do we have library access?"

"Signal coming in from the attacking ship," Aziza told Coy.

"Hold on that a moment," Coy responded, then motioned for the Chief engineer to continue.

"Library access? I suppose we do. But why..?" but Bon was thinking even as he spoke. "Oh, man, do you think they'll buy it?"

"It's worth a shot. File T-107. Call it up fast, and pipe it through to the engineering console on the bridge."

"Yes, sir. I think that I can use our nominal systems control to make a power spike or two. At least for a few seconds."

"Do it," Coy said. Then it quickly tapped its wristcom and said, "Palo, Code Amber, section two."

"Copy,"

"Okay, put me on with him," it said to Aziza. The com officer touched a button and the visage of the attack commander came up on the holovid.

"Commodore Lamont, I have grown tired of your useless attempts. My men have your boarding party surrounded and disarmed. I have your men, and I have your ship. Cease all resistance immediately or I will be forced to execute the captives. "

Lamont paused for just a moment, as if searching internally for some solution.

"Well, Commodore? I'm hardly bluffing. Your answer. Now."

"Get me the rest of the fleet," Coy told Aziza.

The com officer nodded sadly, and complied with the order.

"This is Commodore Lamont to all BlackFleet ships. Cease fire. I repeat, cease fire. Stop all hostilities, and stand down weapons systems." They did so.

"That's much better," their opponent said. "Now, you will immediately surrender yourselves to my crew in control of your bridge. Any further resistance from you will bring the same results I promised. No tricks, and you may actually get to live."

Commander Bon had finally gotten the requested file downloaded to his screen. He looked to Lamont. Coy gave a nearly imperceptible nod, and Bon's fingers flew over the console, executing implied orders.   Coy again glanced at its chrono, waited just a few seconds, then turned again to the com.

"No one takes this ship from me," it said with a snarl. Without another word, it cut the connection.

In the *Raven's* main bridge, the invaders jumped suddenly as loud alarms began sounding. "Sir," one of them said to the leader. "Here, on the engineering console!"

The man strode over to find that the panel was informing them that the fusion reactors had gone critical.   The computer displayed a countdown to reactor breach. The count read one minute, fifty seconds.

"Sir, we've got to get out of here!" the underling shouted. "They've done something---blowing up the ship! We've got to go!"

The leader seemed unnaturally calm, and merely held up the remote transponder he'd been carrying.

"You forget, we've got all their codes. This is probably some self destruct sequence, and I'll just call up all those options and turn it off."

He made some adjustments to his device, scanned for all possible self-destruct codes. There it was. One specific destruct code, designed to bring the ship's reactors to critical. He keyed in the cancellation sequence, and pointed the transponder toward the console.

"Just like that, no more problem," he said. "I simply use their own...." he stopped, realizing that the alarm hadn't shut off yet. "Must have hit the wrong sequence. I hit this, then this, then this, and..." he pointed again, waited. The alarm continued to blare.

The leader leaned over the console, hit a few buttons there. Tried the remote once again. Again no result.

"No," he said finally. "It's---it can't be----we have all their codes! How can----" he stopped dumbfounded.

"Hold position!" The attack leader's voice bellowed from their wristcoms. "We're checking it out. Hold there!"

"What's happening? What can you tell from outside?"

"Nothing definite. As I said, we're checking it. But you are to stay in position! That's an order!"

"What do you mean, 'nothing definite?'" But there was no reply. The attack leader had cut the connection. Panic swelled. The count now read one minute, 20 seconds. One man broke, ran out of the *Raven's* bridge. Then two more. Finally they were all in a panicked flight down the corridor back to the rear lift, fleeing for their very lives.

Coy, however, stood perfectly still. It was watching the external view as an explosion ripped away a cargo bay door on the derelict ship. Several figures were blown out into space by the decompression.

"Get me a close scan on that," Lamont snapped.

The vid image adjusted and Coy saw several black-suited figures tumbling out into space. All of them had their faceplates sealed, and emergency oxygen working. It sighed heavily in relief.

Several other figures, apparently the pirates who had captured them, weren't as fortunate. Obviously they hadn't had someone like Schiff as a training sergeant.

After being left for "dead" by Schiff, Knepp had used some of the special demolition shaped charges that the troopers carry in their packs. After sneaking into position and calling out a code from the trooper's decompression training drill, he blew the upper edge of the bay door. Risky, but it seemed to be paying off so far.

"Only one thing left," Lamont said.

On the monitor, the *Blackbird* came into view. Before any of the fighters could get there, it had scooped all the troopers into its front hatchway. The hatch sealed, and the '*Bird* took only a single hit from weapons fire before her shields went back up. The sleek little ship fired back in all directions, and blasted out of the area at full speed.

On the *Raven,* the invading party jostled one another in the lift. They were consumed by sheer terror. Someone looked at his wrist chrono.

"Forty-five seconds left!"

"What's taking this lift so long?"

"Shut up!" the leader yelled. "We still have time!"

The doors to the hangar bay parted, and the invaders literally fell over one another trying to be the first out. They didn't have to worry about getting back up. Every available BlackFleet crewmember on the ship stood there in the hangar bay. Each one of them had a weapon pointed at the invaders coming out of the lift doors on either side of the bay. The fact that nearly all of them were techs in no way lessened their menace. They had also been cross-trained in the same intruder alert drills that the troopers had gone through, and were glad for the chance to use the training.

The startled invading party noticed that their fellows, left here to guard the hangar bay, had been ambushed as well, and lay in a pile off to one side.

No, the BlackFleet crew didn't look at all happy. They also weren't in any hurry to leave the ship. It became obvious that the emergency had been faked somehow, and that they'd been outfoxed.

Resignedly, each of the invading party stood, unshouldered his or her weapon, and raised their hands into the air. Giorgio Palo walked over to the leader, took the remote transponder from him and stomped it into a dozen pieces.

"I think that ought to be enough of that," he said with finality, motioning the captured group back toward the lifts and the waiting brig.

Coy watched the proceedings on the internal monitors, extremely pleased.

"Virus isolated, sir," Penway said triumphantly. "Purge complete."

"We've regained control of all systems!" Bon shouted.

"Shields up," Coy ordered. "All weapons on line. Give me the--"

"Sir," Aziza interrupted. "The main ship, she's taking off!" Sure enough, the holovid showed the cruiser spinning about, and its engines roaring to full power.

"Lamont to all ships: Pursue and fire at will!"

Each of the BlackFleet commanders centered all their firepower upon the fleeing ship. And for the first time in this battle, the *Raven* was able to join in. Parker targeted the enemy with the heavy dorsal cannons. She fired, sending blasts into their aft shields. Rear shield power on the

enemy ship dropped like a rock. The *Raven* and *Nighthawk* sped forward, surrounding the cruiser on both sides, and cutting off its retreat.

"One shot with the quad and this would be over pretty quickly," Butler said hopefully.

The quad cannon on the nose of the *Raven* was their most powerful ace in the hole. If they used it now that the cruisers shields were weak it would indeed be over. "Tempting," Coy told him, "but as nice as revenge is, I would also like answers. I think we will save it for more dire circumstances."

The small fighters also gave chase, attempting to defend the cruiser. But, by pursing the other craft in the same relative direction, the nimble little ships had lost their speed advantage. Parker, Nathan, and Bard, from their respective ships, easily found their marks.

The cruiser itself began firing back at its pursuers, but now had to divide firepower among three ships instead of only two. It was too little too late. The *Raven* hammered at the ship without mercy and the enemy quickly lost side shielding as well. It began to slow to a halt.

"Get me their leader on the com," Coy ordered.

Aziza tried repeatedly to establish contact. When at last they began receiving a vid image from the ship, it was not what they expected. There were a number of people working frantically on their bridge, but no one was bothering to answer the hail. It seemed that something was terribly wrong.

"Sir," Bon said in alarm. "Scanners show their reactors building to critical mass! Explosion immanent!"

"Not some sort of trick, like ours?"

"No, sir. Scanners have it confirmed!"

"Lamont to all BlackFleet vessels! Retreat! I say again, retreat!"

The four ships peeled away from the cruiser at high speed. The skin on the big ship split in several places, leaking light and debris, as it was racked by internal explosions. It was followed by a terrible eruption of brilliance. When that dimmed, mere fragments were all that remained of the ship. No one made it out.

"Leaving nothing to chance, I guess," Lamont said as Butler caught its glance.

"You think that this 'Boogeyman' blew up an entire heavy cruiser, simply to keep us from learning anything?" Ken asked in amazement.

"How else would you explain that? Their carefully planned offensive was a bust, and we had just about gotten them to heave to and surrender. Think about what that says about whom we're dealing with."

"Skipper," Aziza said. "Getting a message from some of those attack fighters out there. Requesting asylum."

"How many of them are left?"

"Scanners indicate thirteen left intact and functional; four badly damaged and in need of a tow."

Coy thought carefully. It looked at Ken and knew what his vote would be. A look at Bon showed him already going over the schematics of the hanger bay. He was frowning and mumbling to himself, but finally looked up at Lamont.

"Your call, Commodore," he said. Which meant he would find a way if Coy Lamont desired it.

Thirteen functional fighters. "Alright," it decided. " Have them lock down all weapons systems. If even a flicker shows up on our scan, they stay in space. Bring them in one by one and escort them directly to the brig. We'll assess injuries from there." Officers and crew jumped to implement the orders. Coy met Butler's gaze. "Well, I guess you might have your toys after all."

"Hardly dropped in our lap this time. We bloody well paid for these toys."

Coy nodded grimly, knowing how very much they almost paid.

At the White meeting the next day, the massive amounts of damage, names of injured and equipment needs were all listed and reported by department heads. Then a very careful scrutiny of the entire episode was gone over, practically second by second. By combining the Tac records from all four ships, vids from external and internal monitors as well as helmet recorders from Schiff's unit, they had a very accurate recreation of the events.

The number one inescapable conclusion was that they had been blindsided, pure and simple. And Coy was determined that it would **never** happen again.

"In the plus column," Butler remarked, "the evacuation of Bridge, Tac and Sickbay went like clockwork. The emergency Bridge is literally what saved our lives."

"I discovered a few items that should be stored in the emergency sickbay," Ceal reported. "If the injuries had been different we might have been in trouble. Assuming we had to stay there for a while. Anyway, I already have Jimmy transporting the things up there now."

Coy nodded acknowledgement and approval.

"When we finish the 'remodeling' no one will be able to access anything on this ship," Bon said resolutely.

"And speaking of remodeling," Rebel put in, "are we really going to keep all of those fighters?"

"We will keep as many of them as we can get functional," Coy answered.

"The ships I agree with," Hendricks said, "but what about the pilots? We're not going to keep the very people that tried to blow us to atoms, are we?"

Coy thought for a moment before answering. From the looks on the faces around the table, Mara was only voicing the feelings of everyone else. "That depends on why they were trying to blow us to atoms. If they were aware of what they were doing and why, no they will not stay here. The question at that point is what do we do with them?"

Schiff looked up and met Coy's eyes. "They were going to space us." He said simply.

"Whoever was in command of those troopers tried to space you," Coy maintained. "Not these fighter pilots."

Butler frowned. "Is there some particular reason you are defending these guys?"

Lamont gave a very small sigh. "How many people around this table needed someone to defend them not too long ago?"

"Ouch," Rebel murmured *almost* too quietly to hear.

When there were no more responses to the issue volunteered from the group, Coy continued. "A dose of Pentha will sort out quickly enough who was simply a soldier doing what they thought was right and following orders, and who was out for blood for other reasons. If there are no useful suggestions as to what to do with the second category…" It waited a beat, but no one answered… "I will decide that shortly. Meanwhile, Bon , get me some exact parts list and timeframes for converting whatever bays we need . See how the fighters can be spread out between ships. What I need is to figure if we can do this or we have to call in some markers."

Butler perked up at that. As Fleet Exec he was only one of two people privy to Lamont's account balance of favors still owed to them. Lamont dismissed the meeting and as Ken expected nodded him back into his seat for more discussion.

Ceal Byars also hung back and looked at the Commodore with some concern. Lamont returned her gaze with a bland one of its own. After a few seconds of this, she raised one eyebrow in question. Coy gave a miniscule shake of the head in return. She sighed and left.

Ken glanced at the door, which had closed behind her and then at Coy. "Dare I ask..?"

"Why I kept you here?" Lamont asked, purposely misunderstanding the question, "I just wanted your opinion on costs. Asch will be joining us in a minute as well."

Butler knew enough to let it go if Coy was going to all that trouble to misdirect him. He would just have to pin Ceal down later. Not that it would probably do any good. But he could try.

As Lamont said, the Fleet Acquisitions officer arrived just then and they all began to talk business.

Coy sat across from the table in the briefing room, looking at the latest of the 34 surviving fighter pilots and gunners. One Anthony Smith. Coy had to admit it liked the man's cocky attitude. It had seen it so often before in interviews. People who had only made it in life by outwitting everyone around them. Smith had been a war orphan who had decided early on that being a soldier was the only way to improve his lot – and maybe that of others like him. Coy smiled at the Story and signed him on.

The other 33 had stories as varied as they were. Some, like Smith were victims of their world's wars. They were checked off. A few drifters with no particular loyalties or vision. Coy chose one of them – over Butler's disapproval. One had left his rich family to make a name for himself on his own strength. One was a gung ho, self-proclaimed warrior who wanted to win whatever was going on. More than a few simply liked blowing things up. Two had been discharged from their home service when the current skirmish there was over and were lost as to what to do afterward.

Unfortunately, not one of them seemed to know who they ultimately had worked for or why the decision had been made to attack the *Raven*. After joining the supposedly typical merc unit, they had simply followed their orders.

In all Coy kept ten, four pilots and six gunners. The rest, after a second interrogation, were cleared from being hostile enemies, but were still not BlackFleet material. Coy made the decision to drop them off at Alluria Station and let them make their way from there to wherever they wanted to go.

During the trip there, several things were accomplished. One, Bon was able to come up with exact parts and plans needed to permanently house the fighter ships. Two, the new "recruits" were put through an even more intense orientation training than usual. And three, that intense training lost them one more of the pilots who decided to risk abandonment on Alluria to facing Schiff again.

"Skipper, wait up!" Bon's voice followed Coy down the corridor. Obligingly, it stopped and waited. The engineer caught up and waved some data sheets in the air. "I have those stats Vennefron wanted for the com line messages. I think he's right. We can set up a couple of drop spots in different parts of Beta Region where people can contact us. We can collect the messages at will without anyone really knowing the location of the Fleet. Is that the kind of thing you were wanting?"

Lamont looked at him blankly for just a second, as if it didn't know what he was talking about.

"Commodore? Did I misunderstand Venn's request?" Bon frowned.

Coy blinked. "No, that's exactly what we need. Thank you," it turned to continue walking.

"I'm on my way to lunch. We could discuss it more over a bite to eat."

"No, thank you. I'm….I'm not hungry."

Bon studied its face. "You look a little beat. Have you been having those nightmares again?"

"No, I'm fine," it said a little forcefully. "I have things to do, Captain, if you will excuse me."

As it walked away, Bon shook his head. This wasn't the first time a near miss for the Fleet had caused the return of the dreams. He only wished there was some way to help. But the Skipper had obviously been asking to be left alone for the moment. And he would respect that.

Unexpectedly, the commodore did not oversee dropping the prisoners off at Alluria Station. Butler took over and had them transported down in a shuttle, lightly stunned and left them in a docking bay.

"Hey!" a bay worker yelled as Butler started back into the shuttle after the last crewman. "You can't leave people layin' 'round down here!"

Butler took on a drawl of his own. "Th' cap'n says next time they git drunk on duty we leave 'em. So, we're leavin' 'em." With a salute he shut the hatch and yelled to take off. Once they were enroute, he called on his wristcom. "Butler to Lamont."

"Commodore Lamont's quarters," came Asch's voice.

Butler stared at his wrist unit. "Asch? I was trying to reach the Skipper. Doesn't it have its unit on?"

"The Commodore is…indisposed. Is there a message?"

"Is there a…? Well, okay, the prisoners have been safely delivered to Alluria. We are enroute back to the Fleet."

"Roger. The Commodore will be posted. Asch out."

"What do you suppose *that* meant?" Friedhoff asked aloud what Ken was thinking.

But that didn't mean any one else was supposed to think it. "Just what he said, Corporal. The Commodore's work schedule is really not your business."

"Yes, sir."

But Ken still was wondering about it when he got back. He went immediately to I & S to see if any new business had come up. Vennefron was working alone and had no news. He found Bon in the Tac room. "Raeph, anything up?"

"Such as…?" The engineer kept working at a console and didn't even look up.

"I don't know, such as the Skipper being too busy with something to answer its own wristcom."

Bon paused in his work at that and looked at him. "What are you talking about?"

"I tried to report from the shuttle and Asch took the call."

"So? He's the commodore's steward."

"He's never done that before. Coy Lamont could be *swimming* and it answers its calls."

"Is it an emergency?"

"No, just a normal stat report."

"So what is the problem? The Skipper probably just added to Asch's duties again."

"In the last half hour? And why didn't it come with the prisoners? That was the plan."

Bon pursed his lips and frowned. "Are you trying to make a point?"

Butler crossed his arms defensively. "The Skipper is acting funny is all. It wouldn't even argue with me at supper the other night. It just kept staring off into space."

Bon leaned back and crossed his arms as well. He didn't like criticism of Coy Lamont. "It has quiet moods. You know that, as well as I do."

"Yes, but…"

"Leave it." Technically they held the same rank, both being captains, even though Butler was first officer of the Fleet and Bon was second. But more to the point at times like this, Bon had always had a more personal line on the commodore's moods and feelings. Butler glared at Bon for lack of a better target, then begrudgingly, backed down and went off to his normal duties.

The next day, Lamont sent word for Captain Butler to lead the White meeting. Trying to be as nonchalant as humanly possible, Butler did as he was asked. He took department reports, made a few minor changes in staff duty schedules, made a wise crack or two and dismissed the meeting. He stared at Bon as the others left the room but the engineer only shrugged and followed them out.

"Butler to Lamont."

"Lamont," a weary voice replied.

Ken blinked in surprise. Maybe the commodore really had been working day and night on something to sound that tired. "I have the report of our meeting."

"Fine. Down load it to Asch. Lamont out."

Now Butler was just plain angry. The Fleet Exec should be in on anything big enough to cause all of this. Punching the com off, he swung to his feet and headed to the officer's quarters. Standing in front of Coy's door, he paused and listened for a second. Hearing nothing from inside, he pushed the buzzer.

After a few moments, Asch appeared. "Yes, Captain?"

"I need to see La…I wish to see the commodore," he corrected his tone and words.

"I'm sorry. My orders are that the commodore wishes not to be disturbed at this time."

"At this ti…!"

"Good day, Captain. *Please* try later." Asch looked at him meaningfully before shutting the door, but Ken was too mad to decipher it.

Butler sputtered in disbelief. Try later?? Fine. If Coy Lamont wanted something from him, it could bloody well come and look for him itself. He turned and stomped back to the lift tube.

Inside the quarters, Asch went to the huge desk Lamont was sitting at, and had been sitting at more and more lately, and cleared his throat a little to get Coy's attention. "Sir, will you be wanting your meal soon?"

Lamont waved him off. "No, I won't. I had a lunch meeting, so I won't be needing anything."

Asch pursed his lips, trying to decide what was his place to say. "Sir, that was yesterday, and this is dinner not lunch."

Lamont swung around to him at that and stood up, slamming its hands down on the desk. "Why is everyone suddenly so interested in every time I eat or sleep?" it demanded.

"Because we care, sir," Asch answered very quietly.

Coy stared. It seemed to have a hard time catching its breath for just a second. "Just leave me alone," it said finally and went into its sleeping quarters.

Asch stood staring at the closed door for a long while.

"Miss Byars?"

Ceal turned from tutoring Jimmy Dobbs on some medical terms to see Asch standing in Sick Bay.

"Hey, Lieutenant Asch!" the young man greeted the officer.

Although Jimmy was officially assigned to Sick Bay, he occasionally helped Asch out, and the two had become good friends. They shared a painful background of family expectations which neither had ever really had anyone to confide in about.

"Hello, Jimmy. I need to speak with Doctor Byars."

"Sure thing. Later, Ceal. Thanks."

Ceal shook her head, and grinned after his enthusiasm, but lost the grin at Asch's expression. "What is it?"

"I would like you to visit the commodore."

Ceal felt a flutter of fear. "Oh?"

"It doesn't eat."

Ceal relaxed. "Ah, yes, I know. I had the same problem with Lamont when I came on board. It really doesn't need as much ..."

"No, you don't understand. It hasn't eaten anything in over two days, now."

She frowned. "Anything? As in literally anything?"

Asch nodded. "Not a drop of water or bite of food. Privacy is very important to the commodore, I know, and I would not intrude on this lightly. But I am...concerned."

"It won't let her in, you know," Butler's voice interrupted from where he stood leaning against the doorway. He came into Sick Bay and glared a little at Asch. "I've tried."

The steward thought for a moment. "If I were conveniently on another duty at that time, I believe it would answer its own messages."

"You mean it's been deliberately not talking to anyone," Butler said to confirm his own guess.

Instead of answering, Asch turned back to Ceal. "Again, I request you visit and assess the situation yourself. If I am out of line, I will gladly take whatever chastisement the commodore wishes to give."

She looked from one to the other. "Alright. You stay here. I'll go up and see what's going on."

"Stay here and do what? If the commodore asks, I will not lie."

"Finish tutoring Jimmy. He's probably not far away yet."

"Very well. That will do."

Byars left Sick Bay with Butler on her heels. "I'm going to find out as well."

Actually glad of the support, she nodded. Once at the cabin door, however, she said, "Can you wait here? We really don't know what's going on. It might let me know more if I'm alone. Trust me, if I need you, I'll let you know quick enough."

At his unhappy nod, she pushed the buzzer. There was no answer. She pushed again. And again nothing. Taking a deep breath, she spoke into her wrist com. "Byars to Lamont. I know you can hear me. If you do not open your door, as Chief Medical Officer I can override it and come in….I need to talk to you Coy."

There were a few more moments of silence. Just as Butler was urging her to do as she had threatened, the door slid open at a faint, "Enter."

She stepped in and it shut behind her. The quarters were dimly lit. She could barely see Lamont's outline against space as it sat at its desk by the large portal. Slowly she walked over. Even in this light, she could tell it looked awful. It looked more like it hadn't eaten in a week, rather than a day or two. Tears were streaming down its face.

"Coy, what's wrong?" she tried to remain calm.

It opened its mouth, but it was a moment before it spoke. "I lost."

"You lost what?" she took out her scanner and started a cursory exam.

"The *Raven*. They came on the *Raven*."

Blood pressure, pulse….Ceal stared in horror at the readings even as she continued to speak softly. "We didn't lose the *Raven*, Commodore. We're all fine."

It focused on her for the first time. "They came on board. I failed."
It took a ragged breath.

"Commodore, we are going to Sick Bay. And we are going right now."

"I can't command…"

"I'm calling for a pallet."

"No," it stood up. And immediately fell into Ceal's arms.

"Ken!!!" she screamed.

Coy Lamont lay in the bed in Sick Bay hooked up to life support. Ken Butler stood in the door to the private cubicle, arms crossed, trying to hold his fear at bay with anger. If only Lamont had let them know…Raeph Bon leaned on the wall for support and was running a close second to Coy for paleness. Ceal was on the com to the *Nighthawk*.

"I need your help, Rose. As fast as you can get here."

"You don't understand, Ceal. Commodore Lamont does not want me on the case, whatever it is."

Ken looked over at that.

"What do you mean?" Byars demanded in disbelief.

"The commodore hired me. And that's just about the last time it spoke to me. I've called for a conference, I've sent memos…It won't see me. If I'm a terrible doctor I wish it would just say so and let me go."

"Rose, it's the commodore that's sick. Terribly sick. I don't have a clue what is going on. Do you understand, it's laying here dying right in front of me! I need your help."

There was barely a second's delay at that. "I'm on the way. Durand out."

Ceal lowered her wrist and checked Lamont's readouts again. "Why, Coy?" she whispered. "Why did you avoid anyone who could help?"

Lamont's eyes fluttered open. Butler and Bon both leaned closer at the small movement. "You can't help," it rasped out.

"Maybe I could have."

Lamont gave a tiny shake of its head. "I'm not…"it took a breath "…I'm a construct."

"I know, a genetic."

"You don't know. You don't know." It struggled to rally its strength. "I was never meant to be a soldier."

"You said you were a military experiment."

Butler and Bon looked at each other and at her. Then back at Lamont.

Lamont nodded. "But not a soldier. A spy." Another raspy breath. "Confusing gender, bland features, perfect memory. The perfect spy." Its eyes seemed to focus in the distance, almost as if it were reading something far away. "The perfect spy," it repeated, "I can't be interrogated. Drugs don't work. Pain doesn't work." It gave a small imitation of a laugh, "I have a subroutine that would take over if I was tortured. Survive, escape and return with information intact. That was what I was made for." It shut its eyes again. " I never understood... I was never supposed to command....I was never supposed to fail. They couldn't afford that."

"Who couldn't afford that?" Ceal asked desperately. "What is happening?"

But Coy didn't answer. Its thoughts seemed to wander. "I wasn't supposed to care. Spies can't afford that either."

A monitor bleeped and Ceal jerked to look at it. "No..."

It opened its eyes, but didn't look at anything. Its voice was a whisper. "I commanded. I cared. I failed."

"Coy, what's happening?" she asked again unwilling to believe what everything was telling her.

"What do you do with a weapon that's no longer useful?" Its eyes shut and did not open. "Self..." the words were barely audible "... destruct." Coy gasped. Another monitor beeped. And then changed to a steady tone.

"No!" she and Bon shouted together. Ceal's hands raced madly over buttons and switches. Bon's beat in frustration on the wall.

After a few minutes, the monitor stopped the shrill tone and went back to beeping rhythmically.

Butler swallowed. "Is...?"

Ceal shook her head. "I've got it on full life support. Its body will stay alive until I can..." she couldn't finish.

Butler stared at her and then down at Lamont's still features. "Damn."

Bon shook himself, and inhaled. Then he turned away from the bed and faced Butler. "Orders, sir?"

Chapter Six

Captain Butler sat at the desk in his quarters going over the crew roster for the hundredth time. Sixty-nine people. No, he corrected himself sternly, seventy people. But either way, he couldn't figure a way for that amount to run the fleet appropriately. Commodore Lamont had been so sure it could be done. He wished for the millionth time it had left a few more notes or something indicating how exactly he was expected to do it.

The door buzzed, interrupting his thoughts. "Enter."

Raeph Bon came in holding a data disk. "Captain, I've got all the information for the remodeling here. I'm afraid I was right. Only nine fighters will fit on the *Raven* and still leave room for the *Black-Bird* and the shuttles. Now we have to decide whether the other four go on the *Rook* or the *Nighthawk*."

"According to what few notes the Skipper left", Ken gave a mock grimace, "I'm pretty sure it was thinking the *Rook*. It seemed to want to use the *Nighthawk* for ground troops."

Bon nodded. "That's what I thought as well. Also, Asch wants to know if you are going to contact for the Favor or if he is."

Butler sighed. "I suppose I should." He nodded at the small disk in Bon's hand, no bigger than a coin. "Does that have all the contact information as well?"

"Everything you need from start to finish." He put it on the desk.

Butler glanced at the roster and then at the time readout on his wristcom. "Palo's holding down the pilot's chair on the bridge now. He can head us toward the transit point. By the time we're close Hoffman will be on duty."

"Aye, sir."

Butler looked at Bon closely. He seemed a little more rested than he had. And not quite so pale. But still very formal and serious.

"Raeph, we have had a pretty good working relationship from the beginning. I would like to keep it."

Bon pursed his lips, before answering almost in a monotone, "You're my commanding officer. I'll give you whatever you need..."

"Stop that!" Ken sputtered. "Why are you doing this? You're not the only one who misses the Skipper, you know. We've got a fleet to run, here, and you're my first officer for now whether you like it or not."

Raeph stiffened at the mention of Lamont. He said nothing for several moments. "I know everyone misses it, Captain, but not everyone killed it."

Butler stared at him in disbelief. "What are you talking about?"

"You came to me with evidence of something wrong and I blew it off completely. If I had listened and we had gotten there sooner ..."

Butler leaned back in his chair. "Whoa there. Number one, I was there. It was an automatic self-destruct sequence. Nothing anyone did would have stopped it. And number two, it's not dead. As long as Ceal has the life support on, it's technically in a coma...Give yourself a break, Raeph. The people that ki...tried to kill Coy Lamont did it from a lab on Riga thirty years ago."

"That may be but..."

"No buts. I need you Raeph. Whole and operational."

The engineer shook his head. "I don't know, Ken. Every time I see it lying there, I feel so helpless. It's hard to imagine the Fleet going on as usual."

"Maybe you should stop looking," Ken said gently. He had never quite understood the relationship between Bon and Lamont. They had always been closer than he and the commodore, partially because Bon had been the very first person to help Lamont start the BlackFleet. But he had always gotten the feeling that there was a deeper friendship than he and Lamont would ever see. "I said we all miss the Skipper, and we do. And I know we all miss it in a little different way. I also know it will have our hide if we let anything happen to the Fleet. I'm serious about needing you to lean on."

Bon took a steadying breath and let it out. "You're right. The commodore hired me to do a job. I guess I'd better do it right."

Butler smiled. "Thank you."

Bon smiled a little as well. "Funny thing, I thought you might be the one needing the pep talk."

"Trust me, I will."

Ceal glanced up from her monitoring station when she sensed someone else in the room. She didn't expect it to be Ben Edwards. What was the *Nighthawk* engineer doing here? He didn't know she had seen him. He was looking around a little nervously as if expecting to be thrown out. She almost spoke to him, but then decided to see what he was going to do.

Slowly, he made his way over to the chamber where Coy Lamont lay. For a few seconds he looked everywhere but down at the person he had come all the way here to see. When at last he did, his breath caught a

little. He was fidgeting with a tiny object of some kind but Ceal couldn't see what it was without revealing herself.

"H-hello, Skipper," Edwards said in his soft voice. Ben had come to the Fleet in the company of Gus Reinhart, whose servant he had been for most of his life. Gus was now a trooper and Ben an engineer and they were working hard at forging a new, more equal friendship between them. But Edwards had never lost his quiet, polite manners or mannerisms. "I just came to say I, ah, miss...well, we never actually got to finish that game we started. So I brought this as a kind of reminder," he put the object on the stand next to the chamber. It was a chess piece. "When you wake up, maybe we can finish." He said nothing more. He stepped back, gave a salute, and left.

Ceal smiled and wiped moisture from her eyes – again.

Over the following days, the ceremony was repeated again and again as crewmembers came with well wishes. The small table grew crowded with mementos. More than one brought a book disk, another, a real book made out of paper no less. Someone brought music, there were several small pictures, even one lock of hair. Ceal wasn't sure who had brought the string of beads or what the significance was, but it looked old and well handled. Pieces of their lives that the commodore had touched. Fervent hopes that it would be a part of those lives again.

Little by little the visits dropped off as people had to get back to normal duty.

The Fleet docked at a station orbiting Triton to facilitate the remodeling of the shuttle bays into hangers for the fighters. It took one Favor to get the parts needed to do the actual work. Ken soon found it was going to take another to get the workers themselves.

He hadn't expected that. Either Lamont had left out that piece of information, or Butler wasn't as good at negotiating. He had holed up with Asch and Bon for a long meeting about the issue, but neither could come up with a better way to do the work in the time they wanted to spend.

At the moment Butler stood up on the catwalk looking down into the bay, watching the proceedings. He felt a little funny every time they cut into the deck or pulled down beams. He felt like Coy

Lamont was standing behind him saying, 'Ken! What the hell are you doing to my ship?'

But Coy was not standing anywhere. And it had wanted this done. They *needed* this done. The Fleet needed those fighters operational. Which meant the Fleet needed seventeen more pilots and gunners. Well, first things first. It was Fleet tradition to obtain ships long before they had the people to put on them. A little backwards to the way the rest of the universe operated, but then that was s.o.p. for the BlackFleet as well.

One of the things Lamont had mentioned in its notes was that the fighters were to be called *Talons*. Ah, yes, the claws of the bird. Appropriate.

"Aziza to Butler."

"Butler, here. Go."

"Sk…Captain, I have a man who wishes to speak to you. Sounds like someone wanting to join up to me. Actually he kind of talks like an officer of some sort."

Butler stared at his wristcom in amazement. Already? He had just thought about it a moment ago! If the man was a fighter pilot, Ken mused, he just might understand some of Bon's religious leanings. "Have him escorted to my office."

"*Your* office, sir?"

No, Dev, I have not taken over the Commodore's life. Just, temporarily, its job. "Yes, Lieutenant. You do remember where my quarters have always been, don't you?"

"Aye, sir. Aziza out."

Ken pushed off the railing and made his way to D deck. Once in his quarters he called Asch to inform him of the meeting.

"Would you like tea or coffee served, sir?" Asch asked, switching from Acquisitions officer to steward for a moment.

"No tea," Ken assured him. "It's not my…style. Coffee would be okay, I guess."

"Very good, sir," Ashe said approvingly.

Well, at least Butler wouldn't have to worry about accidentally over stepping the line and intruding into Coy Lamont's territory. It looked like the entire crew was out to make sure that didn't happen.

The man who came to the office did indeed have officer written all over him. He turned down the coffee and stood stiff as a rod before the desk. Frankly, Ken was a little intimidated by him.

"Major Gary Michaels, Retired, sir!" he barked out.

Okay, now he was a lot intimidated. "Well, Major Gary Michaels, Retired, I'm Captain Ken Butler, in temporary command of the BlackFleet Mercenaries. What can I do for you?"

"Sir, this station is well known for its expertise in maintaining small fighter craft."

"Yes, I am aware of that. That is why we came here to get our work done."

"Therefore it is only logical that people with interest in that area...collect here."

"I see." At least he was finally getting closer to answering the question. "And may I assume you to be one of those people?"

"Yes, sir. Thirty five years in the service of the Cortiri government training pilots."

Oh, Bon, I think I need to talk to you... "May I ask why you are no longer in the service of the etc, etc.?"

Michaels nearly succeeded in tamping out the anger on his face before answering. "I reached retirement age," he said simply.

A little too simple to let him get away with. "And retirement is always mandatory at a certain age?"

"Not, necessarily. There have been exceptions to the rule over the years."

"But not in your case."

"No, sir."

"Why?"

Michaels actually paused before speaking this time. "The reasons are somewhat personal, Captain."

"They are also somewhat necessary to obtaining a position with this Fleet, Major."

"I'm not sure I understand."

"It's just the way we do things here. Your training and background could be a great asset to us, that's true. But we hire people based on character. It's much more important in the long run. Everyone in the Fleet has told the Commodore or myself his or her Story of why they need to be with us. It goes no further than this room."

"*Need* to be with you?"

"Yes, Major. You could find a spot with a half a dozen merc outfits that use fighters that I know of. If all you want to do is fly around space. But if you want to fly around space and make a difference in the lives of the people around you...then you need to be in the BlackFleet. Heroes need only apply."

Gary Michaels looked at him like he was crazy for several minutes. He didn't say a word. But he also didn't leave. Butler just relaxed in his chair and waited for one or the other to happen.

"My request for extended service was not accepted due to the administration's belief that I was undermining the authority of the government," he finally said.

Oh. Terrific. "All by yourself? How did they think you would do that?"

"By encouraging the individuals belief in their own ...power... their own ability *as* an individual to..." he paused, groping for the right wording.

"Make a difference?" Butler suggested.

Michaels looked thoughtful at that. Again he stood without speaking for several minutes. "And here a moment ago I thought you were a bunch of quacks or zealots or something," he finally said.

"We are," Ken agreed cheerfully. "Want to be one with us?"

Michaels actually *almost* smiled. "Yes, sir. I believe I would at that."

Captain Butler stood and put out his hand. "Welcome aboard, Trainee Michaels."

Michaels was less than thrilled with the "Trainee" status, even though it was the shortest training period in the history of the Fleet. Due mainly to his ability to hand Butler an additional five pilots and two gunners. And also because Schiff agreed with Ken that it would be too awkward for the Major to be in something Walter called "boot camp" along with the very people he was hired to train and lead. What he didn't agree with was accepting all eight of the offered recruits. It seemed a little easy – even for the BlackFleet.

Major Michaels could not in fact speak for their piloting ability. But he had talked to them more than a few times while they were waiting around the shipyards for a break.

"You want me to hire people you found in a bar?" Butler asked. Of course the only person who would get the irony was lying in Sick Bay. In the end, despite Schiff's disapproval and Bon's skepticism, he hired them all. When it came time to, he added the names to the crew list.

Seventy-eight people. His thoughts traveled back to a couple of meetings many months before. 'I don't want a fleet as you mean,' Coy had said, 'I don't want tons of people tripping over themselves.' They had argued long and often about that. Lamont had insisted time and again that the BlackFleet would be no more than the original 20. One ship and 20 people to right all the wrongs in the universe.

Now it was four ships and 78 people. And, hopefully, still growing. Ken had to admit he felt a little guilty about the numbers. About winning. He would gladly go back to losing if it meant Coy Lamont was still in command.

But Butler hadn't hired all of these. Only the last few. Coy itself had upped the number of ships and crew little by little over the months. Ken had only gloated at each step, and had never considered what each change had cost Coy.

'I was never supposed to command…I was never supposed to care…'

Coy Lamont had been programmed pure and simple. The implications struck Ken suddenly. He didn't really understand how one did things like that to a human being – and was quite sure he didn't want to

know. But whether he understood it or not, Coy had lived every minute of the BlackFleet painfully breaking all of its internal rules—for months and months. And all he had done was complain.

Of course he had to admit, there was no way to support something that he didn't even know was happening. He wondered if Bon or Ceal had had any more idea than he what Lamont had been going through.

As if reading his thoughts, Ceal Byars buzzed to gain entrance. She flopped tiredly down in a chair in front of the desk and gratefully accepted his offer of coffee. But she only drank about half of it, then sat looking down into the cup. "I'm surprised you haven't joined the rest of the crew and drink nothing but tea."

He frowned. "I beg your pardon?"

"Everyone I know has switched to tea. I guess it's some sort of tribute to the commodore."

"Huh," Ken leaned back, as usual, this time propping his feet up on the desk. "I don't think anyone wants me emulating the commodore too closely right now."

She nodded agreement. "They're all taking this real hard. It w…isn't only a C.O.. Coy is the symbol of a whole new life for almost everyone in the Fleet. I told Coy once that it was our commander and not to act like our parent. But that's how everyone feels, I think." She scooted up on the edge of her chair to lean on the desk. "And that's kind of what I came to talk about. I don't know who or what Coy Lamont will be like when it wakes up."

"What do you mean?"

"You heard what it said about a subroutine?" Ken nodded. "I think it meant another personality. As a spy that would make sense. A different personality would not know what Coy did. It couldn't give away any secrets even if it wanted to."

"And you think when it comes to, this other personality will be in place?"

She gave a small shrug. "If it was supposed to come on line due to extreme duress, it would make sense. Dying would qualify as duress, I think."

Ken thought for a long time, trying to pretend he didn't understand what she meant. "You're saying that even if Coy woke up today or tomorrow, it may never command the BlackFleet again," he said much more casually than he felt.

"I'm saying it's very possible."

"And there's no way to know?"

Ceal looked back down into the coffee cup and sighed. She sighed a lot lately, Ken noted.

"A long time ago, Coy gave me a file with some of its physical modifications. That plus what it said to us is all I know. And the only way to learn more, that I can think of, is to go to Riga and ask."

Ken's feet hit the floor as he sat up abruptly. "Go to Riga? Nobody just *goes* to Riga – unless you're a customer."

"I know that, too. But it's the only place that would have any information."

Ken thought of something else. "What if ...." He had to word this right. "What if it would rather stay dead than deal with Riga?"

She nodded again. "I had thought about that. I tried to think how I would feel. I've been running from my home for quite a while now. I'm not sure even death would be drastic enough for me to want to contact them." She looked up. "But to be perfectly honest, I don't want to think about it from Coy's point of view. I want it back."

"Have you talked to Raeph about any of this, yet?"

"No. He's been pretty shook up. He seems to feel responsible somehow."

"Still? I thought we had been through that. But anyway, he and the Skipper used to talk, didn't they? Maybe he would have a better idea of what it would want us to do."

There was that sigh again. "Ken, I think we both know what it would want."

"To stay dead."

"I think it has tried before, remember? The card game?"

"Yeah, but that was before the Fleet. Before it had something to live for."

"Caring about the BlackFleet is literally what shut it down."

Ken sputtered in frustration. He hated it when he had no ammunition for a debate. Or did he? "So what if it woke up without the programming? We can't deny it the only chance it will ever have to live life without all the crap in its head running things. Besides, this is a mercenary fleet. It will have countless opportunities to die. But this may be its only chance to live."

She smiled. "Thanks for talking yourself into letting me go. You saved me a lot of trouble."

He blinked and stared at her for a minute. Then he smiled back. "Point goes to Byars. Now the only problem is time. I assume you don't want to wait too long. And the *Raven* is going to be tied up for a while with all the reconstruction and training the pilots."

"What if we transfer Coy to the *Nighthawk* and take it? The whole Fleet can't stay stuck here doing nothing for much longer. People are already starting to snap at each other. We're too used to saving worlds. We need to be busy."

"That's a possibility. Let me think on it. We'll discuss it at tomorrow's White meeting."

"Alright." She stood up. "Thank you, Captain."

Captain Butler had quite a few things to discuss at the White meeting as a matter of fact. He took a deep breath before going into the room where all the other senior officers sat. He was going to get some people mad today.

"Good morning everyone," he greeted them as usual, even though "morning" was relative fiction on a space vessel. Well, then, he reasoned, no one could tell him he was wrong.

He gave everyone the update on construction and crew. He also outlined the plan to take Coy Lamont to Riga to seek medical assistance. No one outside of Ken, Bon, Ceal and Asch really knew what had happened. The rest of the Fleet simply knew it had some sort of attack and was in a coma. Most herms came from Riga though, so no one argued with the reasoning that someone there could help. He then gathered the department reports as usual.

The next topic was what he was dreading. "Now, then, before I outline my next subject, I want a few things said up front. Number one, neither me nor anyone else will ever argue who made this Fleet. And made it work. Nothing I do now or at any other time will change that. Number two, Coy Lamont is in a coma and is incapable of running this Fleet. Number three, said Coy Lamont hired me and put me into the job of Fleet Exec knowing full well that I would assume command at such a time. Number four, I have assumed command and I intend to run this Fleet to the best of my ability. Many of my decisions will be very different than what the commodore would have done. To be blunt, get used to it. Until the time when Commodore Lamont is back in charge, I will be calling the shots. Any questions?"

There were a few sideways glances, but no one spoke for a minute.

"We know the Skipper put you in charge," Schiff broke the silence. "If you are asking for our loyalty, you've always had it."

There were other murmurs of agreement around the table. Michaels was the only outsider in all of this having never even met Coy Lamont. He had, however, heard of little else in the short time he had been with them. All those Stories Butler had mentioned. If they were true it was no wonder this commodore was so revered.

"Thank you Major," Butler nodded at Schiff. "Now for business. The first thing I am going to do is change the hiring. Going over the rosters I have noted some gaping holes that I believe we need to plug. Engineering and Medical both need more help. We still need more pilots.

"I've been thinking that some of our people might want to train for a shot at the fighters. There are several that are good pilots in other types of vessels. I'm willing to give anyone the chance that wants to cross train. But that would mean we would have to fill their current spots. We are also going to need crews to take care of thirteen fighters. And I want full time Tac Com officers for each ship. Altogether, I would like to get the Fleet to approximately two hundred people. Soon."

Another silence met all of this.

"And how are you going to do that?" Bon asked quietly. "Put out an advertisement?"

Come on, Raeph, Ken thought, I need you behind me. "I'm not going to post any notices on bar walls, no. But I am going to encourage, let's call it, word of mouth advertising. Any time we are in dock, we raise questions. Don't always wait for people to come to you. Strike up conversations. Word will get around quickly enough. Send *anyone* with potential to Captain Bon, Major Schiff or myself."

"What about command of the *Raven?*" Hendricks asked, evenly. "It looks like you're going to be a little busy." She looked at him steadily, with no apparent sarcasm or bitterness. The lack of emotion, however, was louder than words.

"I have been considering that issue as well. I would prefer not to move command staff around at this time. Everyone has forged a good working team on their ships. I don't want to interfere with that any more than I can help. I am thinking, for now, I want an Executive Officer, and I will continue technical command. If anyone has a junior officer you think would be a candidate, I will take any suggestions. Otherwise, I might hire from outside for that as well."

"An outsider flying the Skipper's ship?!" Rebel was unable to contain himself any longer.

Butler took a breath and worked hard not to respond in kind. "Every ship in this Fleet belongs to Coy Lamont," he said evenly, "And every single person in this room was once an "outsider" in case you've forgotten that. The next person I interview has as much a right to a second chance as we all did... Any other comments?" He looked them each in the eye as he went around the table. A few nods of support, a couple cool return looks. That was okay. He'd take cool over cold. Michaels, he had. Schiff had already given his word. Byars was okay. Asch would do whatever he asked. Bon he would definitely hear from, he had no doubt about that.

"Sir?" Schiff formally requested attention. "I suggest Lieutenant Tony Knepp to be considered for the position on the *Raven.*"

Heaven bless Walter Schiff two times today. Let Rebel or Hendricks argue with that! Everyone knew it was Knepp's quick thinking that had saved the troopers from certain death. He should have thought of it himself. A war hero. Lamont had even mentioned giving him some sort of commendation. Command of the flagship seemed an adequate reward.

"An excellent suggestion, Major. Asch, make a note for me to discuss it with the lieutenant soon."

"Aye, sir."

"Byars, have the commodore moved over to the *Nighthawk*. Captain Hendricks, prepare to depart as soon as possible. Report daily via direct com."

"Aye, sir."

He looked around briefly one more time. "Dismissed."

It would take the *Nighthawk* a little over twelve days to even reach Riga. According to her orders, Captain Hendricks reported in to the Fleet every morning. The tachyon transmission let the parties talk in real time despite the distance between them. But real time or not the message was the same each transmission. There was no change in the commodore.

Meanwhile, life on the *Raven* and the *Rook* centered on learning to fly the *Talons*. With the nine pilots and gunners Lamont had kept with the ships and the eight Michaels had brought in they still had nine spots to fill. Not to mention crews to take care of the ships on a regular basis. As Ken had said, he opened up the training to any current BlackFleet members who wanted to give it a try. Three men that had come on board with Drake made the list, having already had some time in similar craft. Chen Marcus had requested to stay and train when the *Nighthawk* left orbit. Butler was glad he had granted it when he saw the skill with which Marcus handled the simulator.

Michaels decided to keep the last *Talon* as his personal fighter. Which brought it down to three spots. Sweggert, Pierce, Knepp and McKinney, all having varying degrees of experience with small craft, also requested to try. What they lacked in expertise, they made up for in drive. These were some of Lamont's original recruits. Perhaps it was some of their grief, which drove them to exceed even their own expectations.

Butler took all the candidates who passed the simulator testing and divided them up into three squadrons – two to be housed on the *Raven* and one on the *Rook*. The *Rook's* squad, true to Coy's wishes would be an elite
group. The most cross-trained in the Fleet. Marcus was promoted to Flight Captain and put in charge of them. One of Michaels' finds, one Danielle Cheny, was made Flight Captain for the *Raven*. The new pilots and gunners were immediately promoted to the rank of Lieutenant.

Almost all of the candidates.

Lieutenant Tony Knepp stood in shock staring at the postings on the vidcom. His name was not even on the list. He worked hard to stay modest and humble, but in point of fact he knew he had flown rings around some who had gotten in. He was half way to finding Marcus for a little 'chat' when he was summoned to Captain Butler's quarters. He changed his direction in the corridor much easier than he changed his state of mind.

Taking a breath to prepare himself for whatever, he pushed the buzzer to announce his presence.

"Come."

Knepp went in and found the Captain busy making a pot of coffee. He waved a cup in Tony's direction. "Want some?"

"No thank you, sir."

Butler frowned at the pot. "Nobody ever seems to want my coffee." He poured himself a cup and sat down at his desk. "Sit, Lieutenant."

Knepp sat as directed.

Butler's frown was now directed at him. "I suppose you know what this is about."

What?! Tony swallowed. "I didn't make the fighter squad..?" he ventured.

The captain nodded. "Thanks to that little stunt you pulled on the derelict in the battle for the *Raven*."

He had nothing whatsoever to say to that. Stunt*? Stunt!?*

But Ken Butler carried on as if he didn't notice Knepp's stunned face. "Now on top of all that, another problem has come up as well. You see, with the Commodore on the sick list so to speak, and me in charge of things until…it returns, the *Raven* is bereft of a commander on deck. This is where you come in." Butler counted off reasons on his fingers. "Due to one- your incredible act of quick thinking and bravery which saved the lives of the entire boarding party, two – your perfect record of following orders and adapting to whatever was asked of you, three – your outstanding performance in the simulated battle sequences this week, and four – being one of the few people in this entire outfit with tactical training of any kind, I am offering you the rank of Lieutenant Commander and the post of Exec of the *Raven*."

Knepp sat and stared at him for a couple of minutes. "You have an interesting method of working up to promotions – sir," he finally told him.

Butler smiled. "I'm glad you like them. Think you can deal with my methods for awhile?"

He gave up on the modest and humble and grinned unashamedly. "It will be an honor and a privilege to serve on the bridge of the *Raven*,
sir." They both stood and shook hands. "And I think I'll take that coffee. Now that I know I'm going to have a head to drink it with."

Ceal watched out of the portal as the *Nighthawk* settled into close orbit around Riga. From up here, it looked like a perfectly normal, even attractive planet. Not the blues and greens of her native world, but pleasant just the same. Mostly reds and tans. Very little cloud cover. It was an arid planet with virtually no original life forms. Mankind had taken it over early in Beta Region's colonization due to its wealth of ores, plentiful energy and distance from other inhabited worlds.

The last reason was the real one she was sure.

This was not someplace that she ever thought she would be. As a physician, the thought of experimenting on humans just for money gave her the creeps. Except for Coy Lamont she had never met anyone who had actually been associated with the planet and its less than ethical line of work.

At that thought, she looked behind her at the still form in the medical chamber. The blinking light and soft beeping was the only indication that her commodore lived. And that was only because she had made the decision to hook it up to total life support. Glancing back at the planet below, she wondered if she had been right.

They had been in the system for four days now, waiting for a response. The trip here had been long but that had been the least of their problems. The defense net around the planet had kept them at bay for the first two days while they tried to convince someone on the other end of the com who they were and what they wanted.

The local "law enforcement", Ceal mentally snorted at the description, had finally escorted them to their present orbital position. Then came another two days of trying one lab after another attempting to find someone, anyone who could or would claim knowledge of the decades old contract.

Vennefron had tried every trick in his book to gain the information they needed before they had even left the fleet, but found every path blocked. These people worked on a very strict need-to-know basis. And evidently the BlackFleet didn't need to know.

"Bridge to Byars," Mara Hendricks' voice came over her com link startling her out of her reverie.

"Byars, go ahead."

"Ceal, I think we've made contact with the right lab this time," the captain told her.

"You're sure?"

"No, but at least they aren't outright denying it. That's probably as close as we're going to get."

This was it. "Alright, put them through." She settled in front of her vidcom and tried to look as cool and professional as possible.

The man whose image formed was white haired and gentle looking. Not at all the monster she was expecting. "This is Dr. Floyd-Scot. How may I help you?"

"Dr. Scot, my name is…" she hesitated for a split second. She usually did not go by the honorific since she had never officially graduated from the medical school she had attended. But she figured this man would not respect a mere Med-Tech. "…Dr. Ceal Byars. I have a situation here that I am hoping you can assist me with. A member of our crew has had some sort of physical breakdown and is now in a coma. It is an hermaphrodite by the name of Coy Lamont and according to the medical file I received, it may have originally come from your lab."

The man looked extremely puzzled. "From our lab? Working for a mercenary fleet? I don't believe we have done any work in that area…"

"I don't believe that was the original intent. It was on its own when it came to the BlackFleet. "

"Hmmmm." He rubbed his chin. "Most peculiar. The name means nothing, of course. Probably picked it up along the way. On its own, you say? How interesting. If I understand you correctly, it seems to be a discard – a product that was not picked up by the original contractors. But I'm not sure what it is exactly that you want from us. If you are not the original customer no sort of guarantee would be in effect."

Ceal's train of thought sputtered at that totally unexpected remark. "I'm not interested in arguing about an expired warranty," she managed, hoping she didn't look as surprised as she felt. " We would like our officer back. I need to know what caused the break down, what we can do medically now to assist recovery as well as what long term effects we can expect."

"You said you have a file. Can you send me any information that I can use to identify this particular specimen?"

Internally seething at the words "discard" and "specimen", Ceal smiled through gritted teeth. She would do what it took to get help. "Of course, Doctor. I will send it now."

She sent the information over the link to his vid. Ceal watched his expression as he read go from puzzled to shocked to almost angry.

"Is this a joke, Dr. Byars?" he asked.

She blinked in surprise. "A joke? No, sir. Why would you ask that?"

"I really don't know what you expect to gain from such a deception, but I…"

"This is not a deception!" she exclaimed in anger. "Coy Lamont is lying here in my Sick Bay and needs help. Can you or can you not help?"

He frowned even more. "In your Sick Bay? Alive?"

"Hooked up to life support, but yes."

Another, "Hmm." And then, "May I come on board your vessel and see the ...problem for myself?"

She had been secretly hoping she could get through this without personal contact, but realized it really wasn't a very realistic hope. "Perhaps that would be the easiest way to communicate. I will put you through to the captain to make arrangements." She shunted the com back to the bridge and gave them the request.

"What was all that about?" Rose Durand asked from behind her.

Ceal shook her head. " I'm not sure what he thought I was lying about. "

"I guess we'll soon find out. Are you sure you're ready to deal with these people face to face?"

"No, I'm not sure," she said honestly. "Perhaps you should do the talking. You're more professional than I am in dealing with people."

"You're more professional and ethical and anything else you can name than these so called "doctors". But I'll help any way I can. The thing you know more about is the commodore itself. I know so little of its personal history, I don't think I could answer any of their questions."

Ceal thought for only a moment. "You're right. We'll start with the file and I'll explain as much as I know from there."

Dr. Floyd-Scot stared down at Lamont in amazement. "This should not be. This should never have happened," he muttered over and over to himself as he checked readings and Ceal Byars' notes from the past few weeks.

"What exactly has happened, Doctor ?" Rose asked.

He straightened up and looked at her. And then at Ceal standing just behind her. "I can only tell you what should have happened. This product was designed to be an espionage tool."

"A spy, yes," Ceal interjected, trying to promote Coy from tool to human.

"Alright, a spy. As such it had very specific programming and guidelines. It was supposed to remain aloof, unattached, an information gatherer. Even though the project was terminated and it was on its own, as you say, the programming should have remained intact. Yet you say it was an officer? That should not have been possible. That sort of initiative just wasn't in the design."

"What do we do *now*?" Ceal asked for not the first time.

"If it were me, I'd simply pull the plug." Both women stared at him in utter horror. "This is not a breakdown as you put it, Dr. Byars. It should have self destructed long ago at the first sign of deviation from its programming. We do not allow shoddy work to be connected to our business."

"This is not shoddy work!" Ceal exploded. "This is our commander! How do we undo this self destruct?"

"You can't undo a self destruct. The only reason it has a heartbeat is because you plugged it into your machines. If you want to be humane, unplug it and get it over with."

Neither BlackFleet medical officer could think of anything short of invectives to say in answer to that. No one said anything while they regrouped their thoughts.

"You filthy bastard," came a voice that could only be described as a growl. They turned and saw Mara Hendricks standing in the door. She, it seemed had no objection to invectives. "If it defeated your program enough to become the best damn commander in space, it can bloody well defeat it enough to wake up. Now, you can do something to help or you can go back down to your cesspit and hope I don't blow you and your so-called lab to hell."

Dr. Scot looked quite flustered at all of this. "Really, Captain, insults are not necessary. I'm not sure what you want me to do. I can't change something that was put into effect years ago."

Ceal sat down on a stool. "So there's really nothing to do. No way to help."

The Rigan doctor rubbed his chin for a moment. "I suppose your captain could be right. If the program is degraded to this point anything is possible. There might be one thing I could do for you. I can't do anything about whether it wakes up or not, or what mental state it will be in. But I can surmise that it could be in a great deal of physical discomfort due to the stresses its body underwent during the destruct sequence. Normal medication does not have much effect on our constructs, but I could give you something that would. I am sorry but that is the extent that I can be of use to you."

Ceal nodded numbly.

"Thank you, Doctor," Rose managed a civil tone. "We would appreciate it."

After they returned their "guest" and received the medication, they and their escort, left orbit as soon as possible. No one wanted to make the next report to the *Raven.* The twelve day journey back was going to be much more somber than the hopeful trip out had been.

Butler walked into his cabin, locking the door behind him. He stood in the dark and heaved a great sigh. "I hate you, Coy Lamont," he said angrily to the empty air. But the air didn't believe it any more than he did. What he did hate was the Lamont sized hole in his life.

After a minute or two he let the lights come up partway. Tiredly he went over to the cabinet and started some coffee. Opening a door to get a cup, he caught sight of a bottle in the back of the shelf.

He didn't want coffee. Coffee woke you up, kept you going. He would rather stop for a while.

Just a little while.

He was still looking at the bottle when his wrist com beeped. "Michaels to Butler."

He closed the cabinet door.

"Butler here. Go ahead."

Ken had barely gotten the command to open his door out of his mouth when Michaels marched in and came to attention. Butler was working at overcoming his initial impression of the man and remembering that he, in fact, was the senior officer and the Major's commander. Not something the Major was particularly bothered with.

"Sir, I need to train these recruits somewhere else." He announced as soon as his curt salute had been acknowledged.

"That's what I hate about you, Gary, you always beat around the bush." Ken as usual used his sarcasm to buy a few more moments of time to gather his thoughts. Michaels, also as usual, did not respond. "All right, Major, take it from the top and let me in on what we're talking about."

"Sir, with the latest recruits the *Talon* unit is complete. What the fighter crews need now is intensive training. In the past I would take new recruits to one of our training camps for several months. What can I do that would be equivalent?"

"Months? You want the best defense the Fleet has offline for months?"

"*Sir*, they won't be the best defense anyone has if they don't get the training."

Butler decided he understood why there were times when Coy Lamont would ban the use of any more 'sirs' in a conversation. He thought about the request. Actually, now with the *Nighthawk* gone, and the remodeling of the *Raven* and the *Rook*, the whole Fleet was pretty much off line. It was as good a time as any to accomplish what Michaels wanted.

"Check with Vennefron to see what is close that would do. Preferably in this quadrant. And I want it numbered in weeks, not months."

Major Michaels snapped off one of his perfect salutes. "Yes, sir. Thank you, sir." As he wheeled and exited, Butler was thoroughly convinced the last two 'sirs' were simply to annoy him.

"Com to Butler."

"Butler. Go ahead."

"Sir, message from the *Nighthawk*."

Butler's mood brightened instantly. They must have news from Riga by now. "Send it down, Dev." A few seconds later, the holo-image of Ceal Byars appeared on his desk com. "Hey, Ceal! What..?" His words and mood died when he saw her face. "What happened?"

"They're monsters!" her voice was shaking with anger.

"What are you talking about? They couldn't help?"

"Help?! They told me to pull the plug and be done with it! They talked about Coy as if it were some sort of fungus specimen or something. They...they didn't care at all."

She was so upset, Ken didn't even want to ask the next question, for fear of the answer. "So, what's the Skipper's status now?"

Ceal took a breath to calm down. "No change. No change at all. It might as well be in stasis." Neither said anything for a minute or two. "How's the fleet?" she finally asked.

"Bon is still making a mess down in the bay. He hasn't even started on the *Rook*, yet. Michaels wants to take the *Talons* somewhere to train," he paused. "Everybody is pretty busy, except me."

She managed to look him in the eye. "You, know, Ken..."

"Yeah, I do," he cut her off. "Someday, we might have to make permanent plans, but not yet."

"All right. I'll make regular reports on the way back."

He nodded. "Talk to you then. *Raven* out."

The image faded, but Ken kept looking at the place where her face had been. She was right, of course. At some point, they were going to have to grow up...but not yet.

* * * * *

The squadron of *Talons* flew gracefully through space having been dropped off of the transport ship that had ferried them. They were coming swiftly into the Avalon system where they would be based for their weeks, not months, of training.

Avalon was established toward the end of the second wave of expansion in the Beta region. Because it was along one of the main trade routes, and due to its mineral-rich soil, it had flourished very quickly. A large, bristling spaceport, and an extensive orbital facility had grown up to service the planet's commerce.

The *Talons* approached the orbital facility, slowing at a rate that would allow them to dock. Lieutenant Anthony Smith carefully piloted his *Talon* directly in the glide path provided by his helmet display. Smith had been selected as the third of the BlackFleet's brand new *Talon* fighter squadron commanders. Though designated as a lieutenant, he would still be in charge of three other fighter crews, and he was looking forward to the job.

He watched the station growing larger in his view with a sense of real excitement. They were here at last, finally getting to the difficult, but necessary work of group tactical training.

He knew that Major Michaels intended to do this the right way from the beginning, and he also knew it would take a lot of work to make them a cohesive fighting unit. Smith shrugged off that thought and refocused his thinking as his fighter came in closer to the huge station.

"BlackFleet fighter corps, on programmed approach to docking bay 37," the Major called to the Traffic Controller at Stareye, Avalon's orbital platform.

"We show you on proper approach," the Traffic Controller replied. "Welcome to Stareye."

The thirteen *Talon* fighter craft, and the single shuttle accompanying them, entered the cavernous docking area. As the area repressurized, the BlackFleet crewmembers emerged.

Maj. Gary Michaels strolled over to his fighter crew as they gathered together and stood at attention.

Smith liked the Major. Everybody did. Despite his gruff manner. He expected the best, because he truly believed, deep down that you had it in you. Smith stood at parade rest, along with the other twenty-three pilots and gunners, while Michaels looked them over.

"You may be the sorriest raw recruits this 'Fleet has, but it's time to turn you schoolgirls into a crack fighter corps. Yes, that's right, as of now, the training wheels come off. You will be going through the most intensive seven weeks of your lives. Don't think I'm

bluffing. I don't care if you've been in sixty-five different navies, mi-
litias, or air corps, you are in for something new. We are going to become an effective arm of the 'Fleet. That means, we've got to make up
in skill what we lack in numbers. That's the only way this thing is
gonna work. So, are you ready?"

"Yes, sir!" Smith heard himself reply with the others.

"That sounded weak. I asked , ARE YOU READY?"

"YES SIR!"

Butler hadn't been exaggerating much to Byars. He really
didn't have a whole lot to do. He had hired a couple of people, that he
hoped would turn out to be good Execs for the other ships, looked
over Bon's shoulder until the engineer growled at him, listened to Michael's meticulous daily reports and held staff meetings with what senior staff was still here. So now, rather than look bored and useless to
the crew, Ken decided to go bother Rebel over on the *Rook.*

Adrian Rebel was madly in love with his ugly little ship, and
actually enjoyed showing her off. It seemed to entertain him greatly
that Ken had never learned the magic sequence of switch flips that
turned the ordinary "freighter" into a warship. So he let himself be
taught, even though he figured half of Rebel's enthusiasm was the
commander's way of dealing with the loss of Lamont.

Schiff had wandered up to the bridge partway through the les-
son and was leaning on the doorframe into the tiny tactical room. And
that's where the three of them were when they got the call from
Vennefron.

"A mayday, sir!"

Butler almost laughed. They were not in the best shape themselves right now, either, were they? But he kept the thought to himself.
"Who and where, Lieutenant?"

"From Victoria, sir. I'll put you through," and before Ken
could object, Venn had connected him to a representative of the planet.

The man on the other end was a little dismayed at finding
Commodore Lamont unavailable, but was more than willing to explain
the situation to Butler. "Our Vice President was traveling home from a
routine diplomatic trip when his ship was attacked. All hands were
lost, but we believe that the Vice President was safely launched away
from the battle in an escape pod."

While he was talking, Rebel pulled up the relevant area on his
holo-field. "Where exactly did he launch?"

The rep from Victoria gave him the best information they had, but admitted it was not, in fact, exact. Rebel plugged it in anyway and pointed at the field. "We could be there in a couple of days if he can hold out," he told Butler.

Ken stared at him. "With what?"

"Captain?" the rep's voice sounded a little concerned.

"Just a moment, please," Ken said to him and cut the audio. "Now then," he turned back to Rebel, "What are you talking about?"

Rebel didn't answer. He merely straightened up and crossed his arms.

Schiff said it for him. "We're the BlackFleet."

Butler stared at both of them. A dozen objections came to mind. They were down by half of the fleet, all of the *Talons*, and oh, yes, the Fleet commander. But even while the objections raced through his mind they were followed by answers. The BlackFleet used to do it with only one ship. Of course it was the *Raven*, not the *Rook*. But they did still have the *Blackbird*. And the shuttles. And Rebel and Schiff were still glaring at him.

With a mental sigh, Captain Butler turned the audio back on.

"We're on it, sir. Send us every scrap of information you have." He switched the transmission back to Vennefron to actually collect said information, and raised his wristcom. "Butler to Drake."

"Drake. Go ahead."

"Get the *'Bird* ready to fly. We have a job to do."

To his credit, there was not a split second's hesitation. "Aye, aye, sir!"

Butler looked back at the two in front of him. "I'm going to explain things to Bon and Knepp. Then it's best speed."

"Aye, aye, sir," Rebel said to Butler, but gave Schiff a sideways grin. Schiff didn't *quite* wink back.

Butler paused before dashing out. "You two are dangerous together, you know?"

Rebel saluted. "Yes, sir. Thank you, sir."

The trip took just under two days. During which time they found out that the escape pod had more than likely fallen into an asteroid field. ' *This is beginning to sound way too much like an academy exam,*' Ken thought to himself. It did, in fact remind him of a couple of drills he had had back when he was a cadet. Most of which he passed, come to think of it. That little boost in confidence kept him from whining about how useful the *Talons* would have been and get down to planning their strategy.

The plan was for the *Rook* and the *Blackbird* to circle the outside of the asteroids, using their scanners to try and pick up the escape pod. The two shuttles they had would be flying through the field doing the same. The good thing was that the field was not overly large. The bad thing was that it was very high in ore content, which played havoc with their scanners.

This was going to be much more slow and tedious than Ken had first envisioned. The information from Victoria had included exactly how much air and supplies were in the escape pod. Those numbers kept ticking down in the back of Ken's mind as the search went on.

"Sir!" Rebel called from the tac room.

"You've got something?" Butler asked hopefully, jogging in from the bridge to join him.

Instead of answering directly, Rebel pointed to the holo-field. "Look here, sir. Every ship has had a higher metallic reading from this area. The ore is still making it impossible to pinpoint, but it's definitely more concentrated here than anything else we've picked up."

"Hmm," Butler scowled as he thought. "Why doesn't he just turn on his beacon?" As soon as the words were out of his mouth, an alarm went off.

"Incoming!" Bard called from Weapons station on the bridge.

"I guess that would be why," Rebel answered Butler's question before shouting. "Shields at full! What have we got coming?" What was coming was evidently a low powered warning shot, for it bumped harmlessly against the shielding.

Ken let Rebel deal with the hostiles for a moment while he continued to figure out the rescue. "Butler to Schiff."

"Schiff, go ahead," came the answer from one of the shuttles.

"Suit up. Your troopers are going to have to go out and fine-tune this search after all. I'm sending you the most likely area to check. And by the way, it seems like we're not the only ones looking for this guy." The possibility of an asteroid by asteroid search had come up, and Schiff and his people were prepared.

"Understood. Schiff out."

"We're being hailed," Com announced.

"In here," Butler told him.

In a second a face came on the tac room vid. "Out of our way, freighter. You can haul your ore later. We got business here."

Given the *Rook's* appearance, the mistake was understandable. For a moment, Butler wondered whether keeping up the deception

would buy them any time. Not a lot, considering the *Blackbird* would be joining
in quickly if the fighting got real. But it might confuse them for a little longer, and give Schiff a better chance at being undetected.

"Well, actually, we have business here, too," Butler responded. "And I would appreciate it if you didn't get in *our* way."

The other man laughed. "And what exactly are you going to do? Throw rocks at us?"

Butler muffled the audio just long enough to shout at Rebel, "Adrian, you and Drake pick a point as far away from the search area as you can and rendezvous to 'protect' it."

"And keep them away from Schiff. Got it."

He turned the audio back on. "I'm sorry, can you repeat…"

"Cut the clownin'," the man said angrily. "If you won't move on your own, then we'll help you." The vid went blank.

"He's firing!" Bard told them.

The *Rook's* bridge was jarred only slightly as shields absorbed their opponent's blast.

"Throw a rock at him," Butler said, coldly.

Bard touched three buttons on his panel simultaneously. The large, shielded door on the bow of the armed freighter slid open. Targeting systems locked. And the *Rook's* eight cannons spat energy at the destroyer that had sent the 'warning.' The enemy ship's main front shields flashed, flickered and died.

"Weren't expecting that, were you?" Ken sneered.

The destroyer spun its damaged shielding away from the *Rook*, but its companion craft darted forward.

"Three scout-class ships advancing rapidly!" Bard called from the bridge.

"I see 'em. So we tag 'em Beta, Delta and Gamma," Butler said, closely watching the holo-display in the tac room. His mind kicked into 'academy-exam' overdrive. "Rebel, hold on the misdirection. Stay on that Alpha ship. Give them a heavy broadside with all guns when we're in range. Drake, focus fire on the Beta ship and run some interference for us."

"Aye, sir," came the reply from the *Blackbird*. The destroyer continued to distance itself from the *Rook*, keeping its still-functional rear shields toward her. Jordan, the *Rook's* young pilot, continued to follow it, trying to loop around the approaching scout ships. And then the *Blackbird* came charging in, firing all her guns at the foremost scout ship. The enemy craft twisted and darted, attempting to break away from the new source of fire, but stay in firing range on the freighter.

Ken listened in approval to Drake's steady voice giving commands over the tac com.

"Stay with him, keep firing!"

The *Blackbird* looped and turned, mirroring the scout ship's evasions as it closed in. The *'Bird's* well-timed entry had its effect. The lead scout ship left a more than big enough hole in the maneuver for the *Rook* to charge right through in its pursuit of the destroyer.

"Back in range of the lead ship," Bard called.

"Fire port broadside cannons," Rebel ordered.

This time, the *Rook's* guns hammered at a point on the upper surface of the destroyer, severely weakening shield power in that area. Although the *Blackbird* was keeping one of them quite busy, the two remaining scout ships had turned to follow the *Rook*.

Now, weakened shield power came back up on the bow of the destroyer, and it turned back to fire upon the *Rook*.

The armed freighter shook violently.

"Multiple hits on port, bow and stern shields," Bard reported. "Shield power down overall 38 percent."

"Take us back to the 'protection' coordinates Adrian," Ken ordered. "Drake, follow us and prepare to execute Firing Maneuver Twelve." Both Rebel and Drake signaled agreement, and the two BlackFleet craft knifed in the same direction, firing back at their attackers. They wheeled through the asteroid field, trading shots with the enemy ships, and again drawing them in the opposite direction from Schiff and his team.

"Power down all shuttle systems," Schiff ordered. He stood by the rear hatch, fully suited up in the trooper's space armor. Lights dimmed within the shuttle and the ship itself slid to a stop behind a large asteroid.

"Depressurize cabin and open the hatch. Tight beam transmissions only," the Major added.

When this was done, six troopers from each of the two shuttles leapt into space. They touched off their thruster packs, and headed off in pairs to continue the search.

"Lead ship detaching two shuttles," Bard reported. Sure enough, Butler saw on the tac holo as two small blips left the destroyer.

"Leave them for now," Ken ordered. "They'll be looking in the wrong area anyway. But let me know the second they start to head in Schiff's direction."

"Aye, sir."

"Execute Maneuver Twelve, targets Beta and Gamma." Butler commanded. Suddenly, the *Rook* and *Blackbird* veered off in completely opposite directions. One of the scout ships veered to follow the yacht, while the other three ships followed the freighter. The tac room shook and shook again as the *Rook's* shields were battered.

"Shield power on the port side down 70 percent," Bard reported. "Stern shields down by 76 percent. Bow shielding down 47 percent."

"Reinforce port and stern shields with all energy reserves," Rebel ordered. "And present our starboard only to the destroyer." The pilot officer quickly rolled the ship to comply.

Then, exactly twenty-five seconds after the initial order, both BlackFleet ships turned sharply back to head directly at one another again. And in that twenty-five seconds of approach time, in which one of the scouts had been drawn temporarily outside the fight, both BlackFleet ships pounded mercilessly on the shielding of the other two scout craft. The shielding on one of them ebbed to a dangerously low level on the icon in the tac room. The other showed that its shields had completely fallen. It began trying to move away from the fight.

"Rebel, don't let that one get away!" Ken ordered.

"Bard, target their engines with the forward turret!" Adrian barked.

The *Rook's* guns fired once more, and just before the scout moved out of weapons range, Bard tagged it. It spouted flame from damaged engines and began tumbling helplessly. But the third one rejoined the fight, firing heavily on the dwindling rear shields of the *Rook*. Meanwhile, the destroyer was trying to loop around the freighter to get a better shot at its more weakened shield areas. Jordan twisted and turned the ship madly to deny the shot.

"Drake, link up with us, maneuver four, portside," Ken said into the tac room link.

"Aye, captain," the *Blackbird* commander replied.

In a now time-honored BlackFleet ship maneuver, the *'Bird* sidled up to the *Rook's* shield-damaged port side and stayed there, even through the *Rook's* evasive maneuvering, acting as both a shield and an extra set of guns.

"Rebel, Drake, target Delta," Ken said. "Drake, prepare to detach; reciprocal course, on my order." Butler barked out the orders with a calmness he didn't feel. The *Rook's* shields were dropping fast, despite all that Rebel was doing to reinforce them. And the *Blackbird's* shields, though amazing for a craft her size, were dropping too. This had better work.

"Major! I've got something!" Sren Erhardt's voice came over Schiff's helmet. "High metal reading...minimal power output...it's gotta be the pod!"

"Good work, Lieutenant. Team, hold positions while we verify. Shuttle One, stand by."

"Standing by."

Schiff maneuvered over to the rock Erhardt and Rachel Deszell were hovering near. Sure enough, the silver form of the escape pod was wedged into a crevice of the small asteroid. There was a round port set into the hatch, which Schiff peered into. The dim interior lighting showed a man in a spacesuit, although his helmet was still clamped into its holder on the wall.

"Mr. Vice President?" Schiff used his short range transmitter. The man in the pod nodded warily. "I am Major Walter Schiff of the BlackFleet Mercenaries. We have been commissioned by the government of Victoria to bring you home."

The Vice President closed his eyes in a brief display of gratitude, indicating that he heard and understood. His lips were moving, but nothing came over Schiff's receivers.

"Sir, I am not receiving you. Can you hear me clearly?"

The man nodded again.

"Put on your helmet. We will open the hatch and escort you with our thrusters to a waiting shuttle. Understood?"

The man nodded again and reached for the helmet.

"Shuttle One, pick up at our location. Shuttle Two..."

"We have company!" Liz Gressel announced. "Armed enemy shuttle, heading our way..."

"Target Delta, execute!" Butler ordered.

Both ships concentrated fire on the scout ship directly ahead of them, leaving off firing at the destroyer completely for a few seconds. The scout's shield power dropped quickly.

Butler stared at the tac display as the icons representing his ships and those of his enemies danced around one another. And as the destroyer continued trying to slip around for advantage, the moment came that Ken had been waiting for.

"*Blackbird*, detach! Rebel hit that sucker's topside shields!"

The *Blackbird*, with its greater speed and maneuverability blasted ahead of the freighter to take another shot at the scout ship ahead of them. The scout ship's shields failed completely. Then the '*Bird* performed an 'overhead' loop that sent it straight back at the scout ship astern of them, firing as it went. It scored a lucky hit on a weakened portion of that scout's shields with its first shot, and that enemy craft went into wild evasive maneuvers while the *Blackbird* pursued it.

At the same moment, the *Rook* opened fire once more on the destroyer. Although the enemy ship had reinforced its front shields, they had never managed to do so with the already weakened shields covering her top surface. And in their attempt to jockey into position on the *Rook*, they had just exposed their own weakest shield area again for the first time in several minutes.

Ken didn't miss it. Neither did Bard.

Starboard broadsides and the forward turret hit the destroyer's weakened shield area with perfect precision. Its shields went out as quickly and efficiently as if they'd been turned off by a switch. Another three rapid shots tore into her unprotected hull. She belched flame and her engines abruptly went out. Coasting and on fire, her commander came back on the tac room com.

"You're the BlackFleet, aren't you?"

Butler's smile was anything but friendly. "As a matter of fact we are. And you are..?"

"Go to hell," was the reply before going blank.

"Sore loser," Ken mumbled.

"Sir! Enemy shuttle heading Schiff's way!" Bard called.

Drake, still tied into the tac com, heard it and answered. "On it!" he said and sped his ship in the direction of the rescue efforts.

Schiff looked up to see the approaching threat on the scanner inside his helmet. The scout craft had apparently picked up some energy emission from them somehow, although they'd been very careful not to leak much. It seemed to be heading right for them.

"Schiff to Butler..." he began on the tight beam frequency. "Requesting assistance."

"Already on the way," Butler replied. "Hold on."

"Copy." Then to the troopers, "All squads, take immediate cover. Hostiles en route."

"Roger," came a dozen replies.

Schiff saw Erhardt and Dezell quickly jet to a large outcropping in the face of the asteroid, and hide behind it. Schiff found a large crevice and hustled himself and the V.P. inside. Scanning his helmet display again
he found the reason for their enemies' sudden interest. The escape pod was now transmitting a distress beacon.

"Great", he thought to himself. "Knew this was goin' too smooth."

The scanner image blurred in Schiff's display, then faded altogether as the enemy shuttle passed behind a clump of heavily packed asteroids. When it emerged once more, it was right on top of them. The shuttle came to an abrupt stop directly above the escape pod. Schiff took note of the cannon it sported in its nose.

The Major pushed the Vice President behind him in the crevice, and pulled out his plasma weapon . If the enemy happened to notice where they were, maybe he could protect the VP until help arrived. Maybe.

The shuttle touched off its maneuvering thrusters and edged lower, coming very close to the empty pod. It seemed to hover there for just a moment, then swivelled to face the crevice where Schiff was hidden. For a moment, time seemed to stop as he stared into the cannon.

Suddenly, the shuttle turned to face the oncoming *Blackbird*. The *'Bird's* forward cannons smashed into its lesser shielding, and tore it to pieces. The flaming debris scattered in all directions as the sleek black yacht soared past.

The Major emerged as the *Blackbird* circled back making sure that the troopers were all okay.

"Schiff to Butler," he called.

"Butler, go ahead."

"Objective accomplished. The VP is alive and well. Returning to shuttle… And thank you Commander Drake, for the assist."

"Good work, Major. Good work all around. See you at rendezvous."

Captain Butler read the document once more. Some 'customers' gave a token to represent their obligation to return a Favor. Others gave their signature and still others simply their word and a handshake. Victoria, it seemed, liked to do things more formally. That was fine with him. Whatever made them happy.

He laid the old fashioned paper on his desk, picked up a glass that was sitting there, and leaned back in his chair. "For you, Coy Lamont," he toasted quietly, "Nevermore," and took a drink.

"Durand to Byars!!" the excited voice woke Ceal from a fitful sleep.

Shaking herself awake, she lifted the wrist com to her face. "Byars. Go."

"You need to come down here, Ceal," Rose's voice was breathless.

Ceal could only imagine the worst. She threw her legs out of bed and slipped on shoes. "I'm on the way." She had started sleeping in her work out clothes lately to be ready to run to Sick Bay on a moment's notice. Like this. Her cabin was not far away but even so she made it in record time. "Open!" she commanded the door and skidded into the main exam room.

Rose was standing next to Coy's bed, with her back to the door. She turned around and at first all Ceal could see was her glistening eyes. And then she saw the smile. "Look," she almost whispered and stepped aside.

Coy was no longer lying flat on its back. It was turned on its side, legs slightly drawn up. Its breathing was slow and deep. And on its own.

"When..?" she began.

Rose knew what she was going to ask. "I was just about to do my hourly check and the monitor alarms went off. It's so quiet in here all the time it just about gave me a heart attack. I ran in here and this is what I found. I checked the oxygen first and it's breathing on its own! I've got the rest of the bed set up on back up, just in case."

Ceal went over to the side of the bed. She automatically looked at all the read outs, just as she had been doing for weeks now. Then she looked down at the sleeping form. She knew it was too soon, but she felt like she couldn't wait to find out. Her stomach twitched with nervousness as she said softly. "Coy?"

There was no response.

"Coy?" she said just a tiny bit louder.

"Mmmm," came the groggy reply.

Ceal's knees buckled in sheer relief and she sat abruptly on the stool at the bedside.

"We should let it sleep for awhile," Dr. Durand said reasonably.

She nodded. "You're right, of course." She looked up, returning Rose' grin. "That would be the doctorly thing to do."

Coy stirred and her attention was immediately riveted. "Ceal?" the word came out slowly and a little slurred.

"Yeah, I'm here."

Coy opened its eyes and stared at her for a few seconds. Then it focused on the ceiling beyond her. "I'm on the *Nighthawk*."

Ceal blinked in shock. Half of the time she didn't know where she was when she woke up in the morning. It had taken a few days to adjust to seeing her cabin here instead of her usual one on the *Raven*. To wake up from a coma and immediately recognize the *ceiling* of a ship! Memory was not going to be problem. "Yes." She answered.

Its eyes shut again. "And I feel like hell."

Her grin changed to a more sympathetic smile. "I expect so. Being dead for several weeks will do that to a person."

It opened them again, momentarily puzzled. "Wha...?" Then the puzzled look it had was gone. "Oh, yeah, that." The puzzled look came back. "So why am I talking to you?"

"We haven't figured that one out yet. Our current theory is that you're just too stubborn to go down that easily."

It sighed. "It doesn't feel that easily. It feels like....I don't know what it feels like. Everything hurts."

Happy to be able to do something positive at long last, Ceal picked up the hypo. "I can help with that part at least."

Coy frowned at her. "You know those don't work on me."

"This one will. It was made for you." She checked the calibration. "That's why you're on the *Nighthawk*." She reached for its arm. "We went to Riga..."

Coy slapped the hypo out of her hand. "No!" it cried, then collapsed with the effort of the sudden movement.

Rose stepped up closer and put her hand on Coy's other arm in gentle restraint while Ceal leaned over to pick up the instrument off of the floor. "I know what you're thinking, Commodore. We didn't trust them either. But every test we did came out all right."

"No," it repeated wearily. "I want nothing to do with anything from there."

"Okay," Ceal soothed. "I'm sorry. Rest for now. It's trite, but it's probably the best medicine for you right now anyway."

It nodded. And settled into the pillow in a futile attempt to get more comfortable. The two doctors watched it for a few more moments, then by mutual if unspoken agreement, turned to go into the lab section of Sick Bay.

"I'll need to talk to Butler as soon as possible," the commodore called weakly after them.

"We'll need to rendezvous with the Fleet first if you want face to face. But we can talk about vid com in the morning."

Coy nodded again, and fell asleep.

When it woke the next time, Rose Durand was sitting on the stool. "Good morning. How are you feeling?" she asked in her best bedside manner voice.

Coy mentally inventoried itself. Its muscles still ached, it was stiff all over, felt nauseous, and its head hurt like crazy.

"Better," it lied.

"Good," she acknowledged the answer while not believing it for a moment. " We did do some more tests on that medication, to try to ease
your fears. We did every test we could think of, and even invented a few just for the occasion. We compared it to your original file, to your former baseline record, to your present condition, everything we could."

Coy frowned. "And you found I'm being paranoid."

"And we found you were right," Rose took a breath. "If we had given it to you…"

"If *I* had given it to you, you would be very dead." Ceal came into the room. Her face was pale and her eyes were red.

Coy looked away. It took a long breath, then let it out. "I know they weren't my parents, but they were my creators. I wonder how many times they will kill me?" It looked at Ceal's distraught face. "And at the expense of my own friends. That's more unforgivable than the rest. It's too bad you had to deal with them at all." It gave a small smile. "But I appreciate the effort. This was a long way to come for …"

"Don't you dare say 'for one person'," Ceal let mock anger drive away her grief and guilt for now. "After everything you've done for everyone in this Fleet. You should have seen them, Commodore. I think every single person came to Sick Bay at one time or another. And they left you…things."

Coy's brows drew down. "Things?"

Rose got up and went over to a rolling table. She pushed it up next to the bed. " We brought them for you to see. Pieces of themselves, we figured. Connections to you."

Coy looked in amazement at the collection of items. It picked them up one by one and studied each. Smiles, small shakes of the head and even a tear or two accompanied the study. It knew. Looking at each item, it knew who had brought each one and why. They were right. They were all connected

Ceal pointed to the chess piece. "It started with this one."

"Ah, Ben. He did so want a rematch."

Rose blinked in surprise. "You know who they came from?"

Coy nodded. "Like you said. Points of connection. I tried to forge them with everyone." It looked apologetically at her. "Except for you. I wronged you, Rose. I'm sorry."

"Commodore, you don't have to…"

"Yes, I do. I avoided you purposely. It was just too painful thinking about the whole disaster where we met. I lost so much of myself there. But it was wrong to punish you for my mistakes. Maybe we can start all over again."

She smiled. "Thank you, Commodore. Maybe we can at that." She nodded at the table of items. "You know, I tried to think of something to put there to show what you did for me. You freed me from slavery. I couldn't think of a single thing to represent that."

"So you know everybody's gifts?" Ceal echoed Rose's question.

Coy looked at the half of a sandwich sealed forever in plastic. "Yes, Ceal. I do.

Butler walked into Sick Bay not knowing what he was going to find. As soon as the *Nighthawk* had rendezvoused with the *Raven*, Ceal had said that Lamont was awake and wanting to see him. More than that she wouldn't tell, saying that she didn't want to bias his expectations. Preparation was not biasing he had told her. To no avail.

The Sick Bay door hissed shut behind him, but the person on the bed didn't respond to the noise. The bed was set up in a reclining position, which was better than the flat on its back way Ken had seen it last. It was also out of the formless gray pajamas from before and wearing a standard Fleet issue black T-shirt. Which only accentuated the paleness of its skin. Its body seemed so much thinner and its eyes were underscored by dark rings. Its eyes were also closed.

Ken was deciding between shuffling his feet and clearing his throat, and had just about chosen the throat clearing, when Coy's eyes opened. It looked at him blankly. *"Oh, great,"* he thought. *"Ceal was right about its memory…"*

"Hello, Captain, been having fun with my fleet?" it said quietly, interrupting his inner monologue, and changing his opinion.

"Hello, yourself, Skipper," he grinned. "You look….alive."

Coy snorted. "So I've been told." It waved weakly at a stool near the bed. "Sit."

He sat. And didn't have a clue what to say next.

"I've read all your briefs and reports. I believe the last one was from day before yesterday. I assume nothing has changed since then?"

"The only change is I have Michaels' newest report from the training."

Coy nodded. "I gather this Major Michaels was quite a find."

"Yes, he was." Which brought up the whole recruitment issue.

"And the fighters he brought in. Your notes indicated they were working out as well." Coy settled back against the pillow and closed its eyes again.

"Michaels has reported some egos bumping into each other during their training, but that's pretty normal for fighter pilots. In fact I think it's a prerequisite for the job. Having an ego, that is." He paused and searched for words. "Sir, about the hiring I've done…"

"There are still some holes you plan on filling?"

He took a breath. Even he knew this was not the time or place for arguments. But it did ask. "We need more support structure in every department, yes. "

To his surprise, Coy nodded again. "It will be strange, though, having to get to know members of the Fleet. But putting Knepp on the bridge, that was a great idea. I can just hear Walter suggesting it. You were right to go with it. You certainly needed an Exec under the circumstances."

"*Every* ship needs an Exec. In fact I just hired a couple of people that I'm hoping will be able to fill those slots on the Rook and Nighthawk…When they get done with their basic training I was going to test them more specifically for officer qualifications." Ken paused for a second. "I, ah, know it's not exactly how you did it…"

"You were the one in charge."

"And now?"

Lamont opened its eyes again, but looked at the ceiling a moment before focusing back on Butler. "I've been thinking about that. You seem to have a pretty good handle on the nuts and bolts end of things. I'm thinking seriously about leaving you both where you are for now and concentrating more on the Intelligence end with Vennefron, myself. I'm supposed to be good at that sort of thing. Tailor made in fact if I understand things correctly now."

"Now? You didn't before?"

"I always knew that I was a commissioned product. And I knew that the contract had fallen through. That's why I left Riga in the first place – not exactly with their permission, by the way. But the extent of the programming," it paused and sighed, "I never knew all of it until the end. It was like a cascade of information. Or a high speed download. I take it someone thought I had a right to know why I was dying. The destruct sequence triggered the cascade."

"They *told* you they were killing you?"

"They told me..." Coy paused, trying to put into words all the information. "I knew that I had not fulfilled my...purpose. I had been designed for a specific use and I was not doing it."

"Then why didn't you destruct when your, what did you call it, contract fell through?"

Coy hadn't considered that. "I don't know."

Ken shook his head. "Must be weird to think the people that went to all the trouble to make you would kill you."

"I'm not the only member of the BlackFleet to have problems with 'family', And like you said, I am alive. Although not nearly up to speed. Which takes me back to running Intelligence for a while. I can do that sitting down a lot easier than I can run the bridge or Tac Room. Even now, and don't tell Ceal, I'm working on some ideas from memory. That at least is still intact." It closed its eyes again. "It's going to be a little while, Ken, if even talking to you wears me out."

"Skipper, Tony and I can hold the fort for as long as you need us to," he took Coy's weariness as his cue to leave and stood up. "I'll see that you get the updated reports." Coy nodded its thanks with eyes still closed. "Oh, and, Commodore?" Coy opened its eyes. "Welcome back."

Chapter Seven

When the *Talon* pilots received the word that Commodore Lamont was alive and doing well, the Elite Corps had celebrated long into the night. Michaels, though not actually participating in the party, watched in wonder. He had often had senior officers that he had admired and a few he had liked. But he had never in his career ever found someone who had inspired the kind of affection and loyalty he was seeing. The night was filled with toasts to "Remember the time when the Skipper said…" and "…and when it said I was in, I couldn't believe it!" or "No one ever took me seriously before the Skipper…"

Morning, however brought them all back to reality.

The BlackFleet fighter corps now found itself in the classroom. A tough classroom. The Major threw a barrage of strategies, simulations, exercises, pop quizzes, and training vids at them for 12 hours each day. The entire corps felt as if their brains would burst, if called upon to recite one more stratagem, or to memorize one more set of attack codes. No one more so than the squadron commanders, who had to know everything that the pilots beneath them were being trained in, plus all the command instruction that the Major had singled out for them. Anthony felt his initial enthusiasm waning to a low ebb. Then came this morning.

"I'm gonna tear Harper apart," the Major blared during the morning office briefing with the three of them. "She knows how tight this training schedule is. She was supposed to be here yesterday with those simulators."

"I thought the techs would have been done adapting and programming them by now," Cheny said. "What could have happened?"

"I don't have any idea," Michaels shot back. "But we're gonna have to step up the schedule on actual flying time. I want the techs to have the *Talon*s ready to fly by 1000. We'll have to run our initial drills with actual equipment. She'd better have a damn good excuse when she gets here..."

Chen Marcus spoke up. "What if there's more to it, Major? Some significant problem with the equipment, or an emergency call for the 'Fleet?"

Michaels appeared to think about that for maybe a second before dismissing it. "More than likely some snafu back at the 'Fleet. They could have commed to tell us though." He snorted. "That's head-

quarters for you. I'll call and find out what's wrong. In the meantime, you're dismissed.
Go and get your crews ready to fly. We'll see if they've been paying
attention."

They left the office and split off to get their separate section
crews ready. For Smith's part, not even Capt. Marcus' grandstanding
with the Major---- 'what if there's more to it' indeed---could dampen
the sudden lift in his mood. The only thought on the Lieutenant's
mind was that he could finally climb back into the cockpit of his bird,
and do some real flying. He understood the need for class work, and
preparation, but with some of the necessary groundwork laid, they
were about to get down to what he'd come here for.

The next two hours saw a frantic scrambling about; getting
their gear, doing final inspections in conjunction with the support crew
members they'd brought along, powering up, loading their personal
files and the Major's instructions onto the shipboard systems.

Smith sat with the rest of his section. He mentally smiled with
pride at his crew, designated as Onyx Flight. The lieutenant had been
working with them all week, going over the particulars of their tactical
strategies. He felt that they were ready. They'd shown great ability,
and Smith had encouraged them at every turn. All that remained was
to see how well they'd taken in the huge amount of information.

They began in the morning, flying formation approach tactics,
disengagement maneuvers, and cooperating as a total cohesive unit in
some of the new basic flight procedures. The Major had wanted to get
a feel for how much improvement there had been in this area, and this
was a way to evaluate their learning safely and easily. Smith's divi-
sion slid into and out of formation, performing the basic moves with
ease. He watched as Danielle Cheny's group, and Chen Marcus' group
also performed these maneuvers with equal ease. No challenge there
for any of them. Good. Now they'd get down to business.

The fighter corps brought their birds back to base for servicing
and rechecking of systems while the men and women who'd flown
them went to grab a bite while they could. On the way to the commissary, Smith walked together with Captain Cheny. He was looking
forward to the afternoon's exercise, and adrenaline surged.

"Respectfully speaking ma'am," Smith said to her, "I hope
you've got your E-flares and signal buoy ready for when I splash you
in the exercise this afternoon."

"You seem mighty sure about this, *Lieutenant*." Cheny replied. "I don't think that you should count me out just yet."

"Begging the Captain's pardon; not counting you out, ma'am. I just know that my section is ready. To splash you, that is."

Cheny laughed, then looked at him once again. "You're completely serious, aren't you, Smith?"

"Yes ma'am, that's the truth."

"We'll see, Lieutenant Smith, we'll see."

"Yes, ma'am, we sure will."

Butler stopped at the door of the *Raven's* Sick Bay and viewed the scene before him. Commodore Lamont was back on the flagship but had not been released for duty by Ceal Byars. You would never know it from the activity.

Back in uniform, Lamont had set up a secondary Int/Sec office right in one of the Sick Bay observation cubicles. It and Vennefron were sitting side by side scanning old records of all the attacks they had gathered information about. Except for senior officers, Vennefron was the only person Byars had let in so far. She would not be thrilled with the news he was about to report.

"Skipper," he opened. When Coy looked up he snapped off a salute in his best Gary Michaels imitation. Lamont only raised an amused eyebrow as it returned the salute, but did not mention it. "Sir, we sent Shuttle Two off with equipment for the training pilots a week ago. We've had normal stat reports from them every day. Until now."

Coy frowned and Vennefron looked up from his study in concern.

Butler handed over a data sheet. "We've tried to initiate contact..."

"And didn't get a reply?" Lamont guessed.

"Right. And to top it off we get a request from Michaels just a few minutes ago wondering where his shipment is."

Coy cocked its head at the names on the report. "The JP is...Lynn Harper. I don't know her."

"Ah, no, she's one of our recent recruits. A fairly new pilot, but a good one. There's no reason to think she couldn't handle it – unless something external happened."

Vennefron waved a hand at the information they had been studying. "You don't think..."

Ken and Coy exchanged a serious look.

"Not *my* people," Coy stated, coldly.

Ken nodded understanding. "I'll get a hold of Michaels. They'll have to handle most of it from their end."

Coy raised its wrist com to its face. "Lamont to Bon."

"Bon here. You don't know how great that sounded, Commodore." They could hear his smile even over the tiny speaker.

"Meet me in my Sick Bay 'office' immediately. It's not great. We need to get the Fleet moving."

The levity evaporated from his voice. "On my way."

"So what is up that guy's butt, anyway?" Sweggert asked as he flopped down onto the seat in the commissary for whatever meal this was.

"You can only mean Smith," McKinney said around a mouthful.

"Oh please," Pierce set her tray down and joined them just in time to hear the name. "I want to eat without indigestion." She shook her head. "And to think I thought he was kinda cute."

The other pilots stopped mid bite and stared at her. She may be the best fighter there, in and out of a *Talon*, but Andrea Pierce would never be "one of the guys."

Randy decided it was safer just to let it go. "I'm serious. I would really like to know what the problem is. If we were lousy pilots and holding them back or something that would be one thing, but we're not. We do bad and he treats us like dirt. We do good and he treats us like worse dirt." He stopped his complaints only long enough to take a bite and swallow it. "It didn't use to be like this in the Fleet. Everybody was on the same side. If the Skipper…"

"That's enough, Sweggert." All three pilots turned to see Capt. Marcus standing behind them. "We are one Fleet. But we are three squads. Competition is supposed to improve your edge – not have you whining like infants."

"Yeah, but Cap…"

Whatever argument Sweggert was about to marshal was lost as everyone's screamer went off on their wrist com cutting short their dinner as well as their conversation. "Michaels to all personnel. To the briefing room!" the major's voice came over the units. "Repeat: all BlackFleet personnel to the briefing room immediately!"

Randy stood up and dropped his utensil onto his tray with a clatter. "Nothin' like a good meal…"

Michaels stood at parade rest at the head of the room, as everyone hurriedly filed in.   If anyone thought that this was a drill or some simulated exercise, the severe look on the Major's face immediately told a different story. He counted heads, and began as soon as the last person apologetically ran in and found a seat. He was curt and to the point.

"Pieta was supposed to arrive yesterday with the last flight tech and a set of simulators for training. According to the Fleet, they left on schedule. Somewhere between there and here, they disappeared."

He waited while a buzz of reaction quickly circled the room. Then, he switched on a holo map. "The Fleet has been trying to contact them with no success. This was their last known position," he said indicating a point on the map. "They emerged safely from the transit point, which, as you know, is out beyond the edge of the Avalon system. But they were lost somehow, before arriving here.

"So, we're on SAR. It's for real, boys and girls, because there's trouble of some kind out there. And we're going to have to find out what it is, *and* find our missing crew. The Fleet is coming, but they're still days away. It's up to us.

"Your section commanders will brief you on your assigned search areas---just as soon as I brief *them.* But I want the crews on the field now, seeing to last-minute prep. Dismissed."

It was organized chaos several minutes later as pilots, gunners and crew raced around the field. Pilots and gunners had suited up, and were now running to take their places in the waiting Talons.

Cheny, Smith and Marcus were each detailing the search coordinates to their sections as they all began climbing into their cockpits. Each of the squadrons lifted off in turn, clawing their way through the atmosphere, until they had left the planet far behind.

Racing through space, the three squadrons remained in their practiced formations almost without thought.   When they reached the general coordinates however, the *Talons* peeled off by squadron to conduct the search.

Most of the pilots were searching their assigned areas in empty space between the transit point outside the system, and the core world of Avalon. They were looking for scattered debris, energy signatures, anything that might explain what had happened to their missing shuttle.

Danielle Cheny's Obsidian squadron had been given a different assignment, at the other side of the outer system.

They traveled for quite some distance, before shutting down all power, except for minimal life support. The four tiny ships began coasting silently through space toward a particular target. Their course would bring them easily within low-power scanning range of the small mining planet of Kendrick, on the outer edge of the system. They would simply scan the planet as they floated past, without being picked up on sensors themselves. Then they would loop back, and rendezvous with the rest of their squadron. After another long hour of relative silence, even within the cockpit, Cheny spoke."Here's where we see whether or not the rest of the patrols got the short end of the stick or we did. We're in close enough," she said to her gunner.

"Scanners on receive-only---now. Let's just hope that this works and that no one spots us." The *Talon* squad approached the planet, looped around in a slingshot trajectory, and within several minutes, were on their way, having scanned the entire surface. Only when they were well outside of detection range of Kendrick, did they light off their drives.

"Obsidian One to base," Cheny said over the com. "Seven possibles, repeat, *seven* possibles."

"Confirmed," Michaels said. "Recall all flights. Base out."

Michaels closed the hatch on the remaining shuttle within one of the hangars on the field. The last of the twenty–four pilots and gunners had just walked into it ahead of him. Now all of them watched as he stood just within the hatchway. Then they flinched together as he angrily slammed his fist against a bulkhead.

"Pirates." Michaels said simply. He watched as heads nodded in sudden understanding. He watched also as his own anger was swiftly duplicated around the cramped shuttle.

"I've had Vennefron check," he told them, waving a minicomp he held in his other hand for emphasis. "There have been four other unexplained disappearances reported in this system in the last several months. On the chance that our missing crew might be one of those *unexplained* missing, I had Captain Cheny check out a small planet on the other side of the system from where our shuttle vanished. If it was pirates, they'd have to be operating from a base somewhere, and that's a likely area.

"We were looking for energy signatures from anything other than the established mining facilities on Kendrick. She found seven. The readings eliminated five of them. They were just too small for what we're looking for.

"But one of the remaining two showed a ship landing as Cheny's group overflew, and then being suddenly obscured from the scan, as if hidden under a shielded bunker. My money's on this one. The government here may know something, and they may not. They have done some low-level investigating of the other disappearances, but haven't turned up anything. Just in case there is a problem though, I thought we'd keep this search, and its results to ourselves. I want to keep the rescue to

ourselves, too. That's the reason for our private little conversation here". Michaels then turned to Chen Marcus. "I don't believe that an air assault is the best option here. We're talking about a covert op, and that means you and the Elite Forces, Captain. We need to get in there quickly and get our people out. I'm turning the planning for this over to you."

Marcus stood confidently, and took the minicomp that the Major handed to him. He read its contents before speaking.

"All right," he told them all, "There are a few scenarios that apply to this situation. But any of them would require more manpower than just Ebony flight," he said. "We'll all need to work together to pull this off. Here is what we need to do..."

They timed the attack so that it would take place during the night cycle on that side of the planet. Just as before, BlackFleet craft knifed silently through space toward the mining colony. This time however, they were not simply flying past. Two of the *Talon* squadrons and the remaining shuttle approached the planet from the hemisphere opposite their objective. They came in, skimming the surface by staying only a few dozen meters up, and used a mountain range near the hidden base to mask their final approach from detection. They finally landed behind the last of the foothills, only a few kilometers from their goal.

The Elite forces group had been hard pressed to match the split second timing and maneuverability that the more seasoned pilots displayed in all this. Speed McKinney gave Smith a complimentary nod once they were out of their ships. "When I grow up I want to fly like that," he told the pilot.

Smith took that in silence. Things had moved so quickly in the last few hours that he hadn't had the time to think much about the Elite forces taking over the op. Fortunately, McKinney seemed to be too occupied with getting on with business to expect a reply.

The murky atmosphere of Kendrick was rich in carbon dioxide, but air pressure at this level was close to normal. That meant they hadn't needed to use space armor, only breathers. That helped quite a bit with their ability to move around. After suiting everyone up-Elite Forces in their custom black gear and the others in more typical light battle armor, Chen Marcus, took a team out on recon. Belly-crawling practically to the back door of the base, they got more detailed scans of the layout. They prowled all around the facility, spending two full hours making electronic observations and noting movements and operational patterns in that time as well. After finishing up, the trio returned to the shuttle and the rest of their comrades.

"Listen up," Marcus said as everyone gathered around. He projected a holographic diagram of the base into the air. "There are two main entrances, here and here. They are guarded, but not heavily. These people aren't expecting company like us, yet. There's also the bunker entrance here, where the ships are kept. There are a few remote sensor platforms at various places on the grounds. We've tagged them on your personal scan units, so that you can use scramblers to mask your presence as you get near them.

"Most of the base is underground, and shielded, so even this close, our scans of the interior are incomplete. We do know that it seems to be a large three-level facility with several rooms. We will assume that our people are being kept at the level furthest from the surface, until we learn differently. But the main point of entry will need to be the hatchway on top of this hill here," he said, pointing to a spot on a ridge above the base.

"I'll be leading Squad One; Sweggert, you have Squad Two; Pierce, Squad Three, and Zola, you have Squad Four. One and Two will be going in through the hatch we found, evidently used for receiving supplies. Squad Three will be going in at this doorway entrance, on the other side of the compound. It's the most minimally guarded regular entryway. Squad Four, you're backup, but you know what your primary responsibility is. Operation Bedrest is on. Gear up, and let's go."

Smith found himself in Pierce and McKinney's group. They'd had the normal BlackFleet training in hand held weapons, and in how to move silently, but Smith thought to himself that Pierce and McKinney made it seem easy.

Each of the groups moved into position. Squad Three had crawled to a point behind a small hill, about eighteen meters from one of the entrances. A sealed doorway was set under a shelf of rock, and really difficult to see through the dense atmosphere. The scanner showed that there were two people just inside it, but one of them was heading off back into the depths of the base.

"Shift change," Pierce mumbled more to herself than anyone.

The rest of the team was going to take another fifteen minutes to get into position. Squad Three waited while the night crawled on, but suddenly Pierce noted new movement inside. A second sentry was joining the first at the door.

"What's this? Company on duty?" She silent-signaled the others to remain quiet, but motioned McKinney over to watch what was happening on her scanner. To her amazement the door actually began to open.

The couple of 'guards' at this entrance appeared to be just that—a couple. They were holding hands as they opened the door and came out of the base, for a moonlit walk in the smog, or something. Of course the door sealed shut behind them, but despite that, Pierce couldn't have imagined a more gift-wrapped opportunity.

"Squad Three to One," she whispered into her com unit.

"One, go."

"We have a pair of targets who have just opened the side door to the base. Can't pass up an invitation like that," she reported.

"Roger that, Three."

Pierce had McKinney set up with a stunner, while she crept to the other side of the trail the couple was using to wander outside the base. Several large boulders all over the area helped her to stay hidden from view.

"Set." She whispered to him as she reached position.

Speed waited until they came closer, then tapped the trigger. The male dropped as the beam hit him. Pierce stepped behind the woman at the same instant and put a gun to the pirate's temple.

"Don't try anything funny, or you won't like the punch line," she said. She took her holstered weapon, then frog-marched the woman back to the doorway, and had her open it. Once the door was opened, Pierce shot her with a stunner, and eased her to the ground. She'd be out for a couple of hours. They had enough air in their breathers and that would be more than enough time for their plan.

Pierce signaled for the rest of her squad to join her. They slipped in quickly, and resealed the doors.

"Squad Three to One. We're inside."

"Good work," Marcus whispered. "We've reached the supply doors and are entering the base now. Keep me apprised of your progress."

"Will do. Three out."

Two of Cheny's squadron members stayed to guard the door-way. Pierce made sure that they were set with their "package". The plan was that the Elite force group would station the pilots at the main exits as guards, while they were to actually carry out the op. Pierce had only Smith and one of the techs left, and she intended to station them just a little further inside. So the rest followed as she led down the empty corridor and into the pirate base as they began searching for their crewmates.

Squads One and Two made their way into a corridor from the hatch they had used to enter the base. They were as quiet as humanly possible, and luck was with them this time. Fortunately, no one saw their entry.

At the first corner, they stopped, and checked with their hand-held units. The next room was just some sort of lounge, no further in-formation about how to find their missing crew, here. There were two doorways out of the room however, and both corridors went on for quite a way. Marcus split Squad Two off at this point, indicating that they should take the way to the left. After posting a guard at this posi-tion, the rest moved on.

All was quiet. There was no one, seemingly up doing much of anything at this hour. All of the squads made unopposed progress for a few more minutes. They searched rooms as they went, looking for obvious holding cells, or even plain locked rooms with a handful of persons inside.

So far the search was proving unsuccessful. It was Squad Three once again, that encountered life first.

Pierce stopped at a corner and checked with her scanner, then turned to the rest of her team.

"One" she indicated with her finger, then, "coming this way." She motioned for all of them to back away, then eased her rifle onto the floor, and took a stance at the corner.

The guard approached very casually. He was armed only with a pistol, held loosely before him. Pierce grabbed the guard at the wrist before he was fully around the corner. She stepped inside the man's reach, made a couple of moves so fast that Smith never quite saw them and suddenly the man was on the floor, unconscious or dead. All without making a sound. Pierce picked up her rifle afterward. Smil-ing, she walked back to where Smith still stood, and gently closed his gaping mouth with one of those lethal fingertips.

"Stay here," she whispered to the pilot and the tech. "Guard this junction. If it isn't us, or any of the missing crewmembers shoot it. But I don't want of be a victim of friendly fire on the way back out. So remember—*look* first, then shoot." Then she and McKinney proceeded further into the base. And just like that, Smith's estimation of the Elite forces began to change.

Pierce and McKinney met only one more person in the way of resistance, and he too, was quietly dispatched. A minute later, they found an elevator. Slipping inside, the remnants of Squad Three went down to the next level.

Marcus and Squad One prowled close to an obvious landmark on their scanner info. He crept close enough to the door opening to confirm what the data was telling him. Sure enough, the room was a large, well-lit repair shop. Several people were working the graveyard shift inside. "The repair bay for their ships," he said to the rest of his squad. "The hangar,

and our shuttle must be close by." This would be helpful later on, but they certainly didn't need it right now. The captain backed his team away from the room.

They continued their sweep of this level, and in another moment, the scanner info revealed that the room at the far end of the corridor they were searching was a bit more key to their plan.

"Squad One to Squads Two, Three and Four, report status," he whispered.

"Squad Two; still proceeding from last point of contact. No discoveries."

"Squad Three; we've just made it onto second level. Proceeding cautiously."

"Squad Four; in position."

"We found the atmosphere processing unit," Marcus himself reported. "We'll hold position and coordinate from here. Two, Three: the rest of the operation is up to you. Watch yourselves. One out."

Sweggert's team halted at the end of a darkened corridor. A security detail walked across the end of the hallway. Randy motioned for Grace Wiggins, the other Elite Force member of his squad, to crouch down in the darkness, trusting that their black armor would help them to stay hidden. Had the guards simply looked down the corridor they might have seen the intruders, but they stopped for only a second, then went on their way around the corner to the left. Randy watched them go, and waited for just a moment, to be sure.

To the right, there was another set of elevator doors. He paused only a second before leading the way down to the second level.

Squad Three had met no opposition on the second level so far. They'd stopped and scanned through various doors, but still had not found their crewmen. Pierce tried the next door along the corridor, and stopped cold.

"What?" McKinney whispered.

"Barracks. I count...thirty-seven people behind this door, and the next three doors, as well."

"Terrific. Me and thee against 120?"

"Suggestions?"

Speed thought for only a second. "Seal the doors."

"Right. Odds are there's another way out of the rooms, but this should slow them down some."

Pierce pulled out a packet from one of the fatigue pockets, and opened it. Inside was a gray clay-like compound, which they smeared into the seam of each of the doors quickly and quietly. By the time they finished the last door, the first one had hardened to the density of steel. She checked her chrono.

"That cost us almost three minutes. We'd better move it."

"Speed's my middle..." he said.

Pierce cut him off with a gesture and pointed down the corridor again.

Squad Two waited anxiously at a corner as Sweggert double-checked his scanner. Then his mouth broadened into a wide grin as he found what he had been looking for.

"Control center!" he thought triumphantly. He held up four fingers, referring to the number of persons inside. Then he showed the scanner reading to Wiggins, and pointed toward an adjoining corridor to the left. She understood his implied order, and crept off quietly.

In less than two minutes, she reported back. "Set," she said over Sweggert's helmet com.

Randy consulted the scanner once again. There appeared to be two persons seated against the southern end of the room and two more standing more or less at duty stations, he supposed, on the other side.

"You have the two against the south wall."

"Acknowledged," she said.

"On my mark... " Sweggert whispered.

Wiggins had circled around to the opposite side of the control room, and now they both slipped low and quietly up to the open doorways on either side of the control room, and paused just outside.

"*Go*," Sweggert whispered again into his com.

At that signal, both Sweggert and Wiggins dove and slid into the room on the floor, firing in opposite directions. One of the technicians shouted something as the stun beam hit him, but then he hit the floor, unconscious. None of the other three made a sound at all.

They checked the pulse on each of the downed pirates quickly, then Randy electronically plugged his scanner into the main control panel, and began hitting buttons on the pad. He worked quickly to hack into the system database, and checked in as he was doing so.

"Squad Two to One. We have found base control center and are now querying the central computer."

"Excellent, Two," Marcus said. "Report progress. One out."

A voice came around a corner near the control room preceding its owner. "Hey, I thought I heard something fall in here. The Boss'll have your..."

The newcomer stopped the second she saw the intruders in the room. But she had no time to do anything more. Grace had spun, crouched and aimed before the pirate had even come around the corner. She was dropped with the stunned expression still on her face. Wiggins dragged the unconscious woman inside the control room.

Randy nodded his approval and went back to his work. A chime sounded and he grinned triumphantly.

"Do we do good work or what? Squad Two to Three. I have all of the computer's information for this base. Notes here say that the prisoners are on the third level, Holding Rooms Eight and Nine."

Squad Three acknowledged. "We'll take hostage rescue," she said.

Sweggert planted a device under the main console, then he and Wiggins settled in to wait.

Pierce and McKinney arrived on the third level in an elevator shaft at the other end of the facility. They moved slowly, but purposefully toward one end of the long corridor, now that they knew where they were going. Stopping just around the corner from the guard shack outside the holding area, they listened. The scanner showed one person within, and they also heard the sound of someone listening to a holovid. Pierce nodded to Speed. He stayed low, and crept around the corner, easing his way along under the window of the shack. Then he fished a sample pack from his fatigues and tossed it into a corner, making a loud clatter.

"What was that?" the guard said, obviously annoyed. "Murphy, if that's you playin' around again…"

McKinney stayed perfectly still, waiting.

"Quit clownin' around out there, I mean it."

Still no movement, no sound.

"You can come on out now, the game's over. Look, if I have to get outta this chair, you really ain't gonna like it…"

McKinney sat rock still, but wondered how many hours he would have to wait for the lazy guard to get up. They didn't have a lot of time here. He rolled his eyes with the exasperation of waiting.

The guard swore viciously. "All right, but it had better be a good gag, or I'm telllin' the boss, this time…"

Finally, McKinney heard the man get to his feet and take the two steps to the door of the shack. He opened it and stepped out into the corridor.

"Oh, it's a good gag, alright," Speed said from the floor---just before he hit him with the stunner.

Pierce came up, and helped him drag the guard back inside, and set him back in the seat. After locating the switch on the shack's panel, they opened the door to the holding area. The rooms they sought were the first and second doors inside.

"Boys in here, girls right next door, just like the notes said," Pierce whispered as she read the scanner. "Except there are…three extra prisoners. That will complicate things a little."

They hadn't seen the codes for these doors anywhere inside the shack's computer, so they took two additional minutes to bypass the locks. But they were well trained, being some of the first to undergo Schiff's strict regimen. The locks were no problem. With a satisfied "Ahhh," the doors swished open.

"Clock is ticking," Pierce said as she stepped inside. Pieta rose from the hard mat she'd been sleeping on. She blinked in surprise as light flooded into the room, then took a double-take as she recognized the BlackFleet uniform.

"Calvary here at last?" she grinned in sleepy surprise.

"That's us. So, everyone on their feet, and let's move."

"You'll have to help me with Lynn, here."

"Who…?" Pierce asked, as Pieta helped a young blond woman get slowly to her feet.

"Harper. She's a little groggy. She's the shuttle pilot , and they were filling her with pentha, and other drugs. I guess they thought she knew something about our operational procedures. Then they found out that she was only hired a couple of weeks ago."

"Can she walk? We're going to need to move quickly."

"I can walk," the young woman said groggily, but put her hand to her head. "Just as long as there's no bright lights or sudden ..." she stifled a small belch, " movement."

"They haven't dosed her for a while now," Pieta confirmed, helping Harper to a vertical position. "She should be okay in a little bit. Just a little hung over."

"So what are you guys in for?" Pierce asked, indicating two of the three "extras" she had seen on the scanner.

"Five of us were captured on a freighter a month ago, only three left now. They killed some of us in the attack, and our captain and first officer after we got here. It's been hell. If you can help get us away ..."

"We're all getting out of here, and you're definitely invited, if you care to join us." She motioned with sweeping arms.

They voted with their feet. Harper leaned on Pieta's shoulder, and they all bustled back out into the hallway.

Speed had gathered the other BlackFleet tech, and the remaining member of the freighter crew and stood anxiously waiting.

"Squad Three to One; package secured," Pierce reported.

"Roger that. All squads, second phase of Operation Bedrest is go. Meet all of you at the checkout point."

"Acknowledged," Pierce said. She reached into the carryall and fished out breathers for everyone except the three extra prisoners they hadn't foreseen.

"One of our teams is releasing an odorless sleeping agent into the atmosphere processor," she explained. "Everyone in here not already asleep is going to be doing so pretty soon. I'm afraid that means you as well. Since we didn't know you were in here, we didn't bring enough breathers for you.

We'll have to carry you from here to our shuttle. I'm afraid you'll have to trust me, on that, but I assure you, we won't leave you behind."

"If you're the BlackFleet mercenaries that the rumors are all about, your reputation precedes you, Lieutenant" the man nodded confidently to indicate his trust.

"Good," she nodded back to them as she spoke into her com. "Three to Two,"

"Two, go."

"We're going to need your help down here in a minute. A few extra passengers and not enough breathers to go around."

"Gotcha. On our way."

Pierce turned then to Pieta.

"Is all of our equipment from the shuttle intact?"

"Yes. They hadn't even off-loaded it yet. They were still arguing amongst themselves about what to do about it, and us, once they found out who we were."

"That about wraps it up then. We'll wait here for just a little while."

Sweggert flipped a switch on the device he'd planted under the console. He and Wiggins sealed their helmets before sealing up the doors with the same compound Pierce and McKinney had used. They jogged a way down the corridor, and turned the corner toward the elevator. Just as they were out of earshot however, a red light on the console they had just left began to blink, and a com message came through...

Sweggert and Wiggins arrived at the third level and found team Three with the freighter crew fast asleep on the floor. True to their word, the BlackFleet squads began picking them up to carry them out. The two women were fairly small, so Sweggert and McKinney both slung one of them across their shoulders in a fireman's carry. Wiggins and the male
tech both took the final crewman between them. Pierce led the way, with Pieta and Harper bringing up the rear.

Pierce turned in a different direction from the way they'd gotten onto this level. She was heading for the vehicle bunker, where Captain Marcus was waiting for them. It took a bit of bundling and arranging, but they all managed to fit into the lift. With a final sigh of relief, Pierce hit the button, and the lift took them back to the first level.

As the doors opened, the silence was thick. There had been little noise before, but now everyone around them was still. They passed someone unconscious on the floor, and turned left to head into the final set of corridors before they reached the section of the facility with the repair bay that Marcus had mentioned.

Pierce strode on confidently. She now knew that there were only a few more turns and they'd be in the repair bay, then in the vehicle bunker and on their way

"Don't move!" an angry voice to their right demanded. "Who the hell are you?"

The BlackFleet members whirled in surprise to find seven of the pirates, standing in the corridor, guns drawn. *And* they were wearing breathers.

Pierce's response was immediate.

"Get back!" She screamed to the rest of the group, shoving them back the way they'd come.

She dropped to the ground, snatching at her rifle as she did so. But the pirates fired at the very first motion. Suddenly the quiet hallways screamed and flashed with crisscrossing blaster fire.

Fortunately most of the group had not even made it into the intersection yet. Suddenly an energy bolt smashed into Randy's armored leg. He swore as his leg buckled under him. But the brief second of forward momentum helped direct his fall so that both he and the rescuee he was carrying, fell the right way.

A bolt hit the seam of Pierce's left shoulder covering, giving her a bad shock which partially numbed her arm, but she hardly hesitated to return fire. She too, rolled as she hit the floor, and saw one of the pirates go down as she winged him. She was still firing and rolling until she was also safe beyond the edge of the intersection. Then she shot around the corner wildly, and voice-keyed her com.

"Squads Three and Two to One!" She screamed, straining to be heard over the whine of fire. "Under attack! Seven hostiles have us pinned down on level one, just outside the repair bay!"

"On the way!" Marcus commed back without hesitation. He glanced around and did a quick head count to ensure that everyone else was here, except for Haberny's Squad Four waiting outside. He checked in quickly with them.

"One to Four."

"Go," she said.

"Any activity out there?"

"No sir, we were just waiting for pickup."

"Stay put. And keep an eye out for company. We've got a Situation in here."

"Do you need backup?"

"We'll let you know. One out."

He pointed to two of the squadron members. "You two, guard this doorway," he said, even as he ran toward one of the large doors leading into the vehicle bunker. "You," he said pointing to more, "Guard the shuttle. No one gets in this room until you get the all clear. And you , come with me."

Marty Thomas from Squad One, Smith, and Sam Alexander took up positions to follow him back through the repair shop toward the battle.

Pierce was still firing low around the corner, and McKinney standing, and firing high, when the crack of blaster fire sounded from behind them.

"Some of them have circled around us! Stay down!" Pierce shouted to the rest of the group. Mc Kinney whipped around and helped Wiggins, who also began firing in the opposite direction. Someone was in the hallway behind them, and shooting wildly around that corner. McKinney knew that the fleeing group couldn't stay where they were. He dashed to the back of the group, and dropped to the ground, protecting Pieta and Harper.

Pierce quickly assessed that there were no doorways on the wall they huddled against. There was one however, on the opposite wall.

"Cover me!" she shouted to McKinney, and fired with her rifle in her good arm, as she dashed across the hall, still firing low, and reached up clumsily with her tingling arm to key the lock open. A bolt sheared off a chunk from the wall, which ricocheted into her faceplate. She winced involuntarily, but kept working. Then the door was open. "Move," she ordered the group, and again "Cover!" to Mc Kinney. While Pierce turned and began shooting in the direction of the first attack, McKinney crouched a bit higher, and fired both blaster pistols stiff-armed, looking for all the world like a pre-jump Western gun-slinger. He poured out a rain of continual fire, which made Swiss cheese of the corner. But it did momentarily stop the attack from that direction. When the last of the group had run, crawled, or been dragged into the room, Pierce and McKinney likewise dove into its protection.

Marcus arrived, and stopped short of the corner as he heard the fight just beyond it. He stole a glance around the corner just in time to see the last two Elite force members retreat into the side room, and note where the enemy fire was coming from, then ducked back.

"One to Squads Two and Three, say status."

"We're taking cover in a small room," Pierce reported. "There are no other exits. We're pinned down with fire from both directions."

"I'm just about twenty meters from your position," Marcus told her. "We're on it. Stand by."

He checked his own scanner, noting the layout of their immediate environs. Then he broadened the search to include the whole facility and the environment outside. They appeared to be the only ones moving at all, except for Squad Four and the contingent protecting the shuttle. Assured of that, he looked to Smith and Alexander.

"When I give the word, I want the two of you, one standing, one crouching, to shoot around this corner. Fire along the wall closest to us. And don't stop shooting until...well, you'll know when. Got it?"

"Got it," both pilots replied.

Then Marcus took off in another direction.

Quietly, the two Elite force members circled around until they were in a corridor behind one of the groups of pirates. Marcus checked quickly around the corner, and could see three of them, hunkered down, firing around a corner not twelve meters away. They were shouting at the trapped officers, and seemed to be having a good time. It wasn't going to last.

"Hey, c'mon out and play!" one of the pirates was shouting. "We promise, we won't hurt you. Come on!"

"Yeah, *Chica*. Come on out and let's talk!"

Marcus glanced around the corner at the other set of opponents who were also shooting and shouting similar encouragements, then ducked back around the corner himself to avoid being seen .

"Squad One to Two and Three. In position. Give them a chance," he whispered into his com.

Pierce wasn't sure that she wanted to do anything of the sort. The fact that the blaster fire was continuing didn't help their offer of a peaceful settlement, much. But she quietly acknowledged the order, then screamed loudly to be heard over the noise.

"Lay down your weapons and surrender!" she shouted. "If you do, we promise to take you alive! If you don't, we can't be responsible for the consequences!"

Roaring peals of laughter followed this announcement. The pirates were laughing so hard that they temporarily stopped shooting.

"I mean it!" she shouted. "There won't be another warning!"

Someone stopped laughing long enough to become angry at her nerve. He fired around the corner, even stood for a moment at the edge, firing arrogantly. Pierce pulled back under cover.

"One, to Smith. Now." Marcus said.

Smith had been wondering all this time what he was really doing. He didn't mind a good stand-up fistfight. Cleanly taking out opponents from the familiar environment of his cockpit was the best on many levels. But he wasn't sure what he was doing here. Then he got Captain Marcus' signal.

Immediately, both pilots did as they were ordered, firing around the corner along the wall. The pirates jumped back as fire slashed at them unexpectedly from their right. They yelled, screamed, cursed, and began firing that way as well.

Marcus leaned around the corner and slid two small objects down the hallways so that they hit near the pirates' feet. The pirates, already reeling from the unexpected attack to their right, didn't even have time to react before the objects exploded.

The blasts were just powerful enough to incapacitate, normally. But at such close quarters the unfortunate pirates were thrown bodily against the opposite wall by the explosion.

Two were obviously severely maimed. The rest lay totally still. The reverberations quieted, and the dust settled.

"Sam," Smith said to his partner, "I think we can stop shooting now." Then Smith saw Marcus and Thomas come up cautiously from their place of concealment, and begin to check the bodies.

"Two dead over here," he heard Marcus call out. "And one here."

Smith came around the corner approaching the downed pirates. Marcus was having them stretched out carefully on the floor. The captain double-checked his scanner reading of the rest of the base, and called, "All clear," to the fugitives in the room.

Smith watched Wiggins and Pierce emerge from the room. He winced as he saw that Pierce had been injured. Then he saw Sweggert being helped out by Mc Kinney and grimaced more. Finally, the rest of the former hostages emerged as well. All of them seemed unharmed, at least. McKinney lowered Randy to the floor, and stood back.

"We're going to need help with carrying the other hostages," Pierce reminded the captain.

"Right. After we see to injuries, we'll get everyone to the shuttle."

Several BlackFleet pulled their emergency med kits from their pockets and began checking the figures on the floor.

Smith saw the new pilot he'd heard about over the com,Harper, he believed it was, tending one of the injured pirates. There was a movement to her left, and she only had time enough to gasp as a hand reached out to grab at her.

Even as the heads of the other Elite force members whipped around, a calm voice said simply, "I wouldn't do that if I were you. Put it down, and let her go. Now."

The man's arm had frozen in the motion of raising a pistol toward Harper's head. He hadn't completed the action, because McKinney had one of his pistols drawn and already pointed at the *pirate's* head. The pirate wilted, and allowed himself to be disarmed.

Smith stared at the weapon in McKinney's hand that he would have sworn was empty just a mere second before. He and McKinney caught each other's eye just as the reason for the man's nickname dawned on him. He gave "Speed" a complimentary nod. McKinney merely grinned back.

Marcus strode over and glared at the unfortunate captive.

"What's your name?" he demanded.

"Fields," the man replied. Whether he was telling the truth or not was immaterial to Marcus.

"There's something I could use your help with, Mr. Fields," he said and hauled the man to his feet none too gently.

"McKinney, Smith, you're with me. The rest of you get everyone back to the shuttle. We leave here in ten, pick up Squad Four, the other shuttle, and we'll be on our way back home in time for supper."

The quartet made their way down the corridor, while the rest headed off to the shuttle where the teams were to rendezvous. They had been waiting impatiently for Marcus and the others, when they finally did show up carrying a large sleeping man. "A little get well present for the Commodore," Marcus explained. "In the form of the leader of this rat pack."

The entire group grinned openly at the implications.

"And now if you'd be so kind," Marcus said finally to both Sweggert and to Haberny. Each of them pulled out their scanner/minicomp units. First Sweggert, then Haberny pressed a single button.

Sweggert's signal activated the device he'd left at the control room. Within a few minutes, everything in the entire base's power systems would be useless scrap, with the exception of the life-support systems.

Haberny's signal set off the explosive devices placed over every entrance to the facility. Rock rained down over the doorways, effectively sealing the pirates inside until the authorities and the BlackFleet arrived to fetch them.

Captain Marcus smiled contentedly as he relaxed in the comfortable shuttle seat.

Ceal stood with her arms folded, half blocking the Sick Bay door to the corridor. In front of her, Commodore Coy Lamont fastened its uniform jacket and picked up the hand scanner lying on the work table it had been using for a desk, and a handful of data disks. It turned to the doctor.

"It will be easier to go out if you were standing somewhere else," it commented casually.

She frowned sternly. "You are not ready."

"And you know this because of your many cases like mine that you've dealt with over the years," Coy returned.

She let out her breath in a puff, but stood her ground. "You…"

"I am never going to be ready enough for you, Ceal", it interrupted. "I owe the fact that I am breathing to you. Don't underestimate my debt. But there is no use breathing if I'm not living. I have to get out of here and get back to my life." It stepped closer to her. "I'm okay. And if that changes I swear I will let you know immediately."

"No hiding anything?"

"No hiding. No secrets."

"You promise."

"I promise."

Grudgingly she stepped aside. As Coy passed her, she repeated, "Trust me, you're not ready for what's out there."

Coy turned to look at her as the door swished open. Then a collective gasp made it swivel its head around quickly to the corridor. Coy's mouth gaped open at the sight of every BlackFleet member standing in a line that went the length of the corridor and evidently around the corner as well. Butler, Bon and Schiff stood to one side. At its first step out of Sick Bay a deafening cheer went up. Coy turned again to Ceal, looking more than a little overwhelmed. "When you're right, you're right," it murmured to her.

Then taking a breath it began walking along the line. The first person was Tony Knepp. "Congratulations, Lieutenant Commander."

"Thank you, Sir. Welcome back, Sir."

Next were Aziza, and Parker and Vennefron. "Isn't anyone running this ship?!" it asked in mock horror, as it shook their hands.

Devyu snapped his fingers, "I knew we forgot something. We'll get right on it, Skipper." The bridge crew all saluted and left.

And that's the way it went all the way down the hall. Palo, Swift, McKnight, Hendricks, Torren, Nathan, Edwards, Luka, Penway, Masters, Pedula, Erhardt, Cimini, Reinhart, Dobbs, handshakes, tears, memories and salutes before they hurried back to their duties.

About halfway through, Coy noticed Asch had slipped up into his normal position at its elbow, waiting quietly to assist as needed. "There is a pot of tea waiting for you in your quarters, sir, as soon as you are done reviewing the troops," he said matter-of-factly.

"Bless you," Coy sighed sincerely.

As the last crewmember left, Lamont found that all the senior officers had remained behind.

"Up to a staff meeting?" Butler asked, carefully avoiding Ceal Byars' glare.

Coy smiled at him. "On line and ready to go. My quarters, ladies and gentlemen.

Chapter Eight

"Shipping."

Coy stared at the man before it. The prisoner Marcus had gifted them with was sitting in a chair, bent over forward as far as his restraints would allow. He was sweating and shaking, fighting the truth drug as hard as he could.

"Shipping? Shipping!" Butler slammed his hands down on the table and stood. "We sit here all this time and that's the best you can come up with?"

The man flinched from the loud voice. Fighting the pentha was taking a toll on his nerves. Sound and light were beginning to be painful. A fact that Captain Butler cared about not at all.

"Ken," Lamont said more quietly, "Sit down and relax." It leaned across the table that separated itself from the pirate. "Am I to understand that you were instructed to interfere with shipping lines?"

Gritting his teeth, the man nodded.

"Why?"

"I – don't – know," he bit out.

"What did you get out of the deal?"

"Anything – on – board."

Coy and Butler glanced at each other in surprise.

"You didn't have to give a percentage or cut to anyone?"

"No." The man was panting now.

Ceal, seated just behind the prisoner, motioned for Coy's attention and pointed to her medical scanner. "His blood pressure is soaring. He's dangerously close to a stroke."

Coy nodded understanding, but continued. "So someone instructed you to attack shipping lines, but did not want a share of the, ah, profits. Correct?"

Another nod.

"And you don't know who gave you the instructions."

"'t was – anon – tip." His speech was getting a little slurry.

"An anonymous tip?" Ken exploded again. "You risked your entire crew for an anonymous tip?"

"Good..." pant, pant. "...profit."

"But, you..." Ken began, but Coy cut him off at Ceal's look.

"Administer the antidote. We'll finish this later."

Ceal came around into the man's field of vision. "You won't finish anything if he's dead," she muttered as her hypospray hissed against his arm. "Sir," she added. She checked his vitals and pursed her lips. "Can I take him to Sick Bay now?"

Commodore Lamont shook its head. "He can stay right here until he stabilizes. Then he's going to the brig."

"Commodore…" she began.

Lamont jerked up straight in its chair and pointed a finger at the slumped figure. "He imprisoned my people!" it practically shouted. "If he wasn't potentially useful he would be space debris right now. He goes to the brig!"

Ceal stepped back and blinked at the overpowering emotion in Coy's voice and eyes. "Yes, sir. To the brig. Sorry, sir."

Coy started to say more, then changed its mind. It let out a long slow breath and nodded to Butler.

Raising his wrist com he ordered, "Butler to Security. Enter."

The door opened and the two guards stationed just outside the briefing room joined them. They had remained out of sight and ear-shot during the interrogation as to not confuse the prisoner.

"When Dr. Byars clears this – man – take him to the brig," Butler told them, somehow making the word 'man' an insult with his tone.

"Yes, sir."

Leaving the room, Lamont turned in the direction of I & S with Butler on his heels. Ken could swear he could see the wheels turning in his commander's mind even though it didn't say a word until they reached the intelligence department.

Vennefron was sitting at a console, but leapt to his feet and saluted at their arrival.

"Sit down, Lieutenant," Coy told him. "We have work to do."

"The rat actually squealed something useful?" Venn asked hopefully while seating himself again.

" 'Shipping' was the most useful thing he said," Butler informed him in disgust.

"Oh." His tone indicated he was expecting a little more.

"It may be the biggest clue we've ever gotten," Coy said evenly. "Vennefron, get out the list again. How many incidents involved shipping lines?"

The lieutenant worked for a few minutes. "Directly? Less than a third."

"Why do you say 'directly' ?" Butler came and peered over his shoulder.

"Well, there's a couple more here that were attempted kidnappings and some harassment issues that were owners or CEO's of shipping companies."

Lamont sat down slowly. "How many others were involved in shipping in *any* way?"

A few more moments went by as Vennefron redefined his search. "Three companies that had hits manufactured parts for some main shippers," he read, "Two of the governmental leaders we've assisted were directly responsible for commerce; that young girl we rescued was the daughter of the director of the line fleet for that world..."

Butler straightened up and put his hands on his hips. "Don't you think we're reaching just a little here? For all we know they all liked the color blue too, but that wouldn't make a pattern for pirate attacks."

Coy shook its head. "No, Ken. Any thread that ties all of these incidents has to be more than coincidence. Venn, get some help if you need it. Use that fellow Devyu met at the card game, Kefski. I agree that his primary should be Tac Com, but for now consider him your assistant. I want every one of these people interviewed again. Shipping is our key. Find any link they have."

"Aye, sir." Vennefron spoke into his wrist com and called Gunter Kefski to I & S.

While he was speaking, Butler continued his argument with Lamont. "How would interfering with shipping help anybody?" he asked. "Trade between worlds is the lifeblood of the whole nexus!"

"I don't know, yet. Finding if this is really the link is the first step. If not, then we'll start over again," Coy stood up and prepared to leave Vennefron to his work. "And if you have any better ideas, Captain, please don't hesitate to let me know."

"My pleasure, Skipper," Butler gave a half salute.

Lamont's plan was to take a brief tour around the bridge as it had always had a habit of doing, and then go crash in its quarters for a while. It hated to admit that it still was not up to the energy levels that it was used to. Ceal was confident that with time, everything would be back to normal. Well, at least the things that they wanted to return to the way they had been.

Coy was still assimilating its new self...selves. It had not yet found a way to explain to the others what the changes really were. It was almost as if it had been two separate people all the time, battling for precedence. For the majority of its life, the quiet chameleon spy

had been all it knew. Although the drive for command and its self proclaimed
mission against the Boogeyman had come from somewhere – or some-one – different. A bold, forceful personality that had to win at all cost.

The two warring selves had been in conflict more and more as the BlackFleet had taken shape and become successful. Until the meltdown and reboot. And now… it was still working on that one.

"Commodore!" a voice broke through its thoughts.

It turned to find Major Michaels striding down the corridor to catch up.

"Commodore, may I speak with you for a moment, sir?" he asked after his academy perfect salute had been acknowledged.

Coy smiled inwardly as it recognized the pattern for Butler's new crispness. "Of course, Major. In fact, I've been wanting a chance to talk to you. Can you come to my quarters now?"

"Yes, sir. That would be fine."

Once they were settled in the cabin, Coy in a comfortable chair, Michaels standing at parade rest, and Asch had made his appearance with his magic refilling teapot, they both looked at the other, wondering who would begin. Lamont let him stew for just a few moments before giving in.

"Butler tells me you have over 30 years experience with fighter pilots."

"Yes, sir. I served for 35 and a half years, in point of fact."

"I see. I'm not as clear on why you left."

Michaels gave a very small, very controlled sigh. "I disagreed with my people's tendency to discourage ingenuity."

Coy's brows rose a little. "I'm not aware of many military organizations that encourage ingenuity in their fighting men."

The major pursed his lips. "Perhaps I chose the wrong word."

Lamont waved at another chair. "Perhaps you could sit down to discuss it."

Michaels looked at the comfortable chair for a second before lowering himself down into it. "I must admit, the level of informality around here is still more than a bit surprising."

Coy laughed at little. "Formality is not a large issue with most mercenary units. We're about the best it gets. I guess it's a good thing you ran into us and not another merc unit."

"For a lot of reasons, or so I hear."

Coy waited for him to expand upon that comment, but he didn't seem inclined to. "So, another word for ingenuity?" it returned to the former line of conversation.

"It's just that no one seemed to feel that the enlisted soldiers had any value except as a part of the whole." Michaels seemed dissatisfied with that answer as well.

"Ah," Lamont rescued him. "You believed that the people under you had individual worth outside of the military machine."

The major's eyes lit up. "Yes, that's exactly it. Self worth. When I began my career, each person's life and contribution meant something. But as the leadership changed over the years, blindly following orders became the most important quality in the ranks. I couldn't agree with that."

"This from the man who craves military formality?" Lamont teased.

Michaels opened his mouth, then shut it. "I guess I'm not making much sense, am I?"

"Major, you are making perfect sense. The very foundation of this Fleet is that each and every person has value and worth and the right to improve not only themselves but the little part of the universe they live in.

"Now, I don't mean to sound supernatural, but I do believe that everyone has a goal, a destiny if you will. And the ones that even come close to the path are damned lucky. I think the people who fit in the BlackFleet are some of the lucky ones. I haven't sat down and talked to all the ones recruited in my, ah, absence, but it seems that my officers have been able to keep up with our record of finding the ones who fit. Yourself included."

Michaels cocked his head a little. "You have personally sat and talked to every crew member in the fleet?"

"Of course. I know their names, faces, and usually even their hobbies. What is the use of trying to improve the universe for everyone out there," Coy waved its arm to indicate space, "If I don't care about the worth of the ones in here. It would defeat the whole purpose of the BlackFleet's existence."

Michaels simply sat quietly for several minutes before finding the right words. "Commodore, ever since I stepped foot on this ship, I have heard nothing but flattering things about your vision and plan for this Fleet and its people. I'm glad to know they seem to all be true."

Lamont could think of nothing to say to that, so it simply nodded in acceptance of the compliment.

"And actually valuing my pilots and crews is what I wanted to speak to you about. I saw some damn fine work on that rescue mission, and I was wondering how you went about rewarding them. The only precedent I have seen is Lieutenant Commander Knepp, and I don't think you have enough Exec slots for everyone I wish to acknowledge."

Coy gave a short laugh of agreement. And Butler had claimed the man had no sense of humor. "The BlackFleet is still developing its internal systems, Major. Why don't you and Captain Butler and Major Schiff get together and draft some protocol for such occasions. I'll look them over and take care of your people as soon as possible."

Commodore Lamont walked into the White meeting with a determined expression on its face. This was the first official full senior staff meeting it had run since returning to duty. It had surprised itself by not feeling hesitant. In fact, these days it seemed to have more confidence than it could ever remember having. It had to admit it, dying may have been the best thing that had happened to it in a long time!

The door to the conference room opened and it strode in. All of the officers seated at the table stood and saluted. Carefully hiding a smile it returned the salutes and gestured for everyone to sit. It would never have suspected Butler being in charge would have tightened military formality around the place. And how much of that was due to Ken's secret hero worship of Michaels no one, including Butler himself, would ever know.

"Ladies and gentlemen, if you will open your notes please," Coy told them.

As they each switched on their screen and saw nothing on it, smiles of understanding spread around the table. With the usual exception of Michaels, of course.

"So you want us to do your work for you again," Butler gave an attempt at a serious tone and failed totally.

"Well, you seem to have done such a good job lately, I thought you'd be hurt if I figured everything out by myself," Coy did a better job at a stern face ... if you didn't look at its eyes. "Now then, for those here that are not as familiar with BlackFleet history, this is the kind of meeting when I ask the question and you all come up with the answers."

"And the question is...?" Rebel asked.

Coy put some data on their screens to begin the process. "Our I & S department has found what we think is the thread tying all of the

'Boogeyman's' activities together. They are all, or almost all, connected in one way or another, to the shipping industry."

"Ah," Michaels cleared his throat, "Is that such a reach for pirates to be attacking shipping?"

"Not just shipments," Lamont clarified. "We're talking about the entire industry. Owners, CEO's, ship manufacturers, route scheduling personnel--every aspect of the business."

"Why? Who would gain from disrupting trade?" Hendricks frowned in thought.

"That, my fine officers, is the question. Any ideas of an answer?" Coy leaned back in its seat to physically hand the discussion over to them.

No one said anything for several minutes. They all read and re-read the scanty information on their screens. Lots of head shaking and mumbling followed.

"It still doesn't make any sense to me," Drake said. "Shipping between worlds is what keeps everything going. How could anyone profit from stopping it?"

"What if...," Schiff began, then seemed to change his mind.

The major spoke so seldom that when he did it usually meant something. Everyone turned to listen to his thoughts, but he said no more.

"Come on, Walter," Coy told him, "spit it out."

Schiff looked for a moment like he was trying to decide if that was a direct order he could get out of, but eventually he surrendered. "What if they didn't want to keep things going? If everything went to hell, who would profit by cleaning it up?"

Coy raised its brows in appreciation and exchanged a glance with Butler. "Who indeed?"

"A new shipping company?" Rebel suggested. "If *everyone* else went under someone new would clean up alright."

"So there was no one company or manufacturer of ships that was being targeted exclusively?" Hendricks wondered.

Vennefron checked some of his own notes. "Not apparently. All different names and registries."

Butler rubbed his chin in thought. "Not even related? I mean like parent companies or something?"

"There are a couple that are related, as you put it. There are some that are subsidiaries of other companies, but I am having more difficulty tracking just which of *those* companies might be connected in some way."

"Now," Coy turned back to the rest of the officers, " assume we're wrong. It's not a new company wanting the business. What else could be the rationale?"

"What if the shipping is not the only thread?" Michaels leaned forward on the table with his normal intense expression.

"They all could like the color blue," Butler said only loudly enough for Coy to hear.

"Go on," Lamont told Michaels, ignoring Ken completely.

"Is there any word of some kind of universal police force proposed by anyone? Stirring up trouble in order to stop it?"

"I thought that was our job!" Rebel joked, and at Coy's look, added, "Stopping it, not stirring it up, that is."

Coy shook its head. "I've not heard any rumors of that sort. People have wished for it with all that's going on, but I've heard no serious proposals. I would think that our adversary is more subtle than that, though. That seems a little obvious."

"Unless that's what he *wants* us to think," Butler said dramatically.

Coy did look at him a moment at that one, but still decided not to take the bait. It turned instead to Bon. "Raeph, you've been awfully quiet."

He sighed. "Give me nice clean engineering. Tab A goes into slot B, etc. All this motivation and intrigue is not really up my alley."

"Amen," Ceal Byars echoed the sentiment. She knew she seldom had input at these types of meetings, but had been glad to be included at this one simply to keep an eye on her star patient. Whom even she had to admit was not acting much like a patient anymore. The steady, commanding person she saw before her was a far cry from the lifeless form on the Sick Bay bed not so long ago.

Coy caught her eye and seemed to read the thoughts behind her calculating eyes. It smiled and gave her a small nod.

"Alright, unless someone has more thoughts on all of this..?" No one volunteered any more insight. "Then the Boogeyman discussion is tabled for now. Which brings us to the exciting topic of departmental reports. Major Michaels, have you come up with a plan for commendations?"

The talk continued through all the recent happenings and updates from all the different areas of operation. Butler, in his ongoing campaign for more crew, was pleased to announce that the three techs rescued with the shuttle crew had elected to stay with the Fleet. They were assigned to be the Tac Com crew along with Kefski. So for the first time, all the seats in that department were filled.

The meeting ended with satisfying results. Coy stood, the others following suit and saluting again. As the rest of the officers left for their various duties, Ceal remained behind. Coy looked at her with amusement. "You're not going to keep mothering me forever, are you?"

"And what makes you think that's what I wanted to talk about? You're not the only item on my job description, you know."

"Oh?" As she had made no move to get up and leave, Coy sat on the edge of the table to listen.

"It's just that..."she looked down at her hands. "This may sound a little silly. But when we went to Riga, I called myself Dr. Byars in order to scavenge what respect from them that I could." She paused.

"That makes sense." Coy was admittedly a little puzzled by her anxious expression. It hadn't seen her wring her hands since the early days of the Fleet.

"And after we came back, well I got to thinking about it. I liked being called Doctor, but I'm not one. I have no official credentials to prove..."

Coy held up a hand to stop her. "What is my rank?"

She frowned. "Commodore."

"And how did I get it?"

"You started the Fleet."

"I started the Fleet as a captain. The titles changed when circumstances required."

"That's not exactly the same."

"Actually it is. In fact your claim is probably more accurate than mine. You at least went to school for your learning. Even my very original rank many years ago was simply given to me by my commanding officer at the time. I have no formal training to be a commodore."

"You're saying I should just name myself a doctor whether I am or not."

"I'm saying you don't need a document to prove what you are. Look at me, and Vennefron and Pierce and Erhardt ...people you have literally put back together. How much more proof does the universe need?"

She thought for a few more minutes, and then stood at last. "I suppose you're right," she said without conviction. "I....thank you, for your confidence." And with that she walked out.

Lamont waited about a second before it called Asch back into the room. "Lieutenant, I have a little job for you..."

Coy was interrupted in the middle of its dinner by its screamer followed by Venn's voice.

"Sir, we have a distress call from this very system!"

The commodore dashed out of its cabin even while speaking into its wrist com. "What kind of ship and attackers are we dealing with?'

"It seems to be a military craft. Their message is somewhat fuzzy, but I believe they are saying that they were escorting another ship. They both seemed to be severely damaged, but I can't tell by whom."

"Rally the troops, Lieutenant. Our vacation is over. Lamont to Butler. Prepare all ships for immediate departure on my command."

"Butler. All ships, aye, sir."

At the sound of the screamer, BlackFleet personnel, new and old, raced to their primary positions. Still not knowing what type of situation they faced, troopers and *Talon* crew alike prepared. By the time Coy reached Tac Com, three officers were in their places to communicate directly with the ships each was assigned to. Bon arrived and slid into his

Fleet engineering station and Kefski dashed into place to complete the Tac Com team as Vennefron took over I & S from him.

"We have coordinates?" Lamont asked.

"Transmitting to all ships," Venn acknowledged.

"Captain," Lamont said to Butler on the bridge of the *Raven*, "move the Fleet."

"Aye, sir, moving out."

Coy turned to the Tac Com personnel. "All ships on alert."

One by one the officers reported the shield and weapon status of their charge. Coy looked in satisfaction around the room. The discipline of each person at the stations gave no indication that this was the first the team had functioned together in an actual battle situation. It also felt good just to have enough people to do the job correctly. Score one for Butler.

As I & S had indicated, it took very little time to reach the site of the emergency.

And an emergency it was. A lone vessel drifted, apparently without power, its exterior pocked with holes. It was a Destroyer class ship with definite military markings on the hull. The space surrounding it was filled with debris.

"What the ..?!" Butler's voice came over Coy's command com.

"There's junk everywhere!" Rebel exclaimed from the *Rook*. "Enough for an entire other ship. At least one. And bodies."

"Get someone on the line," Lamont commanded. "And find out where to start."

"Aye, sir, I'm trying," Aziza answered. "I'm not getting any…wait a minute. Damn, lost him."

Coy waited for the lieutenant to regain the signal, which it had no doubts about whatsoever. Meanwhile, Bon was recording scans of everything floating in space around them.

"Rebel was right. It looks as if another ship exploded from the inside out. From the marks on the remaining one I'm guessing it was shrapnel from the exploding ship that tore it apart, rather than a battle."

Coy frowned deeply. "What would make a ship blow apart that totally?"

"Sir, I've got someone," Aziza interrupted. "Visual is pretty degraded, though. On your vid, now."

The image of a young man in uniform appeared on Coy's display. His uniform was filthy, blood ran down his face from cuts and he was holding his right arm at a peculiar angle.

"This is Commodore Coy Lamont of the BlackFleet Mer…"

"I don't care who you are, we need to get people off of this ship before it blows to pieces, too!"

Coy's mouth was still open from the aborted introduction, and now its brows shot up to complete the stunned image. Despite what the officer deemed a tearing emergency, it took a second to compose its voice and features. "How many shuttles do you have that can transport your people to our Fleet?"

"None."

"Excuse me?"

"Our shuttles were docked on the other ship."

"I see. So how many people are we talking about?" it asked, while motioning Bon to start working on the evacuation procedures. The ship was smaller even than the *Nighthawk*, which would preclude their landing in their bay with the size of BlackFleet shuttles. That meant externally docking- hatchway to hatchway.

"How many? I don't know. We had a crew of 60. Half, maybe more are alive. I'm not in communication with the whole ship. And we picked up maybe 25 or 30 survivors from the other ship that had made it to lifeboats."

Bon relayed the information to the shuttle bays of all three ships. Drake and his team got the *BlackBird* ready to launch from the *Raven*. Within minutes there were teams of space armored troops ready on the *Rook* and *Nighthawk* as well. Byars prepped Sick Bay for a possible 60-70 incoming wounded.

"Aid is on the way, ah Captain…" Coy informed the bedraggled image.

"Lieutenant. All of the senior officers are dead. They were over on there. That's why the shuttles…" his voice cracked, and he cradled the broken arm. "We really want off of this ship, Commodore."

"Hang on Lieutenant. We'll have you safe and sound in our Sick Bay as soon as possible." Coy tried to project as much calmness and firmness as possible. "What exactly happened?"

He sighed wearily. "We don't know. The captain and exec went over to have this fancy dinner with the commander of the colony ship, and then all of a sudden it just blew up! We didn't have battle shields up. Pieces of it ripped right through us. "

Coy and Bon looked at each other with identical frowns.

"There must have been some warning," Bon speculated. "A surge in power, a rupture…something."

"You weren't here!" the young man snapped in anger. "You asked what happened. That's what happened. My *captain* was over there. If I knew it was gonna blow up don't you think I, we would have done something!"

Coy couldn't tell from its position on the *Raven* whether the lieutenant was seriously wounded, seriously overwhelmed or seriously lacking in protocol. It suspected a rather newly commissioned officer in charge of the bridge for the first time getting hit with a situation like this. He was as riddled with guilt as his ship was with holes. In any case this conversation was doing nothing to calm him down.

"You're absolutely right, Lieutenant," Coy told him. "Perhaps we should let you get on with the evacuation and we will talk to you when you are on board. Our shuttles will be mating with your ship momentarily."

With that the lieutenant reached out and cut the com. Coy blinked in surprise at the blank vid. Then it looked up to see the five faces around the Tac center registering the same surprise.

"Overflowing with gratitude, ain't he?" LaRue drawled.

"We don't make judgment calls on people in horrific situations," Lamont told him, all the while thinking much the same thoughts. "Let's get him and his people over here and put as much distance between this mess and the Fleet as we can until we know for sure that whatever happened to the first ship isn't going to happen to the other."

Vennefron came on the command com at that. "Are you thinking sabotage, sir?"

Coy started to answer then stopped. "We won't know until we investigate. But I think it's a possibility."

"It certainly would account for an explosion big enough to completely destroy the ship but have no forewarning," Bon agreed. "Except that it would take an awfully well camouflaged bomb to be that powerful and not be detected by someone in some scan."

Coy nodded agreement and then mentally tabled its thoughts on the subject until the immediate situation was dealt with. "Launch the rescue parties. Medical standing by?"

"Standing by, Commodore," Ceal spoke for the entire Fleet's medical staff.

The *BlackBird* and the shuttles launched into space. One by one they mated with the damaged vessel, transported as many of the desperate people as they could, then detached and headed back to their mother ship. As it turned out, there were more survivors on the destroyer than the lieutenant was aware of. In all 93 people were ferried back to the waiting Sick Bays.

Elite Forces and Schiff's troopers were drafted as corpsmen as a large percentage of the rescuees had physical wounds ranging from bumps and bruises to life threatening injuries, and nearly all were emotionally distraught. A great help, however, was the fact that there were four medically trained people among the survivors. One, an actual doctor, was injured himself but oversaw some of the first aid while propped on a stretcher pushed along by a trooper.

Ceal started to object, but realized the frustration the physician would feel at being helpless in the midst of his own people's suffering. She vowed to get him settled and resting as soon as the crush of work subsided, however, even if it took sedation.

Meanwhile, once the ship was totally evacuated, the entire BlackFleet moved to what Coy deemed a safe distance- with shields up. The destroyer and the remains of the other ship were thoroughly scanned, and analyzed, as the engineering staff tried to uncover the reason for the devastation.

With the medical and engineering departments busy with their areas of expertise, Coy, Butler and Vennefron sat down with Lieutenant Conrad-Kurita, arm in cast, and some other representatives of both ships.

"You mentioned the term colony ship," Coy opened, after proper introductions were given.

"Yes. My company was sponsoring the resettling of these people to Esperanza. It is not a new world as such, but it still has quite a bit of land open to a form of homesteading and had advertised for emigrants," Mr. Lin-Speidel explained. "We had settlers from both Katsu and DeGaulle."

"My family was some of them," the other representative said bitterly. He was an older man who had definite signs of Earth Asian ancestry, as did most denizens of Katsu. The only thing keeping the sorrow out of his eyes was the anger that was there. "I want to know what caused this. Was the ship faulty? Should we be suing somebody?"

"No, and no," Lin-Speidel, answered quickly. "The ship was fine. We're a new company, yes, but we stand by our product..."

"Excuse me," Coy interrupted, "A new shipping company?"

"Fairly new, yes. Passengers, commercial trade, we do it all. The competition among the ship making industry is stiffer than you think. It took us several years to get this product out of design and into the market. We knew it had to be the best," he turned from Coy back to the settler. "And it is."

"Was," the man corrected.

Lamont looked at Vennefron with a very distinct 'write that down' expression. It needn't have bothered. The intelligence officer was busy making several notes. Coy gave Butler a grim smile.

"Shipping," Butler whispered the word.

"Mr. Kaneta, I tend to agree with the assessment of the ship. Our fleet engineer tells me that a defect large enough to cause this could not have gotten past the most cursory inspection."

"Then what? What killed my sons?" Tragedy had hit him hard and he needed a target to strike back at. Coy desperately wished it could give it to him, even though it knew from experience it didn't really help.

"We have some theories, but they will have to wait for my people to finish their examination of the site. We have also been in contact with your government and they are sending their own team of investigators. Between us we should discover the answer."

The older man accepted this, but did not pretend to be satisfied. He sat back in his seat with a resigned sigh.

"What will you do now?" Butler asked him out of honest curiosity. "Go back to Katsu?"

Kaneta shook his head. "I really don't know. I sold every-thing. I have nothing to go back to. And I have nothing to start with on Esperanza. My eldest son and I had an accounting firm. We were go-ing to help the others get their businesses established." He sighed sad-ly. "I can't go forward and I can't go back."

"Ah, Mr. Kaneta," Coy said carefully, glancing at Butler just to witness the reaction, "that does leave one obvious possibility."

"I don't see what…"

"Staying here."

The man stared at him. For several minutes. "Join the mili-tary? At my age?"

"Not the military, as you know it. But this crew, yes. There are a lot of different types of jobs that need done on this ship as well as my others. I realize that you and your fellow countrymen have just experienced a horrible situation. But if anyone needs somewhere to belong for awhile…Well, think about it anyway."

Butler was gawking openmouthed. Vennefron nudged him to get him to start breathing normally again.

Coy asked Conrad-Kurita a few more pertinent questions then all three men were allowed to retire to the quarters assigned to them. Vennefron also hurried off to I&S with his notes, leaving Butler and Lamont alone.

"There's a lot of people down there, Skipper," the captain fi-nally managed. "What if they all want to stay?"

"Realistically, all 90 will not stay. Many are crew from the destroyer, after all. But even if a large number do, we have the room and the jobs for them. According to my Exec's notes."

Butler shook his head as if to clear it. "I said this once before for a diametrically opposite reason: make me understand."

Lamont, who had been standing, ready to leave, sat back down at the table. "I can't even begin to explain the differences in my head, Ken. I've spent a lot of time lately trying to analyze the new infor-mation they 'gave' me"

"Your cascade."

Coy nodded. " There were things I had always wanted to do and couldn't. I'm…I've always thought I was supposed to stay quiet, in the shadows…"

"A good spy," Ken interrupted.

"Exactly. At least up until…" it thought back. "About the time I joined Corbett. I signed on pretty low in the crew. But something made me not want to stay there. I'd have these…bursts…of initiative and do something to get promoted. I didn't know where they came from. If I'd had normal human emotions I'd have been terrified. As it was I was merely confused.

"I think," said Ken, "that we've seen some of those bursts."

Again, Coy nodded agreement. "That's how the BlackFleet came into existence. Then the burst was over and I was left holding a ship and crew I didn't know what to do with."

"I didn't help there, did I," Ken began in an apologetic tone.

Coy waved it away. "How could you? I didn't even know what the hell was happening."

"And now?"

Coy sighed. "It's no longer bursts. It's all the time. Except that the old feelings are not gone. It's both. It's…" it was at a loss.

"Melding?" Ken offered. "Combining the two drives?"

Coy looked at him gratefully. "Maybe. But I still don't know why or how."

"Why Riga made you two different people? Or why you're becoming one?"

Now Coy looked at him in amazement. Ken Butler, sarcastic, argumentative Ken Butler had put his finger on it exactly. "Two people. Why would they make me with two different personalities?"

"I have no idea. Unless it was to accomplish two different goals – which didn't happen.."

"Hence the meltdown."

"At least you rebooted sane," Ken grinned. "Ceal and I were kinda worried you'd wake up this completely different person."

"In a way I am. I'm not who I used to be . Literally. I don't even know if you'll want to work for who I end up being." Coy said it casually, but Ken could tell it was a thought that bothered it quite a bit.

"On the contrary, I like the new aggressive Lamont." Another grin. "It likes bigger fleets than the old one did."

Coy raised a brow. "Is that a fact?"

"You didn't even bat an eye at the changes I had made in your…absence." He nodded for emphasis. "Yep, I like it. And speaking of bigger fleets. I was wondering if you could make it big enough to be an admiral so I could be commodore full time?"

Coy appeared to think about that for second, laughed a little, but did not, Butler noticed, answer.

The BlackFleet remained guarding the destroyer and the debris for several days while waiting for the Katsu government to send their team. In that time the engineering staff worked double shifts trying to piece the puzzle back together. Starting with the trajectories of the shrapnel and working backwards they attempted to put the colony ship back together – at least a virtual image of it in the computer. From there they tried to locate the point of the blast that had devastated the ship and the lives on it.

Despite the fact that no one in the crew had ever done anything like this before, they plugged on determinedly and true to BlackFleet tradition, succeeded.

A weary but triumphant Bon called from engineering for Lamont, Butler, Vennefron and Conrad-Kurita to meet him there. In answer to the questions on their faces, he pointed to a tiny blob of melted metal fused to a piece of hull.

"All right," Ken said, "I'll bite. What the hell is it?"

"Accurately put." Bon walked over and picked up the specimen. "I consider it right out of hell anyway." He handed it to Coy. "It's the single most powerful explosive I've ever seen in my life. And most of it seems to have totally disintegrated once it hit space."

"So where did you find some intact?" Venn asked, poking experimentally at the blob with his finger.

"On the destroyer."

"What?!" the Katsu lieutenant yelped, involuntarily taking a step back away from the sample. "I knew we had to get off that thing!"

"Actually, it was only on your ship because it was still attached to the piece of the other ship that landed in yours. We've gone over every inch of the destroyer once we knew what we were looking for and this is about all we found." He paused dramatically. "However it probably wouldn't take a whole lot more than this, in its original state, to make a really big hole. And if it were attached to say the power core in one of the reactors…"

Coy pondered that one for a moment. "What did it look like in its original state?"

Bon shook his head. "Wish I knew. Maybe not a lot different than it does now. That would make it pretty hard to notice. A molecular scan would pick it up, if you knew to do one, but that's about all."

"So there's no doubt it was a deliberate bomb," Butler said.

"No doubt."

"Murder. He's murdered over 200 people this time," Coy's eyes narrowed in fury. "The stakes have raised."

"He?" Conrad-Kurita asked in puzzlement.

The BlackFleet officers looked at each other for a moment before answering. How paranoid would their self proclaimed mission sound to an outsider, anyway? One way to find out.

"We believe we have evidence tying a lot of the pirate activity in the Region together," Lamont told him carefully. "The 'he' is just our way of identifying that we believe this to be part of the pattern."

"You think someone murdered all of those people on purpose?" The lieutenant seemed to have trouble grasping the fact.

"Murder would imply purpose, yes. But I don't think it was those particular people that –someone- had as a target. I think it was simply part of the big picture."

"So what is the target?"

Coy grimaced. "We're still working on that one."

When everyone else had departed Engineering for their own responsibilities, Coy stayed behind to grab a word with Bon. "Raeph, how extensive are the damages to the destroyer?"

He thought for a moment, pretty sure what the commodore was thinking. "You mean can it carry these people back home safely? Or will we end up ferrying them all the way back to Katsu?"

"Something like that," Lamont said evasively.

Bon blew out a breath. "It will definitely take some clean-up. The outside looks like Swiss cheese, but that's all hull damage. Not *too* many internal systems were hit. I mean it's certainly worth the time and trouble to fix….But it's not going to be able to carry people until then. Sorry."

"Hmm," Coy rubbed its chin and thought for a moment more before acknowledging the last remark. "No, that's alright. I was just thinking about…" it smiled, but didn't finish the thought. "Good work on the investigation. We'll download everything to the Katsu ships enroute here. You get some rest."

"Aye, aye sir. No argument."

Coy was a bit surprised by the diplomatic contingent that came with the rescue team. The Katsu ambassador was welcomed aboard the *Raven* with all due ceremony and escorted to Lamont's quarters. He and his staff of four looked around the ship and the quarters with interest, but not, Coy noted, surprise.

"And what may I do for you gentlemen?" it asked as they, Butler and Asch seated themselves comfortably around the long table.

"Well, actually, Commodore, we were prepared to ask that question ourselves, given what we had heard about you and your fleet."

Coy and Ken exchanged a puzzled glance at each other.

"Oh, and what is that?"

The ambassador smiled. "Let me explain. Our government happens to be on quite good terms with the Royal House of Tenetia. We have all heard of your dramatic rescue of the King and his entourage first hand. As well as the terms of payment you requested."

"I see."

"Therefore, I have been sent with the authority to grant you your, 'Favor', I believe it is termed."

"Have you really?" Coy returned the man's smile, but paused for just a moment before continuing. "And you do realize that this Favor can be called in at any time. For anything I request?"

"Yes, yes. I even have it in writing."

Coy took the document disk, inserted it into its scanner and read the contents, nodding all the while. "Ambassador Ryuuzaki, I believe I would appreciate working with you and your government- if we were to have any future association."

Everyone in the room, including the BlackFleet personnel present, blinked and looked at one another in surprise.

"If, Commodore? I don't understand…"

"Well, you see, in point of fact, I already have my Favor decided."

"You do?" Ryuuzaki asked.

"You do?" Butler asked, a little quieter. He looked to Asch, but even he only shrugged.

"Yes, I do. I want the destroyer."

No one said anything for a few moments. Then Ryuuzaki cleared his throat. "You want the destroyer."

"Yes."

"Our destroyer?"

"Yes."

"The one floating outside right now. The one full of holes."

"Yes, Ambassador. That's the one." Coy could tell by the man's unenthusiastic tone that he was not at all happy with this request, and was trying to make the ship as unattractive as possible.

Butler made a little hand waving motion. "Ah, Skipper, could I talk to you for just a second?"

Lamont continued to address the ambassador. "I believe your document entitles you to sign it over to me," it told Ryuuzaki. "I am asking you to do so."

The ambassador spoke to his staff in a quiet tone before turning back to Lamont. "Our forces are not overly large, Commodore. Are you willing to negotiate this?"

Coy shook its head. "No, Ambassador. I sympathize with your need for ships to defend your people. I happen to have the same need myself. This is the Favor I am asking for."

"Very well." Still hesitant, the ambassador took the document back and added his virtual signature and seal to complete the transaction. "There is your ship." He stood, therefore everyone else at the table did likewise. "I believe I will return to mine and co-ordinate the settling of the survivors. The Colonel that accompanied this trip will take care of emptying the computers."

"Thank you," Coy put out a hand.

After a beat, the ambassador put on his best diplomatic smile as he shook Coy's hand. "You are welcome, Commodore. And good luck with your acquisition."

Ken barely waited until Asch had escorted them out before pouncing on Lamont. "What in the universe are we going to do with a junked ship?"

"Fix it up. Find a crew. Put it to work. Same as usual. I have Bon's assurance it's worth repairing."

"Usual? When exactly have we ever acquired a ship that was more holes than space worthy metal?"

Coy wore a perfectly serious expression, "I thought you wanted a bigger fleet, Captain Butler. I get you a destroyer and 90 recruits and all you do is complain!"

"A destroy*ed* ship and 90 *farmers*. Forgive me for forgetting to thank you."

"You're welcome. Now, grab a space suit and let's take a tour of the *Karasu*."

"The *Kar*..." Ken began, then made a surrendering motion, "Let me guess what it means."

Coy nodded to the door. "Are you coming?"

By the time the BlackFleet had made a detailed inspection of their "new" vessel, the Colonel had dumped any data their government thought sensitive and the Katsu ships were ready to transfer the refugee colonists for the trip "home". That is until the colonists gave Ryuuzaki an even bigger surprise.

"They say they want to stay with you," the ambassador told Coy over the vidcom. He shook his head in dismay. "I don't know what gave them the idea that was an option."

"Actually, I did."

"You....?" Now the ambassador frowned. "First our ship, now our people. If I were a paranoid man I would wonder about all of this."

Coy took a breath, wondering itself about how much to try to explain. "The BlackFleet is made up entirely of people who have lost their lives fighting the good fight, so to speak. They want to right some wrongs so that the same things don't happen to others. A tall order, I am aware, but that is our mission. These colonists have quite literally, lost everything. I offered them the chance to belong somewhere where they could do some good for others the same way we tried to help them. If some of them want to stay they are more than welcome."

Ryuuzaki still didn't understand. "These are colonists, not soldiers. What would you have them do?"

"These people are accountants, and cooks, and agriculturalists, and experts in repairing obscure equipment. You don't have people doing those jobs on your military vessels?" Before he could answer, Coy continued. "They gave up their old life just to have their new one stolen from them. If they have the courage to start another one, why would ,or should, you or I stop them?"

The Katsu ambassador started to argue more, then gave up with a small shake of his head. "The next time I think I am well briefed on whom I will be dealing with, I think I will not believe it. Very well, Commodore Lamont. Your "recruits" can stay right where they are. There are some, at least, who have come to their senses and wish to return home. Can you transport them, or shall we send our shuttles back?"

Coy smiled *its* best diplomatic smile and made the arrangements for the transfer. Then it went to meet the newest members of the BlackFleet. Oh, and to inform Captain Butler to add 39 names to the roster.

The scene was very much different than any former BlackFleet interviews. Due to the number of people involved, the meeting was held in the crew mess. The group was directed to divide themselves up by specialty and go to areas around the room manned by Butler, Bon, Ceal Byars, Schiff and Asch. Asch had the largest group and Schiff the smallest, which surprised no one. What did surprise everyone was not only the generous number speaking to Byars, but the gentleman who walked up to Coy with pilot tattoos proudly displayed.

He was an older man, in fact older than most pilots still employed. His story, therefore, was understandable. He had been ready to be dismissed by his sponsoring company due to age. He had requested the job of piloting the colonists as a last effort to escape or at least put off retirement. There was no one else around that would take a chance on him now. Except perhaps, the BlackFleet?

With the understanding that a shuttle would be the most he piloted, at least for now, Jump Pilot Heyob happily went to collect his uniform.

In all they ended up with eight medically trained personnel, eight horticulturalists (which meant that they could at last bring their hydroponics section on line and eat actual fresh food now and then), five cooks (to cook the aforementioned fresh food) 2 more accountants besides Kaneta, 15 that were – or could be engineers, 4 civil servants that Coy had yet to permanently place and one certified Jump Pilot.

Not bad for a day's work.

The colonists had all been in good physical shape in expectation of the work involved in setting up a community on their new world. But despite what Coy had told Ryuuzaki about the civilian type jobs most of them would be doing, they still needed Fleet training.

At the very least Coy meant to see that they could all shoot straight, knew basic self defense and first aid, and could tell the light switches from the self destruct in engineering and on the emergency bridge. And for the ones who looked like they were going to complain, a viewing of the events during the battle for the *Raven* quieted them right down. In the end, they astonished all the senior staff by not only sticking it out down to the last man, but doing it well. But perhaps that wasn't so surprising considering these were people who had given up everything they had ever known to help build a new world. No cowards here.

While the recruits were training, the *Karasu* was towed back to Triton. And for the first time in BlackFleet history, Coy actually had to pay cash for getting a job done. The renovations to the *Raven* and *Rook* had taken all the Favors that could be stretched to include ship repair. Months before, Coy had let Asch loose to do some innovative financing with its personal monies and properties gained in the same card game as the *Raven*. It was now extremely glad it had done so. When all was said and done, the repairs were paid for and Coy was still left with one piece of property on Servati – which was one more than it ever expected to use.

It took longer than Coy had hoped to do the repairs, renovations and obligatory black paint job on the *Karasu*. During the interim, Coy decided to take a few short term, low risk 'contracts'. They received a call on the dedicated drop spot from the government on Tai Han. It seemed they needed to transport some rather important people to Kabale and wanted a little backup. Would the BlackFleet be interested in escort duty?

It seemed a reasonable, and quite understandable request. Coy decided to leave Butler at Triton with the *Nighthawk* to oversee the continuing work on the *Karasu*. The *Rook* and *Raven* with their *Talons* on board would be the most useful if it came to actually protecting their clients.

The trip, however, was nicely uneventful and the most workout the *Talons* got was flying point. It also gave the new crew a much calmer initiation into BlackFleet service than most of the members had ever enjoyed. Nothing like the memorable trial by fire experiences of the *Nighthawk* crew nor triple plus shifts of the original *Raven* team.

It also gave Coy plenty of time to ponder exactly how to man the new vessel. Not that it would ever admit to Butler that it was a problem. And actually, Coy told itself, it wasn't really. Yes, a few departments that they had just gotten up to speed were going to be spread a little thin –again- , but that was nothing new to anyone.

Some personal observations as well as vid com conferences with Ken assured Coy that Tony Knepp could handle still another elevation. This time to commander of the *BlackBird*. When it was docked, Knepp could continue doing his current duties on the bridge of the *Raven* in Butler's absence. But if circumstances dictated that the '*Bird* was cut loose, Butler would be taking over the bridge of the flagship and Knepp would take the yacht-turned-warbird and leave Drake available to take over the new vessel.

That settled all that was left to fill was every other position on the ship. A little creative shuffling of new and old crew and that was taken care of as well. The next highest position, chief engineer was also filled by veteran BlackFleet Hassam Tibai. Jump Pilot Heyob was beside himself with joy at being given his orders to report as J P for the destroyer.

Lynn Harper was put onboard as shuttle and backup pilot having shown tremendous, and untapped talent as a future JP. Com and Weapons chairs were filled by a couple of those rescued by the *Talons* on Kendrick. The Tac Com position for the *Karasu* was given to one of the civil servants turned mercs. Engineering and medical were staffed by an even mixture of new and old.

As Coy sat at its desk pondering not only all the changes the Fleet was going through, but also at its own acceptance…no, it had to be honest with itself…enjoyment at it all. Someday it was going to have to properly apologize to Butler for all the grief it had given him back in the old days. Someday.

It was smiling to itself at that, when a breathless Ceal Byars entered its quarters.

"Ceal? What…?"

"We found him. Finally. Well we could've done it sooner I suppose, but with you being dead and all we kinda put it on a lower priority I guess. But we did it…"

"Whom did you find?"

Ceal took a breath as if making a great announcement. "Hessemen."

Chapter Nine

The room looked much like any other low end bar in any other town on any other planet. Neutral colored walls, inexpensive furniture, cheap copies of cheap art on the walls. Tables and booths were occupied by semi sober people trying to hold conversations with other semi sober people. Tinny music floated through the air entertaining no one. A rather unexciting prize for a long tedious search.

A quick survey of the room showed only one card game being played at present. Coy picked out their target easily enough from the description of his current appearance. If they hadn't had the information, however, there would have been no way Coy or Bon either one would have recognized this as the same person from the game on Alluria. He was much smaller, tan instead of the pasty pale from before, thick dark hair and just a touch of an accent that was impossible to place. His name this time was Cravaack.

Coy nodded to Raeph and Ken and the three of them converged on the game. Bon and Butler both pulled chairs up on either side of "Cravaack". Coy sat down in a space between two players, directly across the table.

"What is going on here?" sputtered one of the players. "Cravaack, are you in some sort of trouble?"

"What? No! I don't know what this is all about," he sounded convincingly innocent.

"I'm sorry, gentlemen, but I need to talk to Mr. Ah, Cravaack, here for a little while. After I'm done he can return to your game, if he's still interested…and able," Coy told them, smiling at them all.

"Forget it," another man threw down his cards and stomped off.

"What business have you got with these…" the first player eyed their uniforms.

"Mercenaries," Butler supplied for him.

"None!" he cried in self defense. "I've never seen them before!"

"Not entirely true, Mr. 'Cravaack'," Coy emphasized the name so that he could hear the quotes around it. "Now, if you will excuse us…" Bon and Butler each grabbed an arm and stood up on either side of him, forcing him to stand as well.

"I am so glad you lost that weight!" Bon murmured to him.

Cravaack stared hard at both of them and then over at Coy. "A herm mercenary," he said slowly, beginning to make connections. "Oh, shit."

Coy grinned at him, and nodded to the door.

Two angry faces watched them exit the bar, sure that they had just been scammed out of some winnings. Hardly anyone else even acknowledged their leaving.

"Where are we going?" Cravaack demanded as they turned down a few streets.

"Oh, I'm sure you'll recognize it when we get there," Coy told him. "After all, it was yours for awhile, I believe."

Cravaack came to a dead stop, dragging his two bodyguards to a halt alongside him. "You don't still have that damn ship do you? Are you insane?!" he choked out. He looked all around him. "What do you want with me?"

"Just some information," Butler told him. "Which we could get a lot faster if you would keep walking."

"Information. You are insane. Just what do you think I can tell you?"

"We will discuss that at length once we are aboard the *Raven*," Coy said in an even voice. "Now as Captain Butler indicated, this would be over more quickly if you co operate."

"Cooperate? I'm not setting foot on that cursed ship!"

"As you wish," Coy said and nodded to Bon.

"What are…" was all he got out before the hypo hissed against his neck. "You're in…" He went limp in their arms.

"Insane, yes, I know," Coy finished for him.

"Now I'm real glad he lost that weight!" Bon grunted, slinging the unconscious man's arms around his neck as Butler did the same on the other side.

Around one more corner they hit the docks. They headed for the shuttle waiting for them in the rented slot, BlackFleet guards standing by the hatch.

"Shore leave," Coy grinned and shook his head at any questioning looks they got from passersby.

From the information that Ceal and Vennefron had uncovered, their guest's original name had been Dominick Tryon. He didn't seem to have used it however for a good twenty years, using about 30 different aliases over that time. Coy figured he must have had a memory almost as good as its own to keep track of all the deceits.

Whoever he was at the moment, he came to consciousness slowly as Ceal's antidote took effect.

He looked around the room blearily for a moment before his memory caught up with him. When it did, he jerked upright on the couch he had been lying on.

"Oh my....I'm really on ..." he turned panic stricken eyes on Coy. "What are you doing? What do you want from me?"

Coy took its time seating itself calmly in a chair across from him. "Why are you so afraid of this ship?"

He paused a moment and surveyed the faces around him. He made a concerted effort to collect himself. "It's not the ship. It's..." he paused again and turned back to face Lamont. "It's not really yours you know."

"I have documents saying otherwise. They do not appear to be forgeries..."

"No, they're real. But, I mean, surely you know by now this wasn't mine."

"I know you were the middle man. The 'fence' as it were. Which brings me to who's on the other side of the fence."

Tryon stared at it for several minutes, his lips shut tightly as if he were afraid something might escape through them without his consent. "Y-you can't pentha me," he stammered.

Coy sighed. "I know. We tested you while you were out. Which leaves us with another puzzle. Most independent fences value their own skin rather highly. It makes me wonder all the more what information you have that's more important than your life?" Coy raised an eyebrow in invitation.

Tryon looked as if he was going to respond to that, but stopped himself.

"It also puzzles me why you are so afraid of him when he's so far away, and yet not afraid of me when I'm right here."

Butler and Bon exchanged a quick glance at each other at the obvious bait.

"He's never far away," Tryon mumbled.

"I meant him personally," Coy told him, "not his hired hands."

"Same thing. Dead is dead no matter who pushes the button."

Coy toyed with the idea of presenting itself as a button pusher, but it didn't want to make a bluff and he call it. It would weaken their position even more. They sat in silence a moment more.

Tryon frowned at Lamont. Coy got up and walked across the room to pour itself a cup of tea as if it hadn't a care in the universe.

Tryon watched it . "I know what you're trying to do with me."

Coy looked pensively down into its cup as it stirred its tea. " I'm doing the same thing I do every day – I give people options of how they want to live – in shame and fear or pride and accomplishment."

Tryon snorted. " You don't have that power."

"I beg to differ," Bon spoke up. "I think so would a whole fleet full of people who are living that better option." He looked at Coy and gave a firm nod of support.

Coy smiled and kept stirring.

"You can't fight him," Tryon tried again.

"Watch me."

"It's too big now. Too many lines involved."

Coy finally took a sip of its overly stirred tea, hiding its attention to even this tiny bit of information. "He can't control all shipping," Coy took a shot in the dark.

Tryon shook his head. "He thinks he can."

All three BlackFleet officers froze in shock of having their theory proved by four such simple words. Then by exchanged glances they all seemed to agree to keep Tryon in the dark as long as possible as to how much he was helping them. Coy returned to the chair it had occupied previously.

"What did the *Raven* have to do with everything? What was the point in giving it to me?"

He shook his head in exasperation. "A mistake. A mistake that has all but ruined my life." He looked ruefully at his captor. "Still ruining it."

"What mistake?" Coy asked.

Tryon glared. "You're the wrong bloody Rigan!"

The conversation halted as everyone digested this revelation.

"So what made you think I was the right Rigan?"

He snorted. "How many Rigans were there on Alluria?"

Coy blinked. "Then what makes you think I'm the wrong Rigan?"

"You must be. You're doing the wrong things."

"Such as trying to stop him with his own ship?"

Tryon, suddenly aware of how much he was talking, closed his mouth with an almost audible snap.

Coy gave him a grim smile. "Well, the Boogeyman may have had this ship once, but thanks to you and your mistake, it's mine now."

Tryon was caught off guard by the reference. "The Boogey what?"

"Besides being a child's nightmare, it refers to an ancient Earth people who preyed on passing ships. It also is my nickname for my, ah, adversary."

Ken stared at it with one of his 'how do you know this stuff?' expressions.

"Adversary." Tryon snorted. "He will destroy you before you can get close."

"At which point he destroys you – because you're with us," Ken pointed out. "Cause the longer you're here the more chance there is that you will tell us something a little more useful."

He dug his hands into the upholstery for emphasis. "I will not!"

"Ah, but will 'he' believe that?"

Tryon suddenly went very, very white under his expensive tan. "Let me go."

Coy shook its head. " Captain Butler is right. I think I had better keep you right here where you are safe."

"Until I talk?"

"At that point we could re negotiate, yes."

Tryon stared at Coy's calm face. "You've killed me. Whether I go or stay, I'm dead."

Coy shook its head in disagreement. "Options, remember? Yes, out there I would agree your usefulness has expired . But here, you can help out a whole lot of people and we can keep you safe. What do you say?"

Tryon began his first day of silent protest in the brig.

"I wonder how many conversations it would take to get another snippet of anything useful?" Coy sighed after Tryon had been escorted out.

"There's probably ways to speed up his conversation," Bon suggested carefully.

Coy's eyes flashed. "We're not torturing anyone!" It blew out its breath. "I came too close to that with our last prisoner. I don't want to repeat that scene."

"So we wait him out?" Butler scowled. They were still sitting in Coy's quarters reviewing the conversation.

"For now."

Ken blew out his breath in frustration. "If you say so." He shook his head.

"Does make you wonder though," Bon mused.

"Wonder what?" Ken asked.

"Who the right Rigan is?"

. Coy paused in its reach to turn on its computer. It looked at him thoughtfully, but didn't answer. Something in Bon's question *almost* connected with something Butler had said lately. And both things *almost* connected with thoughts Coy had had since the cascade. But nothing quite lined up. Nothing quite...

"Skipper?" Bon asked at Coy's expression.

Coy shook its head. Whatever the thread was it would have to wait until a better time to unravel it. For now it turned on the computer set into the conference table, found the information it was looking for and read for a minute. It raised its wrist com up while it read. "Lamont to Vennefron."

There was a very short pause before, "Vennefron. Go ahead, sir."

"I'm looking at the list of shipping line owners. Is this the most complete list we have?"

"That's probably the list of first layer owners. But what I found was that lots of times a few small companies are owned by some larger company. That's the second layer."

Coy mused on that. "How many layers back can you go?"

"Not very many. I started running into sealed documents and silent partners and all kinds of evasive maneuvers so to speak."

"Hmmm. Thank you Lieutenant. I may be getting back to you soon."

"Aye, sir. Vennefron out."

Lamont lowered its wrist slowly, looking across the table at Butler as it did so. "Evasive maneuvers indeed."

Ken perked up as he caught on. "Literally? You think he's hiding behind bogus company names?"

"One person couldn't literally own all the shipping lines, could they?" Bon asked. "I mean that's so illegal they would be easy to catch wouldn't they? And besides, why would he attack himself?"

Butler snorted and pushed himself away from the table in frustration. "We are missing something really important here. And I have the terrible feeling its right in front of us and we're going to hate ourselves when we think of it. If we're going to do any more brainstorming, I think we need more brains."

Coy definitely agreed.

It had been awhile since Lamont had called a White meeting this large. Every commander and department head, as well as a few bridge officers was present. Coy looked out over the group. The cream of the crop. It smiled to itself at Butler's comment if he ever heard Coy say that again.

"Ladies and gentlemen, once again I need your help. We have the facts lined out as we know or surmise them. I need some fresh insight on how it all fits together. That is why some of you are here that haven't been before." Coy turned on all their screens and watched them peruse the information. "Our current main line of reasoning is: Our Boogeyman owns all of the shipping lines. However, he is attacking same said shipping lines. What is he gaining by this?"

"Is he attacking himself or some newer lines trying to cut in on his monopoly?" someone asked.

"Good question. The only way to know that is to find out who owns the newer companies. Venn?"

"There have been several companies spring up in recent years. The one who made the colony ship the *Karasu* was escorting is a good example. Small, privately owned. They have been hit a lot, but not only them. And not all of them directly."

"How indirectly?" Rebel asked.

"The minister of commerce was threatened on one planet when he was considering using a new company."

A few more voices rose with questions, but Coy put up a hand to stop them. "Say that again." It ordered Vennefron.

Venn looked briefly at Butler to make sure he was supposed to literally repeat it. Ken nodded. "I said the minister of commerce was threatened when he wanted to use a new line."

"He didn't want anyone going over to the competitors," someone else voiced Coy's thoughts.

'What line was the minister in question using?"

"Ahh," Vennefron scrambled through his notes. "Here it is, Betalines. Been around as long as the Beta Region has."

"Has it indeed. And who did he want to change to?"

"You got an idea?" Butler asked wondering at Coy's expression.

Venn dove back into his files. "I did make a note of it, even though it wasn't considered the target in that instance. Here it is, Estar Transport."

"Find out who owns it and Betalines and match them to the owners of the other lines."

"Whoever owns Betalines is the Boogeyman?" Drake asked.

"If only it were that easy," Coy said a bit wistfully. "But back to question one, what is he gaining?"

"Hanging onto current customers by scaring away the competition."

"Getting new customers when the new lines seemed unreliable.'

"Selling ships all the time to replace the ones destroyed by the 'pirates'."

"Keeping the profit from all of those things since the pirates were paid off in whatever they were collecting on the jobs." Suggestions came from all around the table.

"Sort of a win – win....win scenario," Butler commented.

Coy looked again to Vennefron. "How many layers does Betalines have between them and the real owner?"

Venn blew out his breath and shook his head. "I'm guessing a whole lot. This guy is not going to be easy to trace. There could be a hundred phony companies and names between here and there."

"Is there any other direction to try to trace him from?" someone asked.

Coy shook its head. "Not unless one of you can think of one. Looking for other directions is what we have been trying all these months."

"The only other lead that we could follow up on is the explosive that we found on the *Karasu*," Bon put in. "And the trouble with that is that it probably would only lead to whatever scum put it on board – not all the way back to the Boogeyman himself."

"Seems like any line is worth investigating," Hendricks said.

Coy nodded agreement. "We don't want to get excited about possibly having a solid lead after all this time and miss something obvious."

There were several more comments and quite a few intelligent suggestions before the meeting was dismissed. Everyone left feeling very good about the advances they had made, which was a rare thing for these "Boogeyman Meetings."

One person however, seemed less than enthusiastic about it all. In fact the longer they went the more disturbed he appeared. But since he didn't offer any ideas Coy left him alone while everyone else was there. It was not surprised, however, when Aziza asked for a private word. Coy waved Butler and the others out and sat back down.

"What is it Dev?"

Morgan L Brautigan

Aziza sat back down as well, looking down at his hands for a moment before straightening up. "I never really told you much about my family, did I, sir?"

If Coy was surprised by this line of conversation, it didn't show it. "Nothing more was necessary. I respected you when you came on board, as I do now, for having the integrity to walk away and make a respectable life for yourself."

Aziza blinked. "You sound as if you already know what they...are."

Coy smiled as encouragingly as it could. "I have a pretty good idea. What brings it up now?"

"Well, I was thinking as you were talking about whoever is pulling the strings in all this and how there must be another angle to track him from."

"Yes..."

"And I was thinking this guy is real dirty. And real secretive. And real powerful." He grimaced. "Just like everyone in my....my father's circle." He took a small breath. "He, my father I mean, might know who he is – or know how to find out."

Coy hid its sigh of relief. It was terrified Devyu had been going to say he thought it *was* his father. "I see," Coy said carefully, "What exactly are you proposing?"

"Well, basically, just asking him."

Coy raised a brow. "At what cost to you?"

Aziza looked down again. "I don't really know. But I know we need to find this guy. And this could be the best way."

"The fastest perhaps," Coy agreed, "But not necessarily the best." It paused and thought for a few moments. "I can't express my appreciation of this offer or the courage I know it would take to do it. I will keep it as a contingency plan. But," it leaned closer to Dev for emphasis, "if this in any way endangers you or your life here we forget it and carry on as we have."

"At the risk of how many lives?" Aziza asked. "No, I'm not pretending having anything to do with him or that whole business is comfortable or appealing. But if it's necessary – it's necessary. We're here to help people, right? Not to be safe and comfortable."

Coy could only smile. "Alright. I will consider it. And you consider it. Come back to me with the way, when and how of contacting them and we'll go from there." Coy stood up so Aziza did likewise. "I thought I was incredibly fortunate two years ago when you walked in here with just the skills I needed up on the bridge. I didn't know then how fortunate. Thank you, Lieutenant."

Aziza saluted proudly and left to return to duty.

"The mafia!" Butler exclaimed when Coy addressed the issue with its inner circle of advisors. "I never knew Aziza was mixed up in that!"

"He's not," Coy reiterated. "He walked away from all that. And he's only offering to have anything to do with them to help us out." Coy paused. "It would be a little like you asking your brother for help."

Butler's head jerked up in anger. He was about to retort in the same manner, but Coy cut him off.

"I only mention it to put his offer in perspective. He could be putting himself in real danger doing this."

"Himself and the Fleet," Bon added.

"The Fleet?" Butler asked, still a little disgruntled.

Bon nodded. "What if they want something in return for this information? Do we really want to end up owing a Favor to them?"

Coy leaned back in its chair. "I admit, I didn't think of it that way. That is definitely something to be weighed carefully. But as the lieutenant reminded me, we're doing this to help others, not to be safe and comfortable ourselves."

Bon shrugged. "I just don't want to see us sacrifice the integrity of the Fleet if we don't have to. I vote to keep on with the angles we discussed and use Dev as an absolute worst case scenario."

"Don't be wishy-washy, Raeph, how do you really feel?"

He glared at Butler. "Maybe you've never dealt with the criminal underground, Ken, but some of us have. It's no laughing matter to get tangled up with them."

If Butler didn't figure out to leave it alone at that, Coy was ready to step in, but fortunately , he did.

"I agree with your concerns, Raeph," Coy told him. "We will not use this line unless everything else is a bust – or unless the Boogeyman turns the heat up any more and we really can't risk losing another ship full of passengers."

Bon nodded reluctantly, and pushed himself up from his seat. "I'm going to go compare notes with Venn on investigating that explosive."

Butler watched him go. Coy watched Butler, watching him. "Leave it alone, Ken," it commanded.

"You're not curious?"

"As curious as everyone in the Fleet is about everyone else's story."

"Yeah, but you know, don't you?"

Coy shook its head. "It's not something he has ever entrusted to me."

"Ah." Ken looked thoughtful. "This command thing is quite a balancing act isn't it? Knowing when to push people and when to back off."

"As I'm sure you found out."

Butler shuddered dramatically. "What I found out is that I'm not ready to do it yet. The only way I got through it was that I reminded myself everyday that you would be back."

"And if I hadn't..."

"But you did. And I don't want to even think about the 'if you didn't'."

Coy looked at him with a mixture of, still unaccustomed, emotions. Pride, gratitude, friendship...and a little concern. "I never meant to make myself indispensable. I meant to choose people who could and would take over as needed." It paused to word it right. "I need to know that if I were blown away in the next battle, my...the Fleet would not die with me."

Ken sat up straighter and lifted his chin a little. "I never meant to imply that I would ever do less than my best."

Coy smiled. "I never meant to imply I doubted it."

Tryon decided to break his silence after only a few days. He opened up and talked about everything but the issue. Loudly. His accommodations. His food. The profits he was losing. Several old girlfriends. When he branched out into his opinions of Coy's mentality his guards got a little testy and threatened to cut off his air supply.

The Tac Com crew, when not in actual battle situations, had become Vennefron's I&S team. Broken up into units, they spent most of their working hours on the main areas of investigation Coy had decided on over the months: tracing the *Raven's* and/or *Blackbird's* movements before coming into Coy's possession; and discovering the connections of all the various shipping and related companies. Both were tedious, time consuming ventures. But the added staff coupled with the urgency everyone was beginning to feel, began to pay off.

"I&S to Lamont!"

Venn's excited voice broke through Coy's dreams and brought it to a sitting position instantly. "Lamont. Go ahead."

"Sir, one of my teams has made some interesting discoveries about the *Raven's* locations during the last couple of years."

Now Coy was up and halfway to the door. "I'm on my way."

"Shall I call Captain Butler?"

It slowed for only a second in thought. "No. Show me what you have now. He'll be up before too long anyway and we'll brief him then."

"Be up..?" Vennefron's voice trailed off in embarrassment. "I'm sorry sir, I didn't think about it being your sleep shift."

"Don't be ridiculous. We've been waiting for this type of information for months. I would only have been upset if you had waited to tell me." By now Coy was dashing down the corridor on the way to deck 'G'. "I'll be there in a minute."

True to its word, in less time than Vennefron would have thought it possible to run to the lift and drop three decks, Lamont appeared at the door to I&S. The only concession to having been woken from a sound sleep was that its uniform jacket was unfastened and its hair was loose instead of pulled back as usual.

"Alright, Lieutenant, what have we got?"

Vennefron and his assistants led the way into the Tac Room where the holographic map of local space had been enlarged to show major portions of the Beta Region. Vennefron pointed to some highlighted areas. "We've been using all of the various means of tracking that we've discussed before; shield frequency signatures, missing technicians, and a few random sightings. And this is what we've put together." Three areas became brighter at some assistant's command. "These three spots seem to have been visited more often than any other. Here out beyond Tai Han, here in the Regional "south" in the Thrackston Nebula, and in the asteroid fields beyond DeGalle. The nebula seems to have been visited slightly more often and for longer periods than the other two. But all three are definitely more often than anywhere else in space."

Coy took control of highlighting the areas over and over again as it thought. "Bases," it finally said. "They're bases of operation." It continued to highlight and think for a few more minutes. When it finally straightened up, its face was set with determination. "Good work, Commander. And to your crew." Coy nodded at each of them in turn before facing a very proud Vennefron.

"Yes, sir, thank you, sir!" he exclaimed, saluting.

Coy returned the unnecessary salute with a straight face. "I'll announce your new rank at the White meeting when you announce your findings." It took just a moment to shunt the information to its office computer. "And now I think you all deserve some down time yourselves." They all grinned or nodded in agreement. "Until White Meeting, Commander."

As Coy expected there was a great deal of excitement at the news of the, assumed, bases. Now the questions became, who exactly was at each of the locations? And were they even still operational after all this time?

"We need some eyes and ears in each of those areas to keep track of who comes and goes," someone suggested.

"Who and how?"

"Transit portal stations?" Butler asked/suggested. "Maybe someone like our bartender buddy on Alluria."

Coy agreed with the line of thinking. "Vennefron has a few contacts here and there who have given us information from time to time. But this would have to be someone who understood the risks they would be taking."

"So do we plant someone of our own, or hire someone already there?"

"I would vote against using someone already in place. We need loyalty we can depend on absolutely."

"Sir," Asch spoke up.

Coy nodded at the unexpected gesture from its steward.

"If you recall, when I was rescued, there were a lot of grateful people willing to repay the Fleet."

"Yes, I do recall that," Coy gave a small smile at the comment. Asch more than anyone besides Butler himself had daily contact with Lamont's perfect memory.

"One of which was a performer of sorts. A singer, I believe, although not of the highest quality." He made a slightly pained face to emphasize this fact. "Someone like that might be able to secure a position at a station bar or club."

"Hmmm. A possibility," Coy hesitantly agreed.

"How would we find him?" Butler asked. "Do we know his name or anything?"

"Taylor Dickenson," Coy 'recalled' instantly. It turned to Vennefron, but he was already digging into his computer in search of information.

"We'll find him, sir."

"When you do we'll arrange a face to face meeting. I don't want anyone going into this not fully understanding all that we may be asking of them."

"What about our other lines of investigation? Anything on the company owners? I would have thought that it would have been easier than tracking the *Raven.*"

"I would have thought so too," Venn agreed. "But every time we think we get something we hit a wall of non information. But we'll keep trying."

"That pretty much confirms that we are on the right trail as far as I'm concerned," Coy said. "A company or two covering up some less than ethical business deals with some smoke would be understandable. But not this number of companies. They can't all have something to hide."

"Which makes the ones that aren't hiding anything cleared of being connected to the Boogeyman?" Drake asked.

" Assuming they really aren't hiding anything and are not simply more clever than the rest," Butler said.

Vennefron moaned slightly at this thought. "I was all set to classify them as clear just to triage if nothing else."

"Go ahead," Coy told him. "We're already working with a lot of assumptions or we wouldn't have discovered any of the facts that we have. If we second guess everything we're going to be at this a very long time."

Four weeks, one rescue, two skirmishes and absolutely zero clues later, it did indeed feel like they had been at it for a long time. Coy's desire to find the Boogeyman and put a stop to all of the destruction was tempered only by the fact that if and when they did find him, it didn't have a single notion how to stop him. Especially if there were pirate forces at each of the three bases equal or larger than the BlackFleet.

" ' You want to be the vigilantes of the universe? Then give me a fleet to do it with!' " Ken Butler had complained many months ago.

Now Coy had to admit, he was right. They needed a fleet. A large fleet. Large enough to deal with three war fronts at the same time. And an idea was beginning to grow as to exactly how to do it. But first they would need a lot more information about the bases. Hell, *any* information about the bases was more than they had now.

Dickenson was found, verified as being Fleet material and set up on the Transit station in the Tai Han system without much trouble. Within a week of his employment covert messages began arriving documenting the numbers and types of ships and personnel that were passing through the station. If his personal opinions of some of said 'personnel' were anything to go by, these could indeed be some of the attackers they were looking for.

And if this base was indeed still active, then they might surmise that the other two were as well. Due to their locations, however, getting information would not be as simple as setting a spy up behind a lounge piano.

Lamont sat in its quarters having yet another strategy meeting with Butler, Michaels and Schiff when the door buzzer sounded. Asch responded as usual and returned escorting a subdued looking Aziza. He hesitated at the sight of the other senior officers before continuing on into the room and over to Lamont.

"What can I do for you, Lieutenant?" Coy asked, knowing quite well the only topic that was likely to bring Aziza here. It had not told anyone outside of Butler and Bon of Devyu's offer, and hadn't been planning to at this time.

"I…" he began, and swallowed. Then he held something out to Lamont. "Here, sir."

Coy reached for the data disk. "What's this?"

Devyu took a breath, but didn't seem to be able to speak.

Its hand froze as the implication sunk in and for a moment the two of them both held the small disk. Carefully Coy took it, forcing itself to breathe normally. The Boogeyman, sitting there in its hand. It looked back up at Aziza. "Just like that?"

The young lieutenant swallowed again. "Hardly, sir. I…I disobeyed you, sir. I didn't wait. I thought if I could do this for you…" he stopped again.

Butler, the only other one in the room with any idea of what was going on swore softly. "What do they want?"

"It, ah , seems, they know our methods of operation."

"They want a Favor," Coy realized.

Aziza nodded.

"And…?"

He took a breath. "And the rest…I can handle."

Michaels and Schiff both sat absorbing the whole, tense, interplay without a word. They knew that they would be informed of anything they needed to know - eventually.

Lamont and Aziza looked at each other for several minutes. Finally, Coy said, "I don't take lightly the risk you exposed yourself to for this. I also don't take lightly the fact that you did not follow my instructions."

"Yes, sir," Dev answered weakly.

"The two, I believe take care of each other. I can think of no more effective discipline."

"Yes, sir," he repeated.

"Which leaves this," Coy held up the disk. "The answer to all of our proverbial prayers?"

"It isn't as much as I would have liked to... I thought maybe he could give me something more specific. But I guess this guy is pretty good at staying hidden...even from his own kind."

Coy nodded understanding. "In other circumstances I would publicly commend..."

"I would like for this not..." Aziza interrupted, then paused.

"To be common knowledge?" Coy finished for him and he nodded. "Request granted. Outside of the people in this room, only Captain Bon is aware. I will keep it as limited as I possibly can. But.." it stood up to look him eye to eye. "every time a ship docks safely in port at the end of its journey, I for one will know who helped make it possible." Its expression softened for the first time in the conversation. "Dismissed, Lieutenant."

Aziza snapped off a perfect salute and exited the quarters, head a little higher than when he came in.

Coy waited only until the doors were closed behind him. "Captain Bon, Commander Vennefron to my quarters, please."

When everyone was present and seated around the table, Coy ceremoniously inserted the coin sized disk into its vidcom. It sat for a few moments, silently digesting the information displayed.

Bon looked across at Butler and frowned in inquiry. Ken just pursed his lips and nodded in Lamont's direction, indicating that they would know soon enough.

At last Coy looked up at their expectant faces and activated their units.

"This is a record of an individual's activities in the shipping industry going back about five years. Notice the last data coincides nicely with our estimation of when the piracy began. My friends, for all practical purposes, we have found the Boogeyman."

"Do we have a name?" Michaels asked.

"The name Dyvees seems to be on more documents than any other, but what that means, your guess is as good as mine." Coy looked bemused for a second. "Interesting old Earth reference, though."

Ken looked up from reading at that. "Reference to what? Something important?"

"It is the name traditionally given to a man who preferred wealth above all else."

Ken stared a moment. "You mean there's someone besides you who knows all this Earth trivia?"

Vennefron was much too focused on the information before him to even notice the exchange. "Still, how..?" he sputtered, as he read.

"He did it," Bon said without inflection. "He got this from...them."

"Aziza?" Michaels asked. "What did he do?"

Bon clenched his hands, noticed it and made himself stop. "He sold his soul to the devil."

"Don't be melodramatic," Ken protested. As one movement everyone around the table turned to look at him in disbelief. "What?!" he asked innocently.

"I gave my word that his method would not be open for discussion, only the results," Lamont said firmly, squelching any more questions.

Vennefron for one was quite satisfied with devouring those results however they had been obtained. "Are we sure, I mean absolutely sure this is him?"

Coy nodded and highlighted something on the screen. "Here is the top of the pyramid of companies he owns. I'm sure it branches out from there to include smaller companies all over the Region. I am also convinced that we are right about his motives. He owns shipping rights on every planet. And when anyone threatened any of that profit by coming up with a competing manufacturer, booking agent, or ship design, he stopped them.

"The amount of pressure and/or malice used was probably relative to the stubbornness of the competition."

"But no one seemed to know why they were being attacked," Butler pointed out. "At least that's what they told us."

"I don't think they did. If he had told anyone what they were doing to upset him, he would have had to admit to owning everything. So he just, shall we say, persuaded them more indirectly to continue using what they always had."

"That's why some of the hits were people like government officials who were just out with their families or something. He wanted to replace them with people who wouldn't change things." Schiff guessed.

"Commander, see if you can plug up any of the gap between the company names we have at the bottom of the list and these names at the top. It would help in the last stage."

"Stage of what?" Butler asked carefully.

Coy leaned back and regarded them all. "Look at what we have. A: The Boogeyman is out to continue his grip on the entire Beta Region by controlling absolutely every interplanetary transaction. B: He is doing that mainly by means of fear, using various pirate and privateer organizations. C: Said pirates and privateers are at least somewhat organized and using three main bases of operation in order to cover the most area of the Betan sphere. D: That's where we need to hit them in order to stop them."

Everyone assimilated this for a moment.

"Three bases," Schiff said. "With five ships and a handful of fighters."

"Hardly." Coy looked directly at Ken Butler. "If we're going to be the vigilantes of the universe, we're going to need a fleet. A really big fleet. Really bigger than us," it quoted.

"But no one is going to loan us a fleet that size," Michaels began.

"No one planet would, no," Coy switched the Boogeyman temporarily off of their screens and replaced him with some names and numbers. "These are the planets we have done 'business' with that I believe we can trust. This is the size of their forces. Most are, unfortunately, rather small. But combine even a ship or two from each with the Fleet and…"

"And we have a war machine," Michaels came as close to smiling as he ever did.

"How are you ever going to get some of these people to work together?" Ken asked, "We've just spent a good part of the past two years pulling some of these guys off of each other's backs!"

"Don't be melodramatic," Bon told him, re-entering the conversation at last. Coy held up its hand to stop the debate before it began even as Ken opened his mouth to retort.

"Trust me, we'll be brainstorming that one in due time. Right now, our main goal in life is to gather as much data on the bases as possible. The only chance we have is in surprise. And for that we need information. Here is what I had in mind…"

Rebel stood before the assembled *Rook* crew, all anxiously waiting to hear what he had to say.

"We have a special mission," he told them, and watched the enthusiasm ripple through the group. "This one is tailor-made for our ship's unique qualities…we're going to contract out as a freighter hauling --- well, whatever we can."

The ripple changed to a room wide thud of disappointment.

Then Sweggert perked up. "It's a cover."

Rebel smiled. "Thank you. Yes, a cover. We are going to patrol the asteroid belt outside of the DeGaulle system, attempting to gather information on the pirate base there."

"There's a pirate base at DeGaulle?" Pierce said, the shock in her voice evident.

"Not only a base. Possibly one of the Boogeyman's hideouts."

Another ripple. Eyes widened. Rebel could swear he almost heard pulses quicken.

"Yes, ladies and gents, we are close. Very close to a direct strike. And for that we need numbers." Rebel turned on a holo map of the asteroid belt. "The *Rook* will hopefully be able to make a slow circuit around the area hauling between ore mining stations and DeGaulle. You, in shuttles or *Talons* will be dropped off here and there to hide and watch and listen. This is one where the Elite Corps has to live up to its name. There can't be any hitches. No mistakes. If he gets wind that we're this close the whole last year of investigation goes out the airlock. Any questions?"

A few people had tactical questions about positioning the spy ships, and a couple wondered about "one" of the Boogeyman's hideouts.

"There are three, as best we can tell," Rebel explained. "Ours, one by Tai Han, and one in the Thrackston Nebula."

"Whew! The Nebula? How is the Skipper ever going to find anyone in there?"

"Fortunately that's not our job. Captain Hendricks, I believe, will be working on that one."

"What about Tai Han?"

"We have a spy set up there already reporting ship and personnel movements," he switched off the holo.

"We're going to have some company for the trip as well. Lieutenant Parker, JP Heyob and Major Michaels will be joining us. As they are all legitimately retirement age, they suit the image of an old freighter scrounging a living—just in case anyone gets too nosey. And we will all be out of uniform for the duration. As of now we are freighter 181 515 11, jointly owned and operated by our group of motley suckers trying to make an honest dollar.

"Now, dress down and prepare to leave the Fleet."

"Aye, sir," Sweggert saluted. "Motley it is, sir," he added winking at Pierce and Speed.

Rebel returned the salute deciding to let them enjoy the parts of this assignment that they could. And hoping they would all live through the other parts.

The *Nighthawk* flew cautiously around one boundary of the Nebula, dropping unmanned recording drones. Once the *'Hawk* was safely away from the area, the signal would be given for the drones to make their way to their designated observation point. This further lessened the chance of anyone noticing what they were doing. On the "opposite" side of the mass, the *Karasu* was doing the same. The *Raven* and the *BlackBird* were in C space, staying out of sight this close to a possible location of the Boogeyman himself.

Not that they were idle. Coy was using the time to personally contact and invite the heads of state, Secretaries of Defense and/or anyone else with the authority, to come and confer about the pirate threat. None of them were told, however, that others were coming as well. The reality of a summit of the entire Region's most powerful people was considered a little too ominous to be chatting about over com lines.

Of course there were a few that were definitely on the not-to-invite list. Such as Tauten Three, whom they knew to be in the Boogeyman's pocket already. And Riga, and Styx whom they simply didn't trust. And there were a couple of other considerations as well.

Coy showed the guest list to Ceal Byars.

"Is there anyone here that you would rather avoid?"

Ceal swallowed and read the list carefully. "Are these all definitely coming?"

"Sorry, yes. Is your uncle there?"

She nodded.

"I see. Well, we have two options, then. You can A: avoid the group session where he will be, or B: stand up to him, with the Black-Fleet behind you."

She sighed. "Ten more months and he's not my guardian anymore. I don't suppose the Boogeyman would rearrange his schedule of galactic domination just for me would he?"

Coy had to grin. "Sorry, I don't think so. But there still might be a way."

"Oh?"

"Remember when we talked about your feeling uncomfortable passing yourself off as an MD?" She nodded again. "It got me to thinking, so I had Asch do a little research. And we found an interesting fact. We didn't know exactly which planet you meant, but we only found one where the legal adult age is 25. We also found that the age can be waived under certain conditions."

She frowned in puzzlement. "Such as?"

"Such as certain professions with a high degree of authority, for instance." Coy spoke into its wrist com. "Lamont to Butler. Gentlemen, if you please."

The door to the briefing room swished open and Butler, Asch, Bon and Schiff entered. Asch held a flat case. All four men came in and stood in a semi circle behind Coy.

"I would have loved to do this in front of the whole fleet, but the whole fleet isn't here, and besides I figured you wouldn't ever speak to me again."

Ceal just stood speechless, wondering what it was talking about.

Coy took the case from Asch and opened it. Inside was a framed document. "We took the liberty of transmitting the files of some of the procedures you have done since joining with the fleet and your notes on them, to your former medical school.

"The response was immediate. You have retroactively passed all of your exams with superb grades. And it is my honor and privilege as stand in for the president of the University of Servati Medical School, to present you with this diploma, certification and all due honors.

"Congratulations, Dr. Byars. And welcome to adulthood. Where your uncle can't touch you."

Coy handed her the case and shook her hand as she stood numbly. By the time the fourth officer had also shaken it, she blinked, came to the realization it was all true, and burst into tears.

* * * * *

Taylor hummed a non descript tune while he idly played his instrument. Very few people were in the bar this early in the day and he didn't want to blow his whole repertoire now. He had to admit he was rather enjoying his current employment. When he had been rescued from the pirate fighters that had attacked the ship, he had wanted to do something to repay the rescuers. But they were a mercenary fleet and he could think of no use that they would have for a piano player.

Even after they had been dropped off safely at the next station and he had gone on about his normal life, he kept thinking about it. What could he do that would be of any use to the vigilantes? All he did was travel all over the Beta Region singing and ....He remembered the moment when the thought had occurred to him. All over the Beta Region. He traveled everywhere – probably to lots of places that would never let a mercenary soldier in the door. But what about an innocent piano player? 'Don't mind me sir, I'm just here to entertain you all.'

Entertain, and listen to everything anyone was saying.

So he had a self proclaimed contribution. Now how would he go about contacting the BlackFleet to see if they were interested? The more he thought about that, the more daunting it became. So he continued simply traveling and singing and listening.

And then the call came. The BlackFleet needed someone to inconspicuously gather information for them on a transit station. Would he be interested....?

His train of thought was interrupted by a handful of men who came in the door just then. One, a little older and grimier than the others, swaggered up to the bar and pounded on it.

"Anybody work in this dump?" he bellowed. When the bartender was not instantly apparent, the man glared around the room. His hard eyes fell on Taylor. "What are you lookin' at?"

Taylor smiled placatingly. "No offense intended, sir. I'm sure the bartender will be out to take your orders in just a moment."

"Sir," one of the others snickered. "He called you sir."

The grimy man punched the other in the arm, hard. "Guess he knows a gentleman when he sees one."

Taylor was saved from further involvement in the conversation by the bartender showing up at that moment. The men got their drinks and went to a table. The room was small enough that the tables were all arranged in the general area of the piano. When Taylor had suggested the arrangement to the owner of the establishment, his argument had been so that everyone could hear him better and he would get more tips. The owner had grinned at the thought of Taylor getting any tips, but let him move the tables.

Now he employed his standard tactic. He started playing just loudly enough that the men had to raise their voices just the tiniest bit to hear each other. Then he gradually quieted down. Gradual enough that the talkers would not realize it was happening and alter their tone. He kept the music going up and down like that the whole time they were there. Every time it softened, he heard more of the conversation before they lowered their voices as well.

"…'nother job…"

"…my fighter needs a new …"

"…hope it's a rich one this time…"

"…back to base…"

At this last comment, the speaker was hushed by his companions. They all glanced over at the piano, he could tell from his peripheral vision, but he resisted the temptation to either look back or raise the volume of his music. Either would tip them that he had heard something. Instead, he just kept singing the same inane little song to its finish. Then he turned around and pretended to be startled at them looking his way.

"Do you have a request?" he asked, nodding his head vaguely in the direction of his tip receptacle.

"Yeah," one said, "Get some singin' lessons."

Taylor smiled one of those 'the-customer-is-always-right-smiles' and began another song. The men tossed down the last of their drinks and left, laughing loudly at their own humor. Taylor looked at the bartender who smiled in sympathy and shook his head.

Then he looked down at the keys, mentally composing his message to the commodore about a group of fighters heading to the base to get information on their next job.

Randy shifted uncomfortably in the shuttle's pilot seat for the hundredth time. "Is it your turn yet?" he asked over his shoulder.

Andrea Pierce grinned at Marty Thomas and held out her hand. "Pay up."

The third member of the shuttle team sighed and handed over an I.O.U. chit. "Sweggert can you just shut-up for awhile? I'm going broke here."

The blond pilot turned around and looked at them. "What are you talking about?"

"We're betting on how often you complain," Pierce told him cheerfully. "Marty here actually believed you could go a whole 20 minutes."

Randy opened his mouth to defend his honor but a readout on the control panel riveted his attention."Shit! We've got company," his voice automatically dropped to a whisper.

Pierce and Thomas moved up beside him to see the information.

"They're coming close. Shut down!" Pierce ordered in a barely audible voice. All three snapped their helmets into place instantly. All systems up to and including life support were switched off. Silently the trio kept their eyes glued to the console. "We're not here, we're just a rock.." they each mentally chanted over and over.

The numbers and co-ordinates on the passive scanner readout changed steadily as the passing ships came closer and closer. Almost involuntarily Randy and Marty looked out of the front portal of the shuttle at open space. Close enough to be a danger was not necessarily close enough to be seen, but they peered into the darkness anyway. As the numbers indicating the distance between them lowered, their breathing slowed almost to nothing.

Pierce, as "commander" of this little team, had her hand over buttons that would start the self-destruct sequence. As Rebel had said, if their identity was discovered by the wrong people, everything that the Commodore had worked for would be gone. She blanked her mind of everything except the readout in front of her. But before it came any closer to a decision, the numbers went up. The ships, whoever they were, were moving away.

All three let out their breath at the same time as Andrea brought her hand back to her side, flexing her fingers in relief. Randy looked over at the others. "Permission to complain now."

Hendricks and Drake continued their patrol of the boundary of the Nebula, transitioning in and out of C-space at random intervals. Life aboard the two ships became routine. But hardly dull. True to BlackFleet standards, drills, training and exercise went on around the clock. Both captains knew that if these information gathering missions were successful, the next thing the Fleet would be facing was real war. This was the perfect time to make sure absolutely every individual on board was as ready as possible.

Mara Hendricks made the habit of working out in the gym herself where everyone could see her. She would never ask more of her crew than she asked of herself. And she asked a lot of herself. But over the months on the *Nighthawk*, Captain Hendricks had earned the respect of everyone on board, and they would no sooner let her down than the Commodore itself.

Over on the *Karasu*, Drake was still working his new crew into a team. He rather wished Schiff were on board with his infamous repertoire of drills. He did the best he could working from memory and what was stored in the ship's library files. But the very best ones, he knew, were only in the major's head. He overheard veteran crew being grateful for this fact more than once.

Drake surprised Coy with a tradition breaking request one day, after giving his normal reports.

"You want what?" Coy asked.

"A ship emblem, a symbol to rally around and help meld my people into a unit."

Coy thought for awhile. It realized that even after everything that had happened, and the growth of the Fleet, it still thought of them all as being one entity. But it had spread the ships out all over the Region, and given, by inference if not order, their commanders more autonomy than ever before. Maybe it was time to start treating the individual ships as individual teams. Each with their own identity and specialty.

"Sir?" Drake asked hesitantly after the long pause.

"What exactly did you have in mind?"

"Well, sir, a couple of my crew had some ideas, integrating the avian theme with the *Karasu*'s heritage. We could send them to you."

Coy had to smile to itself at the enthusiasm in the young commander's voice. "Very well. Let me see them and I'll let you know."

It took less than half of an hour before word had circulated to all the BlackFleet ships that the logo idea was a go and everyone had submitted their proposals to Coy.

It showed them to Ken. "Did you know all this was brewing?"

Butler smirked a little guiltily. "They ran it by me, yes. First Officer and all. For what it's worth, I think it might be good for morale. We're going to be asking a lot of everyone real soon. A little team spirit couldn't hurt."

"So I assume you have your design for the *Raven* all ready to add?"

"Yes, sir, I do, sir," he said as he brought up the file on Coy's console...

By the next duty day, every uniform was sporting a ship emblem on one sleeve, and not to be outdone, Coy added a Fleet emblem on the other. And although the mood of the day was momentarily lightened by the uniform additions, Coy was proud to see that it did not interfere in any way with the business at hand.

During the weeks of duty, the *Karasu* drones reported two sightings of fighters or cruisers entering the Nebula, the *Nighthawk*, one sighting. After extrapolating their courses from the three entry points the I & S team found that they all converged in the same area of the Nebula. Coy closed its hand around the holo image of the convergence.

"You said once, that the *Raven* had visited this site more often than the other two," it commented to Vennefron.

"Yes, that seemed to be the case."

Coy smiled a smile that was anything but humorous. "When we're ready to go in, I want to be here."

"I don't *know* why they wanted this stuff now," Michaels argued with the traffic control officer on one the mining stations in the asteroid belt. "They didn't tell me and I didn't ask. They gave me money to haul it across the belt, so I'm hauling it."

"Well the next time someone gives you money and a cargo, make sure they give you an accurate flight path and schedule," the controller said disgustedly. "I don't have any record of anyone authorizing you to go through our space."

Michaels made quite a show of looking around at everyone else on the bridge. They all went along with him and pretended to be in disagreement about something. Although in quiet enough tones that the controller could not make out what they were actually saying. Finally he turned back to the com. "Are you saying that we have to go all the way around your perimeter just to get to the station right next to yours?"

"You catch on pretty quick for an old geezer," the controller continued his derogatory tone. "Now move that piece of junk along as fast as it can, before one of my people confuses it for a hunk of debris and recycles it."

"I'm not…" the station cut the com on Michael's statement. As soon as the holo vid vanished, so did Michael's hunched stance. He straightened up and narrowed his eyes at the blank vid. "Geezer indeed," he said coldly.

Rebel moved up to his side. "The next time someone calls this ship 'junk' or 'debris' I say we skip the preliminaries and go straight to war now."

Parker shook her head at their posturing. "If you noticed we got what we wanted – an excuse to cruise the perimeter of the belt."

Michaels and Rebel both looked as if they would rather enjoy their wounded pride a little longer, but duty called. Rebel nodded at Heyob, who was sitting in the pilot chair as he did for all such communication scenes. "Go ahead and take us back out and around."

"Aye, sir," Heyob could never quite keep the grin out of his voice when he was given such an order. He had given up on stretching out his usefulness beyond the ill fated colony ship. To be not only a contributing member of the Fleet, but an essential part of this particular mission, seemed to lift the weight of years off of him. He felt more determined and focused than he had in a long, long time.

The *Rook* pulled out of orbit around the station and headed out into space at a painfully slow speed. The crew had plenty of time to get ready to pick up the shuttle hiding out on a large asteroid and put down its replacement. More teams than Pierce's had recorded ships going into the belt at locations where there were supposedly no factories. Ships that were in no way ore freighters. Sometimes alone, sometimes in groups of two to twenty. Beyond any doubt, this was a rendezvous for something far outside the mining industry.

Rebel and company soon found out what was the very worst part of this whole assignment. When those ships would leave the area at full speed, obviously on their way to a "job", and the *Rook* could not disclose their existence, let alone their position to go stop them.

"Trust me, I know how you feel," Lamont answered his frustration at their next communication. "Just focus on the fact of what you are doing there and how it will ultimately stop them all."

"Aye, sir," Rebel replied, trying hard to sound comforted.

Lamont was not fooled in the least. "Adrian, if you didn't care about such things, you wouldn't be BlackFleet. It's your job to care passionately about stopping these guys. It's good to know that my commanders have their priorities right. Pass on my appreciation for jobs well done to your whole crew."

This "Aye, sir," held much more enthusiasm.

Coy nodded, returned the holographic salute, and cut the com. It turned to Butler, who was spending almost as much time in I & S as Coy and Vennefron had been lately. "We're getting a very good picture of what is going on in their area." Coy studied the image of the asteroid field a little longer before switching over to the Nebula. "It's this one I'm worried about. We need a whole lot more intelligence about this base. And if I'm correct in my assumption that this is his main base, then it will also be the best protected. There are probably picket ships all over in there. We are damned lucky none of the drones have been picked up."

"It's a big place, Skipper, and little drones. I think it would take more luck to bump into them," Ken commented.

Coy raised an eyebrow at him. "So when did you become Mr. Optimistic?"

"Me?!" he pretended to take offense. "I've always been completely supportive and …"

Coy was appropriately amused, until it looked beyond Ken to see Vennefron frowning at his screen. It waved a hand to cut Butler short and went over to see what was up.

"Do you happen to know how often you do that?" Butler mumbled.

"A problem, Commander?" Coy asked.

Venn pursed his lips. "I sure hope not, sir. But Taylor has missed two communication times."

Coy's stomach dropped.

Butler lost all flippancy and joined them. "That's not his style."

"Not at all," Coy agreed "Signal him."

"Aye, sir." Vennefron sent the transmission that would make Taylor's wristcom vibrate. No one but the wearer would be aware of the call. There were a variety of silent responses Dickerson could send in return if he were in a situation where conversation would be impossible. No response came back at all.

Coy merely looked at Butler.

"I'm on it," was the captain's reply, even as he was raising his own wristcom. "Butler to Bridge. Best possible speed to Tai Han."

Knepp and a few *Talon* crew, wearing civilian gear, wandered casually into the establishment. They paused just a second before heading straight over and ordering drinks. Tony turned to lean his back against the bar and took in the whole room. The chairs and tables, the tacky artwork…the empty piano.

"What, no entertainment?" he 'teased' the bartender. "When does your singer come on?"

"Find out and we'll both know. Didn't show up for work yesterday or today." He shook his head. "They come and go. Drifters, you know. But…well, he was okay. Sorry to lose him."

Tony grinned at him. "Hey give us our drinks free and we'll go find him for you. We've had no fun at all for ages."

The barkeep frowned at him. "I don't care what you do. I don't hand out free anything….And roughed up piano players can't do much singin'."

Tony tossed his drink down and slammed the glass back down on the bar. "Well, I'm gonna go look. I haven't seen anything on this hunk of metal worth doing anyway. And we're stuck here until…" he acted as if he stopped himself. "Come, on guys. Let's go find ourselves a piano player."

"You're crazy," Milner said on cue. "We just got here."

"And now we're leaving," Tony pretended to push him. He looked over at Smith. "Pay the man, Anth."

"What ! I paid last time!"

"So you're paying again."

Grumbling, Smith handed over his chit for the barkeep to scan. "This better be one good piano player to be worth this."

"Actually," he cringed a little, "he isn't all that great."

"Terrific," Smith rolled his eyes and followed his friends out.

It really only took a couple of hours and a few questions to find out where Taylor had been seen last. A scruffy old dock worker told them about seeing a well dressed young man in the company of some seedier types hanging around the warehouses night before last. Knepp thanked him and they began a methodical search of all the warehouses in the row. The fourth one they tried was nicely dark and decrepit.

Sneaking in, they climbed up to the catwalks as silently as humanly possible in order to get the best view they could. It didn't take long to find them. In the very center of the building, surrounded by ancient crates and broken down machinery, five men stood and one lay on the floor. It didn't take a second look to know who it was on the floor. One of the five was talking.

"I never met a piano player that was artificially allergic to pentha." He kicked Taylor in the stomach. The spy groaned and curled around the injury. "But no matter. When the boss gets here, he'll find out anything he wants to know. He just has that sort of way with people."

The other four chuckled at the remark. "When is he getting back anyway," one said. "I'm starving. Let's send somebody out for food."

"He didn't say. What he did say was to be here when he arrived. You really want to make him annoyed and end up with *him*?" he gave Taylor another token kick.

The rescue team obviously had no time for an elegant plan. Just as Knepp was about to signal the others to get in a better position with their stunners, he suddenly met the sixth member of the group. Rough hands spun him around. "Well what do we have he..." was all he got out before Tony's stunner went off point blank in his gut and he dropped to the metal floor with a thump.

"What the...!" the five down on the floor jerked up straight.

"Shoot anything breathing!" Tony commanded.

Stunner fire filled the room. Graham was hit by return fire, also stunner, fortunately, and was grabbed by Smith before toppling over the railing. It really took very little time for there to be nothing moving on the floor below.

"Knepp to shuttle! We could use a lift."

"Gotcha, Commander. On the way." The pilot lifted the shuttle out of dock and landed it with less grace than he could have on the tarmac outside the warehouse. True a few shipments of something that were inconveniently waiting for loading would never see the rest of their journey, but he really didn't care a whole lot. What he *did* care about came stumbling out of the building half dragging two inert bodies. They practically fell into the open hatch he had waiting for them. The hatch shut and they blasted off, ruining still more of someone's cargo.

Twenty minutes later, a grimy pirate rounded a corner and stopped abruptly. He took in the scorched area and narrowed his cold eyes.

Lamont took a breath and went into Sick Bay. It found Taylor sitting up in bed, being tended by Byars. She got up at the commodore's entrance and let them have some space to themselves. She did, Coy noticed, stay within "mothering" distance.

The entertainer/agent looked up at Lamont with apologetic eyes. "Shorry, Commodore," he said through swollen lips.

Coy shook its head. "The information you relayed to us gave us almost everything we needed to know. It was time to get you out of there." It paused. "A fact we should have thought of a few days earlier."

Taylor started to give a short laugh, winced and changed it to a lopsided grin. "It'll look great in my memoirs shome day."

"Ah," Coy came closer to the bed. "People usually only write memoirs after they retire. How soon will that be?"

"You mean, am I ready to give up?"

Coy cocked its head. "A legitimate question. I'm sure you didn't expect it to lead to all of this when you learned to play music."

"If I didn't ecshpect thish when I agreed to be your lookout then I wash deluding myshelf." He shook his head. "Before, I felt an obligation to repay you and the Fleet. Now, I have a more pershonal interesht. I know I let you down, but I would like to shtay on the team."

"You didn't let me or anyone else in the Fleet down. Your position on the team is quite secure as long as you want it." Coy saw the familiar BlackFleet pride return to his eyes. It gave him a firm, commanding nod and left him to Byars' care.

The man listening to the communication wore quasi military gear and a serious expression. He checked all his scanners and information again as he tracked the owners of the voices he was eavesdropping on.

'How did you say you ended up in the Nebula?' an incredulous voice asked.

The answering voice sounded tired and frustrated. 'I *said* I didn't know. The best our Med Tech and engineer can figure is that the headset had some malfunction. Our pilot is delirious and our back up can't get the ship to respond right. I don't even know how much longer our power is going to last.'

'Don't panic,' the first voice responded with more of a soothing, calm tone. 'Shut down everything except life support if you feel unsure about your power reserves. Just let yourself drift. We'll find you.'

'How long will it take you?'

'From our position, about 3 days.'

'Three days!!'

'Trust me, there's no one else in the Nebula. It's a mess in there. No one likes to be there very long.'

'Including me!'

'In three days time, you will be safely aboard our ship heading out of there. You should be fine until then. If you have any more concerns or something else happens, let us know immediately.'

'Alright....'

The man listening to all of this was still scanning his facts when his superior entered. "Well? Who are they?"

"A small tourist group. It seems to be a small company run by Betalines."

"Hmmm," the other man scratched his chin. "Probably not worth touching. Besides, hitting them now after they've talked to someone would be as good as telling them we're here. Just sit tight and quiet and let them come and go."

"Did you catch who was coming to their rescue?"

He scowled. "No, but I can guess. All the more reason to sit here and let them pass. We'll call off anyone who might have been stopping here in the next few days...Just keep an ear on things."

"Aye, aye."

Butler shut down the com and blew out his breath. "I sure as hell hope this works."

"It should," Coy told him again. "They won't want to give away their position badly enough to try and hit the ship. And while "drifting" they can record with their passive scanners at will. Not to mention what their rescuers will pick up "looking" for them."

"So assuming we get what we need from this, and we already have a good idea about the other two, what next?"

"Next? We talk to all of our friends."

"I sure as hell hope *that* works too. Because if not..."

"I know," Coy sighed. "We don't have a prayer."

Chapter Ten

The night was clear over the southern desert on Avalon, and the Blackbird waited quietly on the sand. Another ship soon came into view. It hovered over the area only briefly, and then settled quietly beside the first. Three uniformed men emerged, accompanying another man dressed in dark, casual clothes. They crossed the short distance between the two ships.

Commander Knepp walked out of the front hatchway on the 'Bird. He greeted the small entourage there.

"Hello Mr. President," he said shaking the dignitary's hand firmly. "I believe we're expected shortly, so if you and your men will follow me..."

The President nodded once, then he and his men walked up the ramp into the armed yacht. Both ships lifted off together. The President's ship veered off, and returned the way it came. The Blackbird clove the air, heading for space---unchallenged by any groundside observers. It had soon left the planet far behind. After reaching a certain distance, minutes later, it opened a transit point, and vanished.

One by one the 28 dignitaries were escorted by BlackFleet officers in dress uniform from their cabins to the main conference room on the Raven. Upon entering they each had the same reaction. Surprise at the size and elegance of the room – and at the number of other guests.

When everyone was seated and their allotted bodyguards were situated, Coy stood up from its seat at the front of the room. There was no need to ask for quiet. Everyone was so skeptical of those gathered around them, that there was virtually no small talk.

Coy felt unnaturally alone at the head of the long, elegant conference table. No other senior officers were present. After consideration, Coy realized Ceal was not the only person that had reason to avoid someone in this prestigious company. Nearly every senior officer in the BlackFleet had come to the fleet after having a parting of the ways with their former government. Coy thought for a moment of what those "deserters" and "mutineers" were ready to do for those same governments. "I appreciate your speed in coming to this meeting," it said formally. "I also appreciate your keeping this meeting an ultra top secret, as each of you has. Some of you are here because your Favors remain unpaid. Some of you are here for other reasons. But by your very presence, you have displayed the courage and determination to attain our objective. Thank you.

"The purpose of this meeting is to do the entire Beta Region a Favor, one which will help every world represented here. Over the past several months we have all seen a rapid and unexplainable rise in the harassment of the shipping industry. Businesses have been disrupted and destroyed, unaccountable amounts of money have been consumed and many lives have been lost. The BlackFleet has partnered with many here today in various portions of our ongoing mission to discover the source and reason behind the attacks. And we have been successful.

"We have traced nearly every incident back to a single individual."

Voices exploded all around the room. Coy let them express their disbelief for a few minutes before raising its hand for calm.

"This person originally owned three companies-under three identities. Each one in turn owned several others, which had subsidiaries, and so on until he had, at one time, control over every facet of the industry. Ship building, engine designs, routing, personnel – everything.

"Then new companies began emerging that weren't on his payroll. The first few we believe he simply bought out. But as they became more plentiful, he had to use other methods. Enter the pirates. The abrupt ending of hostilities in the Alpha Region left him with a vast amount of unemployed para military personnel at hand.

"The hits have been varied in style, size, technique and targets. It has been a challenge to say the least to find the pattern. But the information we have gathered has at last provided us with certain knowledge of the locations of the three major pirate bases in the region."

Coy paused as the various leaders digested these words. Some of them had been trying in vain for at least two years to determine the locations of even one base. Their amazed faces were quite telling.

"We intend to do something about these bases. We intend to eliminate piracy in this sector. Many of you have been trying to do so for a long time. But you've been trying to do so within your own systems. It will take more. It will take a coalition of forces, working together. We simply can't do what needs to be done as separate units.

"What we must do, is to hit these bases in a simultaneous, coordinated strike. Squadrons would be made up of ships representing different systems. These squadrons would attack designated bases at a predetermined time."

Someone raised a hand, and Coy acknowledged the speaker.

"Wouldn't this assault work better if we kept our squadrons separate? Kept the units together that are already used to working together?"

"That is a very good question," Coy replied. "And under normal circumstances it would make perfect sense to do so. But these are not normal circumstances.

"We intend to send a signal; both to those who have participated in this campaign against civilized humanity, and to the one who has personally orchestrated it. We are not fractured and alone anymore. We've learned to fight together. And because we have, their day of preying upon our shipping and commerce is over."

Coy waited once more as heads began nodding in assent, and muttered voices filled with more shock and anger. Coy had thought it was true, and now to see the evidence before it was the greatest encouragement. They were ready.

"The 'Fleet has been investigating this problem, and we are poised to strike in order to solve it. But we need your help. I am asking each of you to contribute from your naval forces. We will form three strike teams. Your C.O.s will submit both themselves and their squadrons to the authority of the BlackFleet. Once the battle commander has gone over the operation details with the coalition C.O., the entire squadron will depart immediately for the attack coordinates."

Coy paused once again, not for effect, not for quiet, but to take a deep breath. "I know what I am asking of you. I am asking you to trust neighbors whom you have had hostile dealings with in the past. I am asking you to work alongside total strangers. I am asking you to free the Beta Region.

"Unfortunately, we don't have time to contact cabinets or committees or however your governments normally conducts matters of this import. We need to act in as much secrecy as humanly possible and we need to act quickly.

"Therefore, I need your answer – now."

There was a moment of silence. Then King Frederic of Tenetia rose to his feet.

"You have my full support, Commodore Lamont."

Coy worked very, very hard at looking solemn and appreciative instead of grinning in relief. "Thank you, Sire."

The Prime Minister of Melan, having been seated by him, stood beside him as well.

"And that of Melan, Commodore."

Person by person, they stood. Some hesitated just long enough to make sure that their nearest neighbors were on board before committing themselves, but in the end, twenty-five stood in support , agreement, and submission, to the BlackFleet.

And in that moment, a terrible, horrifying realization came to it. The Boogeyman was not the most powerful person in the Region after all. Coy Lamont was.

Coy stood gazing out of the portal behind its huge desk as it always did when deep in thought. They were in normal space for the time being and the stars looked especially beautiful after days of the swirling chaos of C space. But Coy wasn't seeing the stars. It was seeing the faces of 25 very powerful people, standing in the conference room, promising the support of their worlds to its plan.

At this moment twenty five worlds, or at least their military forces, were under its personal control. The mixture of thoughts and emotions connected to this fact was impossible to sort out.

A quiet throat clearing from the dark room broke through its reverie. Coy turned around and saw Asch. "Yes, Lieutenant?"

He seemed to hesitate. "Perhaps I interrupted you for no reason, sir, but…well, you've been standing like that for hours. And I was wondering if everything was alright."

Coy paused as well before answering. It tried to decide if it was annoyed at the interruption, amused by Asch's compulsive "mothering", or grateful for the concern. "No imminent breakdown if that's what you mean. But I think I need to talk to someone."

"Whom should I contact, sir?"

"Yourself, for one. Ken, Raeph, Ceal…and Walter."

"Very well," Asch said slowly. It disturbed him that the commodore used first names instead of rank. It seemed to indicate an issue more personal than military. "Immediately?"

"Yes, please," it answered and turned back to the stars.

True to the apparently personal nature of the meeting, the group was sitting on the couches instead of at the long table. Coy was still peering out at space for the first few minutes.

Finally, Ken Butler couldn't stand it any longer. "This isn't another one of your 'I can't lead…' speeches is it?"

Ceal looked at him. "I've said it before and I'll say it again. Shut up, Ken."

"Actually," Coy began, turning from the port at last and joining them, "I hope it doesn't come to that." At their stunned expressions, it continued. "Standing in front of all of those planetary rulers, leaders and advisors, I realized something absolutely terrifying."

"The fate of their worlds was in your hands," Bon said quietly.

"Exactly," Coy breathed in relief that they did understand. "I'm sure even Ken has heard the old saying about power corrupting, and absolute power corrupting absolutely."

"You really think you're going to let all of this go to your head and turn into someone like the Boogeyman?" Butler blinked in shock. "You're a totally different person!"

"I am at the moment."

"You are, period," Schiff put in. "Do you think he has meetings like this and worries about having too much control?"

Coy had to smile a little at the image. "Probably not. But I am. And I am going to continue them. And I want everyone in this room to swear that the first time they see me do anything out of line with our BlackFleet directives they will call me on it."

"Alright," Ceal said with conviction, "if you swear you will call on us the moment that any of this gets too much for you to deal with alone. This is bigger than anything any of us dreamed of when it all started. You need to have outlets – and use them."

"She's right," Bon agreed. Schiff nodded as well.

If Coy had been going to argue in any way with this, it would have stopped when Asch joined the conversation. "Sir, don't think of it as a personal flaw to need this team. When I think back to all of the people I have served in this room in the past year, it has been this particular group that has made some of the most important decisions and discoveries. We represent every facet of the Fleet: Captain Butler is the command staff, Major Schiff the fighting personnel, Doctor Byars the support staff, Captain Bon the hardware and myself the non military functions. Using this, committee if you will, to check what is appropriate action for the Fleet, is simply using the best tool for the job."

They all pondered that for a moment and realized he was quite right. The people here together, except for the somewhat later addition of Asch, were the literal founding members of the BlackFleet.

"So," Ken again broke the silence. "Is this team or committee or tool or whatever we are, really ready to lead this Region in battle?"

Coy looked them over, feeling the determination and confidence it had been doubting just an hour before, return. So this was what it felt like to have people behind you believing in you – this was what it was like to have friends. "Ready or not," it told them, "here we come."

Coy, Ken , Mara Hendricks, and Adrian Rebel, the battle commanders for the proposed three part attack, worked long into that night. In the back of its mind, Coy knew there was no way to plan for every contingency, no plan perfect enough to keep every Black-Fleet member alive and well.

But it could try.

"You're sure about the *Raven*," Ken asked for not the first time.

"Yes, I'm sure," Coy told him, again. "I want to be in the Nebula, but the *Raven* needs to be at Tai Han. Just bring it back to me in one piece if you don't mind." Coy checked its notes. "With the other two battle cruisers..." it was interrupted as a call came through. "Aziza to Lamont."

"Lamont. Go ahead."

"Skipper, we just got a call from...well, you've got to talk to him, sir."

Coy frowned at its wristcom. Now was not a good time for complications. "Talk to him about what, Lieutenant?"

"I think he wants join the war."

Coy frowned in puzzlement. "Another world?"

"No, sir , I believe he is a mercenary."

The three commanders looked at each other. Mara leaned back in her seat. "I gotta hear this."

"Very well, Lieutenant, put him through."

A moment later the holographic figure appeared on Coy's vid-com.

Hendricks sat back up. "I know him! He was the guy that was looking for you."

"Comma...." the figure began, then stopped cold. "Lamont? *Coy* Lamont?!"

"Captain Zachary," Coy answered. It expected to be horrified, enraged, anguished. Instead it felt- nothing. "What can I do for you?"

"Wait a minute. *You're* the crazy mercenary whose been taking over the Region?"

Coy took a breath and spoke very calmly. So calm and controlled in fact that it was scaring Butler. "We are on a bit of a tight schedule, Captain, so if you could please get to the point?"

Zachary took pause at its tone and expression. He frowned as well. "You may be Coy Lamont, but no Lamont I ever knew. Sure don't sound like Aubry's little…"

"The *point*, Captain."

"Alright, *Commodore*. The point is after Aubry's death there was no unity in the fleet. Everybody was getting tired of Corbett real fast. Anybody who wanted to do more than escort service or transit guard duty left. Since I mostly owned my ship, I was one of them. A good number of crew came with me.

"For the past year or so we've been trying to earn an honest living, but with all the pirate activity it's been hard to get anybody to trust us . About the only mercs anyone will trust is the famous Black-Fleet. So I figured it couldn't hurt to see if we could sign on or work out a deal or something. At least I could make a buck to finish paying off the *Starwind*."

Coy had been right. It didn't have time for this. "Captain Zachary, it is not that easy to join the BlackFleet. I personally screen and interview every candidate. We are trusted because we have worked very hard to earn that trust."

"You know me! We worked together!"

"As I recall, you were always a competent captain. That your crew chose to remain loyal to you does speak in your favor as well. But I still do not have time to initiate an entire crew into my Fleet at this moment."

Zachary opened his mouth to protest more, but Coy put a hand up to indicate it was not through.

"I will do this much. Where is your ship now?"

"Servati."

"If you are sincere, take your ship to the coordinates I will send you. We can meet there, and talk face to face."

"Seems like a lot of hoops to jump just to join a merc outfit."

"Then don't. Lamont out."

After the com went silent, Ken looked over at Coy. The only other time he had seen its face this void of expression it had been lay-ing on a bed in Sick Bay. "So do you trust this guy or not?" he asked carefully.

Coy thought for a long moment before answering. "I'll let him come and have a conversation with me and a dose of pentha. After that I'll either use him or disable his ship. I admit his cruiser could come in handy. But I'm not counting on it."

"Why the other co ordinates?" Mara asked.

"I'll meet him on the *Rook,* at a place where he will not see the actual Fleet. In any event, I will take care of Mr. Zachary. You have you own problems."

"Problems. Thanks. How inspiring," Butler grimaced.

Coy stopped them with a dead serious expression. "Take care of my people."

Their salutes were just as serious. "Aye, aye, sir."

Zachary was escorted through the *Rook* and delivered to the waiting Commodore Lamont. He stood gaping at the ancient looking bulkheads of Coy's temporary office.

"Is this a joke? This is the ship that has been striking terror in the hearts of pirates?" he scoffed.

"Perhaps it is not what you have, but how you use it," Coy told him. It wished for a moment that Andrea Pierce was present to prove the point more graphically. "Sit down Captain Zachary. I have some very specific questions to ask you." The crew member who was present, Orson Terrell, stepped up closer to Zachary's chair. "By the way, Captain, do you have any objection to Pentha?"

"To what?"

"Pentha. Truth drug. Are you allergic to it?"

"No, but why would…?"

"I'll take your word for it." It gave a brief nod to Terrell who pressed the hypo against Zachary's neck before he could react. When he was limp and co operative, wearing the typical blank expression, Coy began. It stuck to relevant questions, no matter how tempting it was to find out what the former "Commando" had thought of Lamont in the past. When Coy was satisfied that Zachary was not a pirate plant or operative, it had Terrell administer the antidote.

Zachary was furious. "How dare you!" He lurched out of the chair and stood with fists clenched. "What right…?"

Coy stood and faced him. "I am Commodore Coy Lamont owner and commanding officer of the BlackFleet Mercenaries. And I have a lot of planets counting on me right now to stop the terror and destruction these pirates are causing. I think in the big picture that takes precedence over your personal affront," it said icily. "Now then, if you are serious about joining us, we are on our way to hit the pirate base. Your ship can be added to my battle group immediately."

Zachary stared, shock overwhelming the anger of a moment ago. "Fight pirates! Where's the profit in that?"

"The BlackFleet does not exist to make a profit. We exist to help people. Period. Occasionally we get paid for our efforts, that is true."

"Do-gooders." Zachary scoffed in disgust. "A whole merc unit of do-gooders."

Coy paused. "Let me make myself and my offer clear. I am not asking you to join the BlackFleet. As I have said that is a more involved process than we have time for. What I am offering is a chance to join an alliance of planets and help the Beta Region by ridding it of the pirate activity. If that has been what has been interfering with your getting employment, then it would be to your advantage as well to stop them."

Once again, Zachary was speechless for a second. "Wait a minute. You're telling me you got every planet in the Beta Region to work together!? I mean you, personally, are heading this thing?" he sputtered when he found his voice.

"Not *every* planet. And some that are part of the alliance are not actually able to contribute battleships. Some will help with repairs, some are patrolling the region – doing the job we've been doing for the past couple of years. But a large problem needs a large force to stop it," Coy said casually, downplaying the achievement.

Zachary squinted his eyes and peered at Lamont as if he had never seen it before. "I was wrong. I thought you were someone I used to know. But I would have remembered if I had met anyone powerful enough to order around an entire Region of planets. What happened to you?"

Even if Coy had had the time, it sure didn't have the inclination to tell this person all of the radical changes it had undergone, physical and emotional, in the past couple of years. In fact, it would be impossible seeing as how it had never stopped to figure them out for itself.

"Captain, we could use your help. But we cannot afford your interference. Either you are in on this or you are not. I need your answer. Now." It seemed to be saying that a lot lately.

As he thought, Zachary looked around the room more closely. "This isn't your ship is it?"

Coy allowed itself a small smile of appreciation. "It is one of them, yes. Perhaps you shouldn't judge by outward factors."

Zachary paused and looked at Lamont thoughtfully at that. "I wouldn't usually ask my crew to risk their lives for no pay. But anybody that could accomplish everything the BlackFleet seems to have done and now this…" he stuck out his hand. "The *Starwind* will join your alliance, Commodore."

It was very early in the morning. Although the palace guard stood at full attention outside the door, little else in the royal residence was stirring at this hour.

The ruler of the Royal house of Tenetia had been checking his chrono for quite a while, and it was finally time. He slid out of bed, and went over to his personal com station. After triple-securing the message, he keyed in an address. He waited only a second or so before the naval officer appeared on the screen.

"Mongoose," the Ruler said simply. The officer nodded and cut the com. And with that, the ships began to move…

The *Rook* and its attack group hung motionless, several light–years from much of anything. A ship made transit back into normal space, and approached the group of waiting vessels with the *Rook* at their center. After passwords were exchanged, a shuttle left the new arrival, and docked with the armed merchant ship. Coy, Rebel, Drake, and the rest of the gathered commanders of 9 other ships were seated in the conference room, when the last commander was escorted in. After all were settled, Coy opened up the briefing.

"Each of you knows why you're here. I appreciate your patience with the need for this high a level of security, and I hope to reward not only your patience, but that of your worlds as well.

"I've promised myself to put a stop to what's been going on out here for the past few years. It's finally time, and your worlds have graciously lent me your help. Here is how I intend to use it…"

With that, Coy brought up a holo map for everyone to see. It displayed an area of space surrounding a small planetoid within the Thrackston Nebula.

"According to the extensive intelligence we've been conducting for the last several weeks, this is most likely the main base of operations for the pirates who have been disrupting shipping all over the Region. However, we also know this to be only one of three main bases, and we plan to hit all three in a simultaneous attack. Given tachyon communications, it is essential that none of the three bases warn any of the others about what's coming. And it's even more vital that the base in the Nebula get no warning at all of the other attacks; this one is far more important than the others.

"Therefore in two hours, I will send a signal as we begin our attack. At that signal the other two units will begin their own strikes.

"Many systems have lent the use of ships and crew for the action at hand. Not all were able to, of course, as not all of the systems in the Region even have navies. But of those who have sent ships for the battle, we have, altogether the use of some 5 light patrol ships, 12 destroyers, 4 light cruisers, 5 heavy cruisers, and 2 battlecruisers.

"The battlecruisers especially are valuable assets and I have assigned one of them to the battle we're involved in. The other will be used at DeGaulle. The rest of the ship resources are spread pretty evenly throughout the attack.

"Now, our part of the operation is this:

"The *Rook* will be the first to transit back into normal space out here," it said, indicating the map, "about 125 million kilometers from the main base. Not quite on their front doorstep, but within their outermost defense perimeter."

"They'll immediately know that you're there," one of commanders offered.

"Correct," Coy replied.

"And be quite angry about it too," another said.

"Also correct," Coy replied. "We'll give them a story about being lost and ending up in their space by accident. Something we've done once or twice before."

"Do you expect them to buy that?" yet another commander offered in disbelief. "Especially if you've done it before?"

"No," Coy replied, "I don't expect them to believe it. In fact I'm counting on them not to. I expect them to send out some of their defensive units to 'check us out.' And while they're doing that..."

Mara Hendricks sat at a similar conference table on the *Nighthawk* surrounded by a similar group of ship commanders. After thanking them for coming as well, she began outlining their phase of the three-pronged attack.

"The bad news is that our target is in the asteroid belt outside the DeGaulle system. Navigation and attack strategies are made more difficult by all of the debris in there. The good news is that of the three attacks occurring in this operation we will be working from the most complete intelligence on the target in question.

"It is heavily defended by between 10-20 pirate ships of various classes, and an automated defense net surrounding the base on all sides." She watched as faces winced at this bit of "good news."

"We have been able to determine something of the schedule of rotation for the ships defending this place. That's part of the reason for our timing of the strike. They should be on lowest guard just about the time we set this off."

"We'll come in through the "top" of the asteroid field. Since the field is at the fringes of the system, we should be able to transit into normal space right in their faces. Our attack plan will depend on *speed*. They have to notice our task force only *after* their automated defenses have already engaged us. Then we'll be able to..."

Ken Butler was also busy outlining the attack plan for his group aboard the *Raven*. "We're attacking a moon within the Tai Han system. We have been able to positively locate the base itself. However, we've been unable to pin down the exact number of ships defending it. Extrapolating from the greater knowledge we have about the defenses surrounding the base in the De Gaulle system, we've been planning for between 15-25 ships of classes ranging from fighters to light cruisers. We believe their defenses to be ship-dependant and mobile, rather than the largely fixed defenses surrounding the base at De Gaulle.

"Unfortunately, our plan will depend upon putting a good bit of strain on our JP.s.

"The difficulty in opening transit points increases the closer they are to the gravity well of the central star in any system. The moon which is our target is inside the orbit of Tai Han. We will need to get as close to it as we can in C-space, but the bottom line is that we will have to transit back into normal space while we're still pretty far out from the target. Our Pilots simply could not handle the strain of getting us in as close as would be ideal. So we take it in as close as they can bring us."

"Then what?" someone asked.

"Then, we drive in toward the base, assessing the true nature of the mobile threat as we advance. I know," he said holding up a hand to stop the flood of protests and questions which surged at that statement. "It is a great risk we're asking each of you and your crews to take. But this operation is time intensive. We are coordinating a simultaneous strike against these people, so that we can deal with them once and for all. The other attacks can't wait on us to get all the information we should have about this one. We need to hit them now. Besides," he added, "the *Raven* is...not quite what she appears to be. Despite appearances, she's at least the equivalent of a heavy cruiser.

"The element of surprise in this plan is the key. First, this base isn't planning on getting attacked by anything at the moment, that's another reason we need to get in there as soon as possible. Second, they won't be expecting anyone to put the strain on JPs that transiting back into normal space that far inside the gravity well would represent.

"After we've assessed the number and types of ships that we'll be up against, then we'll..."

The *Rook* sped through C-space. Tension on the bridge was high, but Rebel noticed that people were holding it together. He spoke to each bridge officer in turn, assuring them that they would all succeed in the coming battle with the satisfaction true BlackFleet tradition brought. Now if someone would just give him the same little pep-talk...

Tension had just reached its peak when Jordan informed him that they had reached the proper coordinates.

"Bring us to a relative stop," he ordered the pilot.

"Aye, sir."

Rebel took up position to coordinate the battle from the *Rook's* tac room. This was finally it. Although he had already proven his right to command, now would be the time to really justify everyone's faith in him. He'd been trained, and he was determined to now put that training to optimum use. But that didn't mean that he wasn't terrified.

"Get me the Commodore, please," Rebel said, speaking with a calm he didn't feel. In only a few seconds, Coy's face appeared on the screen.

"We've reached the coordinates, sir. Ready to proceed."

Coy bowed its head in a moment of... what? Thought? Prayer? When it looked back up, its face was also calm. It's eyes, however were anything but.

"It's time to take the head off of the snake, Adrian. Initiate Operation Mongoose."

"Aye sir," Rebel said. He cut the com and spoke to his bridge team.

"I want shield power, life support and engines reduced to 1/5th power the moment we cross back into normal space. Scott, " he said to his pilot, "take us forward at half speed, put us in a slow spin, and then transit into normal space."

"Aye, sir."

A flash of light appeared in the void of the Nebula. A transit point was held open just long enough for the *Rook* to tumble through it. It spun, obviously out of control, and proceeded to broadcast a distress call toward the planetoid close by. They were rewarded within moments by a terse communication from the planet.

"You are in restricted space. Leave immediately or suffer the consequences." And with that, the message ended abruptly.

"Don't send a response," Rebel ordered. "Keep the automatic distress call going. Let's see how far they'll let us in."

They didn't have to wait long. Ten minutes later Bard noticed definite movement on his scanners.

"Captain," he said. "Three destroyer-class ships, leaving orbit and coming this way."

"E.T.A.?"

"Eight minutes."

"Okay, everyone stay sharp. Timing on this is everything."

"Aye sir."

The moments ticked down. The bridge crew peered into their stations, focusing on the job and on their part of the plan.

" 100,000 kilometers and closing," the navigator called out.

"Still not firing missiles?" Rebel asked.

"No sir. No missile launch."

"Fine. Let them keep coming just a little further."

"Yes sir. Now at 80,000. 75,000....60...40..."

"Get ready," Rebel said, gripping the railing in the tac room like a vise.

"30...*20,000!*"

"Now!" Rebel barked. He watched with pride as his crew executed the pre-arranged set of orders with speed and precision. Jordan flattened out the *Rook's* spin and pointed her bow first at the approaching ships. Bard, with the touch of a button, brought all the weapons online, and brought the shields up to maximum power. Palo fired up the reactor and engines to full capacity. And Trevor sent a single, tight-beam message into C-space. That signal acted as both a message in itself, and as a precise location finder.

Immediately after the signal was sent, a rift was torn open in space, just astern of the *Rook* as it raced to meet the enemy ships. The rift opened wide and held, as the patrol ships, destroyers, heavy cruisers, the battleship and the *Karasu*, all poured through in a tight-formation charge. And they came through firing.

Hidden panels and doors on the *Rook* slid open, and it too joined the barrage. The enemy destroyers attempted to return fire even as they sent out an alarm to the main base. They were at least successful in the second action.

The particle beam energy of twelve ships beat their shields down to nothing in a single stroke. The next volley of energy smashed into the ships themselves and finished them off. The *Rook*, *Karasu* and their companions raced past.

Just as planned, all of the violence of the attack group's arrival riveted the attention of the base scanner team to the onset of action. No one noticed two lowly hyper-capable shuttles and two smaller companion craft opening up a transit point far in the other direction from the attack. Just as quickly as they appeared, the four craft shut down all power and vanished from the screens.

Space opened up 'above' the asteroid field outside the DeGaulle system to let ten spacecraft enter, led by the *Nighthawk*, and the Servati battlecruiser *Rapier*.

Captain Mara Hendricks leaned forward expectantly in her command chair, more like a fan at a ball game than a ship commander heading into deadly battle. The '*Hawk* roared into the system with the *Rapier* at her side and the rest of the ships following in tight formation . Hendricks waited several more seconds, her grin broadening with each moment, until she unexpectedly pounded on the armrest of her command chair in a display of pure glee.

"*Nighthawk* to *Rapier*," she said over the com channel. "It worked! We've slipped inside their outer ring defense platforms with no engagements. Well done, Captain."

"To us all," the Servati replied. "But we still have the second and third ring defenses to deal with."

"True. Still, we've hopefully avoided outright one third of the damage they're planning on throwing at us. I'll take what I can get. But you're right, Captain. The rest of the defenses should only be another few seconds away. Get ready."

"Roger that, Captain." The Servati nodded and cut the com.

"Keep us on course, Gil," Hendricks said to the J P. "The field will start to get more dense soon, so stay alert for asteroid debris in our path."

"Aye, sir."

"Time to target?" she asked the navigator.

"Nine minutes," Nathan replied.

"Good. We have only…"

""Defense platforms ahead to port and starboard, powering up and targeting!" Nathan interrupted.

Two elements in the defense net which had been invisible to scanners only moments before came online and fired their particle beams.

"All Alliance ships, return fire," Hendricks ordered.

The 'Hawk and the Rapier were taking the worst hits. The defense platforms hit them twice before the speeding Alliance craft returned fire. The exchange went back and forth. Then the platforms were obliterated as the ships sped past.

"Missile launch dead ahead!" Nathan called out.

"Target incoming missiles!"

The leading ships' forward guns blazed, picking off the swift-approaching missiles with expanding spheres of energy. Still a few of the missiles got through. The Nighthawk rocked once more as hits were made on her shields. "Reinforce forward shields," Hendricks ordered. "Take it from life support on the non combat-essential decks. And find those missile platforms!"

"Got 'em!" Nathan shouted. He fed the coordinates to the other ships in the group, and they struck out at the new threat in another coordinated strike. One volley smashed them. Gil dodged the ship around a pair of asteroids, and the rest of the group followed his path , momentarily hiding the next threat from their view.

"New source! Laser platforms beneath us, and to port. They're firing!"

"Nighthawk to Rapier, target the threat to port. We'll take the other."

The 'Hawk's shields were battered once more from missile attack and by the laser defenses, before those threats were eliminated. Ezra Nathan's hands flew over his board, assessing threat sources of suddenly appearing platforms, and returning fire with one set of guns or another.

"Time now to target?"

"Six minutes, eighteen seconds." Then, "Another particle beam platform to starboard."

"Rapier, you take that one."

"Acknowledged."

"Captain!" Nathan cried out in sudden alarm, "Three mobile defense platforms moving to block our path!"

"Target them and…"

"Sir! They're nuclear mines! Point blank range! *Detonating*!"

"Full power to forward shields!" Hendricks ordered as three miniature suns exploded just ahead of her.

The *Raven* flew through C-space at the head of its task force. Ken wondered once again, not only why Captain Zachary and the *Starwind* were assigned to his attack group, but why the Commodore's former merc "friend" was here at all. Butler shifted his thoughts away from that nagging question, and counted down the seconds.

The strain in Hoffman's figure was apparent as Ken watched the JP from behind. The pilot's shoulders were hunched, and beginning to shake. Butler could also see past Hoffman to the virtual grid of C-space, and the representation of the star at the heart of the Tai Han system. The star that he plunged them closer and closer to.

Butler remembered Bon's comments in the first days of the Fleet about the lack of trust some had in Hoffman. Even being 'worried every time Hoffman made a jump'. Ken saw nothing now but courage, as all the pilots sought to get them in as close as possible. Despite their sacrifice, Ken forced himself to wait until the pre-arranged numbers on the nav board lined up.

"All ships, prepare to transit back into normal space on my order," he said just as the last numbers fell into place. "Now!"

"Course holding. There seem to be twelve destroyer class ships in orbit around the target. No reading yet on fixed defenses."

"Time to intercept?"

"Twenty four minutes."

"Keep an eye on them. I need to know the second they begin to move."

The ships sped on in tense silence, broken only by Ken asking for updates nearly every thirty seconds as they approached the moon. Finally Parker said, "We've got movement Captain. Ten of the ships gathering together. Looks like they're preparing to leave orbit. And I have two other destroyer class ships, a cruiser, and two patrol ships coming in from another direction." Parker gave him the coordinates. "Looks like they were waiting until the other ships could intercept us at about the same time."

"Time to intercept?"

"Seven minutes."

"Okay, crew it's time to start the show." With that, he stood and went to the tac room. The room was dark, lit only by individual screens and by the holographic display which was already online. The officers seated at the stations were in contact with the BlackFleet ships participating in this battle. They were also in contact with the two light cruisers in the attack group, and two of the other participating destroyer ships. Ken stood beside the screen linking him to the *Raven's* bridge.

"All ships: begin braking. Maximum spread."

At his command, the other nine ships in their group began to slow down in their approach to the moon in order to make a relatively low speed pass. Each ship also spread out so as to not be easy targets, yet remained more than close enough to support one another's lines of fire.

"Approaching ships also beginning to decelerate, Captain." Parker announced. "They're forming up into a defensive sphere to block our approach to the moon."

"Roger," Ken replied. "We go with strike plan alpha," he said to the other ships. Then, a few seconds later, Parker reported, "Now in missile range."

"Launch!" Butler ordered.

The *Raven* and both of the cruisers spat out a group of missiles. The approaching pirate destroyers did so as well. Both sets of them sped across space, crossing one another's paths, and found their targets.

Butler felt the jarring motion, and so didn't need the notification when Parker said, "I have multiple missile strikes on the forward shields."

"Shields down 11 percent and holding," Bon said from his station.

"Reinforce the forward shields; they're going to need it." Butler ordered. "Launch the next set."

"Aye sir, launching."

Missiles again flashed through space, taking far less time to reach their targets, as both groups of ships sped toward each other as well. Ken felt himself being jarred again. On the tac grid, he saw at least three of the approaching ships beginning to get dangerously low on shield power.

The task force still made directly for the center of the defensive sphere of destroyers. Butler waited as the two groups continued to close with one another.

"We are... now in particle beam range, Captain."

"Fire!" Ken ordered.

All ships on both sides let loose a barrage of energy. Beams crisscrossed space, smashing into shields. The tac grid showed one pirate destroyer fall out of action, its shields all but gone. Two more of them showed the same signs. Five out of the ten defending ships were out of the fight or close to it. But there were the other five pirate ships approaching from the outer system yet to deal with.

Two of the Alliance destroyers were getting dangerously low as well.

And still they headed for a head-on collision with one another, playing a high-speed game of chicken. The tac room shook with another impact. And now they were only seconds from intercept.

"Go to full speed," Ken ordered. "And…vector to starboard!"

At the order, all ships pivoted together like a flock of birds, turning just a few degrees. Now, instead of heading toward the heart of the defensive sphere, they flew at one of its edges. The defenders began shifting position, moving to block them in their new course. And just as all of them began doing so, Ken barked out, "Back to original course!"

The Alliance ships shifted back now, too late for the destroyers to adjust.

The ships crossed with one another. The pirate destroyer closest to them blew apart as the *Raven* and two of her companions concentrated fire upon it. And another of the defenders fell out of the fight. Then they were through, and racing toward the moon. The pirate destroyers began a long sweeping turn, preparing to give chase. The other five ships coming in changed course to come after them as well.

Butler looked to his group disbursement. "Zachary, Pollard, Freeman, and Patel, you'll act as rearguard. Keep those enemy destroyers off my back while we get this job done."

"Aye, sir," the acknowledgement came back from all four commanders.

Butler shifted uncomfortably in place. He still was not at all sure that he trusted Zachary. His showing up when he had seemed just a little too convenient. Assigning him a role that would keep the questionable captain out of the forefront of his overcrowded thoughts seemed the best idea.

"Begin decelerating again," he said to all ships. "Maintain course for the pirate base."

"The two destroyers that remained here at the base are on attack vector," Parker said. "And there are two large defense platforms in high orbit sending out a jamming signal. They're firing!"

"Jamming us?" Ken mentally questioned as he ordered the last light cruiser he had left, and the shield-weakened destroyer to take the platforms. Then he said to his remaining four small ships, "Target the closest destroyer, we'll take the other one. Kensie, hit it with all broadside cannons."

The *Raven* pivoted to show its side, as it continued to move forward toward the base. All broadside guns opened up and scorched a path across space, slamming headfirst into the pirate destroyer. The ships fired at one another again and again as they approached. Then the pirate ship's shields failed, and the next round of fire tore it to shreds. The other pirate destroyer met the same fate just moments after.

The base now lay before him. This was the moment he'd waited for. Ken said sharply, "*Blackbird* and *Talon* attack wing, launch!"

The '*Bird*, and the *Raven's* two *Talon* squadrons burst forth from the ship with all the speed and coordination gained in many practice drills. They flashed toward the moon ahead of the flagship, weapons already targeting ground defense guns. And Butler also saw on the tac display the instant that the light cruiser and the destroyer took out the orbital defense platforms.

"Good work," he commended them. "Rejoin the..."

"Captain! Parker shouted from the bridge. "Multiple missile launch!"

Butler watched in horror as the same crew members he'd just commended were suddenly swamped with fire. The destroyer exploded .

"Parker! What's launching those..." he stopped, and his horror deepened as two ships resolved themselves on the tac display from where they been hiding behind the defense platforms. Now that they were no longer jamming his scanners, he could see them and see what they were.

"Are those what I think they are, Kensie?"

"Yes sir. Two of the 'Vega' style advanced heavy cruisers that we met in the battle for the *Raven*."

"Bring us about! Fire dorsal cannons!" he said just as the weight of the pirates' combined attack overwhelmed the light cruiser. Just after, it too exploded before his eyes.

As the *Raven* was beginning to return fire, Aziza said, "Incoming com message!"

"Let's have it," Ken ordered. An all too familiar face resolved on the vid.

The grimy looking pirate attack leader stared back at him with cold eyes.

"I'll be accepting your surrender now," he said.

Chapter Eleven

"Damage report!" Hendricks shouted as the *Nighthawk's* violent shuddering began to subside.

Nathan collected himself and concentrated on his panel. It didn't look good.

"All forward and port side shielding, gone. Shield generators in those areas overloaded and offline."

"Get a repair crew over there," Hendricks said. "*Nighthawk* to *Rapier*---come in. Report status."

Hendricks looked with great concern to the blank screen representing her link to the Servati battlecruiser. At the very last second, the *Rapier* had surged a bit ahead of the *Nighthawk*, so that she took the brunt of the triple nuclear blast. Intermittent static came now from the *Rapier's* feed, but it soon resolved into the captain's haggard face.

"All shields offline," he reported. "We have power outages all over the ship, blast damage to the front third of our hull, and the casualty reports are... still coming in. I'm afraid that we're out of the fight, Captain."

"I'll be sure to get 'em for you. My sincerest thanks to you and to your crew."

Hendricks cut the com, and watched on the plot as the rest of the task force began to leave the *Rapier* behind.

"Continue report, Lieutenant."

"We lost only a little forward momentum. Still on course, I think."

"Status of ships still in orbit around the target?"

"Sensors are still being scrambled by the effects of the blast, Captain. Should be back up in another few seconds, although..."

Hendricks interrupted by swearing at herself viciously. "All ships fire forward guns: missile defense mode!"

It was just in time. Missiles fired from the base while everyone's sensors were down had almost reached them. The forward guns got most of them just short of the task force. Three managed to get through, but expended themselves upon three different ships, all of which, fortunately, had operational shielding.

"Scanners becoming functional," the navigator reported. "Ships in orbit around the target are...*leaving* Captain. Heading in all directions."

"What?"

"I show six ships, all smaller classes, pulling out of orbit."

"Are we still on course for low altitude pass on the base?"

"Yes, sir."

"Time to intercept?"

"One minute, thirty seconds."

Hendricks stared at the display. She began designating ships to the rest of the attack group.

"All ships, maintain course, but fire on fleeing ships with long range guns. I don't want one of them getting away if we can help it."

The *Nighthawk*, as well as the others, picked a ship and began pounding the stuffing out of its shields, even as they continued their breakneck pace toward the asteroid base. The enemy craft returned fire, but Hendricks rolled her ship to present its undamaged shields.

Shots were traded. The enemy craft's shields buckled, and the '*Hawk* hit her twice more at extreme range. A shot severely weakened the *Nighthawk's* starboard side protection, but her return shot finally broke through the pirate's shielding. Flame spat out into space. The ship slowed considerably; vital systems on board obviously hit. In the end, only two out of the six pirate vessels managed to escape.

"Starboard shields down 62%"

"Ground defenses opening up!" Nathan said.

"Roll ship!" Hendricks shot back.

The pirates' last gasp was a set of auto cannons set on the outer layer of the large asteroid housing their base. The task force's course was set to have them skim the surface of the asteroid just a couple of miles above the pirate base.

"*Theseus, Valiant,* form up on us: inverted wedge!"

At the last, Hendricks tucked the *Nighthawk* and her damaged shields behind the two heavy cruisers in their attack force where she would be somewhat protected by the other ships' shielding. And now it was the moment of truth.

"All ships, target those ground emplacements. I want them taken out on our first pass."

The base guns blazed, desperately attempting to stave off what their operators knew was coming. The attack force was simply too close now, moving too fast for such measures to be of much use.

"Four...three...two...one...optimum range!" Nathan called out.

"Fire!" Hendricks ordered.

In one stroke, several particle beam cannons lashed out at the ground defenses. A split second later, all of the defense guns were smoking craters. And the top two levels of the pirate base were venting atmosphere in several places. Then an explosion ripped through the surface layer of rock. Flame briefly spouted forth into space before the vacuum quenched it. The attack force rocketed past.

"Braking thrusters!" Hendricks ordered. "Bring us about. Prepare for another pass."

It wasn't necessary. Before the Alliance ships could fully make the turn, a bloodied and desperate looking pirate was on the com screen.

"Alright!" he screamed without preamble or protocol. "We give up! I've got fires all over down here! Do you copy?! We surrender!"

"All ships come to relative stop above the base," Hendricks directed, even as they were all making the long slow turn to come back to the asteroid. She turned a gaze to the com screen that made the already desperate pirate flinch.

"I'm going to be sending several teams down shortly. They'll help you get the fires under control, collect your wounded, and round everyone up for detention. If there is any, and I mean *any* resistance at all to my teams, I will pull them out immediately, and finish what we started with your ground cannons. Do I make myself clear?"

"Perfectly," the pirate quailed.

"This is Captain Mara Hendricks of the BlackFleet Mercenaries with the Betan Alliance task force, out."

She saw the pirate silently mouthing the words 'BlackFleet mercenaries' in disbelief, before the com screen went dark.

The *Rook*, *Karasu*, and the Nebula attack group bore in toward the small planet hiding the main base.

"Not moving, yet?" Rebel asked his navigator.

"No sir. All twenty ships still in orbit around the target."

"But we seem to be detecting a lot of com traffic between them," Trevor offered.

Rebel turned to the part of the tac display that allowed him to communicate with the other ship commanders. "What does this look like to you?" he asked Drake over on the *Karasu*.

Drake peered into his own display on the bridge of the destroyer. Not having been designed to be a task force leader, the *Karasu* had no Tac Room but controlled its part of the action from the bridge itself.

"Looks like we've caught them completely by surprise. And they don't have much time left to figure it out," he answered.

Rebel saw that the cruisers were widely spaced apart as they moved to meet them, and that the other ships in orbit were now moving about in a clearly uncoordinated fashion.

"Looks like you were dead on, Drake." Rebel shook his head in disbelief.

"Being engaged by fixed defense platforms!" the nav announced. The particle beams from four of the platforms opened up on the Alliance ships, spreading their fire fairly evenly throughout.

"All ships! Return fire!" Rebel ordered.

The attack force quickly annihilated the weapons in the automated defense shell, and kept on coming.

"Sir! I have a third cruiser breaking orbit!"

"We're reaching missile range on the first one." Rebel said, watching the tac grid. The first cruiser finally began slowing down to allow the following ships to catch up. Someone over there had finally remembered that they should attack as a group. Especially against a task force containing a battlecruiser. But it was too late.

"Open fire!" Rebel said.

The battlecruiser launched a hail of missiles, which sped on ahead to slam into the pirate cruiser's shields.

It fought back, aiming its counter attack mostly at the battlecruiser. Rebel had the *Rook* and the *Karasu* hold back, saving their limited store of missiles for the battle to come. The larger Alliance ship and one of the heavy cruisers took care of the pirate, just as the other ships reached the area of the battle. The enemy cruiser blew apart, and the hugely unbalanced forces reached particle beam range.

At Rebel's order, all 12 ships hammered their three opponents unmercifully. Shields buckled and fell. "We surrender, we surrender!" one of the pirate commanders shouted over the com.

"Target engine systems and continue to fire," Rebel said into the tac display. The *Rook* and *Karasu* smashed the engines of all three pirate ships into useless scrap. Then the group moved on.

"Seventeen ships are forming up into more of a defensive line, Captain Rebel," Bard reported from the bridge. "They're getting ready for us."

"Then let's not disappoint them. Standard formation. Let's make it good," he said to the attack group, then opening the dedicated channel he reported, "We have engaged and destroyed the first wave of defense, sir. Heading toward the base."

"Acknowledged," came Lamont's voice. "Carry on."

"Aye, aye, sir. Good hunting."

They formed a standard "V" formation with the battle cruiser at its head, and the *Rook* and *Karasu* to either side. The heavy cruisers and other ships formed out from there. They drove in at one third speed decelerating as they went, making for a lengthy, tangled battle with the pirate defenders. Missiles and particle beams flashed across space as they met each other.

On the far side of the planetoid, it was dark, still and quiet. Twenty persons in specialized space armor drifted in a long slow curving arc down to the surface. Their life-support was on bare minimum, and there were no other betraying energy signatures. They had been propelled planetward as tiny projectiles from the hatch of the shuttles, which stayed on station high above.

Schiff, who was in charge of this strike, monitored the passive sensors set in his helmet. The touchiest moment had been when they reached the inner ring defense platforms in orbit above the planet. But whether it was due to the net being set off by the approach of the ships on the other side, or because they were too small for the platforms to notice, they had passed that obstacle effortlessly. Schiff didn't really care which explanation it was, as long as they were through.

Now they curved down in an approach which put them in a low orbit. It was calculated to end with them making planetfall very near the pirate base on the other side. They would have been tiny meteors, except for the lucky fact that there was no atmosphere to trouble them with re-entry.

Now, within only a few kilometers of hitting the ground, Schiff gave the order. All twenty troopers and Elite Forcers fired thruster packs on their backs which slowed their descent. Schiff noticed their approach angle on his display, and made a slight correction, which the others copied. The major watched their final descent anxiously, scanning the horizon for any sign of attack from below. None came. They made a picture-perfect landing behind a set of low hills about two kilometers from the base.

As each person touched down, they jettisoned their packs and unslung their rifles. Schiff signaled for the group to move out. They set out at a trot, making for an area to one edge of the underground pirate base.

The major had them approach quickly, but cautiously. Everyone scanned the ground around them for traps or sensors. At length, they came over a small rise, and made for a set of large rectangular grates with walls 3 feet or so above the terrain. Schiff checked the scanner attached to the left arm of his space armor, and when he saw its reading, he finally broke operational silence.

"Damn," he said with venom. There *were* traps and alarms inside the vents. No way could the scouting mission have detected that for sure, not as far out as they were. Lucky enough to even guess that the things were here from the energy output readings.

"So what now, Major?" one of the troopers asked, "We can't set off the alarms. I thought the op depended on our keeping the element of surprise."

Schiff pointed upward.

"See those flashes of light up there? That's the rest of the fleet distracting these idiots and giving us the chance to get in here with a minimum of risk. So we go into these vents and we go in right now."

As he said the last, he tossed one of the canister assemblies to Marcus, and one to Speed. He motioned them toward the next two vents over. Then, he stepped onto the rim of the vent he'd been crouching beside, and held up a canister of his own. He looked back at the others.

"You comin'?"

The technicians working the late shift in Atmosphere Processing sat idly, watching the monitors, playing cards, or finding some other way to be just plain bored. Boring though it was, however, it did pay great. Whenever the raiding parties came back, they had usually spent a short amount of time making a lot of money, which got distributed all around. .But the techs in question were, at the moment anyway, thinking primarily about how boring their jobs always remained. Until the alarms went off.

Frantic scurrying about followed pretty quickly as they sought to decode the alarm. The giant 5-story-high atmosphere processing unit gathered the diffuse gases of the nebula around them, and converted it to breathable air for the base. It had millions of working parts, any one of which could be critically malfunctioning.

A set of muffled booms went off from deep inside the unit. Then someone noticed that it was the intruder alarm siren that was sounding off. And there was another boom from inside the unit, much closer this time. Someone yelled something about taking cover. And at that moment, in three distinct, widely separated sections, the unit wall exploded inward.

Schiff, Marcus, and Mc Kinney charged through, and others followed close behind each of them. The major motioned for the last four troopers to secure the room. He himself never even broke stride as they ran for the front door.

"Scanners show power conduits in the walls, leading this way," he said. Schiff kept his focus on getting to the door and what lay probably just beyond it. He did notice that Speed McKinney had moved up to cover him on the left, and Cook was on his right.

Max Cook was in a class by himself. He was one of those rare breeds---a true berserker. There wasn't much room in the modern world for people like that.

But Max had gravitated to the fleet and found a home in it. Whatever he did, he did with unmatched intensity.

These thoughts flashed through Schiff's head in the four seconds it took to reach the door. He tapped the open button and it slid aside easily enough. There was a corridor leading down to another doorway about 15 meters away. That door also stood open. And there were two branching passageways leading off in both directions, about halfway down to the other door.

Techs were running back and forth in obvious terror. One was coming around the corner from the passageway on the right, and moving for the open doorway ahead. Schiff checked to confirm that his scanner readings showed conduits above the ceiling and in the walls, all leading toward the room in question. In one smooth series of motions, he charged out, motioned for the rest to follow, aimed his rifle, and dropped the technician who had almost gotten to the power room door.

The alarm continued to blare, and Schiff ran for the door, but paused as he reached the branching corridors. There were three guards, just coming around the corners---two to his left, one on the right. He, McKinney, and Cook all fired before the guards had done much more than raise their pistols.

And that was the moment when the shocked techs inside the power room truly realized that their comrade who'd been trying to get in only a moment before, was dead. Upon having this stunning revelation, and seeing the troopers charging toward them, they prudently began closing the door.

Cook saw it, and reacted even before Schiff did. But the door was closing fast. Cook dove headfirst toward the shrinking opening, as the door scythed downward. He sailed through the air with the speed of a hurled knife.

He almost made it.

Landing on his stomach, he skidded toward the closing power room door as it was slamming downward. He didn't get under it in time.

But the rifle he held stretched out in front of him did.

The door hit it, denting it, but that was all. Max got under it, and using it as a lever, began forcing the door back upward, making some truly terrifying noises as he did so. Schiff, McKinney, and Marcus were there in a second, and jammed their rifles underneath as well. With all of that leverage, the door was forced upward, and the troopers charged in.

To their surprise and amusement, the four technicians in the room were all literally huddled in one corner, scared out of their minds by all this. Cook leaned over one of them and growled and the tech fainted to the floor.

Schiff motioned toward four of the troopers who had come in behind them, and gave them a set of codes. They jogged out of the room, and proceeded to take up positions at the branching corridors. The Major looked around him with great satisfaction.

Commodore Lamont sat in its station chair on the combat drop shuttle monitoring all the battle fronts. It had open channels to the flag bridges of all three commanders. Waiting and watching while others went into battle.

The temptation to be on one of those fronts, leading an assault, any assault, had been powerful. But it had chosen to command a fleet not a ship, and that meant keeping track of the big picture. At one time, it mused, it could have blamed the Rigan programming for the anguish of hearing all that was going on and not being part of it. Of hating that part of command. But no longer.

With each new day since the "reboot" it had been learning more and more about itself, its desires and its goals. This was what it wanted. Occasional anguish and all.

"Schiff to Commodore Lamont," the Major broke into its thoughts. "Power room secure. I have someone downloading all the base information on a hand comp right now. The technicians in this room were quite helpful after having a little chat with Max Cook."

Despite the grave situation, Coy smiled.

"I also have a squad..." There was a muffled boom in the background. "...sealing off one of the only other ways into this area, and setting up a guard on the other one."

There was a brief pause on the line, and then Schiff continued.

"We have his quarters' location, Commodore. Ready to complete this phase on your order."

Coy, as well as everyone else within earshot knew who the 'his' referred to.

"Very well," it said. "Seal up all the doors, shut down all power."

"Aye, sir," Schiff barked a crisp, verbal salute.

"Commodore Lamont!" Sweggert said suddenly from one of the two *Talons* orbiting with the shuttle. "Movement on the surface of the planetoid, about two klicks from the base! A small ship, flying low!" Following Coy's specific orders, the fighters had maintained an intensive scan of the planetoid's surface as they orbited high above it. Looking for exactly what Sweggert had just found.

Coy's heart stopped beating. Then started back up at triple its normal pace.

"Their fearless leader", it said derisively. "I thought he just might find a way to sneak out before the base was taken. *Talon* craft, secure that target. He is not to escape."

Both *Talons* fired off their engines, and began a corkscrew dive directly at the fleeting ship.

The shuttle roared after the *Talons*, but of course, was not diving nearly as fast. The fighters sped toward an intercept.

"Weapons systems coming on line on that thing," Pierce reported from her gunner's seat on the same *Talon*. "I've got a definite power spike."

"Stay on it." Coy ordered "Prepare to return fire, but don't take the first shot. "Let's see what…"

"Commodore!" Pierce interrupted. "Power levels on the target are dropping, rapidly."

"What? Why?" it asked.

"Unknown. Its speed has dropped off too…damn…"

"What is it lieutenant? Report."

"Sir, I've…I've lost it. It's completely gone from the scanners. I'm not picking it up anywhere, now."

Coy shut its eyes, clenched its fist, and pounded the control panel.

"Cut that com channel!" Butler roared. Aziza enthusiastically obliged him, and the grimy pirate vanished.

Tony Knepp called in from his dedicated channel on the *Blackbird*.

"Do we return to base, Captain? Abort the attack run?"

"Negative, Commander. Continue with that attack no matter what."

"Acknowledged."

"So, are we going to surrender, sir?" Aziza asked after that circuit closed, knowing full well what the answer would be.

"Like hell! Parker, stand down on the dorsal cannons. I think this qualifies as a 'more dire circumstance', don't you? Redirect weapons generator energy, and…power up the quadcannon." He studied the tac grid for a moment.

Zachary and the other captains seemed to have dealt with the five destroyers that had tried to block their approach to the moon. Then had gone on to intercept the five ships that had been coming in from outside the system, and those two forces had just begun to engage one another. No help from that quarter. It looked like it was up to the *Raven* and the four ships still with him.

"I want to focus our combined firepower on one target."

The pirate cruiser hit the *Raven's* shields once again. The BlackFleet flagship had turned around to face one of them, and still had not fired yet. The one which was closest continued hitting her port, and then front shields. The other moved in to finish her off if the surrender did not come within seconds. They were quite confident that they had overwhelmed the BlackFleet at last.

Then, a nimbus of energy began to play about the *Raven's* nose. It soon grew blindingly bright. Then, four points of eye-piercing light melded together at her bow, and combined into a huge shaft of energy. It blasted out, slamming into the first cruiser's shields.

The pirate's shields fluctuated wildly, but didn't fall.

"What?" Butler exclaimed truly shocked. "Their shields are still holding after that?"

"Yes, sir," Parker said. "Looks to be 75 percent of normal. Orders?"

"Prepare to fire again," Butler replied.

"The shields on those things are even stronger than when we fought them before." Bon reported. "Looks like they've found a way to enhance their shielding overall by 40 percent."

"Forty percent…?" Butler blew out his breath in exasperation. The ship lurched again as they were fired upon by the first cruiser. The second cruiser was moving in close to the first, and now it too began firing. The deck under him lurched once more.

"Our forward shields down 68 percent," Parker said.

Lamont had ordered him to take this base. Nothing else was acceptable. They were jolted twice more, and Ken hung onto the back of one of the station chairs.

"Message coming through, sir," from Aziza. "He's ordering our immediate surrender."

Butler thought of the pirate's face, and his resolve hardened.

"Parker, target the weakened shield quarter on the first cruiser that attacked us. Fire!"

The quadcannon blasted out again. The other Alliance ships also fired. Despite the second cruiser's attempt to place itself between its sister and the BlackFleet ship, Parker hit the mark with her usual skill. The combined energy broke through the remaining shields and slammed into the hull of the pirate cruiser, punching a thirty-foot wide hole into her bow. The rest of the shields on the enemy ship wavered and then finally fell.

The *Raven* aimed herself directly at the severely damaged ship and charged forward, the other ships following in her wake. Both enemy cruisers began firing on all of them as soon as they began to move.

"Fire it again, Kensie!"

The quadcannon bore into the damaged ship again even as they sailed on toward the pair of cruisers trying to box them in.

"Six seconds from impact, sir," Parker announced.

Then there was a boil of light from within the cruiser ahead as internal explosions wracked it. And a second later, a colossal explosion ripped the ship right in half.

The *Raven* and her companions soared through the fireball, and on into open space. The other pirate ship blasting them from behind began to give chase.

"Quadcannon units overheated, Captain," Parker said.

The one down side to the big gun was that they could only fire it three times in a row and would require a four minute cool down and recharge period before they could use it again. That attack temporarily frustrated, Ken turned his attention to their immediate concern.

"Hoffman, take us out another 12,000 kilometers, and bring us about 180 degrees. We'll keep them guessing." Butler glared at the vid representation of the big enemy ship. "One of us is not getting out of this battle alive. After careful consideration, I've decided that it should be him, rather than me."

The ship traveled only a little further away from the pirate base, then, suddenly wheeled around in its course and headed straight back at its pursuer. Particle beams ripped across space as yet another head-on collision seemed imminent.

The *Blackbird* and the two *Talon* groups dove toward the base. Ground defenses had opened up and begun firing. The BlackFleet team swerved, ducked and banked, avoiding the deadly energy ripping at them from below. But they continued to burn through the moon's atmosphere, approaching the base at reckless speed.

"Distance, 7,000 kilometers, and closing," Danielle Cheny called out to the *Talon* groups. All nine craft were screaming in toward the base preparing to fire.

Tony Knepp watched their approach from his station on the *Blackbird's* cramped bridge. They had to fire at short enough range that the base defenses would have no chance of stopping them. And they were just about to that point, when he looked again at his scanners and got the same nasty surprise Ken Butler was getting at just that moment up in orbit.

Twenty-six fighter craft were lifting off from the base.

"Those are more of the *Talon* prototypes!"

"Yes, and coming this way fast."

In fact the attackers were not even waiting for positive lock up, but were firing beam weapons indiscriminately in the direction of the oncoming ships.

"No choice," Knepp decided. "All craft, fire!"

Sixteen missiles blasted toward the base defenses. Two of them took out two of the enemy "Talons" who happened to be in their path. Most of the rest struck their intended targets.

.Ground defenses, and some bunkers were vaporized as multiple explosions rippled around the complex.

The *Talons* and the *Blackbird* split up into two groups. They looped upward, and then down, changing the angle at which they were attacking the approaching pirate craft. They swerved back and forth firing, and their orderly attack cut through the disorganized ranks of the pirates. Four more of the pirate fighters were obliterated.

Then they crossed past one another in a well-practiced pattern, and curved upward and away from each other, using the extra momentum and speed gained in the dive. They forced the remaining twenty fighters to split up in their pursuit. Which they did quite poorly.

"We've got twelve following us," Cheny said as they looped through the moon's thin atmosphere, preparing for another run on the base.

"And we've got eight," Smith observed.

"Dust yours off as fast as possible, and get back to us," she ordered casually. It didn't seem to matter that she was talking about two-to-one odds.

Smith felt the *Talon* jarred slightly as their shields were getting hit from behind. Smith replied equally casually. "Roger that, ma'am. We're on it." And the BlackFleet *Talon* officers prepared to go to work.

The *Raven* and her companions soared directly at the approaching pirate cruiser.

"Taking massive hits on forward shields," Parker reported. "Shield power in that quarter now down 79 percent."

They wouldn't be able to take many more hits in the front, Butler realized. Although they were giving as well as they were taking, those damnable pirate shields were absorbing everything they could throw. And he still had another minute before he could use their big gun again.

They hurtled in what looked like another suicidal attempt to slam into each other head-on But only for a second or two. This commander was smarter than that. "Vector to starboard, quickly!" Ken ordered.

Both groups knew that someone would have to flinch first. Butler had managed to do so, and at a time of his choosing. Which meant that they would have a little more time to use their port side weapons to best effect. The pirate ship changed direction as well, but too late. Parker had it targeted, and fired as they passed each other.

"Turn us to port, Mr. Hoffman," Butler said, "Keep turning. Try to keep them on our port side."

The two groups of ships began a fighter-like death spiral, looping in a circle which grew tighter and tighter, firing at each other all the while. But not everyone could maintain this.

Ken saw it on the tac grid. The patrol ships were losing shielding, and fast. They were never meant for this kind of fight. He ordered them to pull out, just as one of them sustained heavy damage as her shields failed at last. The other small ship had lost all but her dorsal side shields.

The two destroyers would be next.

And the *Raven* herself was losing shield power on every quarter.

The *Talons* were involved in a struggle with other fighters, down in the moon's atmosphere. Gary Michaels was at that station chair in the tac room, monitoring their progress, urging his outmatched team on. Zachary and their group were still tied up with the outsystem pirates.

The *Raven* continued taking hits which jarred her repeatedly. Ken had Hoffman roll the ship constantly, protecting this side, now that of their dwindling shields.

"Quadcannon online and ready to fire," Parker said.

"Mr. Hoffman, turn us about again. Get us a proper firing angle on that ship."

It was another minute or so, but somehow in their twisting, turning dance, Hoffman managed it.

"Fire!"

The big gun blasted, once, twice. The beams smashed into the cruisers shields. The pirate attack leader was also canny enough to roll their ship and spread the damage around. Even after two such powerful hits, their shields were weakened, but holding.

"Again!" Butler ordered.

The quadcannon fired at the same second that the pirate's cruiser took another shot at one of the destroyers. The quadcannon beam hit the enemy's ship, and the cumulative damage done to each other in their constant battle finally mattered. The shields on her starboard side went down. But the pirate's last shot also broke through shielding in the destroyer's rear quarter, stabbing into its engines. There was an explosion, and the destroyer spun out of control. It grazed the edge of the second destroyer's shields as it went, and effectively took it out of the battle as well.

Butler ordered Hoffman to change course in a direction that would draw the cruiser away from the damaged Alliance ships. It was just the two of them now.

"Quadcannon offline again," Parker said.

"Return fire with the dorsal and broadside guns."

The ships went back to their complicated dance, trying to protect damage, and still trying to fire on one another as best they could. The *Raven* shook, more violently this time.

"Port shields gone, Captain," Parker reported.

"Roll the ship again, present our starboard!"

The ship turned, and they kept on hammering each other without mercy.

"Starboard shields down 92 percent," Parker said quietly. They all knew what that meant. There was another lurch, and then a jarring hit which knocked Ken and anyone else standing off their feet.

"Hull breach, starboard side, Deck E."

Ken clambered back up. If this went on much longer, he and all the crewmembers on Lamont's ship would be destroyed. However, if he was going to go out like this, he would make absolutely sure that a certain grimy pirate leader was going with him. There was another violent lurch.

"Hull breach, port side, Deck C. We've just lost the weapons' fusion reactor."

"Use the backup reactors. Channel all their power to weapons systems. Concentrate fire on that ship."

The ship shook again. And again.

"Damage to port side guns! They're out of operation!"

"Keep on them. Fire with whatever we've got left!" The pirate cruiser looped beneath them, and was angling around for a better shot. Hoffman went the other way, trying to bring their starboard guns into play. The *Raven's* dorsal cannons swivelled, constantly firing. Their starboard guns were almost in place to take one last shot at the man Ken Butler had truly learned to hate. But the damaged cruiser struck again.

"Hull breach! Hangar bay, port side!"

Both ships continued trading shots at a murderous pace. The *Raven* kept trying to make the turn, but the pirate cruiser managed to do it first. It was lined up with the best of its remaining guns pointed right at the *Raven's* already damaged side. "This is it," Ken thought calmly. "Damn, I hate disobeying Lamont's order."

And then, the *Starwind* soared in between the *Raven* and the cruiser.

She came in firing, making the space around them bright as day as she and the pirate traded shots at point blank range.

Her shields were nearly gone too, but Zachary had directly interposed his ship to give the *Raven* a chance. Butler found a surge of adrenaline that he'd not thought was left in him.

"Keep us in the turn! Get us pointed directly at that cruiser! Parker, at my order I want you to fire the quadcannon."

"It's still overheated, and not yet recharged, captain," Parker reminded him.

"Use the manual override on the safeties! Divert all remaining ship power to it. Take it from the other weapons, life support; I don't care! Just get me every scrap of energy you can, and hurry!"

The flagship made the turn. The enemy cruiser kept firing. If she scored a hit on the *Raven's* bow and knocked out his big gun, Butler knew it really would be all over.

"Fire!" Ken screamed.

The quadcannon beam lashed out. It punched into the pirate cruiser's hull. But there was no visible effect.

"Cannon dangerously overloaded, captain!" Parker said.

"Com channel opening!" Aziza reported. "He wants to talk."

Butler strode out of the tac room and back onto the bridge. He stood directly behind Aziza as he brought up the holo-image of the pirate's battered face.

"Wait! Let's talk," he said. "I'll make a deal with you. I have all kinds of information that could help you."

Ken noticed on another display that the pirate was continuing to turn his own ship toward the *Raven*, angling to come between her and the *Starwind*. He also saw that the enemy cruiser's weapons systems were still active. So he wasn't going to let Butler out of this either.

"We can work this out," the grimy pirate lied to him. "What do you say?"

Butler stared into the other man's eyes, his fury tempered now to cold, emotionless determination.

"I say, you've made the wrong enemy today." He nodded at Parker.

The quadcannon beam tore a hole all the way though the length of the pirate cruiser. It smashed through decks, bulkheads, and fusion reactors. The cruiser exploded in a flash of such brilliance, that Ken had to turn his eyes from the display. When he turned back, there was nothing left but slowly cooling dust, traveling in every direction. The *Starwind* sidled up to the damaged flagship, and both moved off to the last front in the battle.

The *Talons* continued in their sweeping, diving battle with the pirate fighters. The fight had slowly climbed into the upper reaches of the moon's thin atmosphere. Smith in Onyx One targeted an enemy at the same moment it was lined it up from Onyx Three. Between their combined fire, the fighter burst into scraps of metal.

"That was ours!" the other gunner shouted over her com link.

"Ha!" Smith returned, as he was lining up his next shot. "Not according to *my* scans."

"Just 'cause you're a flight commander..."

She was cut off by Graham's "Lieutenant! Five of the fighters have split again and are trying for the surface."

Anthony thought for only a split second. "Onyx Two and Four, take 'em out. We'll join you in a minute."

"Roger that."

The two *Talons* took off in pursuit of the fleeing enemy. They chased them for several moments, firing at their tails.

"Something on scanners!" Brasch, in Onyx Two reported suddenly.

"What?"

"Six more fighters, coming from the surface."

"Where'd they come from?"

"I don't know. Maybe they left from the base..." They took a jarring hit from behind as the new arrivals came into range.

"Doesn't matter. Onyx Two and Four to Lieutenant Smith. We could use a little help down here, commander...."

"Finishing up... now." Smith said. "We just got the last one of ours topside. Commander Knepp and Captain Cheny are still busy. We're on our way. Hang on."

Both pilots worked furiously, darting this way shaking off pursuit and striking back. But shield power was dropping fast. Five of the enemy fighters had swung around behind the pair of BlackFleet craft, still flying in tandem.

"Watch it, Onyx Four," Graham said. "Your shields are almost gone!"

"I know, get 'im off of me, will ya?"

Both gunners were firing behind them frantically. Another hit from the pirates took out Estridge's shields completely.

Onyx Four banked hard, trying to throw them off. Graham went with him, and deliberately placed his fighter between his shipmates and the attack from the rear. All five pairs of the pirates' guns focused on them instead. In another three seconds, their shields were gone, too.

There was a blast of fire from above. Smith was tearing down through the atmosphere. Their fire scored a hit on one of the pursuers, and rattled another so that he broke and ran. But the other three stayed on Graham just long enough. Smith's stomach lurched. Even as he continued to fire, even as he hit another of the fighters pursuing his squadron members, the pirates fired one last time.

Graham and Brasch's *Talon* was blown apart.

News of Hendricks' achievement, Zachary's bravery and the loss of the *Talon* all reached Lamont almost simultaneously. The first irreversible BlackFleet deaths hit it like a physical blow and for several desperate moments, Coy longed for the days when it had very few emotions.   With a concentrated effort, it acknowledged the reports and returned its attention to the search on the planetoid below.

The *Talons* and Coy's shuttle criss-crossed the terrain looking for the disappearing fighter. They assumed he landed and shut down all power, including life support, which made him virtually invisible to their scanners. No life support also meant he was in a space suit.

"I have something!" Marty Thomas announced from the other *Talon*. "Possible visual contact." He fed the other ships the coordinates of where he saw the glint of metal down on the surface.

A fly over verified the fact that it was a *Talon* type fighter, parked between two rocky outcroppings. Coy landed its shuttle in front of the ship, at hopefully a safe distance. Randy and Sam Alexander did the same to port and starboard. They had him surrounded.

"Dyvees" Coy transmitted on an open frequency, "This is Commodore Coy Lamont. You are hereby under arrest for crimes against the Beta Region. You have one chance to comply."

There was a moment of silence, then static, then a finally a face to put to Aziza's information came on. "You don't want me dead. You want to know why," was all he said before disappearing.

Coy's brow furrowed in anger. He was right. Alive and spilling information was best, but, Coy reminded itself, stopped was the ultimate goal. "That was your one chance."

At that, the four Elite officers emerged from the *Talons* and began approaching the vessel, weapons drawn and ready.

"I don't suppose he's going to make this easy and come out with his hands up," Sweggert commented on a channel only his colleagues could hear.

"Exit your craft," Coy ordered the fugitive.

Static. "You don't want me dead…" the image began again.

Realization dawned on Coy suddenly. "Take cover!!" it screamed at the four BlackFleet who had nearly reached the ship.

Instantly they turned and dove behind the rock formations. The fighter exploded, shattering the rocks, which rained down on them.

Coy snapped its own helmet down and locked it with one hand, while unstrapping itself from the pilot seat with the other. In seconds it was out of the shuttle and heading for the devastation. The rocks and dust fell down in almost a dreamlike speed due to the lesser gravity of the planetoid. That gravity was Coy's main hope for the survival of the people underneath all that mass. It took several agonizing moments for Coy to locate any sign of life. Peering through the cloud of slowly falling debris, it saw a booted foot. Again, intensely grateful for the lack of weight, Commodore Lamont began digging.

The foot began moving freely, then the leg. A minute later, Marty Thomas sat up, free of the rubble.

"Status", Coy said sharply.

Thomas took just a second to access his medical telemetry. "I seem to be okay."

In answer, Lamont merely nodded to the rest of the pile. "Let's hope…"

"Commo…" a desperate voice broke through."…air..help…"

"Skipper!" Sweggert called.

Coy straightened up and looked all around. It spotted Randy who had evidently freed himself and was hurrying to another pile.

"Over here, sir! It's Sam!"

After extracting Alexander from his deathtrap, Coy's opinion of the gravity changed as they had to fight it trying to race the damaged pilot to the shuttle. Once they had him in , on the pull down stretcher, and oxygen flowing into him, Coy glanced at the other two. "Find her," was all it said.

Keeping busy tending Alexander helped keep all the other thoughts attempting to churn through its mind under control. Where was Pierce? The miracle that even the three of them were alive. How was Butler's final
confrontation going? But foremost, and steadily growing, very intense, very cold, and now very personal, hatred.

"Sweggert to Lamont."

"Lamont. Go."

"Found her, sir. All body parts present and accounted for. Only thing busted is her transmitter."

"Acknowledged," Coy breathed in relief. "Return…"

"Begging your pardon, sir. She seems to think she has located someone you might be interested in."

Lamont, Thomas and Sweggert leaned over the rocks and peered down at the crater like indentation below them. A set of space boot footprints led to a metal door set into the rock.

"Do we have the dimensions yet?" Coy asked Pierce. Due to her damaged com link, she was the logical choice to return to the shuttle and monitor Alexander. While there, she could also use the shuttle's scanners to find out about their quarry's hiding place.

"It appears to be an equipment shack. One door in. Two rooms. Lots of hardware. One lifeform."

"No hidden tunnels or corridors leading back to base?" Coy thought it knew the answer to that since they were on the opposite side of the planetoid from base, but it wanted every possibility covered.

"Apparently not, sir."

"Acknowledged. Keep me posted of any change."

"Aye, sir."

It paused, looking at the 'shack'. How long had it been working for this moment? How many times had they been close, only to lose track of the trail? And what the hell was it going to do with the person on the other side of that door?

"Sir?" Randy prompted.

"We are going down there," Lamont told him evenly. "You two will be on guard on the outside. I am going to go in. If the wrong person comes out—kill him."

"Aye, sir. Count on it."

Coy walked the remaining steps to the door, using its suit scanners to find out as much as possible about what it was walking into. Dyvees seemed to be sitting directly in the middle of the shack, facing the front. What was even stranger; it didn't read a stunner or any other weapon on its opponent. No explosives rigged anywhere in the small building.

Coy stood to one side and pushed the door open. Nothing. It dropped to a prone position before the doorway, weapon drawn. But Dyvees was just sitting there.

The Commodore might have felt foolish, except for all of things this man had done. There was no such thing as being too cautious, here. It stood and walked into the small room. There were tools of various kinds strewn here and there all over the small shack. But the man continued to sit there, in his own space suit, just staring. Although it was hard to tell through the suit, he seemed small and unimpressive.

"Lamont," he said at last. His voice seemed devoid of all emotion. "We finally meet."

Coy took a step toward him, then stopped. The shed was dark, but something else was making Coy feel uneasy. It used the infrared optics in the faceplate of its helmet to look more closely at its surroundings. Not all of the tools in this shack were randomly strewn about. It noticed the muzzles of three power borers, expertly hidden, pointing at the spot where it's next step would take it...

Coy swung the barrel of its gun up, blasting the hidden tools in three short bursts. But in that brief second, it had taken its eyes off of Dyvees.

The man launched himself at Coy, hitting with enough force in the low gravity to slam them hard against one of the shelving units on one wall. At the moment of impact, Dyvees swung wildly and frantically, knocking the blaster out of Coy's grip. Coy scrambled to get leverage enough to push him away, and that was when he brought the knife he'd been hiding slashing in toward Coy's stomach.

Coy blocked the stroke with one hand, and disarmed him with a hard strike from the other. It finally got some leverage, and shoved hard against the shelving, pushing Dyvees away. Coy had taken only two steps and he was back, clawing and swinging like an animal. It was Coy's cool hatred against Dyvees' hot fury.

The conditions were cramped, its opponent was not taking orderly, measured strikes... this was nothing like it's training sessions with Schiff. But it had learned something in all the hours of practice. It stifled it's rage for a moment and waited for an opening in Dyvees' wild attack. When it came, Coy put all of its strength into a punch to the chest, knowing the strike would be blunted by the chestplate on his spacesuit.

Dyvees staggered backward, the wind knocked out of him. Coy swept his legs out from under him, and the second he went down, it was lunging toward the fallen blaster. It touched the handle but was tackled hard from behind. How did such a scrawny little man move so fast?

Lamont was knocked prone onto the floor, and the gun went sliding underneath some shelves. Dyvees gripped the sides of Coy's head, scrambling frantically for the latches on its helmet. It had only a second or two before exposure.

This time the low gravity worked in its favor. Coy shoved hard against the floor, sending its opponent careening into the ceiling. He bounced off, but Coy was ready for his uncontrolled approach. It got just enough room and met him with a brutal front kick. He smashed again into a huge pile of tools, but Coy wasn't waiting to see how he freed himself.

Dyvees screamed and tossed tools about in anger. He took a step and tripped over some of them. He rolled over, and stopped cold as he stared up into the waiting muzzle of Coy's blaster.

Coy stood, breathing hard, holding the Boogeyman's imminent death in its hand. The seconds ticked slowly by as they remained seemingly frozen in position. Scenes flashed through Coy's thoughts.

A stately vessel being swarmed by small fighters desperate to avoid a war; Taylor's bruised and beaten face; watching the intruders come aboard the *Raven;* stone and debris raining down on Pierce and Sweggert; a heroic *Talon* bursting into pieces.

"What," Dyvees panted, "the great Commodore Lamont hasn't the stomach to pull the trigger face to face?"

"On the contrary, I was standing here thinking of all the perfectly good reasons to pull it," Coy spoke with deadly calm as opposed to Dyvees mocking tone. "But I also realized I am being selfish. There are about twenty-five planets full of people that want a piece of you. I have no right to deny them. Get to your feet."

Dyvees barked a laugh. "Ha, you as good as told me you won't kill me. Why should I cooperate?"

In answer Coy pulled the trigger, aiming slightly to the left and singed his spacesuit. Dyvees yelped in fear. "I'm going to keep you *alive* a little longer – I didn't say anything about intact." He stood. "Lamont to Sweggert."

"Sweggert," a very relieved voice answered. "Go ahead."

"We are coming out. He's coming out first, but refrain from killing him for the moment."

"Gotcha. I mean, aye, sir."

Coy grinned at Dyvees with anything but humor. "Let's go."

An emotionally exhausted Butler reported on the final mopping up at Tai Han just as Coy boarded the *Rook.*

"We've taken a lot of damage," he said, torn between bitterness and apology. "Sick bay is full and I don't think Bon has even stopped moving for hours."

Coy nodded understanding. "A hell of a price to pay for victory, eh?"

"Is that what it is?" Butler asked skeptically, "Is it really over?"

"Everyone's objective was accomplished," Coy told him as it pulled its prisoner into vid range, "Including mine."

"Damn," Ken breathed. "Have you decided what to do with him yet?"

"I have a few ideas," Coy replied, carefully not looking at Dyvees. "Perhaps one laser wound for each world he hurt. Or one second naked in space for each."

Butler grinned wearily. "I get the idea. Can't wait to see you at rendezvous, sir. *Raven* out." He saluted and cut the com.

Dyvees leaned over Coy's shoulder to sneer, "You're not scaring me."

Without turning Coy's arm jerked up and its fist exploded backwards into the man's face. Hands still bound behind his back, he hit the deck, hard, nose spouting blood. All it took was a glance at the security team and they hauled him to his feet and half marched, half dragged him to the brig.

A smaller number of ships arrived at the Alliance Force rendezvous this time. Smaller and horribly abused. This had been no easy win. The worlds that had volunteered manpower and materials instead of fighting vessels went to work dividing up the repairs.

Coy's muscles were tight with unexpressed grief as the losses and damages were tallied. It knew that they had planned as well as they could and that everyone executed those plans to the best of their ability. But it still hurt. And unfortunately, with Coy's memory, it knew it always would.

It tried to rally its former sense of triumph as it handed Dyvees over to the newly formed Betan Alliance Security Council. Tenetia, first as always in BlackFleet affairs it seemed, had been designated to head the Council.

"He probably has a ship full of lawyers," Coy warned as the "Boogeyman" was transferred from one set of guards to another.

The Tenetian representative smiled wolfishly. "The Alliance has decided that the Region is still to be classified as a frontier. In other words, we make our own rules. Trust me," he turned the smile on Dyvees, "his lawyers are absolutely useless." The expression when he turned to face Coy was much more somber. He put out his hand. "We owe you much, Commodore Lamont."

And with that it was over. Twenty-seven months of blood, sweat, working, searching and fighting culminated in a simple handshake. Coy collected its troopers and returned to the *Raven*.

Zachary paused before pushing the buzzer to gain entrance to Lamont's quarters. He knew what he had to do, but he had mixed feelings himself – let alone misgivings about Lamont's reaction.

The door was opened by Lieutenant Asch – Lamont's ever present steward/acquisitions officer.

"I ah, need to see the Commodore."

"Yes, sir. This way, please."

Asch led him into an amazing –cabin? The place seemed the size of some of the ships that had been in the recent battle. He followed the lieutenant across the room and down a step. Lamont appeared to be relaxing with a hot drink on a long curved couch. A very tired Lamont.

Zachary took a breath and mentally kicked himself. Great, he was interrupting a commanding officer on personal time.

Coy looked up at Asch's approach and saw Zachary. It took in his anxious face and realized it had to be important for him to come at a time like this. And it had a pretty good idea what it was. Coy nodded at a seat opposite. "Sit down, Captain. Care for coffee or tea?"

"Ah, no, thanks." At that Asch vanished. Zachary sat, though and gathered his thoughts. "Commodore, I have a problem."

"Your ship." Lamont guessed.

He nodded. "It took a lot of damage. You're man Bon helped my engineer with an assessment. In fact he sort of suggested...well, you see, Commodore, I don't have any way to keep going. Even with your Alliance helping with repairs. I still owe back payments and..." He took another breath to bolster his nerve. "Would you be interested in buying her, sir? Bon said that you had acquired ships before in worse condition and renovated them for your use."

Coy's eyebrows rose. "Did he now?"

"Yes, sir. It would solve my financial dilemma and add a good ship to your Fleet." At Coy's look, he added, "Well, after she's fixed up, of course."

Coy put its cup down, picked up a hand comp and appeared to make some calculations. "I have read Bon's assessment, as a matter of fact. The ship is well worth repairing. And my Exec would be thrilled to have it on the team." Coy's voice trailed off doubtfully, despite the optimistic words.

"But..." Zachary supplied the unspoken.

"But if I took on a new ship, it would need a captain and crew." Coy looked him in the eye. "Would you be interested in staying on and commanding a ship that no longer belonged to you?"

Zachary blinked. "Staying on? Joining the BlackFleet?"

"Exactly. Captain Butler has reported on your performance during battle. To do all of that with no promise of payment shows that you are not a mere mercenary. You are BlackFleet material."

Zachary sat speechless. Lamont sat patiently while he thought for several minutes. "I, I don't know what to say. I know I said some things that were out of line when I first contacted you..."

Coy waved it off. "You were right. You had only met the former Coy Lamont. I'm still getting to know the new one myself. And in a way, your very appearance helped me a little further along with that..." Coy paused. "So what about my offer?"

"I think..." he straightened his spine proudly. "I think I would be honored, Commodore Lamont."

Coy smiled and offered a hand. "Welcome aboard, Captain Zachary. Asch will handle the number shuffling involved in paying off your creditors."

"What about my crew?"

"They will be offered a chance at positions with the Fleet as well – although not necessarily on your ship." He gave a reluctant nod of understanding. "Once we explain our initiation process we'll see who's willing to stay. Although," Coy looked thoughtful, "this is one time I might modify the training slightly – seeing what you all went through by helping us out. In the meantime, I'll let Bon get started on the renovations."

"Sorry it doesn't have one of your bird names."

Coy gave another small smile. "That can be fixed easily enough."

Zachary took his cue to leave. He stood and saluted. "Yes, sir. Thank you, sir."

Coy leaned back on the couch and closed its eyes. It was not even aware that Bon had entered as Zachary left until he made a small throat clearing noise. Coy looked up at him and was suddenly struck with the memory of the first time Bon had appeared. "May I help you?" it asked as it had then.

Bon smiled as he too remembered the occasion. "I don't know. Still need engineers?"

"More than ever." Coy motioned at the chair Zachary had vacated. "Six ships and 220 people. How did that happen, Raeph?"

Bon shrugged. "We grew."

"Individually as well as collectively," Coy sighed in agreement.

There was a pause as each thought back over the past couple of years and all the changes they had all gone through.

"So," Bon broke the silence, "now that the war is over, what do you intend to do with this not-so-little BlackFleet of yours?"

Coy shook its head. "The war isn't over. We won a major round, true. And it was one hell of an accomplishment. But people out there are still getting hurt. They are still going to need someone to care."

"So back to the beginning, eh? Daring rescues, dangerous escapes…"

"Exactly. Now that we've cleared the Region of the biggest threat, all of the little threats will move in."

"Well, then," Bon slapped the arms of his chair as he stood up. "I guess I'd better get this bird cleaned up and ready for duty." He headed over to let himself out. He paused at the door just long enough to say, "Good work, Admiral. Good night."

"Good ni…" Coy began before catching what he had said.

Bon grinned and gave a sketchy salute. "Nevermore," he said cheerily and went back to work.

Epilogue

The mood in the conference room on Riga was somber. The men and women around the table wore expressions that matched their conversation.

"Well, Specimen D-17 was completely shut down. Plan A is a total bust." one scientist stated, shaking his head.

"What about Plan B?"

The first man looked disgusted. "Plan B is who shut down Plan A. It seems to have gone completely renegade."

"Is the whole batch faulty?"

"They do seem to have excess initiative," another person scowled across the table at his colleague.

"They had to be able to survive," the offended colleague defended herself.

"So, what do we do? How do we salvage this?" another asked.

"I thought you were going to get rid of this last one, Scot," the first man demanded.

Floyd-Scot frowned. "I did the best I could. I was sure that damned doctor would give it the poison."

"You should have done it yourself."

"I was on their ship! Surrounded by them!"

"You should have…"

"What? Brought them down here? To see what we really do? Is that what you would have preferred?" Scot planted his hands on the table and half stood in anger.

"Alright! That's enough," said one man softly but sternly. "We can sit here all day and toss accusations and blame around the table like a sport. Or we can discuss what to do now." He leaned forward in his usual slow precise manner and switched on his computer notes. "From all the information we have been able to collect, it appears this Lamont, has wiped out any connection to us along with the other specimen. That in itself has bought us more time."

"What about the others? Do we just sit and wait until the program breaks down and they go off course as well?"

He shook his head. "No, although the odds of any of the others surviving the self destruct are extremely low, we can't afford the risk."

The room was quiet for a minute.

"You want us to destroy the whole generation?"

"Abandon the whole plan?"

Another shake of the head. "Not abandon, just adapt perhaps…"

Appendix A

The Cast

Starring:

Coy Lamont — A genetically altered dual-gendered military experiment from Riga

Co-Starring:

Ken Butler — A brash young commander from Mueller's World who ended up on the wrong side of his world's politics

Raeph Bon — An engineer from Harada, dishonorably discharged for objecting to inhumane orders

Ceal Byars — Daughter of the assassinated ruler of her world. On the run from the assassin, who happens to be her uncle

Walter Schiff — Self taught martial arts and weapons specialist

Also Starring:

Anton Vennefron — Brilliant, but alone and chronically depressed

Adrian Rebel — Fall guy in an Academy Scandal

Mara Hendricks — Ship commander who argued morals with the wrong people

Andrea Pierce — Beautiful and deadly guerilla fighter

"Speed" McKinney — Drifter, hand weapon master

Randy Sweggert — Orphaned by pirates, security guard

Rogelio Asch — Scorned by powerful family for his non-military choice of lifestyle

Gary Michaels — Retired fighter pilot

Edwin Drake — Found himself on the losing side of a coup

Devyu Aziza — Left his organized crime family for a more honorable life

Anthony Smith — War orphan, fighter pilot

Tony Knepp — Son of former slaves, put himself through military academy

With:

Myke Pedula	Fighter with untapped Jump Pilot potential
Kensie Parker	Forced into retirement and forgotten after a lifetime of service
Drea Carsons	Daughter of privilege, trying to make a life on her own
Rose Durand	Rescued from inhumane mining conditions by Lamont
Eric Hoffman	Jump Pilot who came with the Raven
Dimitri Luka	Engineer, discharged with Bon
Giorgio Palo	Engineer, discharged with Bon
"Gil" Guillermo	Jump Pilot who came with Nighthawk
Chen Marcus	Enlisted soldier, disenchanted with his planet's government
Heyob	Jump Pilot forced into retirement but still wants to contribute
Neil Zachary	Former colleague of Coy Lamont

Appendix B

The BlackFleet Ships and Their Crews

Admiral Coy Lamont   Fleet Commander

Raven   Flagship of the Fleet   Heavily Armed Luxury
Cruiser

    Commodore Ken Butler, commanding
    Jump Pilot Eric Hoffman
    Lieutenant Kensie Parker, weapons officer
    Ensign Norman Mira, junior weapons officer
    Lieutenant Devyu Aziza, communications officer
    Ensign Alicia Cuffe, junior comm. officer
    Captain Raeph Bon, fleet engineer
    Lieutenant Cori Swift, engineer
      Engineers
          Chief Gio Palo
          Chas Cooper,
          Zebhair Nolan
          Dean Walker
          Kathryn Paxton
          Jerry McCrystal
          Mishele Harsh
          Joel Richards
          Pete Czaja
          Rex Parker
    Doctor Ceal Byars, chief medical officer
    Doctor Mark Jaquay
    MedTech Sara Lanyi
    MedTech Stefan Dobbs
    Med Tech Greta Shermer
    Lieutenant Rogelio Asch, fleet acquisitions officer
    Accounting
          Allen Kaneta
          Chas Soma
    Hydroponics and Food Services
          Doug Hunter
          Geneva Einhorn

Kelli Darre
Lawrence Combs
Mel Burge
Russel Torien
Heiu Lu
Jon Taketa
Susan Saemoon, cook
Commander Anton Vennefron, intelligence
Lieutenant Rodney Parks, security chief
Scott O'Neal, security
Woodrow Siefert, security
Taylor Dickenson, field agent
Tac Com Officers
Veora Kim – Raven
Freda Monroe – Blackbird
Dale LaRue – Nighthawk
Gunter Kefski – Rook
Fouch Philips – Karasu
Karlen Amnell – Starwing
Ensign Layton Tye, shuttle pilot
Ensign Preston Jones, shuttle pilot

Talon Corps
Obsidian Sqadron
Captain Danielle Cheny, flight commander, Talon pilot
Lieutenant Don Milner, Talon gunner
Lieutenant Steph Besl, Talon pilot
Lieutenant Ron Lunsford, Talon gunner
Lieutenant Jess Roig, Talon pilot
Lieutenant Lilli Baker, Talon gunner
Lieutenant Farris Conlon, Talon pilot
Lieutenant Jameson Kowallack, Talon gunner

Onyx Squadron
Lieutenant Anthony Smith, flight commander, Talon pilot
Lieutenant Deb Hake, Talon gunner
Lieutenant Sam Alexander, Talon pilot
Lieutenant Terry Buccigross, Talon gunner
Lieutenant Verde Estridge, Talon pilot
Lieutenant Stefan Joiner, Talon gunner
Talon Ground Crew
Chief James Selesky, crew chief

Liam Cavins
Jim Schaffer
Nabil Saelinns
Luther Lawson
Darrell Hilen
Tracy Furter
Dewey Conter
Willie Bell
Jayne Baer
Phil Terrain
Lex Steib
Natela Shake
Paul Morris
Gerardo Lawton
Troy Davidson
Rico Burns

Nighthawk   Light Cruiser

    Captain Mara Hendricks, commanding
    Commander Dean Ebbing, first officer
    Jump Pilot Guillermo
    Lieutenant Ezra Nathan, weapons officer
    Ensign Rusty Weiss, junior weapons officer
    Lieutenant Drea Carsons, communications officer
    Ensign Robert Larsh, junior comm. officer
    Commander Phil Torren, chief engineer
     Engineers
         Freddy Savalos
         Korey Biggs
         Ben Edwards
         Komeni Doutaz
         John Peters
         Karin Tasso
         Patrick Hensel
         Jeremy Christos
         Tamy Saleh
    Doctor Rose Durand, senior medical officer
    MedTech Jeff Hilton
    Med Tech Gary Turner
    Robert Taing, cook
    Wendy Grady, assistant cook

     Ground Forces
    Major Walter Schiff, commanding
    Lieutenant Sren Erhardt
    Sergeant Larry Treadwell
    Corporal Russ Cornell
    Corporal Karl Friedhoff
    Weapon Spec Ari Cimini
    Weapon Spec Max Cook
    Troopers
         Michael Farr
         Rachel Deszell
         Liz Gressel

Alice Meiser
Felix Ernst
Gus Reinhart
Lucille Mattox
MT Lissa Rae, ground forces medic
Ensign Jerome Burney, ground forces shuttle pilot
Ensign Donovan Joyner, shuttle pilot

Rook   Armed Freighter

Captain Adrian Rebel, commanding
Commander Michael Stearns, first officer
Jump Pilot Scott Taylor Jordan
Lieutenant Dennis Bard, weapons officer
Ensign Aaron Blake, junior weapons officer
Lieutenant Field Trevor, communications officer
Ensign JL Dalley, junior comm. officer
Commander Dimitri Luka, chief engineer
Chief Marc Penway
  Engineers
        Bruce Masters
        Carlos Gaski
        Karen Nogel
        Sheldon Straker
        Cicero Willer
        John Gadd
        Douglas Klett
        Bryon Ligon
Doctor Correll Astria, medical officer
MedTech Orson Terrel
Med Tech Darren Sackett
Sheila Jung, cook
Julie Pannel, assistant cook
Debbie Unser, shuttle pilot

        Elite Corps Ebony Squadron
Captain Chen Marcus, commanding, Talon pilot
        Lieutenant Marty Thomas, Talon gunner
Lieutenant Randy Sweggert, Talon pilot
        Lieutenant Andrea Pierce, Talon gunner
Lieutenant Grace Wiggins, Talon pilot
        Lieutenant Speed McKinney, Talon gunner
Lieutenant Zola Haberny, Talon pilot
        Lieutenant Matt Squire, Talon gunner
Talon Ground Crew
        Chief Chas Omer, crew chief
        Paul Haight

Burgess Lightner
Donna Pieta
Christy Gabbard
Kavid Lynd
Deanna Browne
Hiroyuki Engh
Earl Belfort

Starwing   Light Cruiser

Captain Neil Zachary, commanding
Commander George Radin, first officer
Jump Pilot K.L. Witte
Lieutenant Mel Grein , weapons officer
Ensign Dale Watson, junior weapons officer
Lieutenant Carleen Huang, communications officer
Ensign James Kendall, junior comm. officer
Commander Kurt Schaner, chief engineer
  Engineers
        Lane Dehner
        Vance Barbaro
        Rhonda Yohey
        Pat Salo
        Dan Herderson
        Billy Cox
        Keven Porter
        Carol Hwang
Doctor Dan Stewert, medical officer
MedTech Norvel Mann
Med Tech Brian Strine
Med Tech Gabrielle Kendig
Charles Adoma, cook
Ruth Fields, assistant cook
  Troopers
        Sergeant Cole Greer
        Corporal Jeff Dean
        Corporal Dwight Reaver
        Jason Casey
        Howard Beard
        Nicci Renner
        Herb Mikhail
        Rich Milar
        Sonia Gallaus
        Sylvester Sizer
Ensign Rep Tutas, shuttle pilot

Karasu   Destroyer

     Captain Edwin Drake, commanding
     Commander Darlene McVay, first officer
     Jump Pilot Heyob
     Lieutenant Cietus Huff, weapons officer
     Ensign Jack McSwain, junior weapons officer
     Lieutenant Don Miedema, communications officer
     Ensign Art Taylor, junior comm. officer
     Commander Hassam Tabai, chief engineer
      Engineers
           Lieutenant Alexa Shaw
           Kirlin Nagai
           Richard Lukens
           Francis Davids
           Bobby Jones
           Cecillia Lindley
           Bruce Cutler
     Doctor Scott Gross, medical officer
     Med Tech Don Dakin
     Med Tech Dorthy Skelton
     Sonny Cao, cook
     Berdie McComb, assistant cook
     MedTech Jerry Clift
     Jump Pilot Lynn Harper, shuttle

Blackbird   Armed Yacht

Commander Tony Knepp, commander
Jump Pilot Myke Pedula
Lieutenant Amos Bailey, weapons officer
Ensign Norman Kou, communications officer
Lieutenant Helen McKnight, chief engineer
  Engineers
        Edwin Husky
        Brenda Lykins
Doctor Melanie Stone, medical officer

About the Author:

Morgan Brautigan lives in Ohio, is a teacher by profession, has six children (more or less) and ten grandchildren (for now). Morgan loves the symphony, backpacking, and being a pirate at Renaissance Faires. Oh, and science fiction. Lots of science fiction.

This is the first BlackFleet novel.

Questions, comments and reviews can be posted to Morgan's facebook page or e-mailed to BlackFleet212@hotmail.com

About the Artist:

Tony Branch has been drawing space ships most of his life. After graduating from Cincinnati Academy of Design he has used his talent to make calendars, cards and logo designs. This is his first book cover.

To view more of Tony's work, a complete set of BlackFleet ship portraits and Fleet patches may be seen on Morgan Brautigan's facebook page as they become available.